Hidden Treasures

By the same author:

Fern: My Story
New Beginnings

FERN BRITTON

Hidden Treasures

HarperCollins*Publishers*

HarperCollins*Publishers*
77–85 Fulham Palace Road,
Hammersmith, London W6 8JB

www.harpercollins.co.uk

Published by HarperCollins*Publishers* 2012

1

A catalogue record for this book
is available from the British Library

ISBN: 978 0 00 736271 4

Set in Birka by Palimpsest Book Production Limited,
Falkirk, Stirlingshire.

Printed and bound in Great Britain by
Clays Ltd, St Ives plc.

MIX
Paper from
responsible sources
FSC
www.fsc.org   FSC C007454

ACKNOWLEDGEMENTS

I would like to thank all those patient people who nurtured me and the book to fruition. Kate Bradley, my gentle editor, for staying calm and sending me sweets in the post. Lynne Drew at HarperCollins for having faith in me. My agents, Luigi Bonomi and John Rush, who hold my hand and keep me steady when I wobble. Gorgeous surf genius Windy, who really *does* have the ocean in his eyes. My Mum, who is always the first reader. Karen who keeps the children fed and watered while I'm upstairs typing; Carole who vacuums as quietly as she can outside my office and Bob and Orca whose little pussycat feet have often deleted vital paragraphs.

Finally to Phil, Jack, Harry, Grace and Winnie, whom I couldn't function without. Poor grammar Fern

To my Cornish friends who have welcomed us
so generously.

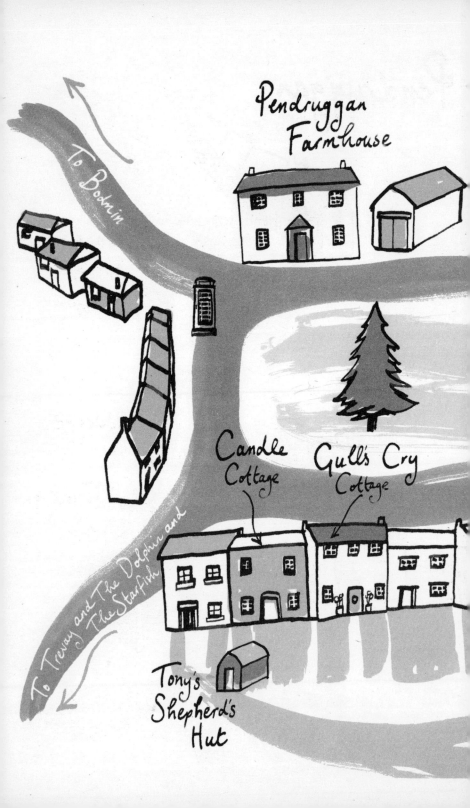

Pendruggan

To Newquay and Truro

Queenie's Village Shop

The Vicarage

Penny's production office

Holy Trinity church

To Shellsand Bay

Prologue

Violet Wingham straightened up and allowed herself the pleasure of feeling the warm evening air on her face. This would be her last night at Gull's Cry. During the seventy-seven years she'd lived in Pendruggan, tending her garden and her cottage, she had always prided herself on being no bother to anyone. Determined that wasn't about to change now, at the age of ninety-six, Violet had made up her mind to place herself in a nursing home until God took her back to her family.

Brushing the damp earth from her fingers, she took one last look at the freshly dug soil. 'Goodbye, my darling. For now,' she said softly, then returned the spade to the old privy which doubled as her garden shed and walked back into her house for the last time.

Part One

1

The sound of a tractor bumping over the cattle grid of the farm across the lane rudely awoke Helen. Yesterday it was the cockerel at the village farm. She wasn't used to hearing such rural sounds. Not yet, anyway.

Lying in bed with her eyes still shut, savouring the warmth of her duvet and the soft cashmere blanket on top (a house-warming present from Gray, her ex), Helen felt more comfortable than she had in years. Nothing to get up for, nobody to deal with and the whole day to herself. She felt her body start to get lighter and was ready to drift off again when the phone rang.

'Who the f . . . ?' she scrabbled for the receiver. 'Hello.'

'Mum, it's me.' It was Chloe, her daughter. 'So how's the new cottage and Cornish life? Got all the yokel men beating a path to your door yet?'

'Darling, I've only just woken up. What time is it?'

'Nine forty-five.'

'Well, that's virtually the middle of the night as far as I'm concerned.'

'Sorry, Mum, it's just that I've been thinking about you so much. Are you OK?'

'Yes, fine.' Helen sat up and plumped the pillows behind her. 'But I'm desperate for you to come and have a look at the cottage. It's so pretty.'

'I can't wait.'

'Well, come and see me. How about this weekend?' pressed Helen.

'Maybe. Sorry, Mum, got to go, a customer's just walked in. Speak later. Love you.'

The lovely Chloe, thought Helen. Wasting her first-class Cambridge degree in Classics by working in a charity shop in Bristol. Her social conscience and a passion to save the world from environmental collapse meant that she recycled everything – even earbuds, if she could. Perhaps she did? Chloe was only twenty-two but seemed so old for her years. A single-minded single woman. By the time Helen was Chloe's age she'd been married a year and had just become a mother to Sean. Chloe came along three years later.

And now they were all grown-up. Sean was something big in advertising and, despite the economic mess, he could apparently afford a Porsche Boxster. Should she worry about her children a bit more, she wondered.

'No,' she said out loud. 'They can worry about me for a change.'

Helen climbed out of bed, and was thrilled once again by the cream deep-pile carpet that her feet sank into. As her mother used to say, 'It's never your extravagances you regret, only your economies.'

Had it been an extravagance to give up her metronome life in West London? She'd amazed herself with the speed and ease of her leap from Chiswick Woman to Cornish Country Woman. One minute she was ironing Gray's shirts and playing the apparently contented wife, the next her marriage had finished. It was almost like a film. They met, they married, they had a family, they had problems, he apologised, she endured, they became friends, they separated. Credits roll, The End. Go home. But home was no longer the London house where she'd raised a family, but a wonky-walled cottage called Gull's Cry in the village of Pendruggan.

How Gray would hate it. The house was not built for anyone over five foot six. He would need to wear a crash helmet to avoid serious head injury. A towering six foot three with a large leonine head and a mane of greying hair worn long and pushed back off his face, he was still a very handsome man. With his bright-blue eyes and a permanent tan, most women found him irresistible; yet he had chosen her. Reliable Helen.

She thought back to the time they had first met. It was the mid-eighties and Helen was supplementing her meagre income from the BBC, where she was a secretary in the newsroom, by working odd nights in a wine bar in Shepherd's Bush. Gray was one of the regulars. He flirted with everybody. He drank rosé wine with ice and was teased by his mates, but he'd just laugh and tell them that only real men drank rosé. He was a partner in an expensive car dealership and drove a turquoise-blue Rolls-Royce Corniche, nearly always with the roof down. Hearing the deep throb of the V8 engine as he pulled up outside, Helen would quickly check herself in the mirror behind the rows of bottles at the bar. One evening he came in alone, ordered a bottle and two glasses and settled himself at the bar. He was waiting for his latest girlfriend to arrive, but she never did. He drained the first bottle, ordered another and turned his seductive blue eyes on Helen instead. He waited for her to finish work, took her out for a curry, and then took her to his bed.

Helen had fallen completely, totally in love. Sure, she'd had a couple of boyfriends before, but no one had ever made her feel so sexy and protected. Gray (who hated his real name, Graham) liked her lack of sophistication and her dogged adoration. Two months after their first night, Helen had missed a period. She told Gray, who immediately went AWOL, leaving Helen to a fortnight of blind panic. Should she tell her widowed dad? Terrified it would kill him, she kept it all to herself for two weeks until one evening, a hungover Gray arrived on her doorstep with a bunch of tulips, a paste diamond ring from Shepherd's Bush market and a proposal of marriage.

They were married within the month and her father had the good grace to say nothing when Sean arrived weighing eight and a half pounds. Even he knew that was a good size for a premature baby!

Helen loved being a mum and a wife. She was a good homemaker and didn't mind Gray's lack of support with nappies or ironing. The dealership seemed to take up all his daylight hours, but she understood. When Chloe arrived they moved from Gray's flat to a four-storey Edwardian townhouse just off the Chiswick High Road. It had a good-sized garden which she filled with spring bulbs and summer flowers.

Then one weekend they had thrown a garden party for his workmates. Her friend Penny, whom she'd met at the BBC, came to help. It was a really warm day and she had put the children downstairs in the cool to have a little nap, taking the baby alarm with her. After an hour's silence, she thought they were sleeping well. But when she went to check on them she heard Gray's voice through the slightly ajar door.

'Sssshhh, sssshh, gorgeous . . .'

This was the first time Helen had ever heard him talking to the children so soothingly.

'. . . She can't hear. I turned the baby alarm off.'

How thoughtful of him. She pushed the door open and saw Gray with his trousers round his ankles, entwined with a woman she'd never seen before, summer dress pushed up to her waist, knickers on the floor, one leg wrapped around Helen's husband and one breast hanging out. She looked at Helen over Gray's shoulder and smiled: 'Hi.'

Gray spun round and fell over. Watching him scrambling on the floor caught up in his trousers and boxer shorts sent such a feeling of violence through her, he should've been glad that she didn't have a carving knife in her hand. Instead, she checked that the children were still sleeping and went into the kitchen, where she sat at the table and sobbed. Penny found her there and, after sending her off to bed with a box of Kleenex and chucking out all of Gray's chinless friends, she launched into Gray with such ferocity that he ran to the pub. He came back at closing time to find Penny guarding Helen's bedroom door.

'I have made up the sofa bed for you in the basement. The kids are asleep and I'll stay here tonight to get them up in the morning. You have got a lot to prove. Not least, that you will never again be this shitty to Helen – or you will have me to answer to.'

He had slunk downstairs.

Penny stayed for a week, filling Helen with good sense and strength.

It took a very long time before Gray shared Helen's bed again or was allowed to touch her. Despite his refusal to talk about what had happened or to answer any of her questions, Helen eventually decided to let her anger and feelings of betrayal go, and to give him a second chance.

The next time it happened, it hadn't hurt quite so much.

Or the next.

That's not to say that his serial infidelity was not a torture for her. Death by a thousand cuts. But she confided in no one. Certainly not Penny, who would have been furious. Besides, Penny had her own problems. She was having an affair with the deputy news editor, who was married.

'I know I'm a hypocrite, Helen,' she confided. 'But his marriage has been over for years and at least you and Gray are back on track.'

If only you knew, thought Helen.

Penny continued, 'They haven't slept together for yonks, but he can't leave her because she's so unstable and he would never forgive himself if she did anything stupid.'

'You deserve so much better though, Pen. How long are you going to wait for him?' Helen said gently. 'Until one of you dies?'

'I keep hoping it will sort itself out. I love him so much. We are meant to be together.'

As these things do, they did sort themselves out. The mad, sexless wife appeared at the office Christmas party with blonde hair, a big smile and eight months pregnant.

This time it was Helen's turn to look after Penny. She rang the deputy news editor at work and gave him what for in no uncertain terms. When Gray heard, he gave Penny a cuddle and said, 'Welcome to the sinners club.'

Over the years, Helen, Gray and the kids, often with Penny in tow, had shared holidays and a friendship that wove a comfortable blanket around them. Helen could always tell when Gray had a fling on the go. It was all very clichéd. He paid more attention to his appearance and was assiduous in bringing home little gifts for her. She didn't know why she put up with it, but the idea of divorce and custody battles exhausted her. Least said, soonest mended.

Penny meanwhile lurched from one unsuitable man to another, but her professional life went from strength to strength. A year older than Helen, she had joined the BBC as a graduate trainee, working as a production secretary in the newsroom, which was where she met Helen. From there she was seconded to *EastEnders* as production assistant to the producer, swiftly working her way up the ladder to director. Her reputation really took off after she directed a historical drama that became a huge hit on both sides of the Atlantic. These days she was head of her own production company, Penny Leighton Productions. Helen was thrilled for her, even though her success meant that now their friendship had to be conducted via email and Skype.

The years had been kind to Gray too. There was always a market for Bentleys and Ferraris among City high-fliers and although the swanky showrooms in Chiswick had long gone, he kept his hand in and sold enough cars privately to keep them comfortable. Sean had moved out to a small flat he'd bought in Tooting and Chloe was settled in Bristol, leaving Helen and Gray on their own. Then, last Boxing Day, she did the unsayable and asked him for a divorce.

*

He fell apart, of course. How could she leave him, what would he do without her? What would the chaps say?

Helen's Chiswick women friends were full of showy compassion for her. Even the one or two who she knew had dallied with her husband.

'Helen, how bloody awful for you. How will you find another man at your age?' etc etc. They hadn't a clue how happy and liberated she felt.

Her father had passed away ten years before. Her mother almost thirty years before, of breast cancer, when Helen was in her teens. She had no dependent children and now, no husband. She didn't need a man to validate her existence, and what's more, she was now financially independent. The cottage was all paid for, thanks to Gray agreeing that she had earned it looking after him (putting up with him, more like) and the children for all those years, and her father had left her his comfortable estate.

After a period of adjustment, Gray discovered he rather liked the single life too, having bought himself a swanky, minimalist Soho flat in which to do some guilt-free entertaining of the opposite sex.

A good deal is one where everybody is happy, thought Helen. And she most definitely was.

2

From her bedroom, Helen stepped out on to the small, square landing. On her left was the only other door upstairs, a second bedroom that she had converted into a bathroom. She headed down the wooden staircase, pausing by the window at the turn in the steps to look out over her wildly overgrown back garden. Like the famous gardens of Heligan, this was her own Lost Garden. Some fifty yards long and twenty wide, it was criss-crossed with mossy brick paths and rectangular flower beds, though it was hard to tell where they ended and the lawn started. Here and there she could see the orange Montbretia licking like flames in the undergrowth. Somewhere amid the tangle of Old Man's Beard and brambles bursting with blackberries was an old privy and a couple of broken-down chicken houses.

It backed on to the graveyard of Holy Trinity Church.

'Very quiet neighbours,' the estate agent had joked.

It didn't bother her at all. There was an ancient drystone wall between her and the dead and she had plans to stud it with primroses and ferns.

At the bottom of the stairs a latch door opened straight into her sitting room. The tall and deep open fireplace cradled last night's ashes, which were still gently smouldering. She stirred the coals, added a firelighter and some kindling, then walked across to the door leading into the kitchen. The September sunshine bounced off the shiny lids of the Aga and made the red roses of the Cath Kidston curtains appear to glow. She filled the kettle, and set it on the hob. Collecting the newspaper from the front-door mat, which was at the opposite end of the kitchen from the back door, she glanced at the front page as she made her tea. Then she loaded everything onto a tray and carried it to her favourite armchair. Plump, patchworked and multicoloured, it sat by the fire and was a startling piece of modern design in her otherwise sedate interior. She added a few lumps of coal and a log to the revived flames and settled down to profligately, deliciously, waste an hour with the headlines, the crossword and her tea.

The warm drink and crackle of the fire made her eyelids droop. Soon she was dreaming that she was back in her old life; Gray had just arrived home bad tempered and hungry, demanding supper. While he poured himself a glass of wine, she rushed around preparing his favourite dishes only for him to announce: 'I had that for lunch. Isn't there anything else? On second thoughts, forget it. I'll have a shower and nip to the pub . . .'

For the second time that morning, the phone woke her.

'Bloody hell,' she complained.

'Darling, it's me. How's life with the pirates?' It was Gray.

'I've been pillaged several times and am waiting for the parson to bring the baccy.'

He laughed. 'I worry about my mate, you know. I do miss you.'

'No you don't. What do you want?'

'Selina is driving me mad. She's filled my flat with her belongings and I need to get out. Can I come and see you?' he wheedled.

'I only have one bedroom, so you'll have to stay in the pub up the road or the Starfish in Trevay.'

'What do I need to do that for? I can bunk in with you. Good God, woman, I slept with you for a quarter of a century – what's the problem?'

'It's the Starfish or the pub. What time is it?'

'Eleven o'clock.'

'Oh hell. I'm expecting Don.'

'Don who? Don Juan? Are you having a little romantic tryst? Darling, you'll make me jealous.'

'You were enough to put me off men for good. Let me know when you've decided where you want to stay. Speak later. Bye.'

*

Upstairs, she ran a quick bath in her luxurious bathroom. Don had done a marvellous job. The Cornish understood what folk from upcountry liked. Years of accepting wealthy second-home owners into their communities meant they were acquainted with all the latest design fads. Helen would have been happy with a B&Q job, but Don soon persuaded her that what she wanted was a limestone tiled floor, huge white sink, a bath with space-age taps and a shower with a head so big its pressure was like a riot hose. This was now her favourite room in the cottage.

Don had said that he'd be with her at just after eleven to take a look at the new boiler and set the thermostat and timer, which was completely beyond her.

By 11.15 a.m. she was bathed and dressed. Her shoulder-length brown hair was still wet and her face free of make-up. She hadn't put make-up on for days. In West

London it was considered rude to be seen without it. Here it was considered rude to be seen with it.

Don eventually rolled up at 12.15 p.m.

'Hello, Helen.'

'Don! Hello, I expected you an hour ago.'

'Yeah. I got here directly. By the way, do you want any bass or lobster? My mate's going out in his boat later. I could drop it over?'

'Well, yes. How much are they?'

'Nothing to me, maid. Don't worry about that.'

'Well, thank you. Anything that's going, please. Shall I put the kettle on?'

'Wouldn't say no. This colour's lovely in 'ere, isn't it?'

Don had his head through the door into the sitting room. Four months ago, when she first got the keys to the Gull's Cry, she had a vague idea of chintz and Laura Ashley, but it was Don who steered her to the soft pastel emulsions and barley-coloured painted floorboards, and it was Don who pushed her into buying her patchwork armchair.

'That's what designers call a hero piece, that is.'

She had met Don when she first came house-hunting in Pendruggan. It had been at the end of May and she had driven her soft-top Mini through the sun-dappled lanes with the roof down. The smell of the wild garlic and salt on the breeze brought back childhood memories that had her hugging herself with joy and excitement, feeling sure that she was going to find her dream home any minute. However, the first few houses she'd looked at were too dark, too damp or too expensive. When she'd seen them all and the sun had gone in, giving way to a few spits of rain, the smile had gone and she needed something to cheer herself up. According to her map, she was some-where between Trevay and Pendruggan. Hungry and needing to regroup, she stopped at the first pub she saw, the Dolphin. It was a proper pub, probably three hundred years old and granite tough. Parking her Mini in the empty car park, Helen walked past the tubs of jolly geraniums, stepped in to the dark of the bar, and immediately liked what she saw. An open fire gently burned in the large grate, a huge copper punchbowl full of perfumed peonies stood on the bar and half a dozen candles flickered in thoughtfully placed bell jars. She ordered a tomato juice and a crab salad from the hand-written menu, then took her drink to a table with two ancient leather chairs and sat down thankfully. When the barmaid brought her the cutlery, she noticed the pages of house details that Helen had placed in front of her.

'House-hunting, are you?' the woman asked.

'Yep. But no luck so far,' Helen said glumly.

'Don,' the barmaid called, 'is Gull's Cry still for sale down in Pendruggan?'

A man with the build of an ex-boxer came through the door behind the bar. 'Old Vi's house? I think so. Why?'

'This lady is lookin', that's all.'

Don, pulled the tea towel from his shoulder and pushed it on to the bar. 'Oh yeah? Needs a bit doin', mind. Is your 'usband good at that stuff?'

'I am looking for myself, actually. I'm thinking about moving down here from London.'

'Holiday 'ome, is it?'

'No. A home home.'

'Pendruggan is a lovely place mind, but the cottage is small. People want lots of bedrooms, see. To let out.'

'How big is it?' she asked.

'Just a little two-up two-down. Wanna look at it? I'll call Neil, the agent who's selling it, if you like.'

'Well, I'm here so, yes!'

Don disappeared back into the gloom behind the bar and the barmaid introduced herself. 'I'm Dorrie. Me and Don 'ave been here for nearly twenty years. There's not much we don't know about round here. In a good way,' she added, seeing Helen's face. 'We look out for each other here, you see. A bit different from being in London, I expect.'

Helen took in the surf-blonde short hair, sawn-off denims and lime-green hoodie with its washed-out, illegible message. She reckoned Dorrie must be in her early forties.

'It's a lovely place to live. We get really busy in the summer and then the winter is quiet, but we love it and the people are really friendly. I take my boys down to the beach to surf in all weathers, and always on Christmas Day.'

'I'm not sure my kids would like that.'

'My two'll show them. Ben's twelve and Hal's fourteen.'

'Well, Chloe is twenty-two and Sean's twenty-five.'

Dorrie's face lit up, 'Perfect! We got gorgeous lifeguards for yer daughter and lots of bar work for yer son.'

Helen thought of sweet and earnest Chloe being pursued by bronzed lifeguards. No way. And as for slick ad-man-about-town Sean serving pints of cider in a pub – absolutely no way!

Don came back rubbing his hands together with pleasure. 'Spoke to Neil up at the estate agents and he'll meet you there in half an hour. I'll draw you a quick map. It's only a couple of miles, but the signposting isn't good. In fact, there isn't any. A cup of coffee while you wait?'

It took her twenty minutes to find the village. The lanes all looked the same, but when she finally found the small village green with a sign saying Pendruggan, and saw the granite cottage with the FOR SALE sign, it was love at first sight. The front drystone wall of Gull's Cry had a wonky gate that drooped on to the brick path and over the years it had worn a groove in the clay. Lavender lined the path to the cottage and the huge pots of tall agapanthus either side of the front door were heavenly. She stooped to look through the brass porthole set in the middle of the door but couldn't see much besides dusty floorboards.

Neil took out the huge old metal key from his pocket, put it in the lock and they stepped inside. It smelled of dust and disuse, but no damp.

'It's been empty a couple of years. The old lady who lived here, Miss Wingham, was in a nursing home till she died. The estate have had it on the market ever since. Too expensive for the local first-time buyers and too small for the upcountry folk who want holiday lets.'

He let her walk round the kitchen, through to the sitting room. She tried to lie down in the wide window seat. Not quite long enough, but perfect to curl up in with a book. Or a cat? She opened the far door, which led to the stairs, and made her way up. Polished oak with a circular bend bringing her out to the landing and two bedrooms. The view from the bedrooms was to the front, overlooking the village green, while the window on the stairs gave a view of the garden and the church. After a quick tour of the overgrown garden, she and Neil retired to the Dolphin to discuss terms.

When her offer was accepted by the executors, Dorrie poured them all a large glass of vodka and cranberry to celebrate.

The vodka left Helen feeling unsure about driving, so Don invited her for supper upstairs in their private bit of the pub. 'Dorrie's got a chicken in the oven for tea. There's plenty to go round.'

Completely seduced by her new house, the village and its people, she followed him upstairs. She had never seen the landlord's accommodation above a pub before, but this was certainly not what she expected. It was like something out of a glossy magazine. Light and airy with a beachy feel to it, the colours were cream and café au lait. The bleached floorboards were strewn with richly coloured rugs, one wall was adorned with a fabulous painting of boats in a harbour, all broad strokes and bright colours. There was a pile of driftwood by the wood-burning stove, and a coffee table made entirely of wide planks. The sofas were deep and squashy and scattered with slightly crazy cushions, each embroidered with a single rose-pink seagull and embellished with real feathers.

'Wow! This is amazing! And look at the view. You can see the sea and the cliffs.'

Don looked embarrassed. 'Dorrie and I worked on it over the winter. Do you like it? The floor's a bit wonky, but after I sanded it we decided it looked all right.'

'It's fabulous! What the London women I know wouldn't give for this! Where's the coffee table from?'

'That? I made it from some old scaffold boards I found. Rubbish really.'

'You did it? Don, I want my cottage to look just like this! Will you do it for me?'

3

D on and Dorrie had sorted out all the building and decorating after that, while Helen set about packing up her old life. She couldn't wait. The London house was lovely, but it held too many memories. The good she could file away, the bad she would delete.

Sean thought she was mad.

'Ma, what on earth do you think you're doing? Lots of older people get an idea in their heads to retire to the seaside, only to find they miss their old life and end up dying lonely.'

'Sean, I am forty-seven. Not quite in my dotage, thank you very much! In fact, still young enough to give you a little brother or sister, if I cared to.'

'Ma, what a revolting idea. And what are you doing with that pile of vintage comics?'

'Throwing them away.'

'They're worth a lot of money. Hang on to them for me, would you?'

'Nope. All your stuff is yours from now on. Take it away or never see it again.'

Within an hour Sean had salvaged what childhood possessions he could fit into his absurdly small car and driven off in a huff.

Chloe had been more understanding. She understood that her mother had had enough of a painful marriage, but she adored both her parents and hoped that somehow they would get back together again.

On her last day, Gray came round to give her a bunch of flowers and a hug. They walked round the old place together and it felt right. He helped her pack her last few things in the car, slipped a wad of notes to the removal men as their tip, and together they shut the front door for ever.

'Bye, old girl. Give me a bell to let me know you got there OK.'

'I will.' She kissed him briefly and with only a quick glance in her rear-view mirror, pointed the snub nose of the Mini in the direction of the M4.

*

And now here she was. Ten days later and everything settled. No looking back and certainly no regrets.

Don called to her, 'Helen, I've set the timer and the thermostat.'

He tried again to explain the procedure to her, but although she nodded at the right moments, she didn't understand it at all. It didn't matter, he'd said she could call him again if she had any trouble.

As he was leaving, she said, 'You don't do gardening as well, do you?'

'Nope. Don't like worms. Ask Queenie, she'll know someone.'

She'd been planning to nip into Queenie's in any case, so she gathered up her things and a few minutes later she was ducking through her low front door. From force of habit, she turned to lock up, then decided instead to leave caution to the cautious. Nobody seemed to lock their front doors in Pendruggan and cars were never locked either.

Don had laughed at her when he had caught her frantically looking for her keys on first moving in: 'Leave them where they're meant to be, maid. Either in the front door or in the ignition. You'll never lose them then.'

*

Queenie's Post Office and General Store was the centre of village life. The day after Helen arrived in Pendruggan she had gone in for a pint of milk and Queenie, thrilled to find new blood in the village, had immediately launched into her life story. She had originally come to Pendruggan as an evacuee from London's East End, but when her parents were tragically killed in the Blitz, the Cornish family with whom she'd been billeted took her under their wing. She stayed with them until she was eighteen, when she left to marry the local farmhand she'd fallen in love with.

'I was married to Ted for fifty-two years, until he died of emphysema in 2000,' Queenie sighed and lit a small roll-up cigarette.

'The only way I'll be leavin' 'ere is in a box. My daughter Sandra wants me to move up to Coventry to be near her, but what do I wanna do that for? This is me 'ome and this is where I'll stay until the day comes when I can rest next to my Ted in the churchyard. Would you like a pasty, duck?'

'Yes, please. They look delicious.'

'Homemade, they are! I do fifteen a day to order. When do you want yours?'

'Can I have one now?'

'No, duck. To order, like I said. Shall I put you on me regular list?'

'Oh, I see. Yes, please. Can I have one tomorrow?'

Queenie took a gnarled pencil from her ear and pulled out a thumbed red exercise book. 'What's your name, dear?'

And Helen found herself telling Queenie her own life story in return.

'That ex-husband of yours sounds like a right bastard, and no mistake. Still,' Queenie adopted a look of wisdom, 'that's men for you.' She paused. 'And now you're 'ere in Miss Wingham's old 'ouse. She was a lovely lady, you know. Very old-fashioned in her ways, and ever so intelligent. She came 'ere to live before the war, you know. Lived in Gull's Cry for seventy-seven years. She was on her own for all of 'em, no fella or nuffink. She never told me, but I fink she lost the love of her life in the war. She never said in so many words, but I could tell. Loved 'er cats too. Her last one was called Raven. She named 'em all after birds – I dunno why. Died peacefully in the nursing 'ome aged ninety-seven. She'll be 'appy to think you've brought the old place back to life. Will you be doin' the garden? She loved it. I'd like to get Alan Titchmarsh down 'ere to give it a going over. If you see 'im, you tell 'im!' She laughed, then coughed a crackly cough that had been cultivated over decades of dedicated smoking.

Now, Thursday had become Pasty Day, and Helen was looking forward to another chat and a chance to browse the shelves, which were lined with greaseproof paper and red gingham. Queenie's stock was extraordinary. Replacement suspenders for corsets and Blakey heel caps sat amongst the more mundane requirements. There was a well-stocked magazine rack, which Queenie devoured – showbiz gossip could have been her specialist knowledge on *Mastermind* – reading at the counter by the dim light of two bulbs suspended from the ceiling, the standard lamp with its pink shade by the freezer and the Tiffany lamp next to the till.

Queenie greeted Helen warmly as she entered. 'Hallo, duck. I ain't seen you much this week – you OK?'

'Yes thanks, Queenie. I did a bit of a shop at Tesco in Trevay yesterday.'

'Tesco? They ain't got nothing in there! I go up sometimes on the bus, but they've never got anythin' I want.'

'Well, it was only to get a few things like balsamic and olive oil.'

'Olive oil? We used to go to the chemist to get that, duck. And Balls Amic? What's that when it's at 'ome?'

'A kind of vinegar.'

'I got malt if you want it?' Queenie turned to look at the gloomy shelf to her right.

'Actually, what I do want, Queenie, is a gardener. Do you know anyone who would help me clear the garden?'

'Oh yeah, me duck. Simple Tony's the one you want.'

'Tony?'

'Simple Tony. 'E's simple, poor lad, but a good worker. Very green-fingered.'

Helen was shocked at Queenie's description of Tony as 'simple', but knew that Queenie's generation had little truck with political correctness. She hoped that Queenie was more sensitive around the poor boy and didn't call him 'Simple Tony' to his face.

'Where does Tony live?' she asked.

'Next door to you. In that shepherd's hut in the garden.'

Helen remembered the hut. The day she moved in,

Polly – the owner of the house next door – had come round with mugs of camomile tea for the unimpressed removal men, who would definitely have preferred a more energising builder's brew. Helen hadn't had a chance to chat to her properly or find out anything about her, but since then there had been several occasions when she'd looked over into the garden and caught sight of a youngish man in a navy-blue boiler suit, sitting on the steps of the hut boiling a kettle on his camping stove. This must be Tony, Helen realised. She was glad to have an excuse to go round and find out more.

'Is that all, duck? Want a magazine? I got some good ones there. Julia Roberts is a lovely girl, ain't she? I like to read about 'er. And Fiona Whatsit what reads the news. Not enough about 'er. She's very popular in my 'ouse, you know.'

'I'll have a bottle of wine please. I'll take it round to Polly.'

'Righto.' She handed Helen a dusty bottle. 'This has been 'ere since the Easter Raffle. Should be good by now.'

4

The smell of woodsmoke drifted over from Polly's chimney and mingled with the damp of the conkers lined up in a row on the doorstep.

Polly opened the door with a smile.

'Hello, Helen. Welcome to Candle Cottage. Don't mind the conkers. I put them there to keep the spiders away – apparently they don't like the smell of them. It's for Tony, the big softie. He hates them! What can I do for you?'

She greeted Helen with a kiss and showed her into a room decorated with beachcombing finds and filled with vintage furniture.

'Polly, what a wonderful room – is that a real crystal ball?'

'Oh, that's my ball to do the village fayres. I like a bit of fortune-telling, but only for fun. Occasionally I'm right. Little Michaela up the way came to see me last year with a broken heart and fretting about her GCSEs. I told her that her life would change in twelve months, and now she's got five grade Cs and is five months' pregnant! We're all very proud of her. Cup of tea?'

'How about a glass of wine? I've brought you a bottle from Queenie's.'

'Proper job! Let me find some glasses from the whatnot.' Polly went to her dark wood shelves and took out two original Babycham Saucer glasses. 'How are you settling in to village life then?' She poured the wine and sat down on a Moroccan pouffe. 'A bit quieter than London, I expect. I'd have come round to see you before now, but I was worried you'd think I was being nosy.'

'It's certainly quieter than London, which can only be a good thing. Polly, I want to pick your brains. I need a gardener and Queenie suggested Tony – the man from your garden. Does he actually live with you?'

'Well, when his mum died, I couldn't bear to see him on his own so I offered him the use of the hut and he loves it. He's a super lad and will get your garden back on track. Don't spoil him, though, and make sure he knows who's boss.'

'Queenie calls him Simple Tony. Is he . . . ?'

'Don't go confusing simple for stupid,' said Polly. 'He ain't stupid. But he does have a tendency to take every-thing very literally. I once told him I was dying for a cup of tea and then had to stop him dialling 999!' Polly laughed. 'I'll send him round to you in the morning and you can show him what needs doing. More wine?'

They sat and talked until it was quite dark outside. Helen filled her in on her previous life and then it was Polly's turn.

'Have you heard about Green Magic? It's all about working with the power of nature and Mother Earth. Any little potion or spell I can rustle up for you? I find it complements my main work as a paramedic with the ambulance service.'

'You're joking!'

'Absolutely not! I'm highly skilled – won awards and everything. So, if there's any magical or medical emergency, don't hesitate to call me! Would you like supper? I'm vegan, mind.'

'That's sweet of you but maybe next time. Thank you, Polly. I look forward to seeing Tony in the morning. Bye!'

*

At 6.45 a.m. Helen was woken by hammering on the front door. Scrambling from her bed she peered out of the window. It was just getting light and she could make out the top of a man's head. He was wearing a thick green check lumberjack coat and carrying a spade. Opening the window, she called down, 'Hello. Can I help you?'

'I don't know?' said the top of the head, crouching now in order to look through the porthole. 'I've come to 'elp you. Polly said that I was to come this mornin' and do gardening? I'm right, I know.'

'Just a minute.' *This has to be Tony*, thought Helen. She ran downstairs and threw open the front door. 'Good morning. It's very early, Tony. I'm not dressed yet.'

'No you're not.'

'Do you want to come back a bit later. In about an hour?'

'No thank you. I am here to do the garden.'

'Well yes, OK. Follow me, then.'

She took Tony out to the back garden, pausing only to slip on her wellies.

'While I'm getting dressed, perhaps you'd like to start on the big bed here.' She pointed at an eight-foot-square raised bed where the brambles were at least six feet high.

'Just weed it and clear it and then I'll be down to help you. OK?'

'Yeah.'

'Would you like a cup of tea?'

'No thankee. I've got me Ribena.' He patted his canvas shoulder bag. 'Don't hurry, lady. Tony will be all right.'

'OK. See you in an hour or so.'

Back indoors, Helen struggled to get her wellies off her slightly sweaty bare feet, put the kettle on and looked at the clock: 6.55 a.m. Realising there was no point in going back to bed, she made herself a cup of milky coffee, opened up her laptop and logged on. There were seventeen new messages, fifteen of which were spam. But there was one from Penny and one from Gray. She looked at Gray's first.

Darling, longing to see you and get the hell out of town. Can you give me a number for the best hotel you can think of? Better book a double in case I can't escape the bloody girlfriend. Thanks, darling. Your Gray.

'I am not your bloody secretary and you are no longer MY Gray!' Helen muttered to herself, but nonetheless she sent a polite email with the number of the swish Starfish Hotel in nearby Trevay.

The Starfish was exactly Gray's kind of place. In summer you couldn't move in the old harbour car park for Porsches and Bentleys, and the Starfish was always awash with visiting celebrities pretending they were staycationing (before they jetted off to the South of France or the Bahamas). The Cornish locals didn't mind a bit. If the townies with more money than sense wanted to spend their bucks down here, well, why not! Never underestimate the commercial nous of a true Cornishman.

Next Helen opened her email from Penny.

Hello, gorgeous, how's it going? You'll never guess what . . . I'm working on a new costume drama based on the books of Mavis Crewe. Have you read them? She's a poor man's Daphne du Maurier, but one or two of her books have cracking stories. We're scouting for a location in Cornwall and, having looked at the map, I've told the location manager to come and recce your village. I might come too – can I stay with you? It'll be in the next month or so. Let me know. Love, Penny

Helen smiled and bashed out a quick reply:

Yes, any time! X

*

After she'd taken a bath and made herself presentable, Helen went out into the garden to see how Tony was faring. There was a bonfire smoking by the compost heap and the rich red soil of the flower bed was turned over neatly with not a weed in sight. Tony was sitting on the upturned wheelbarrow eating a pasty and drinking his Ribena.

'Is that all right for 'ee, missus?'

'Tony, that's wonderful,' said Helen. 'Shall we crack on with some more?'

Together they worked for the rest of the day, stopping only for a quick sandwich – chicken salad for Helen and raspberry jam for Tony – until by sunset all of the large raised beds were cleared.

'How much do I owe you?'

'I'll ask Polly and tell 'ee later, missus.'

Tony collected his jacket, his bag and his spade and jumped over the low wall into Polly's garden. Helen watched as he walked to the steps of his shepherd's hut. He turned and waved to her, then went inside. She could see him turning on the light and drawing the blue gingham curtains.

What a dear man Tony was. Helen thought how fortunate he was to live here and not in a big city. In London he would surely be among the outcast homeless, forgotten by society. But here, among the caring community of Pendruggan, he was protected and safe. She was safe too. Safer than she had felt in years.

Helen turned and walked straight into an imposing male figure dressed head-to-toe in black. She screamed.

5

'Sssh sssh. It's okay.' The man held her arms tight. 'I've just come to introduce myself.'

Helen kicked out at the stranger's ankles and he let go of her, hopping about in pain. She ran to her back door, darted inside and bolted it behind her. Two seconds later, there was a gentle knocking.

'I'm so sorry if I startled you. My name is Canter, Simon Canter. I'm the vicar of Holy Trinity Church here in the village. I've only come to say hello. Actually, I think my ankle is bleeding a bit.'

Helen slid the bolt open and looked at him. Amidst the black of his coat and trousers she saw the distinctive white dog collar.

'Oh my God. You frightened the life out of me.'

'I am awfully sorry. Shall I come back another time?'

'No, it's fine. Come in.' She stepped aside and he walked into the kitchen.

'Would you like me to look at your ankle?'

He rolled up his trousers to reveal a white and hairless leg with a long scrape and blood starting to ooze down his shin.

'Oh God, I'll get a plaster.'

Once he was fixed and she had apologised for her blaspheming, she brought out the sherry bottle and a tube of Pringles. He made himself comfortable at the kitchen table.

'I knocked at your front door, but as there was no answer, and I could see you moving about in the back garden, I walked around the side to find you. Promise! Don't think I'm a Peeping Tom or stalker or anything like that!'

Helen wondered if she would have been able to describe him to a police artist if he really had been an attacker; he had the kind of face you would be hard-pressed to recall. He was slim, slightly under six foot tall, with chocolate-brown eyes enlarged by his spectacles. A shiny bald head made him look older than he was, but she guessed he was about her age. He smiled at her as she looked at him. A lovely smile. Full of humour and sincerity. He had goodness and kindness emanating from him which was instantly likeable.

'I thought I would just pop round, say hello, and welcome you to the parish and the church. Are you a churchgoer?'

'I haven't been for a long time. Not that I'm not a believer! It just hasn't been on my agenda for a while.'

'Perhaps I can persuade you to come along and meet some of the flock? We don't bite!' Simon's Adam's apple wobbled as he laughed. 'Do you play the guitar? Or piano?'

Helen felt panicky. 'No, not really. Not at all, actually. Why?'

'Christmas is nearer than you think and we like to put on a bit of an entertainment in the church. Raise some much-needed funds with ticket sales. The churchyard needs a lot of work. Some of our graves are very old and getting rather dangerous. The parish council are concerned about headstones falling on children or elderly visitors. It all costs money.' He drained his glass and she poured him another. 'We may also have to move some graves and re-inter the remains to make a bit more room. The local archaeologist and county council need to be involved with that.'

'Well, I'd certainly be happy to buy a ticket for the show.'

'Excellent. How many?'

'Just me. And maybe my daughter, if she's down.'

'Can we persuade your husband?' He looked up with something in his eyes she couldn't quite read.

'I doubt it. We're separated.'

'A single lady in the village! Oh my goodness, I wouldn't want you, or anyone else for that matter, to misconstrue my visit here!' More Adam's apple action.

'I am sure your wife wouldn't mind.' She smiled.

'Well, you see,' he coughed, 'I am a single man myself, and as a clergyman I have to be circumspect about my demeanour and behaviour. The village gossips love any excuse.'

Helen, swallowing a laugh, said, 'You are safe with me, I assure you!'

He looked crestfallen.

'Not that I don't think you are an attractive man.'

He perked up.

'It's just that I . . . erm . . . am not ready for . . . anything like that . . . at the moment.'

'It hasn't been my good fortune to find a lady kind enough to take me on.' Simon looked at his shoes. 'Although I live in hope that one day the Good Lord will find a lid to fit my pot, as it were.' The Adam's apple was on a bungee rope.

He took another large slug of sherry. Helen, feeling that she was about to hear his life story, topped up his glass, and then her own. She waited.

He turned his chocolate-brown, magnified eyes to hers, and blew out his slender cheeks.

'I had a disappointment, you see. A few years ago now, but I still think of her. We met on a trip to the Holy Land. One of those organised excursions, you know. We sort of paired up and found ourselves sitting next to each other on the coach each day. Her name is Denise. She's an RE teacher. Or was. I'm not sure what she's doing now. Anyway, I knew I had fallen in love with her and we began writing to each other when we got home. She was in Scotland, not far from her parents. We ended up speaking on the phone every day and after a couple of months we met up in Coventry. The cathedral had a special service and we both thought it was a good halfway point. It was a marvellous day. The service was really inspiring. Wonderful music and singing. I got caught up in the elation of it all and over supper I asked her to marry me.' He looked down at his worn cuffs.

'And she said no?' asked Helen.

'Oh no, she said yes! It was all so exciting. I walked her to her B&B and said goodnight, and in the morning we met briefly at the station before I came back here and she went back to Scotland to make the wedding arrangements.'

'So what happened?'

'The night before the ceremony she said she felt unwell and didn't want to go to the rehearsal. I sat with her and she was crying. I suggested calling the doctor, but she stopped me. She told me she wasn't ill, it was just that . . .' He tipped his head back and looked at the kitchen ceiling. 'It was just that she didn't love me enough to marry me after all.'

Helen leaned forward and held his hand as it cradled the sherry glass.

'I am so sorry,' she said.

'I'm not looking for sympathy.' He took out a hanky and wiped his glasses. 'But it was a blow. I came here a very young man, twenty-one, freshly ordained and full of heroic ideals. A job where I could make a difference to society, the opportunity to meet my soul mate. The vicarage is such a lovely family house. It would come alive with people in it. Children . . . that sort of thing.'

They both sat in silence for a moment. Finally Helen said, 'I think she made a big mistake. I bet she regrets it every day.'

'Well that's kind of you, but . . . it wasn't God's will. So,' he stood up, 'church on Sunday. I give communion at the ten o'clock service, if you're up to it?'

'Yes, I'd love to.'

Simon buttoned up his coat and after apologising again for frightening her earlier in the garden, walked down the path. As he turned towards the vicarage, her eye was caught by Polly waving at her from her window next door and giving her the thumbs-up. Helen returned the thumbs-up and waved back. Two minutes later, back inside and with a fresh glass of sherry in her hand, she wondered what Polly had meant by her gesture. Surely she hadn't thought that there was anything between her and Simon? They'd only just met. She laughed at the idea – what a joke!

6

The following day was Saturday. Helen had survived two weeks of her new life and hadn't once wanted to run back to London. It was a gorgeous day and the September sunshine flooded into her bedroom as she drew open the curtains. Today she intended to rig up a washing line and get some laundry out.

The nearest hardware store was in Trevay so she decided to nip over and treat herself to breakfast as well.

The five-mile drive was a pleasure in itself. Up the steep hill out of Pendruggan, past the Dolphin where she tooted at Dorrie as she swept the leaves from the pub porch, along the cliff road where she could see the surf whipping off the ocean and then down another sharp incline into Trevay. With the roof off the little Mini, she revelled in the splashes of sunlight that dappled the lanes. The local drivers were so different to London ones. They were happy to reverse up the road where it was too tight for two cars to pass, and if she returned the favour they always thanked her. Quite unlike Gray, who was horrendous to drive with. As a passenger he was a bully and as a driver, a dictator. He once shouted at an already nervous Helen when she accidentally curbed the wheels of his latest gas guzzler, 'YOU should NOT have a LICENCE!'

Her journey to Trevay ended without incident and she arrived safely in the harbour car park. She got out and left the car, roof down, doors unlocked, to take in the beauty of the ancient fishing port. Above her, and over-looking the harbour was the Starfish Hotel. Built just before the First World War to accommodate the holiday-makers flocking to Cornwall by train, it had fallen on hard times after Dr Beeching closed the station in the sixties, and cheap, foreign package holidays became all the rage. No rail passengers meant fewer holidaymakers and the old hotel had quietly been allowed to run down. But about fifteen years ago it had been bought up by a stylish and very wealthy widow who persuaded a young, sexy TV chef to take on the kitchens. It was an instant success and was now the shining template for all other faded seaside hotels. Helen thought how much Gray would love it, if and when he came down.

She walked across the road towards the harbour wall. The tide was out and the little fishing boats were resting on their keels in the mud. A seagull swooped down and with a cackle collected up a dead crab from the silt.

Her first stop was the local chandlers and ironmongers. The shelves were lined with cardboard boxes full of every-thing any self-respecting sailor or builder could want. You could even buy a single screw or washer if necessary. She walked up and down the three aisles until she found a twelve-metre ball of yellow washing line. She took it to the counter and asked the young man what he would recommend to fix it to the old brick privy wall and the back door jamb. He found her some metal screw eyes and swively things with some masonry nails and a metal plate with a loop in it. She thought she understood the instructions and tried to pay particular attention when he showed her a useful knot that would withstand a force ten gale.

Pleased with her purchases and the young man's faith in her abilities, Helen left the shop and walked along the road to the inner harbour. She stood for a couple of moments looking at the way the sun sparkled on the emerald-green water. An older couple with a Dachshund stopped and did the same. The three of them exchanged pleasantries and Helen was introduced to Stuart, the dog, who, after sniffing Helen's hand, turned and cocked his leg on her jeans. The couple didn't seem to notice and, saying cheerio, ambled off towards the town.

As the warm liquid travelled into her sock and trainer, she shook her foot and glared at the nonchalantly retreating back of Stuart, swearing under her breath. She heard someone laughing, turned towards the sound and found herself looking straight into the eyes of one of the most handsome men she'd ever seen. Tall and broad-shouldered, he was wearing a tattered and faded red sailcloth fishing smock. A blue-and-white handkerchief was tied round his neck, accentuating the deep fathoms of his blue eyes. A small gold earring glinted in his right ear and his jet-black corkscrewed hair was ruffled in the wind.

'Did you see that?' she asked.

'Oh yes,' he replied, his full mouth and white teeth still laughing. 'That dog must be an excellent judge of character.'

She laughed too. 'Thanks! I feel as if I have half a gallon of pee in my shoe, but it's probably only a teaspoon.'

'Well, I hope your day improves.' And he walked off in the same direction as the incontinent Stuart, leaving

Helen feeling confused. Had she just been teased or insulted?

She couldn't decide whether to head back to the car and go home or nip into a shop for a cheap pair of beach shoes, then look for breakfast. Beach shoes and breakfast won. When she came out of the shop, her trainers and socks tied up inside two plastic bags, she left the harbour behind her and walked into the little town. The streets were narrow and traditionally quaint. Some local businesses like the butcher, baker and green-grocer still survived, but most of the shops were geared to the wealthier holiday visitors. She enjoyed half an hour of window shopping, but didn't succumb. There's plenty of time for me to do shopping here – the rest of my life! she told herself.

Finally she arrived at an all-day café that she'd been to once with Dorrie, when she had treated Dorrie to lunch as a thank you for all her help and input into Gull's Cry. The tables were set outside and she parked herself at a table for two in a sunny, sheltered corner. The waiter came out and took her order for a cappuccino and full Cornish breakfast (just the same as an English one, only better, he said).

Tilting her head up to the sun, Helen closed her eyes and allowed herself to relax. She was aware of how her new shoes touched the cobbles beneath her; the warmth of the sun on her cheeks. Then she tuned in to the sounds around her. She heard voices, a van door slide open, the clip-clop of a woman's shoes on the cobbles and . . . a male voice she thought sounded familiar, coming from inside the café.

'I'll have a black coffee, boy. Three sugars. How's the summer been for you?'

She heard her waiter's voice: 'Handsome. But I'll be glad when the visitors have all gone 'ome.'

'The last six weeks have been heaving, haven't they?' the familiar voice responded. 'You'd think these grockles would want to do more than just mooch about spending too much money in the shops and eating cream teas and fish and chips. Still, if it pays for us to have a good winter, who cares. I saw one just now. Looked arty, like. Expensive handbag and haircut – you know the type. Then a dog peed on her leg. You should've seen her face! Proper townie and no mistake.'

Helen heard her waiter laugh. 'I'd 'ave paid good money to see that!'

The laughter continued. Her veins felt as if they were being flushed through with ice-cold water and yet her face was burning. She reached down to her Mulberry handbag and fumbled for her Tom Ford sunglasses. She must stick out like a sore thumb.

The waiter came back out with her coffee and breakfast, followed immediately by the handsome man she had met on the harbour. His dark, tightly curled hair bounced in the breeze, one hand holding a takeaway cup, the other shoved in his pocket.

'Bye, Bernie.'

'Bye, Piran. Look out for those leaky dogs!' the waiter called to him and, laughing, turned back into the café.

'Bastard. Bloody bastard,' muttered Helen, turning her face so that he couldn't see her.

She ate her breakfast and drank her coffee as quickly as possible. So much for enjoying a leisurely hour people-watching.

She paid the bill, left a minimal tip and drove home, fuming all the way.

*

On her doorstep there was a large bunch of rusty-coloured dahlias, wrapped in newspaper and tied with green twine. A small note read:

Thank you for listening and welcome to our village.
                                    Regards, Simon Canter

Smiling at his thoughtfulness, she carried them into the kitchen and dug out an old Cornishware jug to put them in. They looked just right sitting on the stone hearth of the fireplace.

After putting some laundry in the machine, including the revolting socks and trainers, she collected her brand-new tool box from under the sink and took her new washing line and ironmongery outside.

It was incredibly liberating not to have Gray breathing down her neck, telling her she was getting it all wrong. She hammered and screwed and swore to her heart's content, not caring when she chipped a bit of brick or drilled a hole in the wrong place, and it was fun. After about an hour she tested the whole construction. The knots seemed safe enough and everything appeared secure on the privy wall and back-door frame.

Ten minutes later, she'd hung the first batch of washing out on the line and she couldn't have been more pleased with herself if she'd climbed Machu Picchu.

Back inside, she settled down in her rocking chair by the Aga with a pot of tea and phoned Chloe. They spent a lovely hour catching up with each other's news and Chloe fell about laughing at the story of the dog wee. 'Everyone's a critic, Mum!'

But she felt Helen's humiliation at the hands of the corkscrew-haired man.

'Mummy, how horrible. What a nasty man. I hope you don't bump into him again.'

'I'll make sure to avoid him – not that he'd remember me anyway.'

There was a knock on the door. Helen looked up through the porthole window of the door and caught sight of a faded red fisherman's smock. *No, it couldn't be!*

'Hang on, darling. There's someone outside.' She slid out of her chair and ducked down on her hands and knees so that he couldn't see her. She crawled towards the door and, very tentatively, looked up through the glass to get a clearer view. He was looking down through the porthole directly at her.

'Chloe, oh my God – it's him! He's here.'

'What? Don't answer it.'

'No, I'll have to. He can see me. Stay on the line.'

She stood up, trying to look nonchalant and opened the door. 'Hello. Can I help you?'

'I thought it was you. The dog-wee lady?' He smiled a twisted, sardonic smile.

'Yes, that's me. Ha ha!' Helen laughed awkwardly.

'What were you doing crawling on the floor just now?'

'Erm . . .' She couldn't think of an answer, so said instead, 'I'm on the phone . . . long distance . . . Is this important?'

'Well, no, not to me. But I thought you'd like to know your washing line's broken and your knickers are blowing all over the churchyard.' He looked her up and down slowly. 'Bye, then.'

'Right. Thank you. Goodbye.' And she slammed the door.

'Mum! Are you OK? I heard his voice. Quite sexy.'

'Chloe, he may sound quite sexy, he may look quite sexy, but that man is *not* sexy.'

*

Out in the garden the washing was ruined. She collected it all up and then climbed over the wall into the church-yard to find a tea towel and two pairs of the frilly knickers that Gray had bought her for her last birthday. He had always bought her pretty undies. He loved her legs and was never happier than when they were encased in stockings and suspenders. But then he'd loved any woman in stockings and suspenders. She wished he'd stop giving them to her.

With everything safely in her laundry basket, she hoiked herself back up over the wall and into her garden. She heard a wolf whistle behind her and turned. That bloody man was in the churchyard, looking at her, and laughing. She clutched the basket tightly to her chest and stomped indoors, giving the back door a satisfying slam.

7

S itting at his desk in the vicarage, Simon Canter gazed
out of his study window overlooking the church car
park. He smiled and returned Piran Ambrose's wave as he
drove off in his rusting Toyota truck. Good man, Piran. A
bit surly, but a good heart and he was really helping the
Graveyard Committee in identifying which plots needed
to be renovated, relocated or simply removed all together.

Just beyond the church was the churchyard, and
beyond that Helen Merrifield's back garden. Simon was
in love. She was perfect; a goddess of medium height
with what looked like shapely long legs. He hadn't been
able to see much because of the gardening trousers she'd
been wearing, but he had noticed her full bosom when
she'd taken her coat off and stood there in her T-shirt
looking at his ankle. Her hair was dark auburn with a
natural curl. Her eyes amber. Her creamy skin was scattered with freckles. Her lips stained as if with raspberry
juice, plump and wide . . .

He sighed. Meeting Helen had shaken his orderly
world. He'd felt the same when he first saw Denise and
then, a couple of years after the Denise debacle, when
he'd met Hillary, a woman in her thirties who came to
him for confirmation classes. Week after week they'd sat
here in his study, just the two of them, discussing her
faith and the challenge of believing in a God who didn't

show himself so magically these days; no vivid dramas and burning bushes like in the Old Testament. Her faith had been strong, but she seemed to be having trouble allowing God to accept her as she was. Simon had high hopes of getting her to trust God and eventually trust him too. Then her trust would turn to love and he would have the wife he so very much wanted.

What's that old saying? Simon thought. '*Man plans and God laughs.*' Never had it been truer than when Hillary confessed she was struggling with her lesbian feelings towards one of her married colleagues. Sometimes Simon didn't like God's sense of humour.

And now there was Helen Merrifield. Her name sounded like crystal water sparkling into a little pool.

'Canter S.,' he heard his Latin teacher's voice in his head, 'get on with your work.'

He looked down at the scribbled notes he was making for tomorrow's sermon. All nonsense. 'Come on, man, get a grip.' Living alone was a wonderful excuse for talking aloud to yourself. 'Yes, yes, now where was I? Helen Merrifield . . . did she get my flowers? Did she like them? Shall I go over and see her? Erm . . . no, I'll phone her instead. Drat, don't have her number. She'll phone me. I am in the book. And if she doesn't, I'll see her at church tomorrow. And I'll talk to her about . . . stuff. Yes. Now, what am I doing? Writing tomorrow's sermon. That's it. I'll put the kettle on.'

Which he did, and tried to knuckle down to the task at hand, but Simon was unable to keep thoughts of Helen at bay for long.

'I wonder what she's doing now?' he mused.

*

Helen was on the beach. She'd followed the path from the village green down the side of Pendruggan Farm and walked half a mile across the fields from Gull's Cry to where the Atlantic Ocean swept in and out of Shellsand Bay. It was a beach which the holiday visitors rarely found as it was awkward to trek down to, especially with wind-breaks, cool boxes and buggies. Today it was empty.

She walked down to the tideline and turned over lumps of seaweed with her wellies, looking for interesting bits of wood or shells. She found a cork ring attached to some green fishing net and a beautiful piece of slate shaped like a heart. She put them both in her pocket and then walked down to the sea. The breeze was mild, ruffling her wavy hair, and with every buffet she felt her humiliation at Piran's hands slowly dissipate. The tide was out quite a way, but the swell was big and she spotted two surfers looking like seals in their wetsuits. They were lying on their boards waiting to catch a big wave. She took a great lungful of the salty air and reminded herself that this was why she was here. The wildness of the elements and the freedom of a life without responsibility. She watched as the surfers paddled furiously just ahead of a big breaker and then leapt up on to their boards and expertly rode the wave almost right up on to the beach.

Years ago, when she had come to Cornwall as a child, her father had bought her a little wooden bodyboard. He had spent long, patient hours in the shallows, teaching her how to catch a wave and ride it on her tummy. She so wanted to do it again. Perhaps she could get lessons in real stand-up surfing? She'd ask Queenie.

She stayed for another twenty minutes or so, watching the surfers and then turned for home.

Back at Gull's Cry, the washing machine had done its stuff and she hung the wet laundry on the drying rack above the Aga. Her attempt to fix up the washing line outside was a failure; the bracket had fallen off. The pulley system installed in the kitchen to haul it all up to ceiling height made a satisfying squeaky noise. And at least if that fell down, it wouldn't lead to another ignominious episode with the rude man in the fisherman's smock.

She put a jacket potato in the oven and got the paper out to see what was on the telly. *Rebecca* by Daphne du Maurier. Perfect.

A couple of hours later and she was ready for bed. It was only 9 p.m. A bit earlier than she was used to, but that was country life for you. Wasn't it? She wasn't getting bored already, was she?

8

It was 7 a.m. on Sunday morning and the Reverend Simon Canter was putting on his robes of office. On Sundays he took a no-frills, spoken rather than sung communion at 8 a.m. for those few communicants who wanted the peace of a child-free service first thing, leaving them free to get on with their day.

He'd got up earlier than usual today in order to give the vicarage a bit of a spring clean. His weekly help had been off with her hips for a couple of weeks now and the place was showing signs of neglect, so he'd vacuumed round the vast and largely unused Victorian sitting room and opened the French windows to allow the autumn air to disperse the smell of must and old hymn books that he felt must be hanging around. Then he cut another large bunch of his bronze dahlias from the garden and placed them in a vase on the modest grand piano. Not bad. Next he gave the downstairs loo a quick bleach and the kitchen a wipe.

When he finished getting dressed and came downstairs, he sniffed the air and immediately ran back upstairs to his bathroom. He returned with his aftershave (a Christmas present from Queenie, who'd assured him that David Beckham wore nothing less) and proceeded to squirt it liberally through the rooms downstairs. He sniffed again. Much better. Taking one last look round, he left to tend his flock.

*

Later that morning, walking over to the church, Helen mulled over the possibility that she might be missing London. Or, if not London itself, then maybe her friends. So she resolved to get some dates in the diary and encourage them to visit her.

Getting ready that morning, she'd looked in the mirror and decided she really ought to make an effort with her appearance. Once she'd applied a little mascara, rouge and lip gloss, she realised that it made her look much better than she had in weeks. She had decided on a cream and bronze chiffon tea dress which accentuated her freckles, over the top of which she was wearing a cream cashmere cardigan in case the church was cold. She'd kept her legs bare, with tan strappy sandals on her slim feet.

The church was fourteenth century with Victorian additions, most notably the clock tower. The bell ringers were calling the village to prayers and sending the rooks up into the trees like black plastic bin liners flapping in the breeze. As Helen came out of her gate, Polly and another man caught up with her. They were both in green ambulance uniforms.

'Hello, Helen,' said Polly, walking alongside her. 'We're on call today, but we don't like to miss the service. We've got the pager, haven't we, Pete?' The man on the other side of Helen nodded. 'You do look nice today,' Polly continued. 'I was saying to Pete, I wondered if we'd be seeing you at church today. Seeing as you and the vicar had quite a long chat the other night.' Polly was smiling conspiratorially.

The man with Polly greeted Helen with a grin. 'Hello. I'm Pete. Pleased to meet you. And so's Reverend Canter, apparently.'

'What?' But Helen's voice was lost as, flanked by the couple, she was swept into the church.

The entire congregation of twenty-five turned to look at her. Queenie, who was sitting near the front, waved the three of them over, and they sat down alongside her. For the next five minutes, Queenie, Pete and Polly introduced Helen, very proprietorially, to the entire church until, at exactly 10 a.m, Simon entered from a side door and the service began. As he introduced the first hymn he gave a little nod of hello to Helen and there was a definite thrum of excitement from the congregation.

*

The service was a good and simple one. Apart from a mild hiatus when Pete and Polly were called out to an emergency heart attack in Trevay, it went smoothly. Helen hadn't taken communion for many years and was surprisingly moved by the gentleness of Simon's touch and the blessings as he gave her the bread and wine.

When it came to giving the sign of peace, he made a beeline for her and held her hand a fraction longer than necessary while asking if she'd care to come over to the vicarage after the service to have a glass of sherry with several of the other parishioners. Helen felt she could hardly refuse in front of so many expectant faces.

'Thank you. Just a quick one.'

Simon visibly relaxed and went on to shake hands with the rest of the throng.

*

'Come in. Come in.' He ushered his eight or so guests in to the sitting room. Helen could see that it hadn't benefited from a woman's touch for several years, but she noticed the flowers on the piano and the same musky smell that Simon carried with him. He'd tried hard to make it welcoming. She offered to help him hand around the sherry and small cubes of cheese sprinkled with paprika, from which he'd just taken the cling film.

She was surprised to find she enjoyed herself much more than she'd expected. Everybody was so kind and interested in her. She was definitely the celebrity of the day!

'How do you know the vicar then?' an elderly man in tweed and corduroy asked her.

'Well, it's a very funny story actually.' Simon hovered with a bowl of cashews. 'Tell Jack, Helen.'

As Helen told the story, the room fell silent as all eyes hung on every word. 'I'm glad it was only his shin that I kicked,' she finished.

'So's the vicar,' laughed Jack, elbowing Simon in the ribs.

Within an hour everybody was heading off for their lunch, or to the pub, and Simon accepted Helen's offer of collecting the glasses and washing them up in the sink.

They chatted comfortably about nothing in particular, Helen enjoying his friendly chatter and Simon enjoying the rarity of female company.

'When did you decide the clergy was for you, Simon?'

'It wasn't a road to Damascus moment, I'm afraid.' He smiled. 'I was going to be a vet at first, then maybe a PE teacher, but my heart kept telling me it was people's souls I needed to attend to, not their animals or their bodies. And I have never regretted my decision.'

Helen dried her hands and looked at her watch. 'Golly, it's a quarter to one. I must leave you to the rest of your day.'

As Simon led her back through the dark hall to the front door, she glanced into his office. Books were crammed into the floor-to-ceiling shelves and an ancient swivel chair with a squishy chintz cushion stood in front of a disordered but charming oak desk, which had a view over to the church. Leaning up against the adjacent window was an enormous surfboard.

'Simon! Are you a surfer?'

'A bit. We Cornish boys have to, by law.' They both smiled. 'I might go out this afternoon, actually. The tide'll be coming in about two p.m., so just right.'

'The sea must be freezing.'

'Surprisingly warm right now. October is usually the warmest month. I have a good winter wetsuit though. Boots, gloves, helmet – the lot.'

'Well, Reverend Simon Canter, I never had you down as a surf dude.' He looked at his feet and scuffed one shoe over the other.

'I-I'd be happy to take you, if you wanted to come.'

'I can't surf.'

'I'll teach you. I'm very patient and by next summer I'll have you ready to enter the World Championships down at Fistral Beach.'

She laughed aloud and he smiled back, glad that whatever signals he was sending, they seemed to be working.

'Great,' said Helen. 'Let's go this afternoon.'

*

Helen nipped home to get her swimming costume and a towel and quickly made a flask of tomato soup to warm them up afterwards. This was fun. A friend to play with at last. She loaded up her beach bag and added a packet of custard creams, just in case.

Simon was parked outside, his surfboard on the roof rack. She hurried down the garden path and hopped in next to him. As he pulled away, he tooted his horn merrily at Polly, who was weeding her front garden with Pete. The pair of them straightened up and waved.

Their first stop was the Trevay Surf Shack, a shop devoted to everything surfy. Helen was poured into a skin-tight wetsuit and fitted with a beginner's board, both of which she could hire for the day.

'You'll be wanting these as well, girl,' said Skip, the Kiwi shop owner. Flattered at being referred to as a girl, Helen gladly took the boots, gloves and helmet he proffered.

*

'Right. These are the rules.' Simon was kneeling on the beach with his wetsuit pulled up only to his waist. Helen looked appreciatively at his strong, hairy chest.

Who'd have thought he'd have a bod like that? she thought to herself.

'The water likes to find a deep part of the beach to suck itself back out to sea. Look at it now. You see where the smooth water is? Well, that's usually where the rip or undertow is strongest. Always swim where the water is breaking. It's safer. Once you're strong enough, we'll use the rip to get out to the back of the waves. OK?'

'Is this knowledge something you Cornish boys are born with?'

'No, I used to be a lifeguard.'

'You're kidding!'

'Before I finally chose my vocation.'

'You are full of surprises! Is that how you got those abs?'

He looked down at his body. 'Well, I run a bit as well.'

He stood up and swiftly pulled his wetsuit on.

'Can I just get my balance by holding on to your arm?' Helen asked as she wriggled first one leg then the other into her suit.

Simon was so unused to this kind of interaction with a woman that he accidentally brushed her bosom as he tried to hold her elbow.

'I'm so terribly sorry.'

'Don't worry about it,' laughed Helen, 'Can you zip me up?'

Her slender back was also sprinkled with freckles and his hand felt weak as he pulled at the zip. *Please, please, God. Is this IT?*

Helen was all for jumping straight into the surf, but Simon held her back.

'There's one more thing I have to show you, which is how to stand on the board. Lie down and pretend there's a wave coming. Paddle madly, and at the right moment I want you to jump up on to both feet and stand sideways. OK? Let's go!'

It was much more difficult than it looked. Catching the wave at the right moment was incredibly hard, and as for jumping up on her feet in one smooth movement – ridiculous! Her legs felt like jelly, her arms were pulled out of their sockets and her lungs were full of sea water. Apart from that, it was lovely. Simon was patient and helpful, just as her father had been, but after forty-five minutes, she was getting cold and had had enough.

Her body felt lead-heavy as she walked back up the beach to her bag. She wrapped her big beach towel round her shoulders and sat watching Simon effortlessly catch wave after wave while she drank all the tomato soup.

*

Piran Ambrose stood at the top of the beach with Jack, his terrier, snuffling in the grass of the dunes. What was that woman doing, surfing with the vicar? Piran had known Simon since they were schoolboys together. It was Piran who had got Simon back on his feet after Denise had jilted him. They weren't exactly best friends, but they were mates and Piran would always look out for him. Simon was someone who didn't deserve to be hurt again.

Piran walked down the beach towards Helen.

'Hello, boy! Where have you come from?' Helen tickled the ears of the little Jack Russell who was trying to get a custard cream out of its packet. A shadow fell over her.

'He's mine. He won't pee on you.'

She knew who it was before she looked up.

'I'm Piran Ambrose and this is Jack.' He held out his large, rough hand. She stood up and shook it.

'I'm Helen Merrifield. I'm sorry we met in such awkward circumstances before, and thank you for letting me know about my washing line.'

'That's all right. What you doing down here with the vicar?'

'Oh . . . er . . . he's teaching me to surf, but I got tired. He's very good.'

They both turned to watch Simon as a wave crashed over him and he fell off the board.

'I taught him everything he knows,' said Piran.

She looked at him, raising her eyebrows. 'Oh really? He told me he learnt when he was a lifeguard.'

'That's true. But I was the lifeguard who taught him.'

His full lips smiled, revealing rather nice teeth, but finding she disliked him more than ever, Helen busied herself with picking up the packet of biscuits and stuffing it back in her bag.

'What are you doing down here? You're a London woman through and through, aren't you? Husband divorced you, I expect.'

She stood up quickly, her eyes burning. 'How dare you! I'm divorcing him, actually,' she carried on across his laughter. 'And what I am doing here has nothing to do with you.'

'Well it does when your knickers are flying about my place of work.'

She drew herself up to her full five foot six. 'Mr Ambrose, it is obvious that we have got off on the wrong foot. I suggest that in future we steer clear of each other.'

'Fine.' And with that, he whistled to Jack, waved to Simon and walked back up the beach.

Simon strode, dripping, towards her. 'Has Piran gone?' She nodded. 'Damn. I wanted to thank him for all the work he's putting in on the churchyard restoration plans. He's our local historian, you know. He can tell you things about the families here going back hundreds of years. Lovely bloke. I am proud to call myself his friend. What did he want?'

'I really couldn't tell you,' said Helen, and smiled tightly.

*

Later that night when she was on her own, wallowing in a steamy bath by candlelight, she thought about Simon and Piran. One handsome but horrible, the other not so handsome but sweet. How could Simon be friends with that great Hagrid of a man? She lit a scented Jo Malone candle and tried, unsuccessfully, to banish all thoughts of Piran Ambrose from her mind.

9

The next morning, Helen woke again to brilliant sunshine. The TV weather forecast had predicted a warm, dry week ahead. Good news and excellent for gardening. After breakfast she hopped over the back garden wall and knocked on the door of Tony's shepherd's hut.

''Oo's that?' his voice asked.

'Mrs Merrifield from next door. I was wondering if you'd help me with the garden this week.'

His innocent face with the moleish sleek black hair popped out from the opened door.

'Oh, yes, Mrs M. Lovely. I'll be there directly.'

'Great, see you in a minute.'

She heard an amount of rustling within and assumed he was getting dressed.

Within a few minutes he was at her back door. 'Mornin', Mrs M. Lovely day. This kind of weather makes me feel as happy as a tom tit on a pump handle.'

She smiled at him, and he asked, 'What you got for me today?'

'Well, I'd like to put a lot of spring bulbs in and maybe do some deep digging on those two back beds, ready for the veg plot.'

'I'm good at growing veg. My mum always said I was a proper turnip head.' He looked pleased, then puzzled.

'Which is odd, 'cos I ain't never grown turnips. But I'd be good if I did!'

'Well, in that case we shall grow some. Do you want to come with me in the car to the nursery to get the bulbs and stuff?'

'No thankee, Mrs M. I get grumbly in cars.'

'Ah. Well, I'll go on my own, but I'll be back soon. Perhaps you'd take some shears to that ivy that's covering the privy then? I can't open the door at the moment.'

'Righto.'

*

The nursery was a treasure trove of goodies. She bought three large sacks of daffodils, two of tulips and some smaller bags of snowdrops, crocuses and bluebells. Then she chose seed packets of peas, beans, asparagus, lettuce, courgettes and turnips. While waiting at the till, she spotted an eight-foot Cornish palm in an enormous terracotta pot and a pair of large, blue glazed pots planted, the label said, with agapanthus. She bought the lot with great satisfaction.

She got back home to find the ivy neatly trimmed and her washing line expertly fixed back to the wall.

'Tony, how kind of you to fix my washing line! And the privy looks very smart.'

'I done the ivy all right, but Mr Ambrose fixed the washing line. Said as he thought the weather was so good, you might like to do some washing.'

Piran! Here again. Why couldn't the bloody man keep out of her way? She looked over to the churchyard and there he was. Smiling his cocky little smile and tipping his non-existent hat at her.

'Thought you might like to get some of your smalls out in the fresh air. Don't worry, I've seen it all, so I'm not embarrassed,' he shouted to her retreating back.

Grrrr. She took a deep breath and managed, 'Thank you,' through gritted teeth. 'No plans for laundry today.'

*

It would have been a very pleasurable day if she wasn't so uncomfortably aware of Piran working just a few feet away over the wall. His radio, his whistling, his phone going off and his loud voice as he answered, all served to jangle her nerves. Little Jack came over the wall once or twice to renew her acquaintance, but she tried to keep any conversation with Piran to the minimum.

At lunchtime, Piran and Jack drove off in the truck and Helen breathed a sigh of relief.

'Can I get you some lunch, Tony?'

'No thanks, I've got me sandwiches.'

'Well, sit here with me and we'll eat together.'

She pulled a wooden bench out into a patch of sun, and went inside to make herself a sandwich and a coffee.

When she came out, Tony was sitting in his upright barrow.

'Are you comfortable like that?'

'Yes, Mrs M. 'Tis lovely.'

She settled herself on the bench. 'Tell me about your mum and dad.'

'My dad was a fisherman and me mum was me mum. Dad went to hospital one day and died and Mum broke her heart. Broke my heart when she died 'n' all. People can die of broken hearts, you know.'

'Yes, I believe you.' A silence. Then, 'Do you have brothers or sisters?'

'Nope. Mum and Dad said they broke the mould when they made me. Couldn't have another like me, they said. "Simple Tony Brown, you're a one off, you are." That's what they said. That's what everyone says.'

'You share the name of another gardener. A very famous one called Capability Brown. I think he'd have liked you working with him. You could have called yourselves Brown and Brown.'

'Do you know him?'

'Oh no, only of him. He died a long time ago.'

'Broken heart?'

'I'm not sure. But you are my Capability Brown from now on. May I call you Mr Brown? If I'm truthful, I prefer it to calling you Simple Tony.'

Tony looked at her, weighing things up.

'OK.'

'Thanks. Come on then, Mr Brown, we'll just plant these last few crocus bulbs and then let's get digging the vegetable patch.'

*

Together they dug really deep into the fertile soil, and Mr Brown trundled his old barrow back and forth across the village green at least a dozen times to collect the well-rotted manure from Pendruggan Farm. The farmer and his wife were only too happy to let it go.

Helen took her sweatshirt off, her muscles really warm now. The last bit to go was to dig two trenches for the runner beans and fill them with manure too. She and Mr Brown had a quick drink, he Ribena, she Diet Coke, and then they started.

As Tony thrust his spade into the ground, they heard a thud as it made contact with something hard.

'Ow,' said Mr Brown, shaking his jarred wrist. 'What's this?'

He carefully felt round with the spade, and gradually unearthed a black, painted tin box. It was around two feet across by sixteen inches wide and ten inches deep. He bent down and lifted it out.

'Treasure, Mrs M.!'

'Let's have a look, Mr B.'

They carried it to the wooden bench and brushed as much soil off as they could, revealing a gold pattern in the Indian style which decorated the top and sides.

'It's so pretty,' Helen said, lifting it and shaking it gently, 'There's something in it. I'll wash this mud off my hands and get a damp cloth to wipe it over in case there's something really precious in here.'

Once it was clean, she dried her hands on her discarded sweatshirt and eased the rusty lid open.

No water or rust had got inside to spoil anything. The first object was a beautiful jet brooch shaped like a black bird. It lay on a white blanket, which, when Helen shook it out, looked to be a baby's shawl, the yarn spotted with age but the lacy crochetwork still beautiful. Under this lay a photograph of an Edwardian couple. The woman was holding a baby in her arms, and the man had his hand resting gently on the shoulder of a young boy aged no more than four or five years old. The final item was an ancient Peek Frean's biscuit tin, which was something that looked like crushed ash. Perhaps the cremated remains of something, or somebody.

'Oh my God. What is all this? Who does it belong to?' gasped Helen.

'I don't know,' said Tony, looking a bit pale. 'I think we should bury it again so as not to disturb any spirits.'

'Mr Brown! Don't go soft on me now. This must be so precious to someone that they hid it. It's our duty to return it to its rightful owner so that it has a happy ending. Don't do you think?'

'I don't know.'

'Hmm. Well, I'm intrigued. Leave it with me and I'll have a think what to do next. Maybe I'll ask around – someone might know something. Exciting, isn't it?'

'No.'

'Mr B, this is an adventure for us. What an end to our day! Tomorrow we'll clear out the privy and see if there's anything interesting in there, all right?'

'OK. Bye, Mrs M. See you tomorrow.'

When he'd gone she closed the Peek Frean's tin securely. As she did so, she noticed a small sticky label on the lid. In copperplate handwriting, it said *Falcon*.

A clue? She put everything back into the larger black tin and carried it carefully inside.

After making a pot of tea, she carried the tin box and her mug into the sitting room.

She took everything out again to look more carefully. Who on earth had buried all this and why?

She lit the fire and got on the phone to Penny.

10

'Penny? It's me.'

'Hello, darling. I was going to phone and book some dates to see you. How's it going?'

'Well, I've got quite a lot to tell you. There are some extraordinary people down here. All straight out of central casting! They would be perfect extras for your new programme.'

'Great! We might need them. Anyone handsome caught your eye?'

'No! You're as bad as Chloe. I'm not on the market, as you well know.' She paused to allow Penny's scornful laughter to run its course. 'However, I do have a nice little mystery for you.'

Penny listened to Helen's story of the tin box, only occasionally interrupting with the odd question.

'Wow. How fascinating. How are you going to find out more?' she asked.

'Well, I thought I'd try Simon first. He's the—'

Penny interrupted. 'Simon? A mystery man on the scene already! Come on, don't keep me in suspense!'

'He's the vicar—'

'A lusty vicar! I love it, tell me more.'

'Shut up and listen, will you? He's the vicar who's very—'

'Married?'

'NO! Single. He's very sweet and—'

'You want an excuse to see him so you're going to ask him to take a look at your box! Oooh, matron.'

'NO! LISTEN!'

'OK, sorry. Carry on . . . vicar.' More sniggers.

Helen sighed, 'This is too exhausting. I'll tell you the whole story when you come down. Which is when, exactly?'

They agreed to a date in early October, which was just a couple of weeks away.

'You can stay here with me, but we'll have to share my big bed. Do you mind?'

'I am too old for sleepovers. Can you recommend a good hotel?'

'The Starfish in Trevay is supposed to be THE place, locally.'

'Great. I'll get my PA to book it, and you and I will have a wine-fuelled dinner there. Agreed?'

'Agreed.'

After hanging up, Helen made another call.

*

At 6.30 p.m. every evening, Simon was in the habit of praying for his parish and the wider world. It was a part of his routine that was as important to him as cleaning his teeth. He would light a small candle under his simple wooden crucifix in the study and kneel in front of it. Recently he'd begun using the old chintz cushion on his desk chair to spare his knees. When he was comfortable, he would close his eyes and picture the face of Christ in front of him. He'd thank God for his calling; his home and his friends, and then would offer prayers for those he knew to be having difficulties of some kind. If there was some grim story in the news, he would pray for those involved. Finally he would ask for blessings for the royal family, the government, global leaders, and pray that peace may come to the world.

Very rarely would he trouble God with his own concerns, but since meeting Helen he couldn't help but ask for a sign that would let him know if she was *the one*.

As he was finishing this last PS, the phone on his desk rang. He stood up, crossed himself and blew out the candle, making a final bow to Christ on his cross.

'Yes, yes, hold your horses, I'm coming.' His voice sounded weary, even to himself. He cleared his throat as he picked up the receiver. 'Hello, Reverend Canter.'

'Simon, it's me, Helen . . .'

Simon gave up a silent prayer of thanks. God had sent him the sign.

'I'm cooking a spag bol and wondered if you'd like to share it with me?' she continued. 'There's something I want to show you . . .'

His voice wobbled slightly and his eyebrows danced above his chocolate-brown eyes. 'Yes, Helen, I'd love to. Ten minutes OK?'

'Perfect. Bye.'

*

Piran watched her for a moment through her lighted kitchen window. He had been working late inside the church, trawling through the archives and trying to make sense of the higgledy-piggledy order of the graves out in the churchyard. It was late and he was tired. He watched for a moment as Helen spread the blue checked cloth on the table and grabbed a handful of cutlery from the side. She was a good-looking woman, he had to admit. Now she was opening a bottle of wine and putting out two glasses. Who on earth was that for? He turned the ignition on, ashamed of his prurient interest, but his headlights picked out the figure of Simon Canter, fairly skipping along towards her gate. The man was crazy if he thought a woman like that would be interested in him. Poor old Simon – he was a fool.

*

'Hello, hello. Come on in. Nippy tonight, isn't it?' Helen opened the door wide for him and he stepped into her pretty kitchen. He viewed the neatly laid table. It looked rather romantic and his hopes rose higher. From behind his back he produced a bottle of Rioja, which earned him a kiss on the cheek from Helen.

'Go and sit in the living room. I've got the fire going nicely. It doesn't smoke any more now Don's used some of his magic on it.'

Simon went and sat down gladly, before his legs buckled beneath her kiss. Helen talked to him from the kitchen about Don and the work he'd done and what a wonder he was, then joined him with a glass of cold white wine.

'I'll keep the Rioja for later, if that's all right. I had this open already. Cheers.'

'Cheers.'

He took a mouthful and was grateful for the steadying effect it would have on him.

'It's really lovely in here,' he said. 'You have a home-maker's instinct.'

There was a hissing noise from the kitchen.

'Oops, spaghetti's boiling over. Chuck another log on the fire, would you? And then come and eat.' The last few words were thrown over Helen's shoulder as she went back to the kitchen.

Simon did as she asked, then followed her through and sat at the table.

'Tony and I found some treasure in the garden today.' Steam was billowing around her as she drained the spaghetti into the sink. 'Take a look at that tin box on my desk.' He got up and went to the small desk, more of a table really, in the corner between the sink and the Aga.

'Go on, open it up.'

He did so. 'Oh my. What's all this?' He took each object out carefully and examined them. He was particularly interested in the photo.

'Do you know who any of them are?' she asked, peering over his shoulder on the way to dishing up the pasta.

'No. I have never seen any of them before. It might have something to do with Vi Wingham. She lived here before you came.' Simon reached for the wine bottle and topped up their glasses. 'She was a wonderful woman. Very self-contained and independent. Baked delicious sponge cakes in the old range where your Aga is now. She would donate them to raffles or bring them out when she entertained, although that wasn't very often. A couple of times a year she'd invite me to tea. I enjoyed her company very much.'

'Let's eat and talk – pass me your plate.' Helen spooned steaming pasta on to his plate. 'Queenie told me that Miss Wingham had lost a fiancée in the war.'

'Well, I don't know about that. She revealed very little

71

about herself. After she died, the only thing I found out from the solicitors was that she'd bought this cottage in 1930 when she was only nineteen. She lived here with a succession of cats for seventy-seven years and never modernised it, apart from putting electricity in. You must have seen that she didn't have a bathroom when you bought it, only the privy in the garden.'

'However did she manage? I turned her spare room into my bathroom – I couldn't do without it.'

'She would be pleased for you, I'm sure. But although she was always immaculate, she had more than a touch of the Trojan about her.' He ate a forkful of spaghetti bolognese. 'This is excellent.'

Helen felt very relaxed with her new friend. Conversation with Simon was easy and she liked the way he was around her. No hint of sexual undertones. No hidden agenda. She topped his glass up again.

'Tell me more about Miss Wingham.'

'One morning after church, about three years ago, she invited me round for a quick sherry. She'd never done that before, so I thought, rightly, that it was to discuss something important. She told me that she'd just had her ninety-sixth birthday and, though still able to look after herself, felt it was the right thing to move into a care home. I didn't try to dissuade her because she had always conducted her affairs exactly as she pleased and seemed in full possession of all her faculties. She told me that she had already found the right home, on the road to Newquay, where she would have a room with a sea view, and that she would be going the next day. She asked me to tell the parishioners the following Sunday in my Church Notices. She would be happy to receive visitors, but only if they really wanted to see her. She died a year later, peacefully in her sleep, and two years after that, the house was sold to you.'

'Was her cat still alive? Queenie said they were all named after birds and that the last one was called Raven. Did she have one called Falcon?'

'Not in my time here as vicar, which is almost twenty-two years. There was a Sparrow and a Robin before Raven.'

'Where was MissWingham buried?'

'Ah. Well . . . I haven't discussed this with anyone before, but . . . I don't suppose it matters now. I'm sorry to say that she's in the bottom drawer of my desk.'

Helen stopped, her fork in mid-air. 'I think that needs a bit of explanation.'

'When she died, she left express wishes regarding her funeral arrangements. No mourners, no flowers. She wanted me to give her a proper funeral service in the church and then escort her to the crematorium. It was only myself and the funeral directors at the service where I blessed her and said goodbye. About a week later, they phoned to tell me the ashes were ready for collection, and ever since I have been wondering what to do with them. There was no instruction from the solicitors.'

'Golly, what are you going to do?'

'I don't know yet. I'm sure I shall receive a sign.' He stood up. 'In the meantime, I shall ask Piran to come over and have a look at this box of treasure. He may be able to shed some light on it.'

Helen did her best to disguise her reluctance to this idea, 'Maybe.'

At the front door Simon said, 'I've had a wonderful evening, Helen. You are very kind to me.'

'Not at all. I'm so happy to have made a real friend.'

She reached up and gave him another of her kisses on the cheek and they said goodnight.

Simon waved at the gate before his short walk across the green to the vicarage.

Helen washed up, turned the lights out and went to bed with a good book. Simon walked home as if on air.

11

The next couple of weeks were busy for Helen. She and Tony went to town on the garden. Along the path from the gate to the front door they planted lady's mantle. In the cracks of the drystone wall she pushed violas and primroses. The great Cornish palm looked splendid in its sheltered corner, while the two blue pots containing the agapanthus were placed either side of the old gate. She couldn't wait to see them in bloom.

Tony, meanwhile, took over the vegetable plot. It was dug and composted to within an inch of its life ready for the spring plantings, but he also put in a row of asparagus, and some rhubarb. The rest of the garden Helen filled with roses, daphnes and hydrangeas, with jasmine and clematis left to ramble over the wall which divided her from the churchyard . . . and any spying from Piran Ambrose.

Her final pièce de résistance was a wisteria, which she hoped would clamber over the privy. She and Tony had cleared the privy of its broken gardening tools and rusty watering cans, but they found no other treasure in there. Tony had taken to using it as his main bathroom now, not having running water in the shepherd's hut. The flushing loo and cold water tap served him just fine. It was better than always knocking on Polly's door when he needed to fill his kettle or have a pee. Helen rather liked his presence in the garden.

She had put the tin box under her bed and out of her mind after the supper with Simon. She didn't relish his suggestion of taking it to Piran, but perhaps there would be no alternative.

Anyway, Penny was coming down that weekend, and she might have some bright ideas.

*

It was drizzly with a biting wind when Penny arrived in Trevay at 4 p.m. The journey down had been OK and her comfortable Jaguar XJS had taken all the strain out of the drive, but when she tried to open the door in the Starfish car park, the wind whipped it shut again. She struggled out with her long blonde hair in her eyes and mouth, pulled her warmly padded Donna Karan coat around her, and walked into reception.

The young girl behind the desk greeted her warmly and introduced herself as Kayla. 'I expect you'd like a tray of tea and some crumpets after your long journey?' The thought hadn't entered Penny's head but, now she came to think of it, it seemed like a fabulous idea.

'Thank you so much.' She looked around. 'What a beautiful building.' Outside it may have looked severe, built in local granite by the Victorians, but inside it was as contemporary as any London hotel. Although painted all white, the clever and discreet lighting made it warm and cosy. The slate floor, with vast, jewel-coloured Indian rugs, felt warm underfoot. But it was the touches of designer chic that really brought it all together. Huge four-foot bell jars filled with lime-green apples and twinkling candles, and on the wall above the wide, polished oak staircase was a stunning oil painting of a starfish lying on a sparkling ocean floor.

'Yes, Ms Leighton, we like it. Do you have any luggage in the car that needs bringing in? If you give me the keys, I'll get Darren to collect it and bring it to your room.'

Kayla gave Penny a key attached to a starfish key ring encrusted with Swarovski crystals. 'You're in room 207 on the second floor. The lift is on the left. Anything you need, just give us a call.'

Penny took the lift – fashioned like an old bathing hut; kitsch but cute – to the second floor and found her room. The old adage that less is more applied here. Everything was of the best quality, but not overdone. And the view of the harbour with its fishing boats, from what she could make out through the heavy rain that was now hammering down, would be lovely when the sun came out.

She picked up the phone and called Helen.

'Darling, I'm here! In Trevay! The hotel is fabulous. Shall I book a table for two tonight at seven-thirty? Is that OK for you?'

'Yes, please. I've starved myself all week.'

They chatted a bit more and then Penny ran herself a deep, hot bubbly bath, warming her feet on the heated tiles as she did so. She lay happily in the suds eating her buttered crumpets, drinking her tea and listening to the rain on the windows.

*

At dinner that night, Penny filled Helen in on all the London news. Most of it was about work and a little about friends, but nothing about a social life.

'What about your romantic life? Anyone special yet?' asked Helen.

'No. No one. I'm too old, too set in my ways, too independent, too much of a ball-breaker – or that's what the last complete prat told me. Who understands men? They say they want a woman who has a mind of her own and financial independence. But when it comes down to it, all they really want is someone they can dominate. And I'm not good at being dominated. I wish I was . . . but . . .' She waved a hand. 'MEN! They can go and boil their fat, stupid, chauvinistic heads.'

Helen threw her head back and roared with laughter. 'I'll drink to that! Fancy a margarita before the food arrives?'

One margarita naturally turned into several. Tequila loosened them both up and suddenly everything was funny. When Helen described Simon, Penny did an appalling impression of an ancient, randy old vicar. Helen wheezed with laughter, holding one hand to her ribs and the other to her mouth. Penny, in full swing now, leant back in her chair, tucked her fingers under her imaginary braces and in her vicar voice said, 'I'd be very obliged if I might take a dip in your font, madam.' And with that, she overbalanced her chair and fell straight over backwards.'

'Hello, Mrs Merrifield. You certainly know how to enjoy yourself.'

Piran Ambrose, with a small, large-bosomed, kittenish woman in her thirties on his arm, stopped at the table. Helen jumped up in shock and knocked her glass over. Penny, with the help of a waiter, picked herself up and offered her hand in greeting.

'Good evening. I'm Penny, a friend of Helen's.'

Piran glanced at her and then back to Helen. 'I

remember the first time I had a drink too. Enjoy your evening.'

The kitten woman pulled him away with a parting, malicious smile aimed at Helen.

*

The next morning both women had rather woolly heads. Helen woke up first and turned over to look at Penny. 'I thought we were too old for sleepovers. Thank God you didn't let me drive home.'

Penny opened her still mascara'd eyes. 'Mmm, I took your keys while you and the waiter were dancing on the table. *So* embarrassing.'

'Oh God. I didn't, did I?'

'No, but you asked him to, which was bad enough.'

Helen shoved her friend in the ribs.

'I did not! . . . He was lovely though, wasn't he?'

'Too young for either of us, but nice to look at.'

'Not like that git Piran Ambrose. That's at least three times he's caught me doing something embarrassing.'

'Yes, you've told me that several times, and however handsome he was, you wouldn't look twice at him now, blah blah blah. You weren't happy he was having dinner with someone else though, were you?'

'Was he? I didn't notice.'

'Oh that's right, you didn't notice, So much so, that you couldn't stop turning around and looking at him and asking me who she was. As if I would know!'

Helen opened one eye and looked at her friend, 'No I didn't. I was surprised to see him, that's all.'

'Hmmm. We'll talk about Piran when you're sober.'

Penny hitched herself up on one elbow. 'Full English with room service?'

Helen managed a nod and then closed her eyes for a little more sleep.

*

By lunchtime they felt almost human and took a bracing walk around the town. Penny phoned her PA and told her not to expect her back for the week as she had a lot more research to do than she'd thought.

'Liar, liar, pants on fire!' teased Helen.

'Well, I'm the boss and I don't often spoil myself. And you are my best friend who I haven't seen for ages – so, why not! Ready for a hair of the dog, yet?'

'Penny, you're incorrigible!'

12

Back at Gull's Cry, Helen dragged the large tin box out from under her bed and took it downstairs to Penny, who was peeling spuds for their supper.

'This is it. Have a look and see what you make of it.' She put it down on the kitchen table next to Penny.

Penny rinsed her fingers under the tap and after drying her hands on a tea towel, opened the lid. She took out the shawl first.

'Lovely shawl, I could use this for a period drama. And the brooch. Nice bit of jet . . . touch of rust on the pin though. A photo. What a good-looking couple. They look so old, don't they, but I expect they were only in their twenties, judging by how young the children are. The baby is wrapped in a shawl like the one in the box . . . Have you got a magnifying glass?'

'I think so. Perhaps in my desk drawer.' Helen rooted through the mess and found a small plastic magnifier from a cracker.

'That'll do.' Penny took it from her and, after a few moments screwing her eyes up, said, 'I can't tell. It might be . . . let me look at the brooch the mum has on her blouse collar.' Another breath-holding wait, the boiler made a whoomf noise as the central heating came on, and then, 'Blimey, girl. It looks like she's wearing the brooch we've got here. Look.'

'My God, it is. So could the baby be Violet Wingham, the woman who used to own this house?'

'Why not? Who can we ask?'

'The ghastly Piran Ambrose is the local historian, but I don't fancy seeing him again. I'll phone the little museum in Trevay tomorrow, and ask them if there's anyone other than him.'

'It sounds like a job for Mr Tibbs. He's the hero of the Mavis Crewe books I've bought the TV rights for. They're all set in the early 1930s in a small Cornish parish by the sea, and the widowed Mr Tibbs is the local bank manager. He's very well respected and able to solve all kinds of problems and mysteries, large or small.' She picked up the biscuit tin with the ashes in and gave it a shake. 'These are the ashes, are they?'

Helen nodded and winced as the hangover reared its ugly head again.

'Not enough for an adult, surely? Maybe it's the boy in the photo. Her brother? Mr Tibbs would have this solved in ninety minutes with five commercial breaks.' She looked at a limp Helen.

'You look terrible. Another hair of the dog yet? Or just a cup of tea?'

'Tea, please.'

'Right: tea, bangers and mash, and an early night for you.'

*

Helen was downstairs, showered and dressed, and feeling totally refreshed after a good night's sleep. She had the phone in her hand.

'Hello, Trevay Heritage Museum. How can I help you?' said a cheery voice on the other end of the line.

'Hello, my name is Helen Merrifield. I've dug up an old box in my back garden and it's got several interesting things in it. I wonder if I could bring them in and show them to one of your historians?'

'Oh, we like things like that, don't we! Let me see who's around today. Erm . . . the roster says it's Janet – Janet Coombe. She'll be in around ten-thirty. Shall I tell her you'll be in?'

'Fantastic, thank you. See you then.'

Helen still marvelled at the wonderful service you got down here and how friendly everyone was. And she was mightily relieved that Piran clearly wasn't on duty today.

*

After a quick cup of tea and some toast, she got to the Starfish in time to meet Penny. Together they got the box out of Helen's car and walked with it down to the museum.

By the look of the architecture it must have been the old seamen's mission: 1903 was the date carved into the granite arch above the entrance. The front door had peeling red paint and was held open by a huge brass cabin hook. The sign on the pavement outside said OPEN 10 TILL 6 MONDAY TO SATURDAY INCLUDING BANK HOLIDAYS. A smaller handwritten sign said, *There is no admittance fee, but we rely on donations to keep our history alive. Please give generously.*

Behind a sliding-glass window was a woman in a caramel-coloured twinset, caramel-coloured hair and caramel-coloured glasses. She looked up and, smiling, opened the glass panel.

'May I help you?'

'Yes, I phoned earlier to speak to Janet Coombe?'

'Mrs Merrifield, is it? I would have phoned you to save you a trip, but I didn't take your number. Janet's just called in sick, I'm afraid. But if you're quick, our Mr Ambrose will see you before he goes out to a field study he's working on.'

Helen's heart slipped. 'Oh no, it's OK. I won't bother him. I'll come back to see Jan—'

'Mrs Merrifield and Penny, isn't it?' The rich, sardonic voice was unmistakable. The women turned to face Piran. He looked almost piratical today. The wild curls were glossy, and for the first time Helen noticed a small anchor tattoo on his hand. He was still in his red fishing smock and little Jack was at his heels. 'How are you ladies feeling after your convivial evening?'

'Fine. Did you enjoy your night out, too?' Helen looked him straight in the eye, but he out-stared her until she looked down.

Penny attempted some levity: 'She wants you to look at her box.'

'Really? The pair of you had better come into the curator's office then.'

*

Once he'd silently examined the objects, Piran said, 'So what do you want me to do?'

'I just wondered if we could find out who they belonged to. That's all. But if it's too insignificant for you, I'll do some detective work myself.' Helen went to close the lid and leave.

Piran put his hand on her arm and stopped her. 'Now don't get in a huff because I'm not clearing my diary this minute and getting on with it. I do have a lot of work on. You've seen me in the churchyard, over at Holy Trinity. I'm trying to get a complete survey of the graves done before the winter sets in. After that, I have to report my findings to the bishop and the coroner. So unfortunately, your little box is not a priority.'

Helen gazed out of the dusty window with a look of bored sarcasm.

'Don't look like that, woman. You may be used to having men dance to your tune – your poor husband and the naïve vicar. But not me. I will help you find out about this box, because it is actually quite interesting and there is clearly a story there, but I'll do it when I'm ready, OK?'

'Thank you. That's very kind of you. Come along, Helen, let's give the man some peace.' Penny, realising that Helen was very close to simmering point, yanked her friend out of there before her temper well and truly boiled over.

*

'That bloody man! What is his problem? I have never met anyone so rude.' Helen plonked herself down into one of the comfy leather chairs in the Dolphin. Penny sat down opposite her, feeling the warmth of the open fire on her back.

'He fancies you.'

'I hardly think so.'

Dorrie came over with menus. 'Hello, ladies! Nice to see you, Helen. Are you having some lunch?'

'Dorrie, this is my best friend, Penny. Penny, this is

Dorrie, who is the brilliant interior designer I've been telling you about.'

The women shook hands and smiled.

'Do you know Piran Ambrose, Dorrie?'

'Know 'im! I used to go out with 'im. Before Don, of course. What a lovely man.'

'Lovely man! Are we talking about the same one?'

'There's only one Piran Ambrose. I think all of us are a little in love with him round here. He's very discreet, mind. He'll never let any secrets out about his lady friends. Although I do hear he's seeing someone at the moment. From Truro way, I'm told.'

'He took her out for supper at the Starfish the other night.'

'Did 'e? She must be special then. That must've set him back a bob or two. When I knew 'im we'd collect mussels from the rocks at low tide and cook 'em up in his caravan. We all had caravans then. Lovely memories. You should have seen him when he was young. Hair longer than it is now and a proper surfer's bod. I 'ad a lovely romantic summer with him. I was only eighteen and he was twenty-six, so it wasn't going to last. I was too young for 'im, and anyway I had my eye on Don by then.'

All three women formed their own mental picture of a young Piran wading out of the surf.

Dorrie sighed, and then said, 'So, what can I get you ladies for lunch?'

Without hesitation they both replied, 'Mussels, please.'

*

Over coffee, Dorrie and Don joined them. They were very interested in Penny's work and offered their help with anything that needed doing while she was filming.

'I am sure we can find you some work as extras, if you'd like. And your boys too. If you're up for it, Dorrie, I might need your help in sourcing some original props and design ideas on turn-of-the-century interiors.'

'That sounds ideal! Have you had a chance to look in the Trevay Museum, 'cos Piran's got some lovely original bits of furniture and knick-knacks on display down there.'

'I don't know if that's a good idea.' Helen explained about their meeting that morning, leaving nothing out.

'Piran is a man of hidden depths,' said Don. 'He's the finest friend a man could have. Look at the vicar: he was in a very dark place when his marriage was called off. Piran spent many evenings in the vicarage, just making sure Reverend Canter had food and company. He's a very loyal man.'

Dorrie took Don's hand, 'He's been like a brother to you, 'asn't 'e. Especially after Jenna died.'

'Aye. My sister, Jenna, died when she was only twenty-one. New Year's Eve. A horrible wet, dark night. She was walking up the lane back to my parents' house after a party, and she was knocked down by a hit-and-run driver. Police never found who it was. Piran and I were the first on the scene. He held her so tender like, but she was gone. He helped in every way it's possible to help. My mum and dad love him like a son for what he did for us all.'

In the silence, the fire quietly crackled and hissed.

'So what I'm saying is,' Don continued, 'don't judge him over a couple of trifles.'

Helen felt ashamed at this rebuke and resolved to be less on the defensive when she saw him next. But he had still been bloody rude.

13

The rest of that Saturday afternoon was spent driving along the cliff road between Trevay and Crackington Haven. Helen enjoyed the pleasure of being driven by someone as confident as Penny. The roof was off the Jaguar and the heaters were on full blast. Penny was wearing an emerald Hermès scarf tied Grace Kelly style over her blonde hair; an odd stray lock flying over her dark glasses. Helen had a rust-coloured beret pulled well down over her ears with a large pheasant feather threaded through the front.

'Who are we? Mapp and Lucia or Thelma and Louise?' shouted Penny across the roar of the wind.

'More Hinge and Brackett!' shouted back Helen.

The spectacular coastline and azure sea under the bright October sun sent Penny into raptures.

'Oh my God! We have got to use all of this – the location shots will be just gorgeous. You have so done the right thing in coming down here.'

Crackington Haven, Trebarwith Strand, Boscastle, Tintagel: romantic names steeped in Cornish history and mythology. Penny wanted to walk up the craggy steps to Tintagel Castle and absorb the views that King Arthur and Guinevere may have looked over, but Helen put her off. It was getting dark and cold and Pendruggan was at least an hour's drive.

The sun was now low on the horizon, spreading a Byzantine glow over the waves. The road dipped and wound its way back along the cliffs to Helen's home and as they drove into her village, her headlights picked out the figure of Simon walking towards Gull's Cry. He put up his hand to shield his eyes from the lights and as Penny parked and turned them off, Helen jumped out.

'Simon, sorry I didn't get to church last week.' She looked lamely at her feet. 'I forgot, to be honest.'

She hadn't seen Simon since the surf lesson two Sundays ago and, apart from waving to him as she'd been driving off somewhere, or from the garden when she'd been working with Tony, they'd had no contact.

Simon was painfully aware of this. His every waking moment had been saturated with the thought of when he might see Helen again. He'd had to fight the urge to knock on her door and invite her to supper, fearing the humiliation if she refused. He had hoped she'd be at church, but, as she now so succinctly put, she had forgotten.

'No problem.' He smiled at her, feeling his guts twist.

'Meet my best friend, Penny Leighton. She and I worked together years ago at the BBC. Now she's a big-shot producer.'

Simon's heart plummeted further. He'd had no idea Helen had led such a glamorous early life. Penny certainly looked a television arty type. Make-up a little overdone, her body swathed in some kind of garment made of linen and layers, and a multitude of beads around her neck. All that, plus her ostentatious car made him dislike her immensely. What was she doing here? Trying to tempt his Helen back to the bright lights? His heart pumped hard at the thought of losing Helen now. But he kept smiling.

'I was just popping round with a bottle of plonk to thank you for the other evening.' He proffered the bottle.

'Come in and let's open it.'

'No, you have company. Besides, I'm a bit busy tonight. Sermon to write for tomorrow and all that.' This was a lie. He had written it earlier in the week.

'Oh, go on, just a quick one.' Helen put her arm through his, 'Come on, Penny, grab his other arm. I want you two to meet each other properly.'

Simon had no option but to be bundled up the path and into the house.

*

When they were inside, Penny threw herself on to the feather cushioned window seat in the lounge and let out a theatrical sigh. 'What a day! I've met so many people and seen so much. I'm exhausted!'

Helen, who was just nipping upstairs, said, 'Darling, light the fire would you?'

'Of course.' Simon fair sprinted to the matches on the mantelpiece.

'I think she meant me, but thank you anyway. There are some wine glasses in the kitchen and a corkscrew in the drawer, while you're up.'

Simon, feeling the heat on his burning cheeks, disliked her even more, but was glad to get in the kitchen to allow his blush to fade.

When he came back into the sitting room, Helen was throwing a log on the flames and laughing at something the hateful Penny had said. Were they laughing at him?

Helen saw his chocolate-drop eyes swim behind his

owl glasses. 'Simon, how kind of you to open the wine. Come and sit in my armchair and warm up.' As he did so, Helen pulled up a stuffed pouffe that doubled as a foot rest, and sat down on it next to him. She wanted to make amends for not seeing him.

'Penny, Simon is a marvellous surfer. He took me out the other day. It's much much harder than it looks, but he's brilliant. He used to be a lifeguard.'

Penny lifted her head from its cushion and looked thoughtfully at him. 'Really?'

Simon nodded.

'When are you going again, Simon? Can we watch you?'

The thought of this ghastly woman standing on the beach and sniggering at him was too much to bear.

'I'm not sure when I'll have the time.'

'Oh.' Helen looked disappointed. 'Never mind.' A silence, then Helen again: 'Have you read the books of Mavis Crewe, Simon?'

'No.'

Penny laughed. 'Oh, come on, Hel, Simon doesn't look the detective-novel type. Although I could see him cast as the vicar of St Brewey.'

'Sadly, I don't have time to read novels, though I have heard of her work. I think my mother used to read them back in the sixties.' Simon poured a little more wine into Helen's glass. Penny stretched out her arm, indicating she wanted her glass filled too. Simon grudgingly obliged.

'Yes, they were published in the late fifties and well into the sixties, but they eventually fell out of favour and were forgotten. I've acquired the television rights and we are casting now to start filming in the new year. Helen has been out showing me all the glorious coast locations this afternoon. Tomorrow morning, while she's at church,

I shall have a look round the village here and see if any of it is suitable.'

Simon pursed his lips. Pendruggan was a Cornish jewel of a village, the question was not whether it was fit for this woman's film, but whether she was fit for Pendruggan!

'The St Brewey vicar is a naïve man. Would you say you were naïve, Simon?' Penny tossed this into the conversation while keeping her eyes on her glass of wine.

'If by naïve you mean I only see the good in others, then, no. I am certainly NOT naïve.' He fixed his magnified eyes on Penny with what looked to Helen like a spark. 'Why do you ask?'

'Oh, it's something Piran Ambrose said today, isn't it, Helen?'

'What?' Helen spluttered.

'He said that you may be used to having men dance to your tune, like your poor husband and the naïve vicar, but it wouldn't work on him.' She looked straight at Simon. 'Did he mean you?'

'Penny, Piran was just being horrible, as he normally is. Don't embarrass Simon.'

'I'm only asking.'

Simon got to his feet. 'I really must be off. Things to do, as I said.'

Helen stood too and put her arm on his sleeve. 'Oh, please stay and have some supper. Penny certainly needs to eat and soak up the wine that's making her say silly things.'

'Charming!' came Penny's response from the window seat.

'Thank you, Helen, but I really must go. Goodbye.' He bent to brush his cheek against hers. 'Goodbye, Penny.'

When he'd left, Penny burst out laughing.

'Oh God! You do pick them! First the grouchy historian and now the blushing vicar! Who's next on your list?'

'What are you talking about? Simon is my friend and someone I like very much. Don't be mean.'

'Hmm . . . well, he's got the hots for you, just as Piran does. How many more are there?'

'None. As I told you, I am only interested in making good friends with everybody here. You were rude to Simon, and he isn't used to women like you.'

'You mean he's naïve.'

'Shut up, sober up and, when I've made supper, eat up.'

14

It was cold as Helen walked to church the next day, and almost colder in the church itself. Apparently the oil tank had been drained by thieves. The church warden was to padlock the tank from now on and keep the key on him at all times. Helen was wedged between Queenie on one side, who was wearing an angora tea-cosy hat and a moth-eaten rabbit-fur coat, and Tony on the other, who was wearing at least three boiler suits under his fleece. Within twenty minutes she was so warm, she was glad of the cooling walk to the altar for communion. She smiled up at Simon as he offered her the wafer, but he didn't reciprocate. When he came back with the wine, she tried again, but received only a thin smile in return.

After the service, Helen took her place in the line of people who wanted to thank him and shake his hand, but when it came to her turn he was polite but cool. Helen was mortified; she and Penny had clearly hurt his feelings and now she was going to have to find a way to make up for it.

*

Simon watched her as she walked away. He was tired after a sleepless night cursing himself for his stupidity.

Why had he trusted her when he didn't know her? The phrase 'Fools rush in where angels fear to tread' swept into his mind. He felt a hand tapping his arm.

'Is the oil insured? Only we could have a whip round, if you like?'

He turned to look into the kindly face of Queenie. 'Thank you so much. Yes, we are insured, but how nice of you to think of us. God will provide.'

'That's what my Ted used to say an' all. Got us through rationing did the Lord. I'm making some Bramley apple pies in the week – want a couple for your freezer?'

'Thank you, Queenie. I'd love that. God bless.'

When the last of the congregation had finally gone, Simon went back into the empty church. He locked the ancient door behind him and sat in one of the back pews. He clasped his hands, closed his eyes and prayed.

'Dear God, Can you hear me? I wouldn't normally ask for myself, as you know, but I'm so lonely. Please, if it's your will, help me find a loving woman to be my wife. I feel so much for Helen. But is she the one? Is it possible that she could ever feel something for me? Or am I destined to be a naïve fool? Help me find the way, so that I won't be hurt again. Thanks for listening. Amen.'

He stood, bowed to the figure of Christ at the altar and wiped his eyes with his clerical sleeve.

*

The empty churchyard was cold in the shadows. Penny stopped and read some of the gravestones. A pleasure she wasn't entirely sure about, but compulsive nonetheless. She found one for Eliza Jennings, born 16 January 1827, died 24 June 1834. Penny's own birthday was 16 January.

The rooks in the trees suddenly flew cawing up into the sky, startling her. She looked round and saw the cause of the commotion – it was Simon, leaving by the vestry door, and walking away from her towards the vicarage. She wondered whether she should run after him and apologise, but the moment passed, and he turned the corner out of sight.

The village had surprised Penny with its beauty and traditional charm. Helen's cottage sat on the south-west side of the village green with two cottages to the left of her, one of them Polly's, and four cottages on the right. Two of them were holiday lets and empty at the moment. Dead opposite was the impressively fronted Pendruggan Farmhouse with its limed walls and decorative portico over the front door, which looked to have been added at least a hundred years after the original building was finished. On the left-hand side of the green was a phone box and six council houses, with three post-war prefabs up on the hill above, which were all still occupied. And on the right-hand side of the green was the vicarage and church and Queenie's shop. The entire hamlet was warmly cradled in its little valley. The hills surrounding it were all open farmland with the odd cottage and chapel and barn. She took the footpath up past the church and climbed a stile into a field from the top of which she could see the sea. When she turned round she could see Pendruggan laid out before her like a child's toy village. She took her Moleskin notepad out of her bag and started to draw it for her location manager. Then she texted him:

I've found St Brewey. PL x.

15

Penny was full of excitement and was in such a hurry to get started that she rang her PA to say she would be coming back to London early. She left the following morning with a memory stick full of photographs of locations she'd fallen in love with. She didn't get a chance to apologise to Simon, but she promised Helen that she would return at Christmas and make it up to him then. She had already booked the best available room at the Starfish from 23 December until 2 January, and had been in discussion with the owner about preferential rates for her star-studded cast when they came down to film in the New Year. Now, all she had to do was complete casting and get all the technical logistics into place.

Helen waved her off and felt a sense of relief that she was again able to continue her new life without interruption. The first thing was to go round to see Simon and apologise.

Fortunately, Simon was a very forgiving man, especially when overwhelmed with gratitude at having her all to himself again, and they made another date to go surfing during the week.

As she finished her cup of coffee and got up to go, Simon said, 'Helen, this might be an awful bore, but I have been asked to a diocesan dinner with the bishop in the new year and I wondered if you would accompany me as my guest? It'll be full of dull clergymen and their wives, but I'd be awfully grateful to have you as my companion for the evening.'

Helen, eager to do anything that would cement their friendship again, immediately said, 'Of course! We'll be needing to sober up after Christmas and New Year's Eve! The Bish, eh? Very exciting. What should I wear?'

Simon thought of the clergy wives and their dusty taffeta with ancient pearls. 'Just be yourself. I know they'll be enchanted.'

'That's the worst kind of help you could give me, but hey-ho! They won't meet me again, will they? So it doesn't really matter as long as I don't embarrass you!'

She reached up and gave him a kiss on the cheek. This time he reciprocated, feeling the smoothness of her feminine skin on his lips.

'I really appreciate our friendship, Helen. You know that, don't you?'

She stepped back and looked into his kind face. 'I really appreciate your friendship too. It's lovely to have an uncomplicated friendship with a man. Goodbye, Simon.' Another kiss and she was on her way back to her cottage.

*

They managed to get a couple more surf lessons in before Helen declared the sea was too cold, and that her next lesson wouldn't be until Easter. November was breathing down their necks anyway, and Helen wanted to get started on Christmas preparations.

She phoned the children first.

'Yep, Sean Merrifield . . .'

Helen pictured her son sitting at his desk, tipped back in his chair.

'Darling, it's me, Mum. Have I called at a bad time?'

'No, it's fine. I've got a couple of minutes. Hang on a sec.' He put his hand over the mouthpiece and she could hear his muffled voice telling someone he'd meet them in the pub for lunch in a minute, then he was back on the line. 'So, Ma, how's tricks?'

'All good, thank you. I'm ringing to see if you have any plans for Christmas?'

'Oh, Ma, I don't know yet, I'm so full-on here. Work's gone crazy and—'

She interrupted him. 'Because, darling, I don't have room in my little house for you and I am just trying to get an idea of numbers in order to book rooms at the pub up the road. And,' – she didn't give him time to get any more evasion in – 'I do want you to see my new home and meet my new friends. I want to show you off, that's all.' Was she giving him a guilt-trip? She didn't mean to, but what the hell, she didn't make a habit of it!

'Well, erm, Terri has been badgering me to take her away for the weekend.'

'Terri? What happened to Lucy?'

'Complicated, Ma. But you'll like Terri. She's sweet. A model. Does a lot of PR shoots: drinks companies and motor shows, that kind of thing. Have a look in this week's diary section in *OK!* – she's the blonde in the spray-on red dress.'

'I will!' Helen thought of Queenie and how pleased she'd be to feel she knew someone in her beloved gossip mags. 'Has Daddy met her yet?'

'No! And he won't, if I can help it. You know how

embarrassing he can be when he gets going – trying to chat people up.'

'It's just your dad. And she's not likely to run off with him when she's got you, is she?' Silence greeted her at the other end. 'Is she, Sean?'

'Ask him and Lucy.'

'Oh no.' Helen was gobsmacked. 'Dad didn't make a move on Lucy, did he?'

'Like I said, ask them. I couldn't give a monkey's.' She heard him give a theatrical yawn. 'So, is the old man coming for Christmas?'

'I don't know. But I tell you what, why don't you and Terri come down for Bonfire Night next weekend? Trevay do a great display, I'm told. Then we could have supper at the Dolphin. I'll book you both a room. My treat.'

'Thanks, Ma. I'll check with Terri, but it sounds great. Will Chloe be down too?'

'I'll ask her. In fact, I'll phone her right now. How exciting! Go and have your pub lunch and we'll sort the details out later. Love you. Bye.'

'Love you too, Ma. Bye.'

*

Bloody Gray! How dare he steal his own son's girlfriend. She picked up the phone again.

'Yuh?' Gray's lazy voice.

'You bastard!'

'Hell-o, Helen – how lovely to hear from you. What am I supposed to have done now?'

'Stolen your son's girlfriend, that's what.'

'It was a misunderstanding, that's all, darling.'

'Explain.'

'Well, I met them both for Sunday lunch in the Kings Road and she just kept flirting with me. Sean got all shirty and left us to it.'

'And?'

'And, we . . . saw each other a few times, and now it's over. What's the big deal?'

'The deal is, you don't take your son's girlfriends. No sane, humane father would. How could you?'

'She knew what she was doing. I said to her, "Laura—"'

'LUCY.'

'"Lucy, are you sure you know what you're doing to poor old Sean?" But she was all over me, darling. What can a man do?'

'Behave like a man who is not led by his prick!'

'What a compliment! You didn't seem to mind when my prick led me to you. Did you?'

'Fuck off.' Helen slammed the phone down in a rage. How dare the pig-headed arse behave like that? He'd always been the same. Well, she wasn't going to bloody well invite him down here anytime soon. She would draw the line and have no further contact. She'd tried to remain on good terms for the children's sake, but this was beyond the pale. She picked the phone up again.

'Bristol Home Charity shop, good morning.'

'Chloe, darling, it's Mum. Have you got ten minutes?'

*

By the time Helen put the phone down, she felt a lot better. Chloe had listened and supported her while trying not to be judgemental about her father. But she had agreed that her parents needed to have a cooling-off period and that it would be best not to invite Gray down for Christmas. When Helen asked her about coming down for Bonfire Night, Chloe leapt at the chance. She said she was missing Helen and Sean, and would like to have a look at the glamorous Terri too. Helen couldn't wait to see her children.

*

It was Friday, 4 November and Helen was fretting. Sean had volunteered to collect Chloe from Bristol on the way down so all three of them would arrive together, but now it was 8 p.m. and there was still no sign of them. She was convinced something had gone wrong. Mobile phones and satnavs didn't work well down here, so if Sean had got lost somewhere he'd have no way of letting her know.

She was in the sitting-room window seat, so she could keep an eye on the road. She'd worked hard today; the house was looking its best, a fire glowed in the grate and the kids' favourite curried beef with horseradish stew was in the bottom of the Aga. She hoped that Terri wasn't a vegetarian. Earlier, she had taken two big bell jars with a couple of sturdy church candles in them, and placed them either side of the gate on top of the wonky drystone wall. Helen turned and looked out of the window again. The candles were still lit and flickering attractively. She flicked the television on to pass the time. Sky News wasn't reporting any major pile-ups on the M4 yet . . .

*

Chloe had never been more uncomfortable in a back seat. Sean was driving Terri's Jeep wrangler, which had a kind of tarpaulin roof stretched over the top and the constant flapping made it impossible to hear anything that was said by those in the front seats. She was cold too. It was as if the November night was seeping from the Tarmac, through the tyres and directly into her feet, hands and kidneys. Maybe she'd get the train back to Bristol on Sunday. She looked at the back of Sean's tufty head. She loved her brother and knew that he had been as shocked by Helen and Gray's decision to part as she had. Her father was a rogue, and he'd hurt her mother badly over the years, but Chloe still hadn't believed that the two of them would go through with the divorce. Even now, she was convinced that they would get back together.

She watched as Terri put her hand tenderly on Sean's leg. She was saying something to him which made him take her hand in his and lift it to his lips. Terri was very pretty and her friendliness towards Chloe when they picked her up that afternoon had felt genuine. Chloe was happy for them both. In the meantime, her own love-life was a desert.

Perhaps she was looking for something impossible, someone who was like her father but with all the unfaithful bits taken out. Were men programmed to be unfaithful? At Cambridge there'd been a couple of boys she fancied, but nothing had come of it. Chloe had never wanted to dress in anything low-cut and high-heeled, and as she didn't like the taste of alcohol, getting wrecked and having a tipsy fumble wasn't an option.

She saw herself in the driver's rear-view mirror. Make-up-free, long, shiny auburn hair, inherited from her mother, and an anorak she'd got for a few quid in her own charity shop. She was slender but would never be a Terri.

Terri had perfectly rounded breasts and a super-flat stomach with legs up to her armpits. The legs were currently encased in skin-tight black jeans and spiky-heeled ankle boots. Her coat was lightweight but deeply padded and lined with fur. Terri's hair was model-perfect too. Platinum blonde; natural, according to Sean, for which Chloe had punched him. Too much information.

They came off the M5 and onto winding country roads. The directions Helen had emailed them were in Terri's lap and she read them out to Sean using the light from her mobile phone to see. In the dark it was very difficult to spot any of the little turns into narrow lanes, and the lack of signposts was infuriating, but at last they spotted the Dolphin pub, which Helen had told them was close to Pendruggan.

Eventually, Chloe shouted, 'Look! There! With the candles on the wall. I can see Mum through the window.'

Sean gave the horn a couple of short beeps and they watched Helen jump up and wave out to the two head-lights gleaming in the dark.

As they walked up the path, she threw open the door and the light inside spilled on to the path.

After lots of hugs and kisses and bundling in of bags and bunches of flowers, they were all given the chance to look round the cottage before sitting down by the fire for a drink.

Supper was a success. Terri tucked into the beef stew with gusto – 'Helen, this is marvellous. I could never be a veggie!' – and conversation flowed easily as they exchanged all their news. By half-past ten Sean and Terri had headed off to their room at the Dolphin.

After turning the downstairs lights out, Helen put her arms round Chloe and gave her a big hug.

'I have missed my girl so much.'

'Oh, Mum, it's lovely to be here with you. Terri's nice, isn't she?'

'Yes, I like her. Sean can't keep his eyes or his hands off her.'

'Let's hope Dad can.'

16

D orrie had offered to make the Merrifield family a late breakfast in the pub and she had pulled out all the stops. The table was groaning under dishes of local crispy bacon, eggs, spicy sausages and fresh granary toast. They washed it all down with piping mugs of tea.

'It's a lovely sunny day and the forecast for the firework display tonight is clear and dry.' Don was helping Dorrie to clear the table. 'You going down with the girls to watch it, Sean? Or would you like to join me and the lads for a drink?'

'What time?' asked Sean.

Terri flashed a look at Sean, which Dorrie caught.

'Don, there's plenty of time for that later. Sean wants to see the fireworks.'

Terri cast a grateful glance at Dorrie, who turned away laden with dirty plates and cups. Don gave Sean a covert wink and mouthed 'Later' at him before following his wife into the kitchen.

*

They decided to take two cars down to Trevay, where they spent the next few hours mooching around the warren of narrow streets and shops. Terri liked the little galleries displaying local artists' work and bought a hand-thrown sea-green glazed jug that she had fallen in love with.

'That's really beautiful, Terri. It'll look gorgeous with daffs in,' said Helen.

'Well, believe it or not, it's for putting my paintbrushes in. I have an art degree and I'm putting together some work now with a view to having an exhibition next summer.'

'What about your modelling?'

'It's a money-spinner, that's all. I've been very lucky so far; it's paid the rent and bought my car. It's easy money, and I'm grateful for it, but I have no delusions that it will lead to bigger things. Besides, it's too bloody cold to sit on the bonnet of a car in a bikini indefinitely!' Terri grinned broadly, showing her perfect teeth.

Helen laughed and looked over at her son, who had stopped to buy ice cream for them all. She watched as he beckoned Terri over to collect hers and gave her a hug. Could Terri be *the one*?

After the ice creams, Sean, who had had enough of shopping, spotted the sign pointing to the cliff path and smugglers' caves.

'Heave-ho, me hearties! There'll be doubloons in the offing.'

Chloe and Terri ran after him, rags of laughter falling around them. Helen followed behind, thanking whoever was up there for this perfect day.

The path split in two after about a quarter of a mile, one direction continuing up the cliff path while the other led down to the beach and its caves.

They settled on the caves, which were set in the under-cliff and reached by a steep set of steps, hand hewn into the rock. The old caverns where local smugglers had plied their trade were shrouded in darkness. Sean and Chloe took out their phone torches and tried to see how far they went. Terri and Helen chose to sit on a flat warm rock to watch the yachts in the distance.

After about five minutes the brother and sister returned, disappointed.

'It's all blocked by a rockfall. And anyway, it smells of wee.' Chloe wrinkled her nose and sat down next to her mother. Sean plonked himself down next to Terri.

'Lovely day for surfing,' said Helen. 'I'm having lessons.' Three pairs of eyes looked at her. 'The vicar is teaching me.'

As she had hoped, they all clamoured for more information, which she gladly gave.

'I've arranged to meet him at the fireworks tonight.'

'I shall need to ask what his intentions are towards you, Ma,' said Sean.

'He's my friend, that's all,' Helen insisted.

'Mum, what about the horrible hunk with the dog who had a run-in with your knickers?'

'You mean Piran Ambrose?' Helen felt two pairs of eyes on her. After filling Sean and Terri in on the story, to a loud chorus of disapproval at his rude behaviour, she chose to play it casual. 'I've barely seen him in . . . oh, it must be weeks. People tell me he's actually quite nice. You just need to get to know him.'

'And are you going to get to know him?' Terri slipped her arm under Helen's and squeezed it.

Sean and Chloe looked at each other, then chorused, 'Not if we have anything to do with it.'

*

Later that evening, around 6 p.m., Helen and Chloe were suited and booted in warm shoes and coats. They stopped at the vicarage to pick up Simon, whom Helen had arranged to collect the previous day. He was wearing his usual black coat, but with a checked scarf round his neck and plain black trousers tucked into socks and walking boots. Sean and Terri had gone back to their hotel earlier and they were all due to meet up at the fireworks display.

'Hello. What a super clear night! You must be Chloe.' Simon shook her hand as she jumped out of the passenger seat to nip into the back.

'Lovely to meet you, Simon. You sit at the front, I'm fine here at the back.'

Simon got in and assiduously did up his seat belt. As Helen drove out of the village he turned and gave Chloe a proper look.

'Goodness, Helen. This can't be your daughter. You look like sisters!'

'I know! Uncanny, isn't it?' Helen replied, laughing. 'It's like looking in the Wicked Queen's mirror!'

'Mum! I can see why you like this man.' Chloe was laughing too.

Simon turned back to look at Helen, his heart bumping with pleasure.

*

They managed to squeeze into the harbour car park, although the traffic was already building up, then made their way to join Terri and Sean, who were keeping seats free for them on one of the benches by the harbour railings.

'Well done,' said Helen, hugging Sean and kissing Terri.

'You've got a prime spot here. Let me introduce you to Reverend Simon Canter.'

'Just Simon, please.' He shook hands with them all. It had been a long time since he'd felt part of a family.

The display was due to start soon. In the gloom they could make out a dredger anchored a distance out on the water, with dark figures flashing torches on the deck.

'Is that the hub of the display out on the boat, Simon?' asked Helen.

'Yes. The horizon behind makes a perfect backdrop. It's all done by computer, these days. Jolly clever.'

Would it be appropriate to put his arm round her? Just as Simon was about to send the message from brain to arm, Sean interrupted:

'Fancy some tea and chips? The girls and I are just off to get some.'

Helen shifted slightly away from him to reach for her purse and a ten-pound note. 'Yes, please. My treat.'

Then another familiar face arrived. 'Hello, you two.'

'Hello! Come and join us, Don,' said Helen, smiling warmly.

'Better not. I've left Dorrie behind the bar. I only nipped down to see Piran. We've got a table booked for four of you tonight. Shall I make it five?' He looked at Simon.

'Simon, we'd love you to join us for supper. Can you bear to put up with us all evening?'

'Well, I . . . I'd love to. Thank you.'

'Right you are,' said Don. 'See you later then.'

It was now or never. Simon lifted his arm and was just about to move it casually along the back of the bench and around Helen's shoulders, when she grabbed his hand in her gloved one and said, 'I am so excited! I love fireworks. Brings back lovely memories of parties in our Chiswick back garden when the children were small.'

She thought back to those times, but her smile faded as she realised her memory had played tricks. They hadn't been particularly nice at all. Either Gray would get home late, or not at all; while the children would be overexcited, then bored by her attempts at lighting damp Catherine wheels, which never spun round like they should. By the time Gray eventually turned up, the whole event would have collapsed into screaming kids, tearful wife and a barbecue that reeked of sausage cinders. She pushed it all out of her mind. This was her life now and it was full of promise.

The display was magnificent, huge bursts of colour reflecting in the high tide and the booms reverberating around the old buildings. The final five minutes was a non-stop barrage of rockets, whizzes, bangs and stars. The last rocket soared above everything else and when it exploded it spelled out TREVAY in golden letters.

There was loud and lengthy applause before the crowd turned as one, hurrying to be the first car out of the car park.

*

The Dolphin was packed, but Dorrie and Don had kept a nice table in the corner snug for Helen's party.

Don welcomed them in, took their order for drinks and left them to look at the menu.

He was back quickly with foaming pints for the two men, and a jug of steaming mulled wine for the women.

'We didn't order this,' said Chloe.

'On the 'ouse. It's a Dorrie special. Cheers, ladies! Ready to order?'

The food was excellent as usual and simple in style. Pumpkin ravioli in sage butter, sea bass on a bed of chilli-butter beans, and a plate of local charcuterie with warm crusty bread, all of which were declared delicious. Once that was cleared away, just as they were deciding if they could squeeze in a pudding, there was some excitement at the bar as Dorrie called for quiet. From their corner, they couldn't see Dorrie or the person she was referring to, but a hush fell over the pub.

'Ladies and gentlemen, we've 'ad a great night in Trevay with the fireworks and all the money we've raised for charity, but it wouldn't have been possible without one man. 'E's a special friend to all of us and we wouldn't 'ave 'ad such a spectacular display without 'im. Show your appreciation, ladies and gentlemen, boys and girls, for our own Guy Fawkes – Mr Piran Ambrose.'

An enormous cheer went up in the crowded pub. Simon got to his feet and applauded. Chloe, Sean and Terri stood up and craned their necks to get a look at this man who'd been so rude to Helen.

Helen remained seated.

Piran had heaved himself up on to the bar and, after the applause had died down, looked around at the assembled throng who were sitting down again.

'Thank you, Dorrie, and thank you, Don. Where are you, man?'

Don made himself known behind the bar. Piran continued:

'Don helps raise funds for the show through his tireless committee work and endless raffles, car boot sales, et cetera. He also gets all the licences and safety checks through that we need. I don't know what we'd do without him.' Loud cheers accompanied raucous applause. Piran continued: 'Our chosen charity this year is the graveyard conservation at Holy Trinity down in Pendruggan. It looks like we've raised almost four thousand pounds this year,' – the crowd cheered even louder – 'which is what I shall tell the Reverend Canter tonight, when I go and see him at the vicarage.'

'I'm here, Piran!' piped up Simon.

There was another round of whoops and cheers as Simon stood up and waved. Piran jumped from the bar and strode over to him. He shook his hand and clapped him on the back. 'What you doin' in the pub, vicar? Have you fallen into bad company?'

'No, I'm with Helen and her family.'

Piran turned and at the sight of Helen his face darkened.

'Mrs Merrifield.' He gave a curt nod to the expectant faces of the rest of the party and then, turning back to Simon, said quietly, 'I see you have fallen in with . . . company. We'll speak later, vicar, OK?'

'Certainly, Piran. And thank you so much. What a wonderful donation.'

Piran shook Simon's hand again and turned back to the crowd. 'The Reverend Simon Canter, everyone. He knows he'll see you all in church tomorrow morning! Isn't that right, vicar?'

There was laughter and then Piran was swallowed back into the crowd.

Helen excused herself and went to the ladies'. She closed the door of the cubicle and surprised herself as tears fell silently on her cheeks. Why was this man so horrible to her? How could people like him? What had she done? She quickly blew her nose and tried to pull herself together. This reaction left her feeling completely mystified. Perhaps it was the emotion of having the kids with her. Or maybe the last few months of this completely new chapter in her life had taken more of a toll on her than she realised.

As she left the cubicle and washed her hands at the little sink, she heard a familiar voice outside: Piran.

'What's she doing, hanging around the vicar? Who are those people she's with?'

Don's voice: 'The vicar's fallen for her, I reckon. He's invited her to the diocesan dinner in the new year. Helen told Dorrie.'

'Who's that city boy with the dumb blonde and the mouse?'

'Her son and daughter and his girlfriend. They're staying here. Nice people, Piran.'

'Just keep an eye on the vicar, will you? Don't want him getting hurt again. She'll be off back to London once she gets bored of us hicks – you watch.'

Helen could stand it no longer. Plastering a big smile on her face, she came out of the loo and walked straight into Piran's line of vision. Don had the grace to look sheepish.

'Oops, excuse me! What are you two hicks doing outside the ladies' gossiping like a couple of girls? Dear me, with all this excitement I shall never want to go back to London. Especially as I am so looking forward to my date with dear Simon at the bishop's party.'

Don was looking at his feet. Piran was staring at her with an inscrutable look on his face.

'Good night, gentlemen. If you'll excuse me, I have to get my mousey daughter home.'

Helen turned on her heel, and with all dignity collected up her party and led them out.

17

The next day Dorrie was on the phone full of apologies. Don had told her what had happened and she had given both him and Piran a flea in their ears.

'Don's on the sofa for the foreseeable future, Helen. Like a pair of old washerwomen, they are. Don's ever so embarrassed, but Piran . . . I don't know what goes on in 'is mind at times. He just listened to what I had to say and left. Perhaps 'is new Truro lady's got under his skin.' Helen heard her sigh at the other end. 'Anyway, I hope this doesn't affect our friendship, Helen.'

Helen reassured her that it was water off a duck's back and that this sort of thing happened in small communities. No harm done. But when she got off the phone she resolved not to have anything more to do with Piran Ambrose. Which was a pity, because she wanted to solve the mystery of the tin box. Never mind. She'd sort something out with the other woman from the museum in Trevay; Janet Coombes, was it?

It would have to wait till the spring though. Christmas was looming and she wanted it to be perfect for her and the kids. Chloe was coming to stay with her again and Sean and Terri had accepted her invitation for Christmas, booking themselves back into the Dolphin.

*

In the meantime, much to Helen's irritation, Gray had been phoning again and whingeing about Selina, his latest squeeze, and angling for an invitation for Christmas. Helen had been short and to the point with him.

'Gray, this is not my problem, it's yours. You are a man of fifty-three, not twenty-three. You have plenty of friends you can spend Christmas with. We are separated, remember?'

'Helen, you've changed. You've grown so hard.'

'And not before time.' She heard him tut. 'Why don't you spend Christmas with the diaphanous Selina?'

'She's going to her parents.'

'So?'

'They don't know about me.'

Helen laughed. 'Ha! So they don't know she's hanging out with a man the same age as her father?'

'He's a couple of years older than me, actually.'

'I see. So let me get this straight. Your girlfriend can't take you home with her, your friends haven't offered invitations to spend Christmas with them, and you think you may as well come down here where good old Helen will look after you. Well, it doesn't work like that any more, I'm afraid.'

'Hit me where it hurts, why don't you? Oh, Helen, you really are the perfect wife. Why don't we call the whole divorce thing off? You can still have your life there and I can have my little flat here and we can meet up for romantic weekends. What do you say?' He put an extra growl in his voice. 'You still have the sexiest legs I've ever seen.'

'Gray, you are a cheating, sexist pig who pulled my heart out and stamped it into the dust. You plundered my love, my self-esteem, and my address book for my mates' phone numbers. How can I resist you?'

'Someone got out of bed the wrong side today. Menopause, I expect. I'll leave you to it.'

And he hung up.

*

Later that day he sent a sniffy email advising her that he wouldn't be coming down for Christmas. He was taking Selina to Verbier. Helen pressed the delete button furiously. Then, just as quickly, opened a new mail to him saying, *You are not invited anyway*, and pressed send before she could change her mind.

*

The weather was getting chilly and the skies rather bleak. Her walks on the beach were more of a challenge than a pleasure as she forced her way through the strong buffeting winds, usually getting a faceful of stinging sea spray for her efforts.

Simon was a constant pal. They had fallen into a cosy pattern of mid-week suppers together and catch-ups over a pot of tea. He was a dear friend, of whom she was getting fonder and fonder. He was pedantic and set in his ways, yes, but he was always there and ready to share. He'd be a perfect husband . . . maybe even for her . . . if she could imagine having sex with him, which she couldn't.

*

On a Sunday afternoon walk early in December, they talked about Christmas. For Simon it meant a lot of extra services and diary dates for school carol services and the like. But the major event was the 'Village Entertainment Evening'. Leading the committee this year were Polly and Pete, who had decided to stage 'Pendruggan's Got Talent', a local version of the hit TV show. A handful of acts had signed up already and two of the three judges had been decided on: Simon, because he was 'The Boss', as Polly called him; and Queenie, because of her vast knowledge of celebrity culture.

'We're looking for a third judge.' Simon turned his large, bespectacled brown eyes on her.

There was a pause and then Helen shook her head vehemently. 'No. Not me. I couldn't. I'll make tea, sell tickets, but not that. Absolutely not.'

'I wasn't actually thinking about you. More your friend Penny.'

'Oh!' Helen didn't know whether to feel crushed or relieved. 'Well, I can ask her and see what she says, though I know she is very busy.' Then she remembered how rude Penny had been to Simon when she'd last come down. 'Was she your choice?'

'Well, it was a committee thing. Queenie was telling everyone about the filming that might happen here, and about your friend being in television, so I said I'd ask you.'

'Well, Penny owes you big time after being so mean when she was pissed, so tell the committee that, yes, she'll do it. I'll make sure of it.'

*

Penny had been very sweet about being volunteered for the job and even arranged for her locations manager, production designer and director to come down at the same time. 'We may as well kill many birds with one stone. I'll get my PA to call the Starfish and wangle some rooms.'

Pendruggan's Got Talent was booked for the seventeenth of December and as Penny was coming down on the twenty-third anyway, she decided simply to stay on after the show.

Most of Helen's time in the run-up to the show was spent at the vicarage, co-ordinating press and publicity, printing programmes, and organising ticket sales and the line up of talent. And because Pendruggan had no village hall, the church would have to serve as the theatre, which meant persuading the flower ladies to sort out the decorations.

The main box office was Queenie's shop. No one, not even passing strangers who popped in to ask directions, could get out of the shop without buying tickets. A photograph of Queenie perched behind her till in a gay chiffon hat appeared on the front page of the *Trevay Times,* the local free newspaper, under the headline RIGHT ROYAL VARIETY SHOW. 'Queenie of the box office' read the caption. Helen got a copy laminated and Blu-tacked it on to the shop door.

''Ere, duck . . .' Queenie beckoned Helen over once they'd admired her work. 'Do ya fink that naughty boy Simon Cowell could send us a photo and a few words of luck for the programme?'

'Brilliant idea! I'll see if Penny knows somebody who knows somebody. Don't hold your breath though. It's a long shot.'

But to everyone's surprise a photo and message from Simon Cowell arrived within the week. The photo wasn't signed, much to Queenie's disappointment, but the message read: *Good luck with your talent show. Send me the winner. Yours, Simon Cowell.* It was duly Blu-tacked to the shop door alongside Queenie's photo.

In the end there were ten acts. The Trevay Lifeboat Choir, the Women's Institute Folk Singers, an all-girl pop band called The Ravers, Don doing his Elvis in Vegas act, a magician, Polly reading Alfred Noyes' 'The Highwayman', Pete giving a demonstration of CPR, the Brownies performing a Christmas dance, a muscle man, and Tony singing 'Walking in the Air'.

*

As the big day drew nearer, Helen sat at her desk one night and scratched her head. It wasn't easy, deciding the running order. Where, for instance could you put the CPR demo? She toyed with the idea of putting it second to last before the interval. Maybe after the muscle man and before the Brownies. But who to give the opening spot to? And the closing spot? Helen sighed. Why on earth had she ever agreed to get involved? She must have been mad.

18

'Queenie, meet my oldest friend, Penny. Penny, this is the wonderful Queenie.'

November had passed quickly and before Helen knew it, December had come around and Penny had arrived with her team to prepare for filming.

Now Helen watched as Penny's face absorbed the wondrous innards of the village shop. Queenie put down her copy of *Gossip* mag and turned her beady eyes at the newcomer.

'You're the one what's working on the telly, are you? Let me 'ave a proper look at ya.'

Penny gave a little twirl, rather pleased with her new Ugg leather biker boots, black mini dress, opaque tights and Alexander McQueen black-and-white skull motif scarf. This was her 'country' look.

'Oh my gawd, yes. I can see as you're in the telly. No doubt.'

'Penny is here with her team to decide where the filming will happen.'

'How much?'

'About four weeks I think,' said Penny, who was now browsing the shelves.

'I didn't say 'ow long, I said 'ow much? What will I get if you use my shop for filming?'

Penny turned to Helen. 'You were right, Helen. She's not a sweet old lady at all!'

'No, I'm not. I'm glad we've got that sorted out. 'Ow was Simon Cowell when you spoke to him?'

'I didn't actually get to speak to him. He's in America, but an old mate of mine works for his company, which is how I got the photo and message. I saw it on the door. Has it boosted ticket sales?'

'I've just got the last twenty or so to go and then it'll be standing-room only.' Another thought crossed Queenie's mind. ''Oo's goin to be on this telly programme then? Could you get one of them to 'elp out?'

'It's all top secret at the moment, so I can't say. But we do have our fingers crossed for a very big name.'

'Do you?' asked Helen. 'You haven't told me!'

'Well, she's got a big movie lined up and is just trying to see if she can squeeze us in. We'll know next week.'

'You're talking about Dame Judi Dench.' Queenie folded her magazine and put it back in the rack.

'How do you know?' asked Penny, shocked.

'I read the magazines. There was a rumour in the Scoundrel column. She can't make it 'cos of previous commitments.'

'When did you find this out?'

'This morning. Take a look.' She passed the magazine to Penny.

'Bloody hell! How did this get out without me being told first?' Penny dug in her bag for her BlackBerry. 'No bloody signal.'

Queenie gave one of her crackly laughs with a bit of a cough at the end, and then said, 'So, ladies, ready to talk business?'

*

It was agreed that Jonathan the location manager and Marie, the production designer, would meet Queenie that afternoon and discuss terms for using her shop in the filming.

Slipping her a twenty-pound note, Penny said, 'Maybe you'd be kind enough to tell everybody who comes in here what we're doing, Queenie. It'll save us having to keep explaining.'

Queenie tapped the side of her nose, 'Right you are.' And the twenty-pound note disappeared into her cleavage.

*

Jonathan and Marie were ambling about on the green when the two women came out of the shop.

'So, what do you think?' Penny called as she approached them.

'Lovely spot. Pity about the post-war council houses, but that could be to our advantage.' Jonathan shaded his eyes with his hand and looked at the row of neat houses. 'Marie has an idea.'

'Yes. I think we could screen them out with a false wall, and make that the main St Brewey High Street. Our scenic artists will draw up life-size paintings of the bank, Mr Timm's house next door, and anything else we need. By the time my team have got flowers and trees growing up outside, curtains at the windows, knockers at the doors and rolled out a rubber pavement to walk on, you'd never know it was a complete fabrication. It will be like stepping back in time.' Marie had won umpteen awards, including two BAFTAs and an Oscar nomination, so she knew what she was talking about.

'Brilliant.' Penny turned to Jonathan. 'How are all our

filming permits and permissions coming along? Have we got the go-ahead for using Pendruggan and Trevay?'

'So far so good. The local council are being very helpful.'

'OK. Well, I'll leave you to it. Helen and I have to pay a visit to a friend. Come on, Helen.'

She took Helen's arm and steered her over the green towards the vicarage. 'I must make my apologies to Simon before I turn his village into a living hell.'

*

Simon's beaming smile as he saw Helen at the door dropped the moment he saw Penny. But he ushered them both in and, remembering his manners, offered tea or sherry. 'I'm sorry I don't have anything more exciting for you, Penny. I have very naïve taste in alcohol.'

Penny had the decency to burn at the reminder of how rude she'd been to him the last time they had met.

'A sherry would be lovely, Simon.' She smiled and then rushed on: 'Simon, I owe you a big, fat apology. I was rude and dismissive of you last time we met. I feel ashamed and hope you will accept my apology.'

Simon handed her the sherry glass and looked into her face, which he now noticed was rather attractive. Sincerity shone from her eyes and he couldn't detect any smirking in her plump, smiling lips at all. Eventually he replied, 'You have nothing to apologise for. Any friend of Helen's is a friend of mine.'

He raised his glass to her and she replied, 'And vice versa,' before tipping the drink into her mouth.

*

Over the next few days the villagers got used to Jonathan and Marie taking photos and measurements of Pendruggan. At first the council house residents were not too happy at having their homes hidden away, but when they understood that they'd have a prime view of back-stage goings on, they felt they had a better deal than anybody. All the catering vans, wardrobe trailers and make-up trucks would be between their front doors and the false wall.

Jonathan promised that he would give them all a full tour before the actors arrived, on the strict understanding that when filming started they wouldn't bother them.

The day before the 'Pendruggan's Got Talent' show, the Holy Trinity flower ladies were busy with the final tweaks to the church decor. Marie, taking a wander inside, admired the sprays of red carnations and holly decorating the altar, and the arch of spruce branches being secured around the porch.

'I think it's wonderful, girls!' she told them. 'Would you mind if I came back later and had a little fiddle?'

The ladies' eyes turned in unison to their leader, Audrey Tipton. Audrey NEVER allowed ANYONE to 'have a fiddle' with her designs. EVER.

After a longish pause, Audrey said, 'Well, if you think you can add anything, then do help yourself.'

There was a collective outward breath.

'Great. You can come back tomorrow, but not before noon. OK?'

Grudgingly, Audrey gave Marie the old church key and said, 'Noon tomorrow it is.' She waited until Marie was walking away before whispering to her sidekick, Angela,

'That'll give us just enough time to make it all right again.'

*

What they saw the next day brought tears to their eyes. Even Audrey's. The church had been transformed. Marie had fixed thousands of fairy lights into the spruce branches round the porch and added at least two dozen candlelit lanterns with candles to line the path from the church gate to the building itself. Inside, she and Jonathan had rigged a red plush velvet proscenium arch to mark the boundary between nave and chancel, or, as it was now, auditorium and stage. On the back wall, the altar was hidden by a vast black curtain with a sign saying PENDRUGGAN'S GOT TALENT picked out in chasing lights. A low black Perspex table had been placed in front of the steps leading to the chancel with three silver chairs behind it, ready for the judges. Every pew-end had fairy lights wound round it, and the pulpit, in which the show's compère Mr Audrey Tipton, otherwise known as Geoff, would sit, was swathed and tented in a light sparkly cloth that made it look like an icy snow queen's balcony. The sprays of carnations and holly were still near the altar, but now they rested on white Doric columns which, again, were covered in fairy lights, and from the roof hung an enormous mirror ball. It looked incredible.

'I had it all sent down overnight from the props store. Hope you don't mind. The glitter ball is an old one from *Strictly Come Dancing*. Watch!'

Marie went into the vestry and a moment later the main lights went out and a single spotlight fell on to the motor-driven twirling mirror ball. The church danced in the refracted light and the fairy lights twinkled with mischief. A gasp went up from the flower ladies.

Marie reappeared from behind the vestry curtain. 'Well? Do you like it?'

*

There was one last Christmas surprise that Jonathan had rigged up with the help of a couple of farm hands: a Christmas tree in the middle of the green covered in large multicoloured lights. 'It's the least we can do for the chaos we are going to wreak on you in the coming weeks.' He and Marie hugged everybody goodbye, then set off for London.

Penny, Simon and Helen walked back to the vicarage for a last check on the arrangements.

'What does the winner of the show get?' asked Penny, stirring sugar into her tea.

'A fifty-pound Marks & Spencer's voucher, and dinner for two at the Dolphin,' said Helen, flopping into one of Simon's old armchairs.

'How about that as second prize and first prize could be a proper walk-on part in the filming? No speaking, probably, but a good close-up? I'll pull some strings!'

'That's a fabulous idea,' agreed Helen. 'You're a genius!'

19

The show was due to start at 7.30 p.m. with doors opening half an hour before. The WI ladies who weren't performing were setting up refreshments at the back of the church. Mulled wine, tea, coffee and mince pies. Simon had arranged to meet Penny and Helen in the vestry at 6.45 p.m. They couldn't meet at the vicarage because the whole of the downstairs was being used as a dressing room for the artistes. Queenie was rubbing baby oil liberally into the muscle man's thighs, and a couple of Brownies, dressed as sprites, were delving into the magician's suitcase looking for rabbits. Simon had quietly slipped out the back door and left them to it.

Nipping across his garden and into the churchyard, he gave the clear frosty night sky a nod and said a silent prayer. *Thank you Lord for this wonderful night. Amen. PS Thank you for sending Helen to me.*

*

When he arrived, Helen and Penny were warming their bums on the little fan heater in the vestry.

'I don't know whether it's the night air or nerves making me shiver so much,' said Penny, rubbing her palms together vigorously.

'You? Nervous? Never in my life have I heard you admit to nerves.' Helen smiled at her.

'I have a little something in my pocket, if you're interested, ladies.'

'Now, now, Vicar, you are a one!' teased Penny.

Simon looked at her innocently, 'It's just a little stiffener, as my father would say.'

Penny sniggered, 'Said the bishop to the actress.'

'Ignore my puerile friend. What is it?'

Simon pulled out a hip flask. 'Cherry brandy. Seemed suitably festive.'

All three took a grateful swig and Penny apologised for her lewdness.

'I'm getting used to it,' said Simon with a sigh.

Just then the compère, Mr Audrey Tipton, bustled through the curtain separating the vestry from the church. He gave off rather a strong odour of mulled wine.

'It's a good turnout, vicar. Almost everybody's here. Queenie's settled in her seat and getting impatient. What's the MO?'

'Thanks, Geoff. We'll give it another five minutes and then I'll go out, make a welcome speech, and introduce our guest of honour, Miss Leighton.' Penny reached out to shake Geoff's large hand. 'Then I'll introduce you, and it's all in your hands.'

'Ideal. You put a copy of the running order in the pulpit, did you, Mrs Merrifield?'

'Yes. It's all there, with a little jug of water and a glass if you need it.'

He swept back out into the church. The back door to the churchyard opened, letting in a gust of frosty air, and Polly and the magician came in. 'Everybody's ready,' she whispered. 'They're coming over at timed five-minute intervals like you said, Helen.'

'Excellent! Thanks.'

They all waited in the wings until the dot of 7.30 p.m., and then Simon stepped out to warm applause.

'Ladies and gentlemen, boys and girls, welcome to "Pendruggan's Got Talent"!' He paused to allow the cheers and a couple of catcalls to die down. 'Each year our village entertainment astonishes me with the richness of its talent . . .'

He was stalled momentarily by cries of, 'Get on with it, vicar!'

'. . . And so, tonight I am indebted to my close friend Helen Merrifield . . .' This was greeted by a collective cry of 'Ooooh, vicar!' from the audience, but Simon ploughed on: '. . . who has managed to engage a leading television producer to join Queenie and myself on the judging panel. Please put your hands together and give a warm Pendruggan welcome to Miss Penny Leighton!' Penny stepped through the curtain to several wolf whistles and cheers. She waved to the crowd, blew a couple of theatrical kisses, and then took her seat next to Queenie.

'And now,' continued Simon, 'as I take my seat at the judges' table, I leave you in the capable hands of Mr Geoff Tipton!'

This was Helen's cue to turn on the mirror ball and dim the main church lights. As she did so, she could hear Geoff walking up the pulpit steps.

What she couldn't see, but what she was told later, was that Geoff made his way unsteadily up the steps with his glasses sitting unevenly on his wine-pinkened face. As he got to the top step, he put a hand up to adjust his specs but misjudged their position and knocked them to the floor. Bending down to retrieve them, he hit his nose hard on the brass lectern. When he stood up again, his nose was bleeding profusely.

'Geoff!' shouted Audrey, leaping from her seat, but Polly was already through the curtain and beat her to it. With swift efficiency she checked Geoff over and was calling for ice while trying to staunch the flow.

Simon stood up and, as loudly as he could over the hubbub, asked for a twenty-minute pause in proceedings.

The WI ladies were going to get through a lot of mulled wine tonight.

*

Polly got Geoff mopped up enough for him to be taken off to Casualty by Pete, who insisted the show should go ahead without the benefit of his CPR demo. But as one problem was solved for Helen, another presented itself: Who would compère the show?

To her consternation, she saw Simon stride purposefully towards her with Piran at his elbow.

'Helen, I have asked Piran to step into Geoff's shoes and he's agreed to do it!'

'Reluctantly.' Piran gave Helen a glower. 'And only because Simon's in a tight spot and he knows I'm a safe pair of hands.'

Conceited bastard, thought Helen, but what she said was, 'How kind of you. The running order is in the pulpit, on the lectern. There shouldn't be too much blood on it,' she added sarcastically. 'Obviously, skip Pete's CPR demo.'

'Obviously.' He turned and walked a few feet away to

join the woman he'd had dinner with in the Starfish. They had a quiet conversation and then she kissed him on the lips and gave him a hug, looking over his broad shoulder directly at Helen as she did so.

Yuck, thought Helen. *Ghastly man, ghastly woman.* But she couldn't help but feel the hot prickle of something suspiciously like jealousy as she turned away quickly from the sight of their embrace.

*

Within ten minutes everybody was back in their seats and Simon had introduced Piran, who was instantly charming the appreciative audience.

Helen was just tucking her bag under her pew when she became aware of a strong smell of Chanel No. 5 and someone taking the seat next to her. She sat up and was face to face with Piran's companion, for want of a better word.

'Hello, Helen. I'm Dawn.' She proffered a slender hand. Her generous bosom and curvaceous hips were ostentatiously clad in clingy mulberry-coloured jersey.

Helen shook the hand. It was soft and dry, the nails long and French-polished. She felt slightly intimidated.

'Hello.'

'Isn't Piran amazing? Look at him working the crowd.'

Helen looked up at the pulpit and then around at the audience. They were relaxed; smiling and laughing, clearly thrilled that Piran had replaced the dull Geoff.

'It must help that they've all had second helpings of the mulled wine,' said Helen, meanly. Dawn laughed, oblivious, and then focused adoringly on Piran.

*

The first half went better than anyone could have hoped for. Polly's poem was performed with real verve, and when she got to the bit where the landlord's daughter shoots herself, Helen felt shivers down her spine. The judging panel gave her an excellent critique and Penny praised Polly for her ability to focus after having dealt with a medical emergency. The crowd murmured their agreement.

The magician was next. Billed as The Great Xanardi, he was in fact the local primary school head teacher with dreams of topping the bill at the London Palladium. His wife, the Lovely Letitia, the school secretary, deftly assisted him. The children lapped it up, especially the bit where the rabbit was supposed to magically emerge from the cake tin, but resolutely refused to do so.

Queenie, taking a leaf out of Louis Walsh's book, told them, 'You owned that stage and Letitia's satin Chinese dress is very exotic. Reminds me of Princess Diana.'

Third on the bill was the Trevay Lifeboat Choir singing a medley of Christmas hymns in close harmony. After their performance, Simon told them it was an honour to have such brave men supporting the church tonight and that they were certainly in with a shout of getting the top prize.

The first half closed with the Brownies' Christmas dance. Dressed as shimmering faerie sprites they pirouetted and thumped about the makeshift stage in a way that can only make a parent proud. The finale was the wholly unexpected sight of the magician's rabbit hopping across the floor to centre stage and sitting on its hind legs, twitching its little whiskers at the laughing audience.

Fearing the wrath of mothers, all three judges praised the girls effusively.

'Ladies and gentlemen,' boomed a handsome, Helen begrudgingly acknowledged, Piran from the pulpit, 'we shall now have a short intermission. Drinks are available at the back and the vicar has made his vicarage cloakroom available to those who need it, although to save queuing I dare say it'd be quicker for you to nip home. See you back here in twenty minutes for more "Pendruggan's Got Talent"!'

Helen immediately set off for the vestry. Aware of someone following her through the curtain, and thinking it was Penny or Simon, she said without turning, 'Well done. Very professional.'

'Thank you, Helen,' came Piran's voice in reply. 'Coming from you, that's a real compliment. I'm glad I've got you on your own. I was wondering if—'

'There you are, you naughty man!' Dawn came sweeping through the vestry curtain. 'What are you two gossiping about?'

Piran gave Helen an apologetic look and then escorted Dawn back into the church. As the curtain fell back into place behind them, Helen was left wondering what it was he was going to ask her.

*

The intermission over, the audience took their seats with mulled wine fumes settling upon them like smog over New York.

Piran took the pulpit steps two at a time. He had lipstick on his cheek, Helen noticed, and the fragrant Dawn was smirking next to her. Double yuck.

The second half opened with The Ravers. The all-girl band were dressed in hot-pants so skimpy they immediately elicited wolf whistles from the young farmers standing at the back. After watching them gyrating filthily to, and murdering the lyrics of, The B52's 'Love Shack', there wasn't a person in the church who didn't have a strong opinion of them one way or another.

Helen glanced at Piran, whose piratical smile and glinting earring looked evilly lascivious in the warm lights, as he nodded along to the music. She then looked at Dawn, whose smile had tightened a fraction.

Jealous of a few teenage girls, are you? Grow up! was Helen's silent thought.

Again the judges were kind and suggested that The Ravers should audition for *The X Factor*.

The Women's Institute folk singers were much as you would expect, and the muscle man – Mickey the Mussels of Mousehole, as he was billed – gave an eye-popping display of body-builder poses to 'Ding Dong Merrily on High'. The crowd loved him and so did Queenie, who found herself lifted into his arms and given a kiss at the end of his routine.

It was now down to the last two acts. Don, wearing a white catsuit and sideburns, gave his rendition of 'It is No Secret (What God Can Do)' from Elvis' 1957 Christmas Album to an audience who sat in awed silence as if in the presence of the King himself. As he left the stage to cheers and applause, Piran quipped, 'Don has left the building.' More laughter as Don popped his head back on stage and took another bow.

The last act was Tony Brown, Helen's very own Mr B., singing 'Walking in the Air'. After much agonising about where to put him in the running order, she had felt that there would be so much goodwill towards him that he'd be the ideal act to close with. She had helped him choose an outfit for the evening too. He was wearing his newest jeans with a Viyella shirt and tweed jacket that they'd chosen together at the charity shop. Helen would have bought him something new, but he insisted that he pay for it himself and that he liked the feel of clothes that had been worn in. 'New clothes make me itchy,' he'd explained.

As Piran began his introduction, Tony walked through the vestry curtain and straight up on to the stage. Someone from the back of the church shouted encouragingly, 'Get on, boy!' then Tony smiled, took a deep breath and, without any musical accompaniment, opened his mouth to sing. For the next three and a half minutes the crowd sat transfixed, listening to the simple purity and musicality which he poured into the song. At the end there was a short hush before the crowd slowly rose to their feet for an ovation that lasted several minutes. Tony smiled and waved broadly, his lovable, sleek, black-haired head bobbing in little bows of thanks.

The winner was decided by who got the loudest cheers and applause from the audience. Mickey the Mussels and Polly came joint second. She chose the M&S voucher and Mickey chose the dinner for two at the Dolphin because, as he explained, he'd just got engaged and wanted to take his fiancée out somewhere special to celebrate. Helen thought she detected a slight air of disappointment in Queenie's reaction to this news.

The overwhelming cheers and applause for the first

prize of a walk-on part in the new Mavis Crewe drama went to . . . Tony. Everybody hugged him or pumped his hand in congratulations. When asked if he wanted to say a few words, he came to front of the stage and said, 'Thanks to my mum.'

There wasn't a dry eye in the house and Helen thought that Tony coming first was the nicest and most heart-warming thing she had ever had the pleasure of being part of.

Soon after, people started to shrug themselves into their coats, collect their programmes and gloves, and brave the cold night for their own cosy beds. Queenie was comman-deering Mickey the Mussels to escort her home and Polly was collecting up the beaming Tony. As he left, he caught sight of Helen and, like a shy young school boy, he walked up and sort of leant into her, burying his head in her shoulder while his arms hung loosely by his side. She put her arms round him, gave him a squeeze and kissed the top of his moleskin head.

'I am very proud of you, Mr B. Well done.'

'Thank 'ee for helping me with my new clothes, Mrs M.'

'My pleasure. Off you go. Polly's waiting.'

The crowd had thinned out by this time. Just the few good souls who remained to tidy up the mulled wine and mince pie detritus. Helen saw Simon and Penny talking to Piran, who had Dawn draped over his arm.

'Helen!' Simon called her over. 'I was just telling Piran how we couldn't have coped without him.'

Helen took a deep breath and smiled as sincerely as she could. 'Simon's right. You were marvellous.'

Dawn looked up into Piran's face and fluttered her eyelashes. 'If I was looking for people for a TV drama, I'd cast you. Not that simpleton of a village idiot.'

Piran turned on her so fast it made all of them jump. 'If you think that young man doesn't deserve to have won tonight then you, my dear, are the idiot.'

Freeing himself from her arm, he said, 'Simon, Helen, Penny – would you care to join me for a drink at the Dolphin? I promised Don I'd see him before closing time.'

'Oh yes, do join us,' Dawn asked breathlessly.

'No, Dawn. You go on home. I'll call you.'

Dawn haughtily collected her bag, pulled her coat more tightly round her, and reached up to plant a large, red-lipsticked smear of a kiss on Piran's face. 'Don't forget what you're missing, gorgeous.' She gave Helen a malevolent glance. 'I know how you like to do your bit for the older folk.'

Piran grabbed her by the arm. 'Insult other people if you must, but not my friends. Helen and Tony have done more for this evening than you ever could or would. I'll see you to your car.'

Helen was rather impressed by Piran's show of manliness, and more than pleased by his comments about her.

'What a cow,' whispered Penny. 'I hope he's dumping her. We'll find out in a minute.'

They waited for about ten minutes. Then Penny, who could no longer stand the suspense, went out to see what was going on. When she came back she had disappointing news.

'They've gone. No cars left outside. No sign of anyone. Is he always that outrageous?'

'No,' said Simon, 'Yes,' said Helen in unison.

20

With just a week to go before Christmas, the days were short and extremely cold. The night frosts lingered through the daytime and Helen was concerned for her palm tree. It rustled its frost-nipped leaves loudly in the easterly wind, but at least remained upright. She bought several strings of outdoor fairy lights and wound them round the garden walls, up the path and over the frame of the front door.

She had asked Tony to go out and buy a Christmas tree for her and he came back with a fat little one which fitted snugly into the right-hand nook of the fireplace. When they'd secured it inside a weighted wicker basket, Tony nipped out over the back wall saying he'd be back in a minute. He returned with a shoe box tucked under his arm and a parcel wrapped up in newspaper in his hand.

'Happy Christmas, Mrs M.' He handed her the shoe box. Inside were about two dozen tree decorations made entirely of shells and driftwood.

'Mr B.! These are gorgeous. Did you make them yourself?'

'Aye. My mum and I used to make them together, but I made these special for you, see.'

'Help me put them on the tree.'

The end result was rustic and charming. Tony put a

couple of strings of fairy lights round the branches as a finishing touch.

'I got this too . . .'

He opened the newspaper-wrapped parcel. This was also made from shells but stuck on to a piece of plywood and shaped like a cross.

'It's to go on the top, see.'

They sat back and admired their handiwork.

'Mr B., I couldn't have asked for anything better.' She gave him a kiss. 'Do you have any more of the crosses? I'd like to give one to the vicar as a Christmas present.'

'I'll make 'ee one tonight.'

'How much will I owe you?'

'Nothin to you, Mrs M.'

'Well, in that case, how about you and I have some Christmas cake and a drink to celebrate?' She got up to go to the kitchen and put the kettle on. '*It's a Wonderful Life* is on the telly in a minute. Shall we watch it together?'

'I watched telly before and it don't agree with me.'

'Does it make you grumbly? Like the car?'

'No. It hurts my eyes. But I'll have the cake and a Ribena, then I'll be off.'

Helen dished them both up a generous slice of cake and they sat in companionable silence admiring the tree as it twinkled attractively in the approaching dusk.

*

A couple of days later and Helen was sitting on the floor in front of the fire, writing her Christmas cards. There were many old London friends who had bothered to send her a card, and as many again who hadn't. She crossed them off her list. It was a good feeling to cut the dead wood from her life.

Once the cards had been done, she turned to wrapping up the presents she'd bought that day in Trevay. She hadn't gone mad but had tried to choose thoughtfully for her new Cornish friends.

Simon was easy. Tony had been as good as his word and had made a stunning cross out of mussel and limpet shells. It was about twelve inches high and made to stand on a shelf or desk. She wrapped it in tissue paper and lay it in a box covered in glitter, tying it with red ribbon.

Tony was easier. She got him a pair of new secateurs, a spade and a fork. She had them engraved TO MR B. WITH LOVE MRS M.

For Terri, Sean and Chloe, she had bought a selection of typically Cornish bits and pieces for their stockings. Pots of Cornish salt, slate coasters, shell wind chimes and thickly warm hoodies individually printed with their names on the back and the legend TREVAY LIFEGUARD.

She'd picked up some little gifts for her other new friends too, Dorrie and Don, Polly and Pete. But she had something special in mind for Queenie, and couldn't wait to surprise her. They'd all done so much to help her settle into Pendruggan and Helen wanted to show them her gratitude.

*

Cards posted, presents wrapped, all she had to do was get the last-minute food shop done and she was ready.

The phone rang. 'Hello, sexy, thought you might like my contact details in Verbier. I'm off tomorrow lunchtime.

Can't wait. All those fur rugs and log fires. I'll be thinking of you all the time.'

'Hello, Gray. Presumably your mobile will work over there, so if the children wish to ring you, they can. I don't need the details, thank you. You just enjoy yourself with the luscious Selina.'

'Oh, darling, don't be jealous. Anyway, Chloe tells me you have at least two suitors drooling over you.'

'Do I?'

'The limp vicar and a rude pirate, apparently.'

'It's none of your business, but Simon is not limp, he's a good man who happens to be coming to share Christmas lunch with us. And Piran is nothing at all.'

'You're making me jealous now. If a woman says a man is nothing, it means he's definitely something.'

Helen sighed. 'Oh, do shut up.'

'But haven't I spoiled you for any other man?'

'Happy Christmas, bon voyage and goodbye.' She put the phone down.

21

During the three days running up to Christmas Eve, Helen braved the battle of the fruit-and-veg aisle at the supermarket, filled her car with petrol, reorganised the fridge, changed her sheets and towels and double-checked the Dolphin room bookings for Sean and Terri. Don and Dorrie had decorated the pub with fresh holly and mistletoe and three beautifully dressed trees. The fire was never allowed to die and the big copper punchbowl was filled with scarlet cyclamen.

It was all arranged that Helen, Sean, Chloe, Terri and Penny would have Christmas Eve supper in the pub and then go down to midnight mass. On Christmas Day, Simon would join them all for lunch at Gull's Cry.

Helen hadn't felt so excited about Christmas for years. She hadn't seen too much of Penny, who was using her room at the Starfish as an office to finalise casting, shooting schedules and budget calculations, but they usually managed a catch-up for elevenses or afternoon tea.

*

Christmas Eve dawned with the promise of snow showers on the local weather report.

Helen immediately rang Sean, who told her, 'We're

leaving at about midday, picking Chloe up on the way and we should be with you by early evening.'

'There may be some snow coming in down here, so do drive carefully and don't take any risks.'

'Ma, I'm a big boy now. See you later.'

Later that morning, a satellite TV van pulled up and Helen raced outside to join the engineer, a capable chap called Jim. Helen had racked her brains to think of the perfect present for Queenie, then it had hit her. It was rather extravagant, but satellite TV would be ideal for the celeb-hungry pensioner. No longer would she miss seeing the Oscars live; she could sit up all night and watch them as they were actually happening.

Helen and Jim went in together to surprise Queenie with her Christmas present.

'Oh my good gawd! What you gone and done that for!' Queenie wiped her eyes free of her tears. 'It's wonderful, that's what it is, and no mistake! Wait till I tell my Sandra!'

Jim did his job skilfully and, when he'd finished, Helen manned the shop while he showed Queenie how to use the remote. She got the hang of it pretty quickly. Before departing, he left his phone number with her in case of problems.

'Helen,' she shouted from the top of the stairs, 'pretend to call me down.'

'OK . . . Queenie, could you come down a minute, please?'

'Yes, I'll just pause me *Celebrity Cash in the Attic* first.' Helen could hear her to talking herself: ''old on. Right. I press this one 'ere and Gloria Hunniford can wait a bit.' Footsteps. 'Yes, Helen, how can I help you?' And then one of Queenie's special crackly laughs. 'This will keep me busy all Christmas. Marvellous what they can do nowadays innit.' She sat on her stool behind the counter and rolled one of her skinny cigarettes. 'Thank you, 'elen. You 'ave made my day.'

'It's my pleasure. You deserve it.'

As Helen left the shop and walked back to Gull's Cry, she felt the cold brush of the first snowflakes falling on her face. Turning, she looked at the Christmas tree on the village green. The snow had started to fall in a little flurry and the handsome green branches were catching the flakes.

Helen thought of Sean, Terri and Chloe battling up the motorway. 'Please hurry up and get here, kids, before the weather does,' she whispered, 'then Christmas can really start.'

*

The traffic had been holiday heavy and as the temperature dropped, the snow started again, but Sean and the girls arrived safely around 6 p.m.

Sean and Terri dropped Chloe off and then set out for the Dolphin. There was just time for everyone to unpack and get settled before supper at the pub.

By the time Helen drove out of Pendruggan, the lane had a good covering of snow and the Mini's wheels were struggling for grip, but the sky was crystal clear with a canopy of stars twinkling in the heavens.

The pub was busy and Don was working hard behind the bar while Dorrie was edging through the tables to take orders while delivering steaming plates of delicious grub to the diners. Sean and Terri hadn't come down from their room yet, so Helen and Chloe got settled at their favourite table, the one in the snug with a view over the fields and the lights of Trevay.

'Cheers, my darling,' said Helen, raising her gin and tonic to Chloe. 'A bit different to last year's Christmas, isn't it?'

The two women looked at each other, remembering. It was on Boxing Day last year that Helen had told Gray she wanted a divorce. She had meant to wait until the new year, so as not to spoil the holiday for any of them, but trying to keep her unhappiness from bubbling to the surface was like battling to keep a lilo underwater. A couple of weeks before, she had found a Tiffany box on Gray's desk in the study. She hated herself for looking, but she couldn't help herself: it was a beautiful single diamond set on a platinum chain. She'd never been an acquisitive sort of person, but it was a wonderful gift and she was looking forward to being surprised by it on Christmas morning. Instead, she received a pair of lacy knickers and a sewing machine. The sewing machine was just what she wanted; she had ordered it herself online and had it delivered for Gray to wrap and put away. But where was the beautiful necklace? Not under the tree, or in her table cracker, and not under her pillow that night.

A grit-sized piece of ice formed in her gut. And it was growing.

Boxing Day morning was spent having a lie-in and then a lazy breakfast. When the phone rang, Gray leapt up from the table and dashed into the study to answer it.

Feeling paranoid, her pulse rushing in her ears, Helen lifted the extension in the kitchen, and listened.

*

'God you are such a cliché!' Helen spun round as Gray came and nuzzled her neck ten minutes later when she was at the sink.

'I can't help but fancy my sexy wife.' He gave her one of his seductive smiles.

'I'll tell you what you can't help. You can't help getting a hard-on talking to your latest shag on the phone. Well, if you think I'm going to relieve your frustrations in her absence, you can think again.'

'Darling, what are you talking about?'

'I heard her voice on the phone.'

'Who? Sally? She's a client. Thanking me for getting the car she'd bought her husband for Christmas. I had to pull out all the stops to get it delivered on Christmas Eve. Still, the customer comes first, eh?'

'Nice try. Are you in the habit of throwing in Tiffany necklaces as well?'

Gray let go of her waist and stepped back, deciding which tactic to employ. He chose to attack.

'You're mad! What are you talking about?'

She gave him a look of heartbroken defeat, collected her coat and went for a long walk.

That night she asked for a divorce.

*

Chloe broke the silence. 'Are you happy, Mum? No regrets?'

'No regrets, darling.'

'Hi, Ma, budge up a bit.' Sean and Terri had come down at last.

The atmosphere grew warm again and the jolly mood of the pub soaked into their little group as they raised a toast to each other.

Later they drove back down to Pendruggan, Terri's four-wheel-drive jeep leading the way in the crunchy snow. They convened at Gull's Cry for hot chocolate and a sprawl in front of the television before gathering themselves up for midnight mass.

The church was lit entirely by candles and the central heating was on full blast. Helen's gang found Queenie, Polly, Pete and Tony, and sat in the pew behind them. Queenie regaled them all with how many channels she had on her new telly and how handsome Huw Edwards looked in HD. The happy group engaged in cheerful chatter until the organ struck up 'O Little Town of Bethlehem', and the congregation rose to their feet.

The Merrifield clan gave gusto to the hymn while Queenie joined in with a surprisingly low, Lee Marvin rumble.

During the reading about Mary's pondering on her fate, Helen heard the latch on the back door open. Several heads turned, smiled at the newcomer and then resumed listening. Helen didn't look round but heard the footsteps coming towards her. It was clear that, whoever it was, was looking for a seat. She shifted up a bit, leaving the end of her pew empty. She was taken aback when it was Piran that sat down next to her. He glanced in her direction, gave a tight smile and bent his head in prayer.

At the sharing of the peace, Piran shook the many hands offered his way. Helen had been ostentatiously avoiding it by shaking any and everybody else's, including Simon, who had held her hand with tenderness and given her a warm embrace.

When Helen and Piran finally got to each other, he took her hand, kissed her cheek and whispered in her ear, 'Peace be with you.' She looked up at him and their eyes met for a moment, then they both smiled.

With a quiet laugh, Helen replied, 'Thank you. And peace be with you too.'

After that, the warmth of his thigh and shoulder so close to her own was palpable – and it flowed through her in an exquisitely, deliciously disturbing way.

As the last organ chords of 'Hark! The Herald Angels Sing' echoed round the vaulted ceiling, Helen was one of the last to leave her pew, thinking of Piran's unspoken olive branch. Should she ask him back to Gull's Cry for a festive glass of something? Distracted by a hug from Tony and then another from Queenie, Helen realised with chagrin that Piran had already left his seat. She looked around and could just see him at the door talking to Simon, then he walked off and out into the night. She hurried over, but when she got to Simon, there was no sign of Piran outside. Helen momentarily felt something akin to disappointment, but was then annoyed with herself for her foolishness. *Stop behaving like a schoolgirl. Piran is NOT for you!* Taking hold of Simon's shoulders, she gave him a big hug and invited him over for a drink.

'I'd love to, Helen, but forgive me, I can't. I have to be up early.'

Secretly relieved, she said, 'No problem. Lunch is at one, so see you at about twelve-thirty for an aperitif?'

'Perfect. And, Helen, Happy Christmas. God bless you.'

22

On Christmas morning Helen awoke to the sound, drifting up the stairs, of someone making a pot of tea. A few minutes later, Chloe came quietly up into the bedroom and put the tray on the blanket box at the end of the bed. She moved towards the window and opened the curtains.

'Happy Christmas, Mummy!'

Helen opened her eyes. 'Happy Christmas to you, Chloe darling. Is that tea I spy?'

'Yep. And that's not the only surprise. It snowed during the night and we have a winter wonderland outside.'

They drank their tea, Chloe opened her stocking, with much oohing and aahing, and they slowly got themselves and the house ready for lunch.

Sean and Terri rang to wish them Happy Christmas, as did Simon, who was very gracious about them not coming to church that morning.

For the next couple of hours, mother and daughter boogied round the house to songs on the radio and Helen drank a little too much brandy and lovage, a Cornish drink which Don had introduced her to; excellent for tummy upsets or sea sickness, but very alcoholic. Teetotal Chloe sensibly drank fruit juice. By midday, Helen was quite merry. Polly and Pete popped by and they exchanged presents with Helen: sloe gin from them and a thermos flask each from her, perfect for warm soup when they were out in their ambulance on cold nights. They couldn't stop as they were on call, but shortly after, Queenie and Tony knocked at the door to wish them Happy Christmas before walking up to Pendruggan Farm where Sylvia the farmer's wife always gave them lunch. After letting them in, Helen's unsteady legs carried her to her rocking chair.

'Happy Christmas!' Not wanting to risk getting out of the rocking chair, Helen gestured to Chloe. 'Darling, can you get Mr B.'s present by the fireplace?'

Chloe passed the wrapped garden tools to Tony. When he opened them he was lost for words. He could only manage to nod in gratitude, but his face beamed with such pleasure, it touched Helen's heart.

'I've just got the kettle on for coffee, Mum could do with one. Would you two like a cup as well?'

'No, we'd better be off,' said Queenie. ''appy Christmas! Careful in this snow. Bye.'

As Chloe closed the door behind them, she laughed affectionately at her mum, who was still in the rocking chair and really was quite tiddly now. 'Here, Mum, best get this coffee down you or you'll never get through the day.'

*

Simon arrived promptly at 12.30 p.m. and walked into the kitchen, having carefully knocked the snow off his boots by the door. He had a small plastic carrier bag in one hand and his gloves in the other. 'Afternoon, all. I hope I'm not too early.' He looked around. 'Oh dear, am I the first? I thought I might have kept you waiting.'

This was a lie. As soon as his service was over, he had dashed back home to change, unable to wait a second longer to see Helen. He had even tried to kill a bit of time by walking the long way round the village green.

Chloe took his coat and gloves and they wished each other Merry Christmas. He walked over to a rosy-looking Helen, ensconced in her rocking chair by the Aga and bent down to give her a kiss. She smelled of brandy.

'Hello, Simon. Would you like to put your gifts under the tree while I finish my coffee?'

'Happy Christmas, Helen. Don't get up.' He crossed to the door leading to the living room. 'They're only tokens, you know, but heartfelt nonetheless. It looks lovely in here, Helen. Really lovely.'

They heard the sound of a sports car pulling up outside. Two minutes later, Penny barged in carrying three large bags of extravagantly wrapped gifts, a magnum of Krug and small drifts of snow on her shoes.

'The road from Trevay to here is treacherous! Good old Jeremy the Jaguar managed it, but once or twice it got quite hairy.'

'Let me help you with those, Auntie Pen,' offered Chloe. 'I'll put them under the tree, if you like?'

'Yes please, gorgeous girl. Merry Christmas!' Penny let the bags, champagne and her coat fall into Chloe's care.

'And Simon! Happy Christmas on the busiest day of the Christian year! Packed 'em in this morning, I bet!' She swaddled Simon in a Thierry Mugler-perfumed bear-hug.

'And Happy Christmas to you too, Penny. Thank you, we've had a marvellous turn out for the services.' Simon wriggled out of her grasp and pushed his glasses back up his nose. 'Can I get you a drink? Helen?'

'I think I may be all right for a moment,' replied Helen carefully.

Chloe came back in. 'For the moment? I think you'll be all right until Easter! Mum hit the bottle a bit early and I am trying to sober her up.'

'Poo to that!' said Penny. 'Simon – open that champagne!'

Simon had never been taught how to open a bottle of champagne, so Penny gave him a quick lesson: 'Twist the bottle NOT the cork, but hold both firmly and the cork will gently pop into your palm.'

Simon did as he was told and was rather pleased with himself as the bottle opened in a pleasingly James Bond sort of way.

Chloe had the glasses ready but, spotting Sean and Terri walking up the path, she produced only four champagne flutes, deciding that her mother had imbibed quite enough Christmas spirit already.

Sean and Terri, entering laden down with gifts, were greeted with more hugs and kisses. There was now quite a crowd in the snug little kitchen.

Terri helped Chloe take the coats upstairs, leaving Penny to carry the drinks tray into the living room where the fire glowed and crackled invitingly.

Once Chloe and Terri had rejoined them, there was a lot of toasting each other. Having decided she had better relieve her mother of the hostess duties, Chloe declared that lunch was postponed till 2 p.m. so that they could all open their presents and relax.

'I'll play Father Christmas,' volunteered Sean, who was nearest the tree.

Helen received a vintage, turquoise Hermès scarf from Chloe's charity shop, a couple of novels she'd been wanting from Sean, and a special-edition DVD of *Little Women* from Terri. Penny gave her an enormous jar of Crème de la Mer moisturiser and a Donna Karan cashmere dressing gown. Simon's gift was last and in a small envelope.

'What's this?' Helen peered into his smiling brown eyes. She opened it and read, *Dear Helen, You are hereby entitled to make your choice of a full surfing outfit including accessories. Happy Christmas from The Trevay Surf Shack and Simon x x x*' She looked up at him with undisguised pleasure. 'Thank you, Simon. What a wonderful gift! Thank you all – I am so spoilt, I think I might cry.' And she promptly burst into tears.

'More champagne!' ordered Penny, who was lolling on the rug by the fire, wearing the necklace and earrings Helen had given her.

Chloe and Terri were thrilled with their presents, and Sean couldn't wait to try his new fishing rod. He had always been keen on fishing and on his last visit, Don had promised to take him out on his boat.

'Thanks, Ma.' And he got up and kissed her. 'You're the best. Oh no, don't cry again!' he fretted, as Helen's lips started to quiver once more. 'Tissues, someone, quick.'

Finally, Helen gave Simon his hand-made cross of mussels and driftwood. This time it was Simon who was blinking back the tears.

'Oh for God's sake! What's wrong with you all!' Penny was up on her feet, sharing the dregs of the bottle while everyone laughed.

'Right. I'd better check the spuds and get the veg on.'

Chloe stood up. 'Oh, Mum, there's one more thing – from Dad. Here.'

Helen opened it with dread. A square box about twelve inches tall. She undid only the top end and read the words on the packaging. Standing up, she walked to the kitchen, where she threw it in the bin.

23

Lunch was excellent. Nobody mentioned Gray's present in the bin. Instead, they concentrated on praising Chloe's cooking. Helen poured the red wine that had been warming by the Aga and took a large slug as she toasted Chloe.

'Here's to us and those who love us and bugger the rest who don't. Cheers.'

There was much chinking of glasses, and concerned looks passed over Helen's head by Chloe, Sean and Penny. Then the table relaxed into the passing of dishes and gravy and the satisfying murmur of people enjoying good food and togetherness.

Later, when Sean and Terri insisted on doing the washing up and Simon had left, clutching his cross, to prepare for evensong, Penny sent Helen to bed to have a forty-five minute snooze before going over to the church. 'Up the wooden hill to Bedfordshire for you, my girl. Chop chop.'

'You will wake me, won't you? I like to sing carols.'

'Yes, yes, just have a lie down first.'

As soon as Helen had gone upstairs and the others were all ensconced round the telly, Penny nipped into the kitchen and opened the bin. Empty.

'Looking for something?'

Sean was in the doorway.

'No, no, I was just erm . . .'

'Looking for Ma's mystery present? I took the rubbish out so that none of us would find out what it was.'

'Good idea. Yes. Good idea. I just wondered . . . if there was anything I could . . .'

'No, there isn't. Forget it. Ma obviously has.'

'OK.' Penny attempted to look unconcerned. 'I'll put the kettle on then, shall I?'

'Yes please.'

*

Helen felt worse when she got up. She hadn't been able to sleep. Her mind was churning over Gray and his bloody stupid gift. She ran through all the rude names that she could think of to describe him, then got up, cleaned her teeth and went downstairs.

Dusk was falling and they walked over to the church under a yellowing sky. As they got to the churchyard, big, fat snowflakes started to fall faster and faster. They walked into the welcoming warmth of the candlelit church and found their usual pew, just in time, as Simon was already standing in the chancel.

'Good evening, everybody. I hope you have had a wonderful Christmas Day, and I think we can all thank God for his many blessings. I'd also like to thank Helen and her family, who shared their Christmas lunch with me.' He smiled over at Helen and once again a frisson at the possibility of a blossoming romance fizzled through the congregation. Helen shook her head, smiling. Simon continued, 'Walking from the vicarage just a few minutes ago, I was struck by the beauty of our village

Christmas tree on the green, and I wondered if you'd all like to go outside so we can sing our carols around the tree, all the better for God to hear. Who would like that?'

'All of us!' said Tony, immediately standing up.

And amid the swell of laughter, the congregation got to their feet and walked out into the snowy darkness, clutching their orders of service, and the candles that Simon was lighting and handing out at the door.

As Simon started the singing, curious villagers heard the activity and came to join them. The snow fell thickly, the candles guttered, but for the first time in many years Helen felt at peace. Loved even. By her family, her oldest friend, and her new friend, Simon.

She put her arm through Penny's and smiled at her. Penny gave her a squeeze of acknowledgement. Helen looked over at Simon and caught his eye. He beamed at her and she gave him a wink. What a difference a year makes.

*

'I'm starving,' said Terri as they all returned to Gull's Cry, stamping their cold feet on the kitchen flagstones.

'Me too,' said Penny, rubbing life back into her toes while warming them by the Aga. 'Shall I rummage in the fridge?'

While the other women got busy assembling a feast of pork pie, cold ham, cold roast potatoes, salad, bread and cheese on the kitchen table, Sean and Helen sat talking quietly by the fire in the other room.

'What did Dad buy you, Ma?'

'I can't remember.'

There was a silence. Then, 'Yes, you can.'

'Yes, I can. Let's just say it was one of your father's inappropriate jokes. OK?'

'Supper's ready, you two,' Terri called from the kitchen.

'Coming.' Sean leant over and kissed Helen on the head. 'Love you, Ma.'

'Love you more.'

'Not possible.' They smiled as they remembered the old childhood game of words they used to play.

'Sean?'

'Yes, Mum?'

'Do you love Terri? Properly, I mean?'

'I think I do. Yes.'

'Good. Then look after her, won't you.' She hugged him. 'Come on, I'm starving.'

*

'Simon's a really decent man, isn't he?' said Penny, munching through a piece of pork pie and piccalilli.

'Yes, he's sweet,' agreed Terri. 'He certainly has a soft spot for you, Helen.'

'We're just friends, good friends. That's all. What he needs is a nice young maiden who will adore him and give him the family he craves.'

'Or an older woman who can show him the ropes!' sniggered Sean.

Helen threw a spring onion at him.

'Oh, do grow up,' Chloe said crossly, scraping her chair back to get some fruit juice from the fridge.

'It's all right, darling. Sean's teasing me. You are not about to get a stepfather of ANY kind. Let alone the vicar kind.'

'It's not that, I just think you should all stop being judgemental about Simon. He's a human being, after all.'

'Ooooo!' sang Penny. 'I think you lurve him, you want to maaarry him!'

This time it was Penny who got the spring onion in the face.

*

Later, when the dishwasher was whirring and they were all sprawled around the living room lit by fairy lights and firelight, Helen finished off another bottle of wine. Her head was gently foggy and her body felt light and relaxed. She was just starting to doze off when, to her delight, Penny, Sean and Terri started to make moves to go.

The snow was a good six or seven inches deep now and Penny was cadging a lift in the Jeep with Sean and Terri, rather than attempt the drive in her Jag.

They were all trooping out of the door, ready to brave the night when the phone rang.

Helen answered, 'Hello?' There was a pause, and the others listened, wondering who it could be at this time of night.

'No, you cannot come down here, Gray. I don't care if you are on your own.' Another pause. 'How dare you try to dump your emotional guilt on me!' Helen was starting to shout. 'Just piss off, Gray! Do not even ATTEMPT to come down here, because if you do, I'll stuff your bloody Christmas present up your flabby arse! Happy Christmas.' And she slammed the phone down. Four pairs of eyes looked at her expectantly.

'Do you know what that pig gave me for Christmas? Shall I tell you? A vibrator!'

For the final time that day, Helen burst into tears. And after her friends had given her hugs, words of comfort and then quietly crept away, Chloe gently escorted her mother up the stairs to bed.

24

B oxing Day dawned. Chloe tiptoed into the bedroom with a tea tray, Marmite on toast and paracetamol. She opened the curtains and the flood of white light from the snow and frost outside burned into Helen's sealed eyelids like an oxy-acetylene torch.

'I am never going to drink again,' Helen groaned.

'Come on, Mum, I'll help you sit up.' Chloe plumped up Helen's pillows, crossed the room to close the curtains halfway and then proffered Helen the contents of the tray. 'I remember how you used to look after me when I was little. How quickly the roles reverse.'

'Did I behave very badly?'

'Not too badly . . . not as badly as Daddy.'

'Did I badmouth him? I'm sorry, darling.'

'I'm not a little girl any more, Mum. I realise my parents are fallible human beings.'

'Selina has dumped him. How dare he assume he'd be welcome here! Stupid man.'

'I think he's too afraid to come now . . . knowing what you'll do to him.'

Chloe got into bed next to her mum and held her hand.

'Mum, I know he has behaved appallingly, but do you think you might ever forgive him?'

'Forgive, maybe. Forget, never.'

'You're not properly divorced yet, are you?'

'No. But I should get that finalised once and for all and apply for the decree absolute. I'll do it in the new year.'

'Do you have to?'

'Yes, of course. Why?'

Chloe lay looking at her feet moving under the duvet. 'Do you hope that Daddy and I will get back together?'

'Yes, I suppose so.'

'It ain't going to happen, Chloe.' She saw the tears in her daughter's eyes and felt her own eyes begin to swim too. 'It just ain't going to happen.'

*

Penny was treating them all to Boxing Day lunch at the Starfish. Terri's Jeep was once again the only vehicle that would navigate the lanes safely, so Sean collected his mum and sister at midday.

As they walked into the reception hall of the hotel, Terri's appreciative eyes took it all in. 'Wow! What a place – and what a view!' She walked over to the huge picture window overlooking the harbour and the open sea beyond.

Helen asked the receptionist to call Penny's room and let her know they'd arrived. While they waited, they settled into the large squashy sofas grouped by the huge open fireplace.

An attractive, slender woman in her mid-sixties came towards them. 'Hello, are you Miss Leighton's party?' They nodded in assent. 'Welcome. Lovely to have you all at the Starfish. I am the owner, Louise Lonsdale.' They all introduced themselves and found glasses of Buck's Fizz materialising at Louise's insistence.

'Penny – Miss Leighton – has told me so much about you all and the television crew that she is bringing down from London. It sounds so exciting! And very good for the Starfish, too, so your lunch today is on the house. You may have seen our chef, Orlando Tavy, on *Top of the Chops*? An execrable television cookery show from which I rescued him, but it made his name, though he is far too talented for that rubbish. He's doing a special tasting menu today and I'm sure you'll like it. Ah, Penny, there you are. I was just getting to know your friends.'

Penny was sweeping down the stairs in long black boots and black lurex hot-pants, with swathes of cream chiffon around her top half. 'Sorry I'm late. I've been on the phone to Dahlia Dahling's agent. It's not quite in the bag, but I think we may have just cast her as Mr Tibbs' secretary sidekick. Very exciting! Keep your fingers crossed that we pull it off. Louise, darling, will you join us for lunch?'

'Too busy, sadly. But go and enjoy! My treat.' The two women air-kissed graciously and Louise hurried over to greet more newcomers.

'She's starstruck but bloody good at her job,' Penny whispered to Helen. 'By the way, how's your head?'

'Better after paracetamol and Buck's Fizz,' Helen replied.

'That's my girl.' Penny turned to the wider group. 'Come on, everybody, let's eat!'

Orlando Tavy's taster menu ran to eight courses of minute but delicious dishes. Mostly local seafood cooked simply, and well worth the Michelin star he was hoping to get in the new year guide.

After a pudding of the lightest spotted dick with home-churned ice cream, the chef appeared in the dining room to glad-hand the guests. Helen watched him move round the room. He looked tired. His face was pasty and his skin had a slight sheen of sweat, which he mopped with the tea towel thrown over his shoulder. However, none of that could detract from his angelic blue eyes and the smattering of freckles across his perfect nose. He had a mop of blond curly hair kept off his face with a tortoiseshell hairband, and strong hands with well-shaped, spotlessly clean nails. Penny couldn't take her eyes off him.

'Isn't he gorgeous.' She leaned towards Helen conspiratorially.

'Does he like the older woman?' Helen judged him to be in his late thirties.

'I hope so.'

Orlando approached their table and gave a charming bow to Penny, who practically licked her lips with desire.

'Miss Leighton, we missed you for lunch yesterday, but how was it for you today?'

'Delicious, thank you. May I introduce you to my best friend and her family.'

There followed a lot of handshakes and words of appreciation before Orlando turned to Penny and murmured something that no one else could hear. Penny blushed slightly and smiled into his eyes. 'Is that so? Maybe we should discuss that further another time.' He kissed her hand and moved off to another table.

'Tell me what he said immediately,' Helen demanded in Penny's ear.

'He said, "If madam would like a little extra on the side, she only has to call for room service."'

'He didn't!'

'He did.'

'And would you?'

But before Penny could answer, Helen heard Chloe saying, 'Daddy! What are you doing here?'

25

'Hello, everyone.' Gray stood across the table from Helen. The shock must have been clear on her face, because he quickly said, 'Helen, forgive me for turning up when I know you asked me not to, but I really need to be with my family right now.'

He looked so lost and crushed that she couldn't trust herself to speak, not knowing whether tears or vitriol were more likely to pour forth. Chloe salvaged the situation.

'Daddy, I'll get another chair. You're too late for lunch, but let me get you a drink.'

He turned to her and cupped her face in his hands. 'My darling daughter. What would I do without you? A large Scotch would be very reviving.'

As Chloe went in search of a chair, Gray threw himself into her empty seat. He put his elbows on the table and sank his head into his hands. He sighed deeply, then ran his fingers through his long, thick hair.

'You look terrible,' said Penny.

'Cheers, Pen. You look gorgeous too,' he answered.

Helen, who was scrutinising him closely for signs of play-acting, asked, 'What's happened?'

'Sadly, Selina is a young woman who can't shake off Mummy and Daddy's apron strings, so she dumped me.'

'You mean, once her parents found out she was sleeping

with one of their own generation, they vetoed her plans for Christmas in Verbier.'

'Elegantly put, Helen darling. Yes. I am humiliated and feel like an old fool.'

'Which you are.' Penny smiled without irony.

'Thank you again, Pen darling.' He reached into his pocket and produced a handkerchief with which he wiped his eyes, and loudly blew his nose.

A waiter arrived with the extra chair. 'Where do you want to sit, Daddy?' asked Chloe. He looked across to Helen, 'Next to Mummy, darling.'

Everyone, except Helen, shuffled their chairs to make space. When he was settled next to her, he took her hand and kissed it. 'Sorry you didn't like my present. It was a silly joke. I'll make it up to you, I promise. Happy Christmas.'

*

Helen couldn't recall much of that afternoon. She seemed to be floating outside herself. Watching herself making conversation and smiling, noticing how happy Chloe and Sean seemed to be, seeing both their parents apparently comfortable in each other's company.

Penny, reading her thoughts, decided that alcohol was the best way to get Helen through the afternoon.

Helen gratefully accepted a large brandy and stopped counting after the third. She was surprised when she found herself, along with everybody else, back at Gull's Cry. Not long after that, Sean, Terri and Chloe set off for the Dolphin, saying they'd had enough of oldies, and Penny must have collected her car and gone back to the Starfish. Helen remembered going upstairs to the loo and thinking that she might have a little snooze. She washed her hands and teeth and went into her bedroom. The curtains were closed and in the gloom she could see that the bed was a mess. How did that happen? She thought she and Chloe had made it that morning, but she stepped out of her dress and pulled off her tights, hopping slightly to keep her balance. Then she slipped off her bra and pants.

'How I've missed those stretch marks.'

Helen leapt with fright and saw the bedclothes moving. Now she could see an apparently naked Gray lying on her pillows, pulling back the covers for her to join him.

'Come on, darling. No funny business. I just think two old mates need a hug. What do you say?'

Helen wondered what the correct response should be, but her brandy-addled brain couldn't be bothered to find one. She got into bed and felt Gray's arms around her. She turned into his body and let her fingers touch the hair on his chest. She couldn't resist burying her nose in it and breathing in the deeply familiar smell.

'Have you missed me as much as I miss you?' he asked.

She didn't bother speaking and within moments couldn't have anyway because he was kissing her gently. Helen surrendered to his caresses; they both knew the moves so well, and soon he was making love to her in the old way.

Later on, as Helen slept, Gray heard the key in the front door. The tread on the stairs was light, and when Chloe quietly opened the bedroom door and breathed, 'Mum? I'm home. How did it go with Dad?' he answered for her: 'Very well, thank you, darling. Mummy's just having a little sleep.'

Chloe withdrew from the bedroom, and couldn't resist a little smile as she retreated back down the stairs.

*

For the second time in as many days, Helen woke with the king daddy of all hangovers. She turned over slowly, wondering if Gray was still next to her. He was.

'Hello, sexy.' He stroked the dip between her hip and breast. 'I'm glad you're awake. I have to head back into town this afternoon and I'd hate to leave before you woke up.'

'What?' She struggled to sit up on her elbows.

'Yes, I have to have drinks and supper with some mates. All very dull, but you know what it's like.'

She stared at him, feeling a fool.

'You're going?'

'Yes, darling.'

'And what was last night about?' A horrible sensation was filling her ribcage and boiling into her brain.

'We've still got the old magic, haven't we? And you've lost weight. It suits you.' He wriggled up the bed towards her and attempted to kiss her neck. She pushed him away.

'What did last night mean to you?'

'It meant,' he started nibbling again, 'that we can be the most civilised divorced couple I know.'

Helen leapt out of bed as fast as her nausea would let her. 'Get out, you bastard! What a bloody idiot I am, and what a bloody shit you are.' She threw his clothes, folded so carefully on her small dressing-table chair, at him. 'Put those on and piss off.'

Then she ran to her bathroom and slammed the door.

She looked at herself in the mirror over the sink. Her hair was a mess, there were dark circles under her eyes and her mouth tasted sour and dry.

'You stupid cow,' she said to her reflection. 'You let him in again, and he almost got you. But not before discarding you like last night's dirty dishcloth. You are a disgrace to womanhood.'

She remained there, sitting on the side of the bath until after a little while there was a gentle knock at the door. 'Piss off back to some other poor cow, you arsehole, but leave me alone.'

'Mum?' It was Chloe. 'Are you OK? Dad seemed a bit upset when he left. I was sleeping on the sofa and saw him go.'

'*Dad* seemed a bit upset?' Helen wrenched the door open and pushed past Chloe.

'He doesn't know the *meaning* of the word.' Helen could hear the shrillness in her voice. 'I have to go out to clear my head.'

She went into her bedroom and began pulling on tracksuit bottoms, T-shirt and a warm hoodie. 'Don't follow me, Chloe. I just need some space. See you later.'

And with that she ran downstairs and disappeared out of the front door.

*

Shellsand Bay was deserted apart from a couple of families with dogs and children enjoying the winter sunshine. But by the time she got to the water's edge they were leaving. The beach was her own. Helen took a great lungful of air and tipped her face up to the sun. The gentle waves were lapping her wellingtons. Her brain hurt from alcohol, shame and the glare of the winter sun. A sudden surge of self-pity assaulted her and she was unable to stop herself breaking down into great gulping sobs with a river of tears flowing down her cheeks.

Her anguished crying was lost on the breeze with only

the gulls to hear. At length, the ragged noises ceased and her headache grew worse. She was suddenly exhausted and felt terribly cold and alone. Turning to walk back up the beach, she saw a little Jack Russell running towards her with its owner striding closely behind.

'Helen,' Piran called, 'are you all right?' He was close now. 'My God, you look terrible, woman. Here, put this on.' He took off his long padded jacket and tried to wrap it round her.

'Get off. I don't need your help. I don't need a man at all. You are all a bunch of shits. Laughing at me and taking me for a fool.'

'OK.' He took his coat back and put it on. 'If that's the way you feel.'

He took a step away from her, turned his back and began throwing a ball for Jack, who was enjoying the thrill of jumping up as high as he could to snatch the ball from the air.

'I don't know, Jack,' he said, bending down to ruffle Jack's ears as the little dog returned with the ball and dropped it at his feet. 'I'll never understand women, especially the ones who look as if they're upset and could do with a friendly ear, but then when you try to help they tell you to piss off.'

Helen rounded on him. 'I don't need you – why don't you just go back to being your usual unpleasant self, then we'd all know where we are,' she said angrily.

She then reached down for Jack's ball, which had rolled towards her, and threw it towards Piran's shoulder blades as hard as she could.

'Ow! And then, Jack, they throw balls at you, just to add insult to injury – or is it the other way round? Go fetch, boy.' He threw the ball again, then watched Jack retrieve the ball and return with it in his mouth, his whole body quivering with pleasure.

'Take my advice, boy. Never go to a woman's rescue. That Helen Merrifield, for instance. I found her knickers blowing all over the county, but did she thank me? No. Looked at me as though I was depraved. Me! Her knickers are too small for me anyway.'

'I've had enough of this!' Helen was just about to stomp off, more miserable than ever, when Piran turned quickly towards her, and caught her wrists in his strong hands, preventing her from escape. His sea-blue eyes ringed with long, dark lashes looked deep into her face. His dark curls rippled in the wind, exposing the small gold ring in his ear.

'What is your problem, Helen Merrifield?' he said quietly.

Helen lowered her eyes, brimming with tears, and remained silent. He let go of her, took his coat off again and wrapped it around her shoulders, then slowly and gently took her in his arms. Her tears flowed freely into the warmth of his thick jumper. After a few minutes, he led her to a rock and they sat down, his right arm holding her shoulder warmly.

'I'm a good listener.' He bent his head to look into her still downturned eyes. 'Here—' He dug in a pocket for a couple of crumpled tissues. 'I used them to clean my windscreen, but they're clean enough.'

She smiled and took them gratefully. Her eyes were sore, her head hurt and her pride was hanging out of her like guts out of roadkill. Taking a deep breath, she told him all about her failed marriage, her reasons for coming to Pendruggan, and then Gray's sudden arrival and his unexpected materialisation back in her bed.

'I've made such a mess,' Helen groaned. 'Drink played a part, or maybe it was having the children around again, but just for a moment it seemed like the easiest thing in the world to just slip back into our old ways.'

'And is that what you want, Helen?' Piran asked, studying her face keenly. 'To go back to the old life?'

For a moment their eyes locked, and Helen was acutely aware of the space between them, and how easy it would be close the divide and lean in towards him; to feel his lips against hers.

Piran broke the spell and turned his face out towards the sea.

She studied his strong profile, then answered, 'No, I love this new life. I'm going to make it work, but sometimes the past refuses to disappear.'

'Why did you put up with him for so long?'

Helen thought for a moment. 'Most of the time I was too exhausted by the situation to think clearly. It was easier to make others happy and forget my own unhappiness. And there were happy times, too. It wasn't all bad, you know.'

Piran sat, almost motionless, looking out at the horizon. Jack whined in boredom. Helen looked at her watch and realised they must have been talking for quite some time.

'Thank you for listening.' Without thinking, she put her hand on his leg and kissed his cheek.

He threw a stone for Jack and when he turned back to her, he looked troubled.

'What is it?'

He seemed about to speak, but then shook his head. 'Another time, another place . . . maybe.'

'I'm a good listener too, if you ever need one.' He gave her a small smile, whistled for Jack and then stood up.

Helen followed suit. 'Here's your coat back. I'm much warmer now.'

'That's all right. I'll collect it the next time I'm passing.'

'I'd be very grateful if you didn't tell anyone the stuff I just told you.'

'I'm not a gossip, Helen. And you're not the first woman to do something stupid.'

She looked at him sharply. What did that mean?

'Do you think I'm stupid?'

'Yes.'

Helen glared at him.

'Don't go all sulky on me, woman. You asked my opinion and I gave it.'

She started off up the beach at a fast pace, her fury at him reignited.

'There you are, you see,' he called after her. 'Typical bloody woman, doesn't like hearing the truth.'

She carried on walking, not looking behind her until she got to the top of the path that led away from the beach. When she turned around, she saw Piran and Jack striding purposefully off in the distance, without a backward glance.

26

As Helen opened the front door of Gull's Cry, she saw the note in Chloe's handwriting on the table.

Dear Mum,
We are all worried about you. We waited as long as we could for you to come back, but we have to hit the road now to get back to town for work tomorrow. Love you so much, and don't worry about anything. I'll phone you when I get in.
Chloe (and Sean and Terri) xxx

She put the kettle on, swallowed a couple of painkillers and went to bed.

By the time Chloe rang that night, her headache was a lot better and she was sitting by a warm fire in her new dressing gown and old slippers reading one of the books Sean had given her.

'Hi, Mum. Thank you for a fabulous Christmas. Sean and Terri send their love and will ring you tomorrow. I put them off calling you tonight, thinking you may want a bit of peace. Are you OK?'

Helen sighed and ran her hand through her unwashed, salty hair. 'I feel much better. I am so sorry about this morning, darling. Everything just got on top of me and the hangover didn't help.'

'What happened between you and Daddy?'

Helen groaned but gave Chloe the briefest details.

'So, I'm confused, does this mean Daddy's trying to get back together?'

'Ha! If you're confused, imagine how I feel. I think he wants to have his cake and eat it, like he's always done, and I am not interested. I will always love a bit of Dad, but I am carving out my own life now.'

'Oh.' Chloe's voice was childlike in its disappointment. 'I understand. I just couldn't help hoping somehow.'

'It'll all be OK, darling. It's early days. We've had our turn!' Helen put a smile in her voice. 'I'm looking forward to seeing what direction your life's going to take!'

'Nobody's interested in me.'

'That's not true. You wouldn't know if anyone was interested in you because you aren't looking.'

'Really?'

'Really.'

They chatted a bit more, Chloe reassured that Helen sounded fine, and Helen full of love for her kind and gentle daughter. When they'd said goodbye, she settled back to her book but was soon interrupted by a knock on the door.

'Simon. Hello, come in. Forgive my dressing gown.'

'You look very fetching, Helen.'

'Would you like a drink? I'm on tea. My liver needs a break from alcohol.'

'Tea would be lovely, thank you.'

'Did you have a good Boxing Day yesterday?'

'Yes, super. The parish gatherings can get quite lively.' Helen tried to hide her sceptical look.

'We had a canasta tournament. Great fun and very competitive.' He took the mug Helen offered. 'Queenie was cheating outrageously, but no one challenged her. You must come to the next one.'

'Hmm.'

They sipped their tea as they moved to the warm fire. Helen sat down in the window seat, leaving Simon the big armchair.

'Talking of which,' he continued, 'you haven't forgotten the diocesan dinner, have you?'

'It's a week on Friday, isn't it?'

'Yes. If I pick you up at about five-thirty, that should get us there in time. A bit early, I know, but the bishop's wife likes to eat at seven.'

'Perfect. At least it means we'll be home early!'

As Helen showed Simon out, he said casually, 'By the way, a bit of joyous news: Piran and Dawn are engaged.'

Helen felt her world tip slightly.

'What?'

'Yes. It surprised me too. Isn't it marvellous! Bye.'

Helen shut the front door and opened a bottle of wine.

*

The days between Christmas and New Year passed uneventfully. Helen spoke on the phone to Penny a couple of times, but only briefly, as she was up to her neck in filming schedules, design meetings, costume fittings and final castings. When Helen asked her about Orlando the chef, Penny replied, 'Room service is to be recommended!'

Helen did not tell her about the Gray incident or Piran's news. It could all keep for another time.

Dorrie and Don wanted her to come up to the Dolphin for New Year's Eve, but she feigned a cold and was in bed early instead. She left her bedroom window open to hear the ship's horns hoot in the new year in Trevay. It was a tradition carried out in ports around the UK and she was delighted she was able to hear, at exactly midnight, the whistles and blasts carried on the breeze straight into her room.

She was glad the old year was over and wondered what the new one would bring.

27

Helen's kitchen table was covered with Penny's laptop, iPad, script, schedules, a cup of coffee and one of her two BlackBerry phones.

It had been this way for the three weeks since the new year began. The casting of *Mr Tibbs and the Hidden Treasure* was now finally agreed and contracts signed. Mr Tibbs, the star of the series, was to be played by David Cunningham, a well-respected British Hollywood star who, having reached his early forties, had found happiness with a make-up lady called Sonia. They had settled down, got married and had twins, breaking the hearts of many fans and previous leading ladies. His brand of old-school gentlemanly charm, intelligence and humour were perfect for the role. His attractive secretary sidekick, a slightly older woman called Nancy Trumpet, was to be played by veteran siren Dahlia Dahling.

The other BlackBerry was even now clamped to Penny's ear as she tipped boiling water into a coffee mug and mimed a pouring action at Helen and pointed to the fridge. Helen duly fetched the milk.

Mouthing 'Thanks', Penny continued with her phone call. 'John, darling, I promise I've booked Dahlia *the* best room in the Starfish . . . Yes, the kitchen know she's vegan . . . yes, the air conditioning has been off for the specified seventy-two hours . . .' She looked over at Helen and rolled her eyes. 'The room is very quiet, yes . . . I'm not sure we can do anything about the seagulls making noise too early . . . Yes, we are *so* looking forward to seeing her for the first read-through tomorrow . . . She is mine and Sven's dream Nancy Trumpet . . . Wonderful! See you then. Bye.'

Setting the phone down on the table, Penny sank into a chair and ran her fingers through her tangled blonde hair. 'My God, he's a good agent. Not only for getting Miss Dahling a whacking salary, but for dealing with the tricky cow in the first place.' She took a sip of the hot coffee. 'God save me from pain-in-the-arse actors.'

'You love it! You know you do.'

'Maybe. I like the initial idea and the end product. It's just the messy bit in the middle, dealing with spoilt actors and actually making the bloody thing that I hate.'

One of the BlackBerrys started ringing. Penny's tired mascara-smudged eyes looked into Helen's. 'Oh, make it STOP!' Then, in a flash, she manufactured a giant smile, picked up the phone and said, 'Hello, Sven . . . Yes, the witch queen is on her way . . . She'll be here by six . . . Yes, I told John, her agent, four o'clock because I know she's always late . . . Yes, it's a Bentley, not a Merc . . . Well, thank you, and you are the best director I have ever worked with . . . Yes, I do mean it . . . OK, drinks in the hotel at five-thirty before Medusa descends . . . Ha ha . . . love you, bye.'

Helen proffered a packet of chocolate fingers. Penny took two and stirred her coffee with one.

'Is there anything I can do to help you, Pen? When does your PA get here?'

'Charlie? She's on tonight's train,' Penny said through a mouthful of soggy biscuit. 'She only left on Friday afternoon for a couple of days skiing in Cor-so-posh or whatever it's called, but when she's not here, even for a couple of days, I realise how bloody good she is. By tomorrow morning, she'll be back in harness. Thank God.'

One of the BlackBerry's chirruped with an email, and Helen left Penny to it.

Upstairs, she opened her wardrobe door and pulled out a couple of outfits for the diocesan dinner. The first was a five-year-old draped jersey Armani trouser suit. The jacket was shaped like a tuxedo and the trousers slim over the hips with a liquid flow to the wide legs. Were trousers allowed at vicars' dos? The other choice was a gorgeous *Mad Men*-style fifties dress. She'd bought it for a wedding last spring. It was petal pink with three-quarter-length sleeves and, although demure at the front with a boat-shaped slash neck, it plunged at the back in a deep cowl. She took both outfits downstairs to show Penny.

Penny was still at the table with the empty coffee cup by her elbow, a glass of Scotch in her hand, her face white.

'Penny, what's happened?'

'What am I going to do?' Two large tears rolled out of her reddening eyes. 'It's Charlie – she's broken a leg and both wrists. Snowboarder ploughed into her. Not a fucking scratch on him. She can't come home till she's been operated on. She'll be out of action for weeks.' She slugged back the remains of the Scotch and started sobbing theatrically.

Smiling, Helen moved to her best friend and put her arm round her. 'Is that all? I thought someone had died, or Dahlia Dahling had pulled out, or you'd lost your Birkin bag . . . Or something really serious.'

'Ha bloody ha!' Penny spat, knocking Helen away. 'The whole production is in jeopardy and you stand there making jokes.' More sobs.

'I'm just saying that it's not the end of the world.'

'Not the end of the fucking world!' Penny looked coldly at Helen and then something seemed to switch inside her and she launched into a tirade:

'I'll tell you what's the end of the fucking world! This village and your life! Take a look at yourself. You haven't had a haircut in months. Your eyebrows are overgrown. You have a definite moustache and I'd be ashamed to be seen with you in London. In fact, I shall be ashamed to be seen with you when the cast and crew get here. I've been meaning to say this for some time. You are a mess. You haven't got off your fat backside since you married Gray. You've been very lucky. No money worries, wonderful parents who had the decency to drop off the perch without a fuss and leave you financially independent. OK, Gray was, and is, a shit. But look what you got in return. A comfortable home, a man to make love to, two gorgeous children . . . people to go on holiday with. And . . . I . . .' she began to break down in sobs 'I . . . have worked my heart out . . . and . . . have NOBODY. You even have Simon fucking Canter *and* Piran shitting Ambrose panting after you . . . And you say doing without my PA is nothing more serious than losing a Birkin BAG?'

Helen was expressionless watching her friend descend into this self-pitying morass. She had seen this hysteria and heard the cruelty many times before and always during a work crisis.

She took a deep breath and said in a calm voice, 'Penny, I didn't mean to upset you, but let's get this into perspective. There must be another PA in London some-where who could match Charlie. Maybe even better her.'

'NOBODY knows me the way Charlie does. I have spent five years honing her, moulding her, to my very own specifications! I haven't time to train up some gorm-less temp.' Penny stood up and started sifting the piles of papers into her briefcase.

In a quiet voice, Helen said, 'I know you. And I can type. Could I help a little?'

Penny snapped her laptop shut and sat down heavily. She wiped her black-streaked cheeks on one sleeve and her dripping nose on the other. After a long moment, studying the kitchen floor, she looked up at Helen and said,

'You'll have to have a lip wax first.'

28

The world of a film set is a magical universe, Helen thought as she stood staring out of her bedroom window, drinking her morning tea. It was only 7.30 a.m. but through the winter gloom she could just make out the goings on around the village green.

The council houses to her left had disappeared behind a massive timber wall on which the scenic artists had painted two beautiful thatched and terraced eighteenth-century cottages. Next door to them was painted Mr Tibbs' bank, the South-West Friendly, an imposing Edwardian red-brick building with a pillared entrance and curlicued window sills. Next to that were a couple of Victorian buildings: the post office and the village shop.

Helen watched Queenie as she collared a young male crew member carrying a walkie-talkie. Whatever she was saying to him, he clearly couldn't help her. Shaking his head in apology, he moved away, leaving Queenie to walk as quickly as her rolling gait would allow back to her shop. Apparently it was there her problem lay: two red double-decker buses had been parked right in front of her entrance. As Helen looked on, a breathless Queenie reached the buses and started gesticulating at the bus drivers. Though they were smiling and piling on the charm for her, it didn't look as if they were going to budge.

Smiling, Helen checked her reflection in her cheval mirror. She hoped she'd chosen the right image for her first real day on set. Her skinny black jeans, black suede trainers and black cashmere roll-neck jumper set her newly bobbed auburn hair off well. Her eyebrows had new definition and her top lip and chin were as smooth as the proverbial baby's bottom.

Penny had apologised for speaking the truth so cruelly and had treated Helen to a day at the Starfish spa to make it up to her.

Downstairs, she collected her all-weather anorak from the hook by the back door, a large cardboard box from the front door and went out into the biting late January air.

She didn't have far to go. Turning right out of her gate, she had only to walk the fifty paces to one of the two holiday cottages next door.

The front door was wide open to reveal the Mavis Crewe location production office. Booking the cottage had been one of the last things Charlie had managed to arrange before the disastrous events of the skiing weekend.

A couple of young men were huddled round the tea urn chatting and waiting for orders. Helen recognised the director, Sven, whom Penny had introduced to her the night she'd volunteered to fill in for Charlie. He was sitting in an armchair with his feet up on a low coffee table, stroking his wispy beard and listening intently to a young woman with Titian hair wound up on her head and secured with a bulldog clip. She was wearing baggy jeans with a walkie-talkie radio clipped on to the back pocket and her small feet were clad in green Doc Martens. The whole look was topped off with a short, navy quilted jacket. She had a clipboard and was going through the day's schedule.

'The art director, lighting director and DOP want to talk to you in five to set up exactly what you want for tomorrow's scenes.' The young woman's walkie-talkie crackled and a voice said, 'Jim to Gilly. Meet you and Sven in the dining bus in two minutes.' Gilly looked at Sven for confirmation. He nodded and pulled his lanky legs off the coffee table to stand up.

'Gilly to Jim. See you there. Travelling now.'

The pair of them strode past Helen, ignoring her nervous smile.

'Morning,' she addressed the two young men by the tea urn.

'Morning.'

'I'm Helen – Penny Leighton's PA. Well, the temporary one.'

'I'm Jako and this is Haz.' They all shook hands.

'I suppose you know all about this filming stuff, do you?'

'A bit.'

'Then I'm hoping you can tell me, because I'm a complete novice.'

In the course of ten minutes, the boys gave her a quick and dirty lesson on the essential things she needed to know. The pair of them were twins, freshly graduated from the National Film School, and this was their first major job. They were runners, sometimes known as gofers. Whatever was needed, they did it. The girl with the bulldog clip in her hair was Gilly, the first assistant director, or in film-set shorthand: First. It was her job to organise the schedules, the cast, the crew and anything else the director might want her to do. The DOP was the director of photography or cameraman. The double-decker buses blocking Queenie's shop were the dining rooms. The large white lorry was the catering truck and the mobile loos were the honey wagons.

'What you don't know, just blag. You'll be fine,' Haz said cheerfully as he and Jako left to find bacon butties.

*

Helen commandeered one of the three tables as her desk and sat down. There was a phone and little else. She had bought everything she could think of in Ryman's yesterday, and now she began to take it all out of her cardboard box. She was so absorbed in the pleasure of new stationery that she jumped when her mobile rang. It was Penny.

'Where are you?'

'In the holiday cottage. I'm setting up my desk.'

'Good. Stay there until I call you. Are the computers in yet?'

Helen looked around. 'No.'

'Stay put. The IT man is on his way. He said he'd be in by half-eight.'

'Right, bye.' But Penny had already gone.

Ten minutes later, Haz and Jako returned with meal vouchers for her – 'You can't get any food without handing these over first!' – and a bacon butty with a polystyrene cup of surprisingly good cappuccino.

'Thanks, lads.'

'No probs, Hel. Gotta go – Gilly's calling for us. See ya. Good luck!'

Over the next hour or so, Penny rang many times with queries and orders. She was at the Starfish, waiting for Sven to come over. The basement of the hotel had been hired as a rehearsal room for the cast. It would be the first opportunity for the actors to meet and read through the script together. Penny was nervous.

'Thank God they're all here under one roof, at least. But no one has come down for breakfast yet. The read-through starts at ten. I hate it when we get behind schedule on the first day.'

'When will you rehearse? You start filming tomorrow.'

'It's not like a play. They don't need to learn the lines or rehearse until the last minute because we'll shoot everything out of sequence. But we do need to get them all together to read the script through so that they know how a scene plays and have met the rest of the cast before shooting begins. God, I hate act—'

Helen heard the sound of Penny's hand being clamped over the receiver, followed by her muffled voice saying, 'Dahlia, how lovely to see you! You look great.' There was the sound of air being kissed, then, 'Helen, got to go. Once the IT man has been, come straight over here. I need you.' She hung up.

*

The IT man came soon after. It was apparent that he'd be quite some time, so Helen left him to it and went over to the Starfish with her own laptop, a notepad and a fistful of pens and pencils.

The receptionist showed her down to the basement rehearsal room where she finally entered the heart of the showbiz world.

Sitting on chairs arranged in a circle were roughly thirty people. She recognised Dahlia Dahling immediately. An attractive woman in her late forties, still strongly exuding sex appeal. She sat with her toned, silk-stocking-clad legs crossed neatly and her tight pencil skirt riding up to reveal the lacy line of a stocking top. Her white, tailored shirt was unbuttoned just enough to expose a sumptuously milky cleavage. One black stiletto hung invitingly from the toes of a foot that was crossed over her left leg. A scent of lily of the valley, and possibly sex, hung around her and filled the room.

Wow, thought Helen, *she is gorgeous.* She looked around the rest of the company. They were all entranced, listening to Dahlia's sensual voice reading one of the scenes.

'Darling Mr Tibbs, if we don't find that missing necklace soon, Jack will go to prison and Hetty's heart will be broken.'

A good-looking man, also in his forties, sitting next to Dahlia, began to speak. 'My dear, I am well aware of the consequences should we not locate those pearls. If only we had at least one clue.'

Dahlia waited a beat then, 'I noticed Lord Trimsome's maid – Nell, I think her name is – being comforted by Doctor Cochran in the tea shop the other day. Maybe I'll go up to the house to enquire after her and see if there's anything else I can find out.'

'Nancy, if there's anything to discover, you're the woman to do it. Now pass the garibaldis . . .'

There was a brief silence when they reached the end of the scene, then Dahlia and the handsome actor looked up at Sven with smiles on their faces.

'Great!' Sven started to clap and everybody joined in. When the noise subsided, Sven continued, 'Let's take a short break for coffee. Fantastic first half.' He turned and started a quiet conversation with Penny, who was on his right.

Helen joined them. 'How's it going?'

'All good so far. Dahlia is perfect as Nancy Trumpet, and David is just so charming and easy-going. He's already nailed the part of Maurice Tibbs.' Penny put her arms round Sven and gave him a squeeze. 'I think we're going to pull this off! This could be the start of a licence to print money.'

Sven hugged her back. 'Don't tempt fate, love! How many more books did old Mavis write about Mr Tibbs?'

'There are eighteen all together, and Penny Leighton Productions has the TV rights to every last one! Ker-ching!'

Helen laughed. 'I hope my wages will reflect your success.'

Penny hugged her too, then, 'Depends how well you do your job! It's not too late for me to get someone else, you know.'

*

A quarter of an hour later and they were all back in their seats to read through to the end.

'Right, let's read on,' called Sven from his chair, and they did.

Having read the novel as part of her preparation for the job, Helen was already familiar with the plot, but she watched transfixed as the actors breathed life into the characters: Nell Smith, the penniless lady's maid, three months' pregnant after being seduced by Lord Gerald Trimsome. Trinsome's slimy chauffeur, Harold, who stumbles upon Nell's secret and blackmails her, demanding £250 or else he will go to Her Ladyship and tell all. Jack Smith, Nell's brother and the manor's handyman, who has the misfortune to be pruning the wisteria around Lady Trimsome's window on the afternoon a valuable pearl necklace goes missing from her dressing table. Pompous Chief Inspector Leslie Whistler, who deems the theft an open-and-shut case and wastes no time in arresting Jack.

Fortunately for Jack, amateur sleuth Maurice Tibbs, the St Brewey bank manager, and his glamorous secretary Nancy Trumpet are determined to prove his innocence.

Standing in the basement of the Starfish Hotel, watching the actors in their modern-day clothes, reading from scripts, Helen found herself transported to 1930s St Brewey. Though she had yet to see all the locations, she could picture the interior of Mr Tibbs' office as a chance remark from Mrs Trumpet had him springing up from his desk in excitement: 'Nancy! That's it! Quick, get the car out, we are going to Trimsome Manor.' As she listened to Tibbs gently extracting the truth from Nell and then demanding an audience with Lord Trimsome and his chauffeur, she imagined the contrast between the servants' quarters and the grand surroundings of His Lordship's library, where the final denouement would take place.

While Dahlia assumed the soft tones of Mrs Trumpet comforting poor Nell, David Cunningham was majestic in his cross-examination of the philandering Lord Trimsome and his blackmailing chauffeur. Shaken by Tibbs' revelations, His Lordship invites Lady Trimsome to join them in the library, and it emerges that she has known all along about her cheating husband and Nell. Hoping to get the girl dismissed before the scandal of the baby could be discovered, it had been her intention to hide the pearls and accuse Nell of having stolen them. On learning that Jack's heartbroken sweetheart Hetty has attempted suicide, Lady Trimsome breaks down and confesses.

'My work here is done,' read Cunningham. 'I have important business at the police station. You stay here, Mrs Trumpet, and look after the women. I'll pick you up once I have reunited Jack with Hetty.'

Dahlia now took centre stage as Nancy and set about persuading Lord and Lady Trimsome to provide Nell and her baby with a home and income by allowing her to stay on as Her Ladyship's personal maid. Lord Trimsome, having thanked his wife for her kindness and understanding, excuses himself and leaves the room. Some minutes later, a gunshot is heard in the library. His Lordship has done the decent thing.

The final scene featured Mr Tibbs and Mrs Trumpet leaving the graveyard after the funeral.

'A sorry business, Mrs Trumpet.'

'Yes indeed, Mr Tibbs. But at least that poor child will have a wonderful life.'

'There's a new tea shop opened by the river. Fancy some tiffin, Mrs Trumpet?'

'I thought you'd never ask, Mr Tibbs.'

There followed a short silence, then David Cunningham began a deep, joyful laugh. 'That is the best ending ever! Hilarious. Bless old Mavis Crewe.'

Everyone was laughing now.

Penny nudged Helen under the table and whispered, 'This is a good sign. If they feel it's fun from the off, the shoot will go a lot better.'

Sven was back on his feet. 'Congratulations, everyone. Play it straight like that, and the warmth and humour of Miss Mavis Crewe can't fail to delight the viewers. If this doesn't win a BAFTA, or at the very least a National Television Award, I shall eat my director's hat.'

More appreciative laughter. Sven shushed them with

his hands. 'And I am delighted to tell you that Mavis herself is hoping to visit us when she gets back from her world cruise. OK, that's it, everyone. Lunch!'

*

With the exception of Miss Dahling and Mr Cunningham, who were shown into a waiting Bentley, the cast were taken by minibus down to Pendruggan's location catering, the double-decker buses that had now been moved a suitable distance from Queenie's, for their lunch. The afternoon would be spent in final costume fittings and wig checks, ready for tomorrow: day one of filming.

Helen and Penny walked down the broad steps of the hotel to Helen's car. 'What a great day,' said Helen. 'What time do you want me tomorrow?'

'This day has only just begun, girl. You knock off when I tell you to. Drive me down to the location production office and we'll get stuck into some real work.'

29

Helen had never worked so hard in her life. Not that it was hard physical work, like running around after a toddler all day, but mentally, and emotionally, it was exhausting. Penny, on the other hand, worked like a machine, her brain apparently faster than the super-fast Internet connection newly installed in the location office. The demands on her to make speedy decisions came every few minutes:

'I don't like the blue of Trumpet's office. More lavendery . . . And the wig is too strawberry . . . I want Trumpet's hair to be platinum . . .'

Helen's only respite was the ringing of Penny's BlackBerry, announcing a new interruption.

During a brief lull, Penny motioned Helen to pull up a chair next to her and said, 'I am now going to give you the blueprint of a day's shooting schedule. Write it down, and commit it to memory. ANY schedule can be worked into this. If it's a night shoot, just insert p.m. for a.m. And vice versa. OK? Ready?'

'Right, yes, let me just get my pen—'

But Penny was off, 'Five forty-five a.m.: wake-up call for cast and crew. Six forty-five: everyone on set. Seven: breakfast – no one works well on an empty stomach. Seven-twenty: crew start setting up, actors to make-up and wardrobe. Eight: check that SA's are in position.'

'SA's?'

'Supporting artistes. A fancy name for extras. Otherwise known as Background. They are always hungry and trying to get themselves in shot. Eight-thirty: call actors on set for rehearsals, then release them back to wardrobe and make-up. Nine a.m.: hopefully first shot of the day. One p.m.: break for lunch. Try to be first in the queue or you'll wait for ages, and I like my lunch hot.'

'Right.'

'One-thirty: crew back at work to set up again. Seven-thirty p.m.: wrap for the day – we don't want to pay overtime and have union squabbles. Sven will give notes on the day's work to cast and crew alike, then the cast return to the hotel to learn their lines and have an early night. Although by week two they're usually in the bar till late and bed-hopping for the rest of the night. Eight-thirty: crew to make the set safe and secure before leaving. Nine p.m.: crew in bed and lights out . . . One hopes.' Penny looked up at Helen. 'Got that?'

'Yes, I think so.'

'Good. Don't forget it.'

'Penny, please don't speak to me like that. I am your friend, remember, and doing you a favour.'

Penny smiled sheepishly. 'Oops. Sorry, Helen, I am grateful.'

Then she was off again.

'Another thing you need to know is about actors. They are insecure, charming and dangerous. DO NOT fall for one.' Helen glanced up from her notes. 'Don't give me that butter-wouldn't-melt look, lady. On your current form, you'll be beating them off.'

'Oh, shut up.'

Both women laughed.

'Let me continue. Actors work perfectly well in the real world. They can drive cars, work kettles and open doors. On set, they can do none of these things.'

Helen laughed again.

'No, I'm serious. They will blame everyone but themselves if things don't go their way, and they will also have some sort of emotional breakdown at the slightest criticism of their performance, costume, wig et cetera. AND they will expect to sleep with whoever they choose.' Helen's eyebrows shot up in disbelief. 'It's true! Even you, Helen. And they make some quite extraordinary demands too, you wait and see.'

Penny leant forward and added in a more serious voice, 'Having said all that, actors are brave and hard-working, and the good ones are incredibly gifted. Can you imagine a job where you put all your thoughts and emotions, not to mention your body, out there for the world and his wife to adore or criticise without mercy? To learn lines, to pretend to be in love with your co-star, even though you actually loathe each other. It's a hard and cruel profession, but if you get it right the rewards, emotionally and financially, are huge. Get it wrong and you're yesterday's man – or woman.'

'Blimey. No wonder they have a reputation for being tricky to handle.'

'Quite, but don't go soft on them. They need boundaries, regular meals and an early bedtime.'

'Like kids?'

'Yes, Hel, just like kids.'

*

The two friends worked well into the night. Helen typing up endless notes and schedules while answering emails, getting coffee and trying to sneak a proper look at the transformation taking place in Pendruggan. A couple of weeks ago it had been a twenty-first-century village. But now it was a quintessential 1930s village. The false row of buildings masking the council houses were fully dressed with wisteria up the walls, quaint front gardens and curtains at the windows. The stately South-West Friendly Bank had its sign up, hand-painted in wood to look like solid brass, but if you walked through the front door you'd meet nothing but the scaffolding that was keeping the whole lot standing.

Beyond the scaffolding was the crew village. Wardrobe trucks, make-up trucks, lighting, and props trucks were parked on the grass between the wooden set and council houses. The residents of the council houses had become firm mates with all the crew. Cups of tea were shared at first, followed soon by invitations to the pub, which were gladly accepted, and there were even a few burgeoning romances going on between residents and visitors.

Across the green from her office, Helen had watched as Pendruggan Farmhouse had its satellite dish removed, and later most of the inside furniture too. The farmer and his wife were renting the house out to be used as interiors for both the bank and for Trimsome Manor.

'Very 'igh and mighty they're gettin',' Queenie had sniffed. 'Sylvia keeps telling me their 'ouse is an architectural gem.' More sniffs. 'I told 'er I wouldn't want no strangers pickin' through my things. Oh no.'

'Nothing to do with your shop not being used then, Queenie?'

'Do me a favour! I haven't a resentful bone in me body, but I don't like people gettin' above themselves. Anyway, I'm filming my scenes soon. Got costume fittings tomorrow. That'll show 'em.'

Queenie had been the first to put her name down for supporting artist work. She had set the list up herself, on her counter, so that she could vet applicants. When thirty people had signed up, she closed the list and delivered it to Helen's office in person.

''ere you go, darlin'. Got you some good 'uns 'ere.'

Helen scanned the names. 'All your friends, I see!'

'Don't know what you mean. Them's talented people.' She gave Helen a hearty wink and with a crackly laugh went back to her shop.

*

All the preparations were virtually finished now, and tomorrow would be the first day on set. Finally, at 10 p.m., Penny called it a day. They locked up the office and Penny headed off to the Starfish, while Helen said good night to the two security guards doing their rounds and walked gratefully home.

When she got back to Gull's Cry, there was a note on her mat from Simon.

Dear Helen,
Everything still OK for 'The Bish's supps', as you call it? I'll pick you up as we arranged. Hope you aren't too tired tonight. Looking forward to seeing you.

Yours
Simon x

Only two nights away. This was definitely one of those arrangements Helen was regretting accepting. Not because she didn't want to spend time with Simon but because she was so tired. At least she had her outfit ready and hanging on the back of the bedroom door.

After sniffily dismissing the black trouser suit and the pink dress, Penny had generously offered Helen the run of her wardrobe. They had settled on a sleek midnight-blue crêpe jersey dress. It just touched the top of her knees, and with some matching tights and very high Gina heels (also Penny's), she would look pretty good.

Simon had been wonderful to her and Penny since New Year. He had helped get all the filming permissions past the parish council and the local authorities, had helped put up the signage directing the film trucks from the main road to the village via the maze of lanes, and had offered the vicarage to Dahlia and David whenever they wanted to get away from the buzz of the crew.

He had even taken to bringing round hot suppers to Helen and Penny when he knew they might not have time to cook.

He had really become a fixture in the women's lives, adapting so well to the invasion that Helen no longer saw him as a diffident man with cripplingly good manners, but more as a capable man to whom one could turn in a crisis. Even Penny couldn't make him blush any more. Without realising it, they had become the Three Musketeers.

Of Piran she had seen little. He was back, working in the churchyard, but as she had no need to go out into the winter garden, their contact was limited.

A couple of days earlier, over morning coffee at the

pub, Dorrie had filled her in on Piran's forthcoming nuptials with Dawn. Apparently he was in no hurry to get married, but Dawn had booked the first of September with Simon and was busy planning guest lists, dress-makers and flowers. The reception, to be held at the Starfish, was for five hundred of their closest friends.

'Piran don't have five hundred friends! Five, maybe – but that's at a push. He's a private man, see. We all love him, but he rarely lets anyone into his little circle. Must be Dawn's friends, I suppose. Can't see him putting up with it myself,' Dorrie told her.

Helen found herself thinking about how much she'd like to be a friend of Piran's. In truth, she'd like him to fancy her so that she could turn the pig-headed git down. But oh how delicious it would be to have that raven-headed varmint after her. How wonderful to feel his hands round her waist and his lips on hers . . .

'Are you listening?'

Helen came back to the present. 'Er, yes, sorry.'

But the moment Dorrie resumed her monologue, Helen slid back into her thoughts. My God. What was wrong with her – fantasising about Piran? She laughed to herself. It must be the stress of life on set getting to her! Piran Ambrose might well be dangerously attractive, but she would be a fool to want to be involved with the man. No way.

Running her fingers over Simon's note now, she thought of Piran again. The way he'd held her so protectively on the beach, the feel of his leg beside her in church, his delicious teasing of her . . .

'Get a grip, woman,' she said to the empty room. Then she put Simon's note on the kitchen table, made herself a cup of Ovaltine and went to bed.

She dreamt of Simon finding her and Gray making love in the church. He had been pleased for her and agreed to remarry them. Once he'd gone, she looked up at Gray, but it wasn't him. It was Piran.

Part Two

30

Day one of filming, 8.45 a.m. They were inside the farmhouse. Sven was standing looking at a monitor and stroking his beard.

'OK, Gilly, when you're ready.'

Gilly stood, legs slightly apart, walkie-talkie in hand, headphones on, and boomed at the crew and actors around her.

'Ladies and gentlemen, listen up. We're going for the first take. Final checks, please.'

The make-up artists and costume team stepped into the pool of light surrounding Mr Tibbs and Nancy Trumpet. They smoothed Nancy's wig and brushed invisible lint from Mr Tibbs' shoulders. The art director had transformed the farmhouse's little-used dining room into the interior of Mr Tibbs' office in the South-West Friendly Bank. Noses powdered and lipstick refreshed, make-up and wardrobe retreated.

Gilly called out, 'Quiet, please! Shh shh shh. Turnover.'

'Running,' said the camera operator.

'And speed,' said the soundman.

'Mark it,' the cameraman again. A young man with a clapperboard put it in front of the camera.

'Scene seven, shot one, take one.' He clapped the board's arm.

'Set,' called the cameraman.

'Action,' shouted Gilly.

MR TIBBS: Mrs Trumpet. Have you been tidying my files
again?
MRS TRUMPET: I may have moved one or two items from
the floor to your cabinet, yes.
MR TIBBS: You are marvellous in every way, Trumpet, but
your annoying habit of hiding my per—

The soundman interjected with just one word, 'Airplane.'
'And cut,' said Gilly.
Helen and Penny stood quietly in a corner of the room
watching.
'I couldn't hear that plane,' she whispered to Penny.
'It's amazing what tiny sounds the equipment will pick up.
They are the bane of the soundman's life. Very annoying
when a scene is going well. You'll see, we'll stop for cars,
tractors, chickens and even squeaky bikes.'
The make-up artists quickly nipped in and repowdered
both David and Dahlia's faces.
'She's only just done that,' whispered Helen again.
'It's the lights. When you are directly under them, as they
are, you start to shine very quickly. Now shush.'
'Scene seven, shot one, take two.' Clap.
Someone sneezed off-camera.
'Keep rolling and quiet PLEASE,' shouted Gilly. 'And,
action.'

MR TIBBS: Mrs Trumpet, have you been tidying my files
again?
MRS TRUMPET: I may have moved one or two items from
the floor to your cabinet, yes.
MR TIBBS: You are marvellous in every way, Trumpet, but

your annoying habit of hiding my personal papers is really not your responsibility. I distinctly remember putting a buff envelope on my desk this morning, and now it has gone.

MRS TRUMPET: Do you mean this one? *[Nancy bends over giving Mr Tibbs a perfect view of her perfect posterior and extracts a buff envelope from the rubbish bin]* It must have fallen off this higgledy pile of post I asked you to sign yesterday.

MR TIBBS: Ah. Dear Trumpet, what would I do without you? *[Mr Tibbs sits]* Coffee time, I think. Don't you?

[Nancy smiles indulgently and leaves the office]

'And cut,' cried Gilly.

Sven stepped into the set. 'David, that's great. I love the way you gave Nancy that little twinkle. Dahlia, darling, you're tremendous! Great performances. But in the next take I want to see a little less sexual tension. We must keep the audience guessing for as long as possible. Will she, won't she? Will he, won't he? That kind of thing.' Sven looked at Gilly. 'OK. Let's go again.'

Dahlia called him back. 'How does the wig look on camera, Sven?' She was pulling at the back of her head. The make-up lady, standing slightly off set, crossed her arms with annoyance.

'Really good.'

'Is it set a bit too tight? Could I loosen the bun a little and have some soft tendrils?'

'Good idea. But not for this scene.' Sven came off the set and had a quiet word with the make-up lady. 'She thinks I'm telling you to loosen it for later, but I'm telling you to leave it the way it is. You've got it just right. Any problems, I'll deal with it.'

The make-up lady thanked him and managed an innocent nod to Dahlia, who looked pleased to have got her own way.

'Scene seven, shot one, take three.' Clap.

With each take, and there were many, Helen's admiration for the patience and good humour of the team grew. David and Dahlia were word perfect each time, but modified their performance with each take in order to give Sven what he wanted, though much of it would end up on the cutting-room floor. Helen could see a real on-screen chemistry between the two actors and said so to Penny.

'I felt they'd be good, but this is better than we could have hoped for. Especially on day one. Let's just hope the audience like it. If we can get a commission for a whole series, I can retire!'

And so the morning went on. Every scene had to be shot from several points of view with just the one camera. By the time they had three scenes in the can, what with filming the reverse angles, over the shoulders and cutaways, it was lunchtime.

Walking out of the warm fug of the farmhouse and back into the bleak cold, Helen saw Jako and Haz carrying trays of hot food over to the respective Winnebagos of David Cunningham and Dahlia Dahling.

'All right, Helen? It was a good morning, wasn't it,' Jako shouted over.

'Yes. It seemed to go really well.'

Penny touched her elbow. 'Darling, I'll have my lunch in David's winnie. I want to congratulate him and make sure he's OK. Have to keep the talent happy, you know!'

'Are you asking me to get your lunch and deliver it to you, you lazy cow?'

'I'm sorry, I thought you were my *paid* PA?'

'Yes, ma'am.' Helen pretended to tug her forelock and walked across the green towards the throng of hungry actors and crew.

The queue for lunch was long, but Sven ushered her to the front: 'Exec producer and director's perk.'

Lunch was cooked inside the catering lorry, and served through an open side like a hot dog van at a fête. The menu was extensive, and not a burger bun in sight. There was Thai green curry, shepherd's pie and cod mornay, with Eton mess, sticky toffee, and syrup sponge for pudding. Helen chose for herself and Penny, then staggered back to the imposing Winnebago. Taped to the door was a laminated sheet with a large star on it and 'Mr David Cunningham' typed underneath. She knocked and heard 'Enter'. She climbed in.

*

David was lying on a masseur's bench while a young man worked on the muscles of his back.

'Oh, Mr Cunningham. Sorry to disturb you. I was looking for Penny. I'm Helen, her PA.'

'She's in the loo, love. Just leave it there,' said David.

'Right. Is there anything I can get you while I'm here?'

'Yeah. Who supplies the charlie round here?'

'I'm not familiar with all the film language yet. But if you can tell me what the charlie is, I'll get it.'

David Cunningham and the masseur fell about laughing. Hearing the noise, Penny opened the door at the other end of the winnie, still drying her hands on a paper towel.

'What did I miss?'

'Your PA isn't entirely au fait with the lingo, bless her. I just need a little charlie to keep the old performance up.'

'Cocaine? Absolutely not, David! This isn't LA, and I am not allowing my staff to be your drug-dealers. Got that?'

David laughed again. 'Whatever you say, boss.'

Leaving David to the rest of his massage, Penny and Helen headed off outside to some nearby tables and chairs that had been put out so the crew could sit down to eat.

Penny was furious. 'How dare he expect you to get him his filthy drugs! He's been in Hollywood too long,' she ranted, through a mouthful of cod mornay. 'Asking *my* PA to get him his fix, indeed! Unbelievable!'

She took a deep breath and then said pragmatically, 'He knows that's the runner's job. Gilly can get Haz or Jako on to it straight away.' Then she stomped off, leaving her lunch half-eaten.

*

The afternoon shoot went slowly. Dahlia was having a wardrobe crisis.

'Sven, this skirt is much too long. I can't move in it. It's like a hobble skirt. Really.'

'Dahlia, it's correct for the period and looks sensational on your cute little tush.'

'Well, that's something, I suppose.' Dahlia smiled seductively and then looked quite serious. 'But when I walk up the little steps to reach the old files, you can't see my "correct for the period" suspenders and stocking tops.'

David's pupils almost popped out of his head, 'She's right, Sven. Old Tibbs would like a glimpse of those.'

Sven shot back, 'Not in this scene. Now come on, people, or we'll get behind schedule.'

'Final checks, please, ladies and gentlemen,' Gilly called. 'Let's get this in the can.' And on they went again.

*

Helen couldn't believe how painfully her feet ached when she got to bed that night and it seemed as though her eyes had only been shut for a few moments before she was up at a sparrows fart to face a day very much like the one before.

It was the day of the bishop's dinner and Penny had agreed, after a lot of grumbling, to let her go early so that she would have time to get ready. Never had her bath been more welcoming. She lay in the suds listening to Radio 4. It was only when the six o'clock pips went that she realised she had dozed for almost half an hour. She leapt out, dried herself and was somehow ready for Simon's knock on the door at six-thirty.

31

Simon stood on the doorstep looking almost trendy. He'd been to the optician and chosen some new tortoise-shell, Arthur Milleresque frames. With his balding head and newly close-cropped sides he looked most distinguished.

'Wow! Look at you!'

'Are they too much? Do I look silly?'

'No! You look great. And is this a new suit?'

He stepped back in order for her to get a really good view.

'Yes. The most expensive I think I've ever bought. A gents' outfitters in Truro kitted me out. My other suits were getting a bit shiny and an evening with the bishop *and* you, called for something new. New dog collar too, see?'

'The smartest clergyman in England. It's an honour to be your date for the night.'

Simon's chocolate-button eyes shone.

'I can't tell you how much I'm looking forward to taking you out. Sorry it's not to the opera or the ballet.'

'Good. Because I can't abide either. Lead on, Macduff.'

*

Even though it was the beginning of February, the evening held a hint of early spring. The headlights picked out primroses studding the hedgerows, and early ferns were in tight curl.

It was a clear night and the stars twinkled in the heavens. Simon had a CD of classical music playing quietly.

Helen felt totally at peace. 'What's this?'

'Rachmaninov. Beautiful, isn't it?'

They let the music enfold them as Simon drove his elderly Volvo to its destination. He glanced at Helen. Her eyes were closed. There were dark shadows under them, but her lips were tilted up at the edges in happiness. Simon allowed himself a little longer to look at her, and then turned his eyes back to the road and concentrated on the drive.

*

'Ah bless you, bless you. Welcome. Come on in out of the cold.'

The bishop was standing in the grand hallway of his official residence. The housekeeper had opened the front door and was gathering up their coats.

'My lord, please may I introduce a dear friend of mine, Mrs Helen Merrifield.'

'Mrs Merrifield, it's a pleasure to meet you. And it's good to see you too, Simon. Come into the drawing room, we have a fire going.'

They followed the rounded, jolly shape of the bishop and entered a room in which waited two other clergyman and their wives, and the bishop's wife, Ruth, who bustled towards them with her hand outstretched.

'Dear Simon . . .' she kissed him on both cheeks '. . . introduce us to your lovely companion.'

Simon did so. Helen smiled, noticing how very over-dressed she was. The women in the room were only a little older than her but were competing to see who could look most like the queen . . . on a budget.

'You are so lucky to be able to wear such high heels. Running around a parish requires comfy flats, sadly,' said Diana, wife of the archdeacon.

'My bunions wouldn't put up with shoes like that,' offered Valerie, wife of the dean.

'I think she looks smashing. Well done, Simon!' said the bishop, clapping Simon on the back. 'Don't you, chaps?'

Murmurs of 'rather', And 'What do you see in old Simon then, Mrs Merrifield?' followed until the housekeeper appeared and announced that dinner was served in the dining room.

Helen realised it was clear the bishop and his guests thought that she and Simon were something more than friends, but tried to quiet the alarm bell ringing in the far reaches of her mind.

At dinner, she was seated between the dean and the bishop; Simon between Ruth and Valerie.

There was polite gossip about diocese happenings and an impending visit from the Bishop of Bristol, then, over pudding, the bishop asked Simon how the survey of the churchyard was going.

'Very well. Piran Ambrose, our local archaeologist and historian, has catalogued all the graves we can find. There are a few that need exhuming and re-siting, but many of them can be renovated. I have to organise that with the authorities. Piran has written to the families involved to let them know of our plans, but tracking them down is, of course, tricky. We have asked for all the families to get back to us by the first of March, and we're hoping that some of them may contribute to the cost. At the moment, it's estimated that we need a quarter of a million pounds.'

'That's an awful lot of coffee mornings!' said Ruth. 'Why are the renovations so important?'

'The churchyard is getting dangerous. I feel uncomfortable about allowing elderly people or children to wander in case they fall into a hole. As for the dead, they deserve their eternal resting place to be in good condition. When it's done, the stones will be upright, the grass will be easier to cut and children will be able to play safely. In our secular world, so fearful of death, I want to encourage our young generation to see death as peaceful, not taboo.'

'So where will you get the money from?' asked the dean.

'Funds are being raised from all the events we organise. The Trevay fireworks and the Christmas talent show helped a lot. Our next big fundraiser is the Pendruggan spring carnival. But,' Simon sighed, 'it'll take us about thirty years to raise all the money, by which time I'll be in the graveyard myself.'

'Let me have a chat with our bursar and see if we can't help a little.' The bishop tapped the side of his nose. 'I may know a man who knows a man!'

The table laughed and the conversation moved on to Helen.

'And how did you meet dear Simon, Mrs Merrifield?' asked Ruth, the bishop's wife.

'I moved into the village about six months ago and he terrified me in the back garden!'

'I was on a pastoral visit. To welcome the newcomer to our fold.'

'And scared the shit – sorry, the living daylights out of me at the same time.'

'And how long have you been widowed?' Ruth asked, politely ignoring Helen's use of the S-word.

Helen gave a small laugh.

'Oh, he's very much alive. We are separated and the divorce is going through at the moment.'

'Oh?' Ruth looked at Simon. 'And where do you stand on the remarriage of divorcées in church, Simon?'

Simon looked down at his napkin, then at Helen, then at Ruth. 'I think God teaches us many things, even through the painful process of divorce. Ultimately he wants us to recognise and share love, so I'm all for divorcées remarrying and,' he looked again at Helen, 'I'd be happy to remarry them at Holy Trinity.'

There was a small pause while Ruth pursed her lips, but the bishop rescued Simon.

'Bravo. Well said. We have lost sight of the message of God, which is the simplest but hardest of all: love thy neighbour.'

But Ruth wouldn't let go. 'Indeed! So, Helen, what are your intentions towards our Simon?'

'Well, I . . .' Helen felt all the eyes in the room bear down on her.

'That is enough, my dear,' interrupted the bishop, looking directly at his wife. 'Tell me, Simon, how's it going with the TV people in Pendruggan?'

Helen looked gratefully at the bishop as Simon answered: 'Helen has helped me no end. If it hadn't been for her and her friend Penny, we wouldn't have had any of this excitement.'

'I hope some of those wealthy actors will contribute to the churchyard fund,' said Ruth.

'If it's God's will, then certainly,' responded the bishop.

*

Soon the evening came to a natural end. On the journey home, Simon took Helen's hand.

'Thank you, Helen.'

'I enjoyed it more than I thought I would. Mrs Bish gave me a few tricky moments, but the Bish himself was terribly sweet.'

He held her hand just a little bit longer before letting it go and driving home in silence.

At her front step, Simon took her key and opened the door for her. As she turned to say good night, he put his hands gently on her shoulders and kissed her lips. It was a short, soft, dry kiss, but one that Helen could easily interpret.

'Simon. Please. Don't.'

'Helen, I have so much to say to you. You were amazing tonight. I have never met anyone as wonderful as you. I want us to share more evenings like this. Dearest Helen, I have grown so fond of you, and that fondness has grown into something much more. Hear me out, I . . .'

Helen, whose heart was now beating with shock rather than passion, quickly put her fingers over his lips.

'Simon. Don't say it. Please don't. You are my dearest friend. Please say nothing more. You are too important to me to spoil it with . . . Complications. Go home and let's be as if this moment didn't happen. Please.'

Simon took his hands from her shoulders so fast that she felt he was going to hit her. Then she saw the pain in his eyes. He blinked rapidly and pretended to search his pockets for something while saying, 'Helen, oh my, ha! What a fool I've made of myself. I'm so sorry. It'll never happen again. Good night. Forget I said anything,' and he walked back to his car.

32

'Good old Simon!' smiled Penny across her desk the next morning when Helen confided in her. 'He's grown some balls at last. And you, you heartless wench, have sliced them off again in one fell swoop.' Penny, dressed in warm clothing from head to toe, hugged her coffee mug in her mittened hands.

'Please don't take the mickey. Out of him or me. He means so much to me, but . . . when he kissed me, I just knew it wasn't right. And if I were ever to have another relationship, it would have to be perfect. No more compromise. It has to be true love, lots of great sex and complete faithfulness.'

'Does that sort of relationship even exist?' Penny sipped her coffee.

'David Cunningham and his wife Sonia seem OK.'

'Yes, but only because he's sown every wild oat he has and his cocaine habit has rendered him impotent. Sonia had been his make-up artist and part-time lover for years. She nursed him through all his affairs with the world's most glamorous leading ladies They never saw her as a threat. More fool them! She was in it for the long game and won. Sonia's got her head screwed on. She's got him on a very loose chain and he doesn't feel the need to yank it.'

'I was the same with Gray, but it didn't work.'

'He was hardly impotent and you were just stupid.'

229

'Thanks for reminding me!' Helen wrapped her thin scarf a little tighter over her chin. 'I haven't heard from him since the Christmas blip.'

'What Christmas blip?'

Helen scrunched her face up in shame. 'I didn't tell you, but I had a little accident with Gray . . .'

*

When Helen had finished telling Penny the sorry tale, Penny got up and put her arms round her friend. 'You silly woman.'

'Yeah, that's what Piran said too.'

'You told him but not me! Charming. How come he got to hear it?'

Penny sat silently listening to how Piran had attempted to comfort Helen on the beach. Finally she said,

I think this is a conversation we need to have over a bottle of wine. I think he could be bonkers about you . . . or just plain bonkers. And what the hell is he doing with Dullard Dawn? Bloody men, eh? Let's make time in the next few days for a long supper and a good chinwag. But now, my friend, we have work to do.'

*

The weather forecast for the next three days was dry and bright, but still cold. Sven had decided that they should crack on with as many exterior shots as possible while they had the sunny light. All the crew were wearing thick outerwear and, Helen felt sure, thermal underwear too. She made a note to self: *Must get down to M&S for some warm socks and vests.*

230

Pendruggan Farmhouse was now transformed into the exterior of Trimsome Manor. Artificial wisteria hung in heavy clusters from the eves and window frames, stained-glass sides made from Perspex adorned the grand porch and the garden frothed with fake cow parsley and blue-bells. An old ladder was resting on an upstairs sash windowsill. A props man was leaning out of the window and making sure the ladder was firmly secured. Huge lights were set up in the garden, bathing it in the sunny glow of a May day, rather than the keen nip of a February one. As Helen watched, men with thick gloves were hiding the black power cables and electric junction boxes under yards of astro turf.

She felt a shadow on her back and a familiar voice said, 'Hello, Heather. Got your eye on the muscle, have you?'

Helen didn't need to turn round to know who it was.

'Oh, hello, Dawn. My name is Helen and I am admiring the excellent work of true professionals – actually.'

'If you say so.' Dawn was looking immaculate, if not ridiculous, in a snow-white ski jacket with a fur trim round the hood, yeti boots and large sunglasses on her head. 'Have you spotted Piran with your beady little eyes?'

'My beady little eyes haven't been looking for him.'

'Good. He's here somewhere, getting ready to play a fisherman bringing his catch into the village shop or something. Perfect casting. He's going to look even more handsome than usual. I might ask him to bring the costume home – we could play pirates and wenches together. Ha ha ha.'

Dawn's studied, tinkling laugh made Helen want to grab her by the throat and bash her perfect teeth out on the granite surround of the village pump. Instead, she said,

'What a vulgar idea.' And went off, ostensibly in search of someone, but really just to get away from bloody Dawn.

It was sod's law that the first person she bumped into as she rounded the corner to the crew village was Piran, stepping out of the wardrobe truck fully kitted out in his fisherman's garb.

He had the decency to look a little embarrassed.

Helen said, 'Well! Hello, sailor!'

'Hello, Helen.' He looked around him to see if anyone could hear, then said, 'How are you? Feeling better than when we last talked?'

'What? Oh, that.' She tried a tinkling laugh of her own. 'I was making a mountain out a molehill. All sorted . . . water under the bridge and all that.'

'It didn't look that way to me. I've been thinking about you.'

She looked up into his ocean eyes. 'Have you?'

Their eyes locked for a moment, but then Helen was brought back to earth when she heard the grating voice of Dawn break in.

'Piran! There you are. And Helen! I was just saying how I'm going to persuade you to bring your sexy costume home to play.' Dawn pushed her hand through Piran's arm and attached herself like a barnacle.

Piran looked uncomfortably down at his old fisherman's smock, moleskin breeks and oilskin boots. 'I feel a right chump in this get-up, but I promised Queenie I'd do my bit.'

Gilly, armed with a megaphone, stepped out of the make-up truck behind them. 'Where are all the other extras?'

'There are a few still getting changed in the wardrobe lorry.'

'Right, I'll gather them up.' Putting the megaphone to her lips, she boomed, 'Listen up, everybody. Would all SA's still in the truck please go and stand on the village green in one large group. From there we can place you in the set and show you what you need to do. Understood?' A vague murmur came from the lorry. 'I said UNDERSTOOD?' 'Yes,' came a slightly louder reply. 'Good. Off you go then. You're all going to be movie stars. Chop chop.'

Piran untangled Dawn's arm from his.

'Good luck, darling. Dawnie's watching!' She attempted to plant a kiss on his retreating face.

After two paces, he turned and said, 'Helen, I'll catch you later.'

Dawn's face was inscrutable then, her voice dripping with malice, she said, 'Oh yes, he told me you'd had a bit of a breakdown at Christmas. He's so good with lame ducks. I *adore* that man. He's Heathcliff, Rhett Butler and Marco Pierre White all rolled into one, isn't he?'

But Helen didn't stop to listen. She had already made her escape.

*

The rest of the day was enormous fun for Helen as she watched Dahlia on manoeuvres. Piran had done his bit for the day and had changed back into his levi's and guernsey sweater, plus warm boots and jacket, but he was still hanging about chatting to the riggers. Little Jack was sniffing around their heels. Dahlia, by extraordinary coincidence, made sure her personalised canvas director's chair was within tickling distance of Jack.

'Hey, little doggie. Who do you belong to, sweetie?' Jack

wandered towards her and sniffed her hand. She tickled his ears and he let rip a poisonous fart before returning to an oblivious Piran.

'We're going for a take,' called Gilly. 'Dahlia, David, we're just on final checks in the garden scene, then we'll go. OK?'

Putting down his *Times* crossword and surreptitiously wiping his runny nose with his thermal gloves, David got down from his chair and called affectionately to Dahlia, 'Come on, you silly cow. I want to be back in time for *The Apprentice*.'

'David, darling, how I love it when you talk dirty.'

As she hopped off her chair, Dahlia managed to elegantly trip over the cashmere rug that she'd wrapped round her knees, going over on one ankle and slipping to the ground.

Jack's bark of surprise alerted Piran.

'For God's sake, woman, be careful!'

Piran strode over to her and helped her back up into her chair.

'Where does it hurt?'

Dahlia gave him a powerful, liquid look. 'Silly me. It's fine, I'm sure. Let me just try it.' She got down from the stool once more and tried her weight on the ankle, immediately falling on to Piran's shoulder. 'Oh dear, I don't think I can put any weight on it. Maybe you could just walk me into the farmhouse and through to the back garden?'

Helen watched as David Cunningham nudged one of the crew, and she overheard him say, 'Aye aye, Mata Hari's working her charm!' Both the men and Helen watched as Dahlia did a lot of wilting on Piran's shoulder as he half carried her to the farmhouse.

Dawn was sitting a little way off on a three-legged canvas camping stool and her eyes took in every movement the pair made. As soon as they went into the farmhouse and out of sight, Dawn was off her perch and hurrying in pursuit. Just as she got to the front door, Gilly came out and stopped her.

'Sorry. I can't allow unauthorised people into the house. It is a film set and access is restricted.'

'But my fiancée is a performer.' When Gilly looked questioningly at her, Dawn continued, 'He's just helped Miss Dahling in. After she hurt her ankle?'

'No doubt he'll be out in a moment. Now, if you wouldn't mind waiting somewhere else, thank you.' Gilly began steering Dawn out of harm's way as two scene hands came in loaded with heavy equipment, 'Mind your backs, please,' Gilly said. 'I'm sorry, you'll have to get out of the way, we need to leave this entrance clear.'

Looking peeved, Dawn walked back to her stool, picked it up and marched off to Piran's battered truck.

Helen, observing all this from about twenty yards away, was highly amused. Poor old Dawn, poor old Dahlia and definitely poor old Piran.

*

Helen saw very little of the rest of the day's filming as she had a load of emails and calls to catch up on for Penny, but at six o'clock she heard the end-of-day broadcast from Gilly's megaphone:

'Listen up, everybody. That was another great day. Sven wants me to thank all the SA's who have worked so tirelessly and have been absolute troopers. Thank you so much.' There were loud cheers and applause. 'Even though you have eaten the chuck wagon empty!' More cheers and catcalls.

'Now some important notices. Our wonderful star, Mr David Cunningham, or Mr Tibbs as we know him better, has a birthday next Tuesday, and he wants me to let you know that you are all invited to a party he is throwing at the Starfish. Sadly, we cannot extend the invitation to partners unless they are involved in the shoot. Bring your swimming costumes as we have exclusive use of the roof terrace hot tub.' More whistling and applause.

'On the door of my van, you will find a piece of paper headed DAVID'S PARTY. Please put your name on it by the end of tomorrow, so we have an idea of numbers. Now go get some sleep, and we'll see you tomorrow.'

33

The following morning, sitting in her empty production office with a fan heater blowing on her chilled ankles, Helen was thinking about phoning Simon. She had avoided the inevitable, awkward conversation for the last twenty-four hours, hoping that maybe he would break the ice first. After all, she told herself, he was the one who had spoilt things with that clumsy declaration. On the other hand, she felt desperate that she had hurt his feelings or led him on in some way. She took a deep breath and rehearsed the conversation in her mind.

Simon, it's Helen here. I want to apologise for any misunderstanding the other evening. You are a wonderful friend and I don't want there to be any discomfort between us, so, assuming we can carry on as before, would you do me the honour of being my partner for David Cunningham's party?

Yes. That should do it. She dialled the number, sat up straight and put a smile on her face. She waited, then . . . the engaged tone. A tiny wave of annoyance lapped at her lungs. She put the phone down with unnecessary force. The door banged open and Penny arrived, talking on her BlackBerry as usual.

'That's great. I am so pleased. Come straight to the hotel and I'll meet you there. Thanks, Simon. Byeee.'

Penny threw her large Mulberry bag down on Helen's desk, 'Fancy a cuppa? I'll put the kettle on.'

Penny went into the small galley kitchen at the back of the cottage and Helen could hear the tap being run and the click as the kettle was turned on at the wall. Penny came back in to the front-room office, humming irritatingly, and flopped into her office swivel chair, putting her feet on the desk. She looked at Helen's pinched face.

'What's the matter with you? PMT or menopause?'

'Nothing's the matter.' Helen tried to keep her voice light.

'Good. Let's crack on. The weather is holding and we're shooting all the driving scenes with the "action cars" today.'

The kettle whistled and clicked off. Penny jumped up, whistling to herself now, and Helen heard the clatter of mugs and teaspoons. 'Do you want a biscuit?' Penny yelled.

'No thanks,' Helen replied, aware that her breathing had grown shallow and fast. 'Who was that you were speaking to?'

Penny came back in and passed over a mug of tea with Snoopy on it.

'Simon. Why?'

'Our Simon?'

'Yes. vicar Simon. He's coming to David's party with me.' Penny stirred her tea nonchalantly.

'Is he?' Helen started to sweep imaginary crumbs from her desk. 'Who asked who?'

'I asked him, if that's all right with you.' Penny stopped stirring and stared at Helen. 'Unless you have a problem with that?'

'Why? should I?'

Penny relaxed. 'No. And that's exactly what I told him.'

'So, you've been discussing me?' Helen could feel a flush of anger find her cheeks.

'Well . . .' Penny looked challengingly at Helen. 'He didn't want to upset you after the other night's shenanigans.'

'What shenanigans?'

'Calm down, Helen. Cut the jealous woman act. You blew him out.'

'I am *not* behaving like a jealous woman. I just don't want him getting hurt or getting the wrong idea about you.'

Penny carefully placed her cup of tea on the desk and, looking straight into Helen's eyes, said very slowly, 'What Simon and I think of each other is none of your business.'

'Simon is a dear, sweet friend, and while I may not feel the same way about him as he does about me, I still don't want to see him eaten for breakfast by a piranha!'

Penny looked incensed. 'Are you comparing me to a carnivorous fish? I'm shocked that you feel that way about me!'

'Oh, don't look so innocent!' Helen snorted. 'You're hardly the shrinking violet where men are concerned, and I just think Simon deserves to be treated a bit more sensitively, that's all.'

'Oh, just like you did when you dashed his hopes the other night,' Penny retorted.

Helen looked down into her lap, feeling the sting of Penny's words.

The two women sat in furious silence for a moment before Penny broke the impasse.

'Look,' she said, 'Simon is a grown man who is taking me to David's party. And that is that.'

'So be it.'

'Excellent. That's that sorted out.' Penny picked up her bag and went to the door. 'I thought you'd make much more fuss at my next bit of news, actually.'

'What's that?'

'Gray is organising all the "action car" hire. He's on his way down now with a low-loader. Should be here in about half an hour. He's found us Mr Tibbs' car, Lord Trimsome's car and a police car.'

Helen looked at Penny in shock.

'What?' she said.

'His rates were really good. Great, isn't it! And as a special surprise for you, he's bringing Chloe down with him. Gotta go. See you later.'

It took Helen several minutes to file all this information correctly. Simon and Penny were going to David's party. Together. Helen couldn't work out what she was feeling. Hurt? Discarded? Clearly not the love of Simon's life after all. How dare he move on so quickly, and to Penny! Helen didn't want him. But really, Penny?! What was that all about?

Anger started bubbling up again, sending a furious heat through her limbs. And bloody Gray! Why the hell had Penny got *him* involved in the filming? She, Helen, was the PA! *She* should have been the one to make that particular phone call. Or not. Ah yes, that was it, Penny hadn't wanted her to put a spanner in the works by refusing to deal with Gray! Well, she'd show them who was professional around here! She could damn well do her job and stark naked with a BlackBerry up her nose if she had to! Let them play their silly mind games. She would rise above it.

She stood up, knocking the table with her knee, and

tipping the contents of her Snoopy mug inside her handbag.

*

And that was how Chloe found her. Sitting with many sodden tissues on the floor and one more clenched to her crying eyes.

'Mummy! What's happened? Aren't you feeling well?'

Chloe put her arms round her mother and hugged her. Helen looked up with gratitude.

'Oh, darling. You're here at last. Auntie Penny only just told me the wonderful news that you were coming and I am crying tears of happiness.'

*

'Keep her coming. Straight back. Stop. Left-hand down a bit. That's it. Well done, mate.' One of the crew was helping the low-loader driver to unload the cars.

Helen had been given the task of making certain that none of the classic 'action cars' were damaged as they were driven off the lorry. Gray was standing with his hands on his hips, sunglasses on his head, chatting to the props team. He hadn't even bothered to acknowledge Helen.

'Fabulous car, that: 1935 Rolls-Royce Landaulette. Two hundred thousand on the clock and the engine's barely run in.' All the men within fifty metres were standing looking at the creamy yellow classic as it was delicately parked in a cordoned-off area to the side of the green.

The actor playing Lord Trimsome, Tim Watkins, walked over and stroked the bonnet. 'Welcome to Papa, old girl. Lord Trimsome certainly has style.'

Next off the truck was a black Wolseley Wasp with a POLICE sign on its roof. The two actors playing the policemen applauded its arrival, and immediately jumped inside. Finally came Mr Tibbs' car, a Morris Eight Series 1. Dark green and pretty with its sit-up-and-beg silhouette.

David Cunningham strolled over and looked at it. 'Hello, my beauty!' He opened the door and a waft of old leather leaked out and up the noses of several appreciative bystanders.

'You can keep your Roller, Tim,' he shouted across. 'This'll do old Tibbs fine.'

'Yeah, but this baby will get Trimsome into Nancy's knickers quicker than that old tub.'

All the men laughed at the sexist, bawdy joke and as quickly stopped when Dahlia sauntered over in nothing but a silky dressing gown, nipples pointing like chapel hat pegs, wearing wellies with her hair tightly pinned under a stocking net.

'Oh, very amusing, boys. Tim, darling, Nancy needs a man not a mouse.' She gave him a vampy gaze under faux eyelashes. 'Has anyone seen the blessed wig woman? She pinned me up and then bloody vanished.'

Spotting Helen, Dahlia undulated in her direction.

'Helen!'

'Hello, Dahlia.'

'I'm glad I've found you.' Dahlia dropped her voice a little. 'I hope you don't mind me asking,' she started, 'but who is that man playing the fisherman? I noticed you were talking to him earlier.'

'That's Piran Ambrose,' Helen answered, 'our local man of mystery.'

'Yes, he looks it. Darling, those eyes!' Dahlia clutched

her surgically enhanced bosom and breathily asked, 'Is he married?'

'No, no . . . no.' Helen hesitated and then added wickedly, 'Ladies aren't his cup of tea.'

'Really?' Dahlia looked surprised.

'Hmm. Lots of people have tried, but he's definitely what they call a confirmed bachelor.'

'You'd never guess.' Dahlia looked crestfallen. 'Shame.' She paused, then looked back at Helen with a glint in her eye. 'Still, there's no harm in trying, is there?'

*

Later on that day, as the cars were being buffed to within an inch of their lives and the men on set stood around, still apparently transfixed by the gleaming vintage cars, Helen ran into Dahlia again.

This time her wig had been sorted by the make-up department and she was looking a million dollars in a tweed twinset that perfectly brought out her hour-glass curves.

'Ah, Helen – I ran into that handsome Piran at lunchtime. I happened to be in the churchyard enjoying the sun and there he was! I asked him to take me to David's party. But he said he couldn't. I asked him if it was because he was taking somebody else, but he just laughed and said he'd see me there. Does he have a partner?'

'Er yes. He does have a partner, but he won't be taking them to the party because it's someone who isn't working on the show.' Helen knew she was leading Dahlia up the garden path but she didn't care. It was fun, and what the hell: Piran deserved a little trouble.

'Interesting. Watch this space, darling. There aren't many men I couldn't conquer, straight or gay. Ha ha.'

Dahlia sashayed off, perfectly aware of the effect her curvaceous bottom, wobbling like a perfect panna cotta, was having on the watching men.

Helen was thinking: if Piran was going to the party, it would have to be without Dawn, who wasn't cast or crew so was therefore ineligable. But what were the chances of Dawn letting him go on his own?

So deep in thought was she that she was unaware of the figure approaching her from behind.

'Her bottom's not a patch on yours, my darling.' She felt familiar fingers pinch her bum. Without turning round she said, 'Hello, Gray. Thank you for bringing Chloe with you. Now please fuck off.'

34

As it turned out, Helen managed not to run into Gray or Penny over the next couple of days. He was staying at the Starfish, and Penny was in London on a flying visit to TV7. Helen was stuck in her office with a million calls and emails to make to the production accountants (expenses were getting dangerously close to the limit), agents (whose clients were bitching about the size of their parts), the travel co-ordinator (could Helen please cut down on the number of taxis to and from the Starfish) and local police (about the closure of certain lanes where filming in the cars would take place). The locals were very helpful and completely succumbed to the invasion. In return, the film crew were generous with their time; giving the odd unscheduled tour of the set and the interiors of the make-up and wardrobe trucks, while also having endless photos taken with babies and whiskery grannies.

It was February half term, and many holidaymakers, having read the local papers, made the pilgrimage to Pendruggan, following the neon production location signs. The dads came to glimpse Dahlia Dahling and the mums to sigh over David Cunningham. Helen was amazed to see how patient the stars of the show were with their fans. She had worried that Dahlia might be a woman-hating diva, but, from the little contact they had shared, she detected a woman who was tough, funny and talented, and she was starting to feel a bit guilty about having given her the wrong impression about Piran.

Helen particularly admired the way Dahlia handled a tetchy David Cunningham on the days when he was more than a little wrecked after a night of chemical abuse. She saw the pair of them at lunch one day when, after a frustrating morning spent fluffing every one of his lines, David began spooning custard instead of mayonnaise on his poached salmon. Seeing this, Dahlia, in a voice she knew would be heard around the village, remarked, 'Darling David, improvising your lunch now, as well as your lines. How creative!'

Everybody fell about laughing and to his credit, after a beat, so did David, replying, 'Darlings! It's the latest taste sensation. Have you never been to London?'

*

The weather was holding up well. The early spring sun actually had some warmth in it and Queenie was doing a roaring trade in ice creams and pasties. Don and Dorrie had opened up the sheltered courtyard at the back of the pub to serve cream teas and the speedboats down in Trevay were rarely idle.

Even the daffodils were sunning themselves in the steep hedges of the lanes.

Helen was longing to walk on the beach. It lay not even half a mile away, but she was tied to the office during daylight and when she locked up she was just too tired.

Chloe, on the other hand, was having a ball. Helen had introduced her to Haz and Jako on her first day, over morning coffee.

'Boys, meet my daughter, Chloe. Chloe, this is Haz and Jako.'

'Hi, Chloe. Good to meet you. Do you surf?' asked Haz.

'No. I've never tried.'

'Well, you're in the right place and with the right people now, so no excuses. We have a day off tomorrow. Pick you up at nine,' said Jako.

'Won't I need a wetsuit or a board?' asked Chloe, laughing.

Helen stepped in. 'Simon gave me a voucher for a wetsuit for my Christmas present. Remember? We're the same sizeish, so go and get yourself kitted out and hire a board for the day.'

After that, Helen saw Chloe only for breakfast and supper. Jako and Haz had introduced her to all the surf boys and girls and life was now all about partying in each other's clapped-out caravans, sited on very basic but wonderfully bucolic beachside fields, and catching the waves.

*

On the day of David's birthday, Sven, Gilly and Penny walked into Helen's office and made themselves comfortable. Helen looked up from her typing. Nothing more had been said about Penny's date with Simon, and Helen was determined to look as carefree as possible.

'Hello, you lot. Can I get you anything?' she asked, smiling as broadly as she could.

Penny, also studiously avoiding the subject, said, 'Three cappuccinos and three almond croissants please, Hel.'

'Certainly. Is this a private pow-wow, or can I come back and finish these emails?'

'Yeah yeah, it's fine. Come back. We're only sorting out the schedule. The shooting is going so well we may be able to break early today and get ready for David's party in good time. We haven't told the cast or crew yet, just in case it's not possible.'

'Sounds good. Back in a minute.'

When she returned, only Penny remained.

'Gilly and Sven have gone to tell everyone the good news. We are going to break an hour early tonight. We're on schedule, pretty much on budget and the weather is looking good again tomorrow so we should be able to complete all of our scheduled outdoor scenes. In forty-eight hours it can piss down for all I care, because we're doing interiors from then on.'

Penny took a step towards Helen and put her hands on Helen's shoulders. 'You are my best mate and I don't honestly think I could have got through these past weeks without your help and brilliance. I really don't want us to fall out over Simon.'

'Neither do I, but you can't treat his feelings lightly, you know.'

Penny drew Helen to her. 'He's a mate, that's all. A mate who had his heart broken by another mate. I'm a sucker for a sob story.'

'What about Orlando the sexy chef?'

'Oh god. Too young, too athletic in the sack and too aware that he was doing an old lady a favour. My mother always used to say, "Better to be an old man's darling than a young man's fool."'

Changing tack, Penny continued, 'How are you getting to the party? Would you like a lift in with Simon? Or do you have other arrangements?'

Helen sighed. She wasn't sure she could bear to be in

the same car as Simon and Penny. 'I may not come actually. I'm knackered and . . .'

Penny held her at arm's length and said sternly, 'It is your duty! A mandatory part of your job! Who are you coming with?'

'Er, well, nobody.'

'Excellent! Single gorgeous female on the pull. Every party needs one and you are it. I am officially giving you the rest of the day off.' She looked at the pile of paperwork on Helen's desk. 'As soon as you have cleared your in-tray.'

Playfully shoving Penny away, Helen said, 'Even the ugly sisters weren't so horrible to Cinderella.'

*

By the time Helen had cleared her desk, it was six o clock. The cast and crew had long since left the village. She locked up and walked quickly to Gull's Cry. The lights were on, which meant that Chloe was home. She opened the front, 'Hi, darling.'

The door to the small lounge was shut and she could hear voices. Assuming that Chloe was watching television, Helen turned the handle and walked in. Chloe was lying on the rug by the glowing fire. A young man with sea-tangled blond hair was leaning over her and kissing her daughter passionately. Helen was relieved to see that they were both fully clothed.

Who the hell is he? she wondered, then coughed politely and said, 'Hi. Anyone want a cup of coffee?'

Chloe sat up quickly and the young man jumped to his feet.

'Mrs Merrifield. Hello.'

'Hello.'

'Mum, this is Mack. He's a friend.'

'Yup. I guessed that. Hello, Mack.' She stepped forward and shook his strong hand.

'Could I put the kettle on for you, Mrs Merrifield? Chloe told me you were going out tonight so maybe you want to get ready?'

'Yes. That would be very kind,' she said slowly.

When he'd left the room, Chloe mouthed, 'Sorry, Mum.'

'What for! He's a bit of a creep, sucking up by making tea like that, but he is gorgeous. Has he . . . Do you . . . Are you . . . ?'

Helen couldn't bring herself to ask if Mack had actually defiled her virgin daughter, but Chloe, pinkening, helped her out. 'Mum! We just surf together!'

'Good, that's important, isn't it? Well, have a nice evening and, erm, don't do anything you are not comfortable with . . . especially in *my* bed.' Both women giggled and Helen sped upstairs before she caused any further embarrassment.

*

The Starfish Hotel was bathed in sapphire-blue floodlights, its palm trees standing stark against the starry night sky. Helen had never been to Cannes, but guessed it couldn't be any more splendid than this. Voices, laughter and the sound of swing music drifted down from the roof terrace. Walking up the wide steps to the front door, she glanced over her shoulder to the glassy water of the harbour. It shone with the reflection of the building.

Helen sang the Black Eyed Peas *Tonight's Going To Be A Good Night* to herself.

Stepping out of the beach-hut decorated lift, on to the roof terrace, the breeze caught her hair and made her shiver. She was wearing a long turquoise fine-knit cashmere dress. Very simple with little cap sleeves. It set off her creamy skin, freckles, and glossy auburn curls to perfection. She took in the faces, now so familiar, gathered around, smiling and talking.

'There you are, darling.' Gray strode up to her and, taking her in his arms, whispered in her ear. 'I must say, you look sensational. Very fuckable.'

She pulled out of his embrace and looked at him. A number of possible responses occurred to her, but she held her tongue and said, 'Good! Thank you.'

'Let me get you a glass of something. The white is superb.' With his hand in the small of her back he guided her to the bar and, cutting across everyone else waiting, called, 'Rob, a bottle of the white and two glasses, please.'

'Coming up, sir,' nodded Rob the bartender.

'We'll be at my usual table.' Another nod from Rob and several tuts from the queue. Helen noted that Gray hadn't lost his touch with the bar staff.

Gray took her hand, and Helen allowed herself to be led towards a small table set in a quiet corner overlooking the sea. A trellis of ivy surrounded it and acted as a windbreak to the cool night air. On the bleached wood table stood a lighted storm lantern.

'Sit here, darling.' Gray motioned to the double bench seat with gaily striped feather cushions on it and a warm fleecy blanket hung over each arm.

She sat, without comment, and he took one of the fleeces, flapped it open and draped it over her legs. He sat next to her just as Rob arrived with a tray, ice bucket, wine and glasses.

'Cheers, my darling.'

They each drank and Helen realised that, despite everything, she was grateful that Gray was there to spare her the unnerving experience of hanging around at the edge of the action like a spare part.

'Gray . . .'

'Yes, love?'

'What exactly are you doing here?'

'Earning some money with the cars and enjoying time with you and Chloe and Pen.'

'Why can't you let go of our marriage?'

He put his glass down and held his hands in his lap. His gaze drifted towards the party, 'I wasn't the one who started divorce proceedings.'

'Not if you don't count sleeping around repeatedly – or doesn't that constitute the end of a marriage?'

'Helen, please don't.' He turned his face to hers. 'My behaviour towards you shocks me whenever I think of it.'

'Is that why you drag your heels over replying to the solicitor's letters?'

He looked uncomfortably into her eyes, 'Yes. I suppose. I'm just waiting for you to have enough of this women's lib stuff, and come home where you belong.' He shifted his body round to her and in a low voice said, 'When are you coming back to me, darling?'

Helen looked at him for a long moment. 'I am no longer your wife, Gray. Maybe by law I still am, but not in my heart. I can never come back to you. Nothing would change.'

'It would, I promise—'

'Hush. This is the first time since leaving school and meeting you, that I've had an opportunity to find out who I am and what I believe in. I am contented in a way that

252

living with you never made me.' Gray's face pinched into a hurt expression. 'Three decades have gone by and I find myself with a blank page in front of me. A chance to discover a life that doesn't include washing, ironing, cooking and shopping for a family who thought it was all I needed. And I find that what I needed was someone who was a friend to me.'

'I am your mate.'

'Mates don't treat mates the way you treated me. Mates are loyal and kind. They listen and share. They don't demand supper and sex when you're knackered, or leave a trail of shaving scum and laundry in their wake.'

'What's got into you, darling? All this Germaine Greer stuff isn't you. Have you been listening to too much *Woman's Hour*? This is all very peevish and, if I may say so, childish.'

'That's something you can easily recognise.'

'Well, what about you?' He sat straighter, picked up his glass and took a large mouthful. 'All those months of refusing me sex after you had Chloe and Sean. What's a man supposed to do when his wife is frigid? I tried to encourage you. What do you think all that sexy underwear was for?'

'You.'

'No! It was for you. To help you feel sexier towards me.'

'Ha!' Helen tipped her head back and barked out a mirthless laugh. 'I'd have felt sexier towards you if you had brought fish and chips home for supper instead of expecting me to cook, or if you once emptied the dishwasher without saying, "I've emptied the dishwasher for you." What did you expect, a medal?'

'Oh this is pure kindergarten. You are being absurd.'

'No. I am just trying to get into your thick, emotionally unintelligent head the realities that could have kept us together. And if I ever meet someone again with whom I wish to spend my life, it would have to be on the basis of complete trust. You couldn't even keep your hands off your own son's girlfriend. To betray your wife is one thing, but to betray your son is quite another.'

'Helen, I have taken just about enough of your insults. I've never laid a finger on you. I never kept you short of money. In truth, I am glad to be shot of you. That dear young girl I once knew has turned into a harpy.' During the final few words, he stood up, tucked his shirt into his belt, pulled his waist up and knocked several ivy leaves on to the table.

'I feel sorry for you, Helen. And so do your friends. Your true friends, back in London. Not this bunch of pathetic vicars and hippies. You need help. If you need a doctor or a therapist, I'll find one for you, but I am not certain things would ever be the same between us again. It's a burden to have a partner with mental health issues. A burden that would be hard to bear, even for a man as strong as I.'

He topped up his glass of wine and walked back towards the party.

35

Helen wanted to leave immediately. Go home to her little nest and cry pitiful tears. But she couldn't. Chloe was there. She could call a friend and ask to come over, but her friends were here, at the party. And anyway, she wasn't sure if she wanted to confide in Penny or Simon right now.

She didn't regret a word she had said to Gray, but this hadn't been the time or the place. How did Gray always manage to turn things round so that she was the guilty party? Gray, the man she had loved so very much, the father of her much-loved children. Gray with whom she'd had the best of times and the most painful of times. Gray who had sex with other women, who penetrated their bodies, kissed their nipples, gave them oral sex. Gray who would then come home to her, saturated in the essence of these other women, and want to do the same with her. A huge wave of white-hot anger managed to breach her wall of resentment and denial.

Tears welled in her eyes. She turned her back on anyone who might see her and faced out towards the sea. Her eyes were burning now and she screwed them tight shut whilst trying to breath normally. Was she mad? Did she need help? She thought about those friends who Gray said were worried about her. Not one of them had phoned her since her arrival here. She'd received a handful of

Christmas cards, but none with any messages of real interest or concern for her. She opened her eyes and a stream of tears rolled down her cheeks.

Rummaging in her bag, she found a small packet of tissues and a mirror. When she looked at her reflection she saw a woman who, apart from soggy eyes and a nose wiped free of make-up, looked OK, really. No dark circles, no extra wrinkles. She examined her hairline – no grey hairs – yet. And why did she look OK? Because, she told her reflected self, you are doing what you want to do, and you are happy, aren't you? Happy to be free of responsibility. Happy to have dumped your old life, no matter how much it hurt people. Happy to have hurt even your new friends, like Simon. Happy to be a selfish cow who wants it all her own way?

Her head was pounding now and the tears came again. She had to go home. Any control she had over herself was slipping away. With a final wipe of her eyes, she picked up her bag, stood up and turned to make her escape.

*

The party-goers were in full swing. The band on the other side of the terrace had struck up 'Boogie Woogie Bugle Boy' and bodies everywhere started to dance. Others were standing in small groups, laughing and drinking, and a couple of the make-up girls were already in the steaming hot tub, calling to David Cunningham to join them. 'Come on, birthday boy. Don't be shy.'

'Later, my beauties! Later!' he called back. 'I have a little business to attend to first.'

The smoke from the barbecue was imbued with the

rainbow colours of the carnival lanterns strung above their heads.

Helen kept her head down and, sticking to the dark edges of the crowd, made her way round to the door leading to the lift. Just another half-dozen paces and she'd be there.

'Helen!'

Oh God, who had seen her? She pretended not to hear.

'Helen!'

Still keeping her head down, Helen saw a pair of beautiful ankles in very high black suede killer heels. 'Look who I've found!'

There was nothing for it but to look up. When she did so, she was confronted with the dazzling vision of Dahlia Dahling, resplendent in a backless, strapless, possibly bra-less, red jersey dress that gave new meaning to the word 'figure-hugging'.

'Hi, Dahlia.' She looked up a little further and swallowed hard. 'Hello, Piran.'

The sight of Piran took her breath away. He was wearing a black dinner jacket complete with black bow tie. His hair was super clean and shiny. He'd shaved and the musk of his cologne made her want to lean in and kiss him with a terrifying intensity. Dahlia broke the spell.

'Piran was just going to get me a drink. Would you like one too, Helen?'

'I was just going, actually. A bit of a headache.'

'Oh, don't be a spoilsport! Have just one drink before you go. Piran, we'll be waiting for you on those two chairs. Don't be long, now!' Dahlia waved a graceful hand towards the bar.

Piran gave Helen a searching look and extricated

himself from Dahlia's arm, which was around his waist. Both women watched him walk to the bar.

'Quick, darling. Tell me everything you know about him . . . I can plan my strategy then.'

'Strategy for what?'

'For seduction, of course! I won't let a little thing like his being gay get in my way, you know!'

'Ah, well, you see, I may have given you the wrong end of the stick—'

'Oh, do look at David! Will he never learn?'

Helen followed Dahlia's gaze and saw David and one of the waiters exchanging money for a small paper wrap.

'What an idiot! I must stop him. Keep Piran here till I get back.'

Dahlia had leapt to her feet and was following David to the gents' loos.

Surely now, if she was quick, Helen could escape. But just as her brain was telling her body to stand up, Penny and Simon appeared, both giggling, and Simon very pink in the face.

'Hello, darling Helen. Are you having a lovely time?' gushed Penny. 'Simon's an amazing mover on the dance floor. Did you know he could jive?'

'West Country champion 1988.' Simon beamed. 'Helen, you haven't got a drink. You need a drink. I'll go and get you one. And another one for you too, Pen? Got to keep your jiving legs oiled. Ha ha.' He turned a little too fast and lost his balance slightly, but kept his path to the bar.

Penny sat down and gave out a huge breath. 'That man is amazing. He dances like a demon. And he's very funny when he's had a drink.'

'You look as if you've both had a couple of glasses!' Helen snapped wearily.

'Well, we had a bottle in my room earlier. Don't look at me like that! I was finishing some phone calls and so he waited upstairs with me rather than in the lobby like a spare pr-pr-priest at a wedding.'

Penny laughed loudly at her own joke.

'Anyway, Miss Femme Fatale,' she continued, 'how is the evening going for you? How is the hunt going for the future Mr Merrifield?'

Helen tried to answer, but Penny kept going: 'I see the ex-Mr Merrifield is here. He's plying all the girls with drink and regaling them with his interminable stories. They are lapping it up, the poor saps.'

'We had a bit of a row earlier. And, Penny, what are you doing getting Simon drunk? He isn't one of your London playboys, you know.'

But Helen had already lost Penny's attention. 'Well, hello, Piran! I didn't know you were coming tonight.'

'Good evening, Penny.' He passed Helen her drink. 'It's a St Clements. I thought alcohol wouldn't help your headache.'

'Thank you, Piran. I'm off in a minute, actually.'

'That's one of the few sensible things you've said. This isn't my sort of thing. I'd rather be in the pub.' Piran pulled on his tight collar.

Penny stopped them. 'Oh, you party poopers. You can't go until you've had at least one dance.' She caught sight of Simon, weaving his way unsteadily towards them with three glasses in his hand. 'Simon, take Helen to the dance floor immediately!' she commanded.

'Righty-ho, milady.' And he hauled Helen to her feet. She gave Piran a pleading glance but his attention was taken by an advancing Dahlia. Too late, she had him by the elbow and, too late, Helen found herself being twirled vigorously by Simon.

After three fast-paced numbers, Helen was puffing, perspiration running down her back. Her hot breath steamed in the cooling night air. She was no partner for Simon, whose dance technique was rather novel and quite unrelenting. He shouted at her above the noise: 'I thought I'd forgotten how to do this. My mother was very keen on dancing. A jitterbug champion during the war. Perhaps we'll start a dance class in the village. What do you think?'

He picked her up above his head and swooped her back down to the floor before she had time to reply. Her burgeoning headache was now bouncing around inside her skull. At last the band came to the end of the number and, breathing heavily, Helen told Simon she really ought to go.

'I have to be up early,' was her lame excuse.

'Certainly, of course. Penny told me you all have to catch up on the hour off you've had today.'

As they walked off the dance floor the band started up again with 'Big Spender'. From somewhere in the crowd came the sound of a powerfully deep woman's voice, singing along to the lyrics. There were several whoops from the crowd, and Penny heard David Cunningham's familiar voice cry out, 'Go, Dahlia!'

As the partygoers stepped back to create a space, Dahlia stood in the middle, looking like Rita Hayworth in *Gilda*, her hour-glass figure filling her clingy, red silk jersey dress, her brunette hair tumbling in careless curls around her face. She had one arm above her head, her face in silhouette, the other hand was holding up her skirt, revealing black stockings and a hint of bare thigh. As she sang she began to bump and grind her way towards Piran, who watched her darkly. He was leaning on the bar, close to the now-empty hot tub. The crowd melted from around him and Dahlia, the mongoose to his cobra, kept singing and undulating towards him. As she reached the steps of the hot tub she slipped her shoes off and, without stopping, still singing, stepped right into the bubbling water, her dress riding up to expose lacy stocking tops and black ribboned suspenders. She sank deeper into the water, still singing. Piran remained at the bar, a dangerous expression on his face.

Dahlia was now purring the last few bars of the song and, as she reached the final lyric, she stood up revealing shapely breasts clearly outlined beneath her clinging wet dress, reached towards Piran, took his hand and pulled him towards the water.

He shook her off immediately.

'What are you doing, woman? Get out, get dry and stop making a damn fool of yourself.'

Dahlia looked as if he had slapped her. 'What did you say?' she replied with menace.

'I said, get out and get dry. This isn't an 18–30 holiday.'

Dahlia leapt out of the pool like a tiger and flung herself at Piran.

'Piran, what the hell do you think you're doing?' A new voice joined in.

Piran, Dahlia and the crowd turned as one to see who the newcomer was.

'Dawn. I told you not to come.' Piran was struggling to grab Dahlia's wrists, but she was now winding herself round him like a Russian vine. 'What is it with you bloody women?' He finally threw Dahlia off and as she staggered towards the open, welcoming arms of Gray, Dawn advanced with speed.

'What are you doing with my fiancé?'

'Dawn, once and for all: I am not your fiancé.' Piran stood firm between the two women.

'Your fiancé? Honey, you're barking up the wrong tree.' Dahlia screamed. 'He's a faggot. Didn't you know?'

'Whaaat?' Dawn pulled herself up to her full five foot four inches and, with lightning speed she slapped Dahlia hard. Gray attempted to get between the two women but Dawn was pretty nifty with her knee too and he fell to the floor in pain.

'Come with me.' Helen grabbed Piran's hand and ran him out of the hotel and into her car.

36

They had driven out of the car park and were on the road leading out of Trevay before Piran spoke.

'I don't know about you, but I could do with a beer. We're too late for the pub, but I've got some at home if you want one.'

Helen thought for a moment. 'I'm not sure about a beer, but I'd love a cup of tea before I go home. Chloe has got male company and I'd rather stay out until the coast is clear.'

'In that case, take a left here.' In the dark, Helen swung her little Mini down a narrow dirt track with a dead-end sign on the corner.

She was very aware of Piran's bulk in the tiny front seat. The curls on his head flattened against the roof. She had never been this close to him in a confined space before. She was aware of his thigh almost touching the gear stick, the smell of him, fresh air after rain, seasalt mingling with his musky aftershave, starting to warm up something long cold in her being.

'Just here. Park on the grass by the gate. Or are you a typical woman who can't park?'

If these words had come from Gray, they would have been an insult. She looked at Piran and detected a teasing twinkle in his blue eyes.

She smiled. 'Yes, I can park and drive on motorways

and round Hyde Park corner without mishap, thank you.'

'Well, that's one better than me then.' He smiled at her and hauled himself out of the car and towards the gate. 'Come on, before I change my mind.'

He opened the unlocked front door and turned on the inside light. She stepped into the unmistakable room of a single man.

The slate floor was mostly covered with a threadbare rug and Jack's little basket. He toppled out to welcome them. The ceiling was low-beamed and drooping in the middle. A large, sagging sofa was covered in cat hairs. The owners of which, one black-and-white moggy, the other a tabby, were sprawled on the cushions. They looked sleepily up at Piran, then at Helen, then put their heads back on their paws, eyes shut. By the sofa lay a pile of newspapers and a shoe box of fishing lures. In the grate was a neatly laid fire, which Piran was now putting a match to. There was an old TV on an upside-down lobster pot, and above the fireplace a photo of a much younger Piran with a pretty girl.

Piran was loosening his bow tie. 'Put the kettle on and get a beer out of the fridge, would you?'

'What did your last servant die of?'

'I'm sorting out the fire for you.'

She shrugged and did as she was asked.

The kitchen was simple and relatively clean. The fridge held nothing more than a few bottles of beer, two mackerel on a blue-and-white striped plate, a carton of milk, six eggs and a lump of cheddar.

Jack came in, clicking his claws on the slate, and looking hopefully for a snack. Helen broke off a corner of cheese and gave it to him.

Looking for the mugs and beer glasses, she opened cupboards containing a car battery, fishing reels, a couple of bottles of sauce (red and brown) and a mis-matched selection of crockery and cutlery.

Carrying the tea and beer back into the other room, she found the cats tipped off the sofa and standing in disbelief on the rug. Piran had cleared a space for her and he motioned her to sit next to him.

'Here you are.' She handed him his glass and sat down. 'Cheers.' She raised her mug of tea in salute. 'Who's that young girl in the photo?'

'An old friend.'

'Ah.'

Silence but for the crackle of the kindling wood in the grate, and a gurgle from Helen's stomach.

'Are you hungry, Helen?'

'I am a bit. But I'll have something when I get home. I'll be off when I've had my tea.'

'Don't be so damned stupid. I'll make an omelette for you, if you like?'

Helen looked at him, her head on one side. 'Can you make omelettes?'

'I wouldn't offer if I couldn't. Stay there and tickle the cats. Black one's Bosun, the Tabby is Sprat.'

From the kitchen, Helen could hear the symphony of pots, pans, cupboard doors, plates and bowls as Piran set to work. Within what seemed like moments, he was back with steaming plates for both of them. They ate their cheese omelettes quickly and hungrily, and Helen had to admit hers was pretty good; she said as much.

'Comes from years of looking after myself.' He wiped his mouth on the kitchen-roll napkin and put his plate on the floor. Bosun and Sprat set about washing it clean.

'Piran, can I ask you something?'

He gave no acknowledgement of hearing the question, so she ploughed on.

'Why are you engaged to Dawn?'

Piran sighed. 'We are not engaged. She is vulnerable and needy, and I have got myself into a difficult situation. I'm a bit of a coward where relationships are concerned. But I have to tell her soon.'

'Yes, I could see that she's not really your kind of woman.'

'Ha.' He gave a short laugh. 'What is my kind of woman then?'

Feeling braver, Helen expanded: 'Well, someone not so high maintenance. Someone who isn't jealous and suspicious and . . . well . . . frankly, someone who isn't a bitch.'

He looked into his beer, and then back up at her. 'I did know someone like that. It was a long time ago . . . but it didn't work out.'

'What happened?'

He got up and put a log on the fire, then picked up the photo on the mantelpiece. 'This is Jenna – Don's sister. She died. It's a long time ago. I keep this picture so I'll never forget her face.'

Helen remembered. 'Dorrie told me a bit about that. Wasn't it New Year's Eve?'

'Yes. A hit-and-run. Never got the bastard. Dorrie and Don and her parents were devastated. We – Jenna and I – hadn't told them that we were going to live here in the cottage together. We were waiting till we'd signed the lease.'

'I'm so sorry. Were you going to be married?'

'I don't know. I'm not the marrying kind.'

'Dawn thinks you are. She's been talking to Simon and Dorrie about the service and the reception.'

'What Dawn says and what I know are two different things.'

'You mean, you're really not engaged?'

'No. And I'm no poof either – not that I'm anti-gay or anything, before you jump down my throat.'

Helen looked sheepish. 'I'm afraid that's my fault. I was trying to save you from Dahlia by throwing a few red herrings in her way. It didn't work though. She was determined to seduce you.'

'I should put you over my knee for that, but . . .' He was smiling and the smile soon turned to bubbling laughter, 'but, I've never seen anything so hilarious as Dawn and Dahlia brawling like that.'

Piran couldn't contain the guffaws which were bursting out of him. 'Ha ha . . . and that poor sod Gray, getting one between the legs . . .' He was wheezing now and Helen was laughing too. The cats were crouching with their ears at right-angles to their heads and their eyes as round as owls.

'What a tosser that Gray is! Whatever did you see in him?'

'God only knows. Do you think I'm insane and in need of help? Because he seems to think so. On account of my having left him.'

'No more mad than the average woman, no.'

'OK, let me run this by you: should I be angry with a man who spent twenty-five years cheating on me?'

'Yes.'

'Good. And do you think I'm crazy not to go back to him?'

'No.' He stopped laughing and smiled gently at her. 'I like you being here.'

'Do you? You could have fooled me.'

'Just a bit of teasing, Helen, that's all.'

'So if I'm going to stay here and stick to my guns, what are you going to do about Dawn?'

Piran walked over to Helen and sat next to her again. 'What would you have me do, maid?' He leaned into her and cupped her face gently with his hand. Helen felt a delicious tingle as he brushed her lips with his own. He pulled back and stood up again, smiling.

'Perhaps admitting to Dawn that I'm gay is a good idea after all?'

As Piran said this, there was an almighty bang and the front door crashed open, startling the cats, who skidded out into the night, and Jack who barked loudly. There, standing in the doorway, was a furious-looking Dawn, with a rather dishevelled Dahlia standing next to her.

'There, you see, he is gay!' Dahlia exclaimed dramatically to the rather wild-eyed Dawn by her side.

'You bastard!' Dawn yelled at Piran. 'Take that!' She pulled off the ring from her engagement finger and threw it at him. 'You owe me five hundred pounds for that. The wedding is off.'

With that, she stalked out of the cottage and into one of the two taxis waiting outside. The three left inside stood looking at each other, listening to the rattly diesel engine as it reversed back up the lane.

Dahlia broke the silence. 'I could do with a drink. What a night!'

*

Sitting on the floor with her back against the sofa, Dahlia wolfed down the last of her omelette, and wiped her lips on her ruined dress. She reached for her beer. 'That was delicious. Piran, thank you for making it.'

She bowed her head in a show of gratitude and raised her glass to him. 'I also have an apology to make to you. I am so sorry that I questioned your sexuality in such a public manner. No, no . . .' She held her hands up to stop him interrupting. 'I behaved appallingly. I wasn't quite myself. You see, I followed David to the gents' in order to stop him having his usual little toot of charlie, and found the only way from stopping him taking the lot was to share it with him. I haven't had any coke for years, and the buzz quite took me over. It doesn't excuse my behaviour, but I hope it explains it.'

Piran smiled wryly. 'You're not my type any way. Flighty, headstrong and an actress – recipe for disaster.'

'Your charm knows no bounds.' She bowed her head again. 'After the altercation with Dawn, she sped off in a taxi, and before I knew it I was commandeering my own taxi with the clichéd line, "Follow that cab!" I didn't know we'd end up here! Our dramatic entrance, just as you declared yourself to be gay, couldn't have been timed better . . . I take it you are not gay?'

'I am not.'

Despite her rather unkempt appearance, Dahlia was still able to bat her lashes flirtatiously in Piran's direction. Then she turned her gaze to Helen.

'You crafty cow! You could have told me that he was a) spoken for, and b) that you had your eyes on him.'

'Excuse me! I do not have my eyes on anyone. I have just come out of a very difficult marriage and am looking for nothing but friendship and peace.'

'Tell it to the birds, darling!' Dahlia took a deep draught of beer, tipping up the glass until it was empty. She let

out a satisfying burp. 'I understand that Gray is your
ex-husband?'

'Yes.'

'Not gay?'

'Definitely not.'

'Available?'

'Always – any time, any place.'

'Excellent. So you won't mind if I give him a whirl?'

'Be my guest. But the most reliable thing about him is
his unreliability.'

'Don't you worry about that. I'll give him a good run
for his money.' Dahlia looked at her watch and groaned.
'Oh god, look at the time! I have to be in make-up in five
hours. Can I crash here tonight?'

'No,' Piran answered quickly. 'Get in Helen's car and
we'll drive you back to the hotel.'

Piran took Helen's car keys and drove first to Gull's
Cry to drop Helen off. Since Dahlia was snoring in the
back, they left her there while Piran escorted Helen to
her front door.

Inside, they found a very drunk Gray waiting on the
sofa, with a very tired Chloe.

Gray stood up and, with all the belligerence he could
muster, slurred, 'Where the hell have you been, and why
is he here?'

Piran stepped in. 'Helen's just fine.' He turned to her:
'You'd better get some sleep. Thank you for an interesting
evening.'

They smiled quietly at each other before Gray interjected, 'What are you doing with my wife?' He had clumps
of spittle in the corners of his mouth.

Piran turned back to Gray. 'Come on, buddy. I'll give
you a lift back to the Starfish. I've got someone in the

car who'll be very pleased to see you.' He got a shoulder under Gray's arm and gathered him up.

'Goodnight, Chloe. Helen, I'll bring the car back tomorrow some time.'

As the door closed behind them, Chloe turned to Helen excitedly.

'Mummy, I'm going surfing in Sri Lanka with Mack.'

37

'Who would have thought that Dawn could pack such a punch! After she kneed Gray, the men wouldn't go near her. She turned again on Dahlia, forgetting that Dahlia had done all that kung fu training when she was a Bond girl. She was brilliant! Got Dawn in a headlock between her fabulous thighs and half-strangled her. When Dawn finally begged for mercy and was released, she ran off to the fire escape with Dahlia close behind. We looked over the roof and saw Dawn jump into a taxi, shortly followed by Dahlia. My God it was funny. The guys loved it. What a party!'

Penny was reeking of last night's booze and behind her enormous sunglasses her face was make-up free, with a couple of spots on her chin.

'What time did it all break up?' asked Helen.

'Late. But if you think I look terrible, you should see Simon.'

'He was already pissed when I found you. The last party he went to was the beetle drive. I wonder how he got home?'

'Well, don't go jumping to conclusions, but . . .'

'Oh my God. He stayed with you, didn't he?'

'No, no . . . Well, yes.'

'What?'

'In the sense that we shared a bed and slept in it, but all very chaste.'

'Yeah! You *chased* him all the way upstairs.'

'No. He was a bit tiddly, so was I, it was three in the morning and it seemed the sensible thing to do. He was a perfect gentlemen and treated me like a lady.'

Helen threw Penny an old-fashioned look.

'Anyway, now I've confessed, have you got any aspirin?'

'Yes, here.' Helen rummaged in her bag. 'Well, thank you for telling me. Poor Simon. Was he mortified when he woke up looking at your raddled mug?'

'No, actually. He was very sweet and endearingly shy. He got out of bed, wearing his pants – I did have a quick peek. Great bod!'

'That's the surfing.' Penny said automatically, trying to picture Simon in his pants. 'What kind of pants?'

'Cotton trunks. Grey.'

'I'd have taken him for a boxer man.'

'Me, too. But let me finish. He took his clothes into the bathroom, and once he was dressed he said goodbye and sped off.'

'Golly. Do you think he has ever spent the night in a lady's bed before?'

'I really don't know. And by the way, your quite detailed interrogation is making me feel uneasy.'

'It's just, I don't know, so adventurous for quiet old Simon.'

'Yes, well, quiet old Simon has another surprising talent. He's a great kisser.'

'Whaaaat?'

'Well, I wasn't going to tell you that bit. But, yes, he's a great kisser and, really, if he had given the signal . . . Well . . . who knows?'

'Oh my God, you were going to take advantage of him? But he's celibate. It's a solemn vow he's taken, Penny!'

'A definite elephant in the room.' Penny giggled.

'It's not funny.' Helen frowned in thought. 'You have to take this more seriously. Simon wants something permanent in his life, someone who loves him, and can fit into his church life, not some old London lush who is just after a good time. This is all my fault. I should have seen he was falling for me. I woke something up inside him.'

Penny pulled a face of disbelief. 'Hey, Mrs Big Head. It was me he was snogging in a five-star bed, not you! And why must you assume that I am just out to selfishly have a good time? I am capable of finer feeling, you know. And by the way, where did you and Piran piss off to? I saw you running off like a pair of schoolkids. Hand in hand.'

'We did not run off – and don't change the subject.'

'Yes, let's change the subject! What happened with Simon and me is our business. And you, Miss Helen the Pure, ran off into the night with the best-looking man at the party! What happened?'

'Promise you won't tell anyone?'

'You can trust your best mate.' Penny opened her arms wide and beamed at Helen.

'Yes. But since she isn't here, can I trust you?'

'Oh, very funny. Come on, fill me in – the set is off to a slow start this morning, due to the collective hangover. Let's talk now before all hell breaks loose.'

For the next half hour Penny listened as Helen told her about the row with Gray, the confidences that Piran, Dahlia and she had shared, the news that Chloe was finally spreading her wings and what had happened between Piran and herself.

'How did he kiss?'

'Pretty good. It wasn't full-on snogging, just lips touching, but there was a definite tingle between us.'

'And he's coming over today?'

'He's got to drop my car off.'

'And . . . ?'

'And what?'

'What are you planning for tonight?'

'I thought I'd just see how the land lies in the daylight first.'

'You're bloody useless.' Penny glanced out of the window and saw Gilly walking across the green towards the office, walkie-talkie in hand. 'I've got work to do. Text me when he turns up.'

*

Helen was finding it hard to concentrate on her work. In the end, she gave up and stood by the office window to watch for Piran to turn up with her car. At elevenses she wandered out to the catering truck for coffee and toasted teacake. She scanned the perimeter of the green. No Piran. She decided to eat her snack on the top deck of the dining bus, the better vantage point to scout for her familiar little Mini.

Her quietly ordered life had turned upside down in the last twenty-four hours. Her best friends, Simon and Penny, were on the brink of something that Helen really wasn't sure she was happy about. She loved them both, but individually, not as a couple. And now her heart was doing pole vaults every time she thought of Piran. What the hell was happening to her?

Within moments she was joined by Dahlia, who enveloped her in a perfumed air-kiss.

'Mwah, mwah, darling. How's your head?'

'I'm fine. How are you coping with yours?'

'I ignore it. It's the professional in me. I am never late and I never pretend to be ill.'

'Apart from feigning a sprained ankle to pull Piran?'

Dahlia pulled a sorrowful face. 'You've got me there. Anyway, don't you want to know how your ex behaved when we got back to the Starfish last night?'

'Not particularly.'

'OK. If you don't want to hear the latest on Piran, that's your business.'

Dahlia made a move as if to leave. Helen looked up and stopped her.

'OK. I'm interested. Tell me.'

'Well, I think I must have had a little doze in the back seat . . .'

'You were smashed.'

'. . . but when we go to the Starfish, I woke up to hear Piran and Gray talking about you and me. Naturally, I pretended to still be asleep.'

'Naturally. What were they saying?'

'Piran was being rather sweet about me, actually. He told Gray not to mess me about, as he could see I was a nice woman who—'

'What did he say about me?'

'I'm getting to it! So, he was doing a really good job of pointing out my attractions to Gray, who, rather sweetly I thought, said that I was "a walking wet dream". Isn't that lovely?'

'Well, that's Gray all over. He's about as useful as a wet dream.'

'Now, let's not fall out. You did give me permission to toy with him, didn't you?'

This was clearly a rhetorical question, so Helen didn't bother to answer.

'Anyway, then Gray starts arguing with Piran about you. Really angry. Accusing Piran of using your fragile mental state to—'

'Oh, for God's sake! I am NOT mad!'

'Listen: using your fragile mental state to take advantage of you. He said, "Keep your hands off my wife, and her money. Which happens to be *my* money anyway."'

'The little shit! It's *my* money. How dare he!'

'Wait, there's more. Piran told him to get out of the car and go to bed before he did something he'd regret. So Gray got out of the car and shouted to Piran, "Why don't you marry your sister. Isn't that what you inbreds do down here?" Well, that was it. Piran moved like a bullet. He was on to Gray like a flash and threw him on to the bonnet of the car.'

'Oh my God! Is he all right?'

'Well, I leapt out of the car – you really need a bigger one, darling. It's jolly difficult in a tight dress to—'

'Get on with it!'

'I ran up the steps to the hotel and roused the night porter, who took one look at the brawl on his doorstep and rang the police. Not what we needed at all! I ran back to the boys, still both slugging it out, but now on the pavement. I told them the police were coming and to scarper PDQ. By the time the cops arrived – two adorable young men, by the way – Piran had driven off and I had given Gray my room key and told him to mop himself up.'

'He's got his own room at the Starfish.'

'Never mind that. So, when the police arrived I was waiting for them on my own. I apologised for wasting their time and told them that a couple of fans of mine had got a little rowdy. Nothing to worry about. It turned out that my Bond film was one of their favourites, so we had photos all round, a couple of autographs, and Dahlia saved the day.'

'How does Gray look?'

'Ghastly. A bruised cheek and, when I looked this morning, some rather angry-looking red scratches on his back. Mind you, that might have been me.' She smiled innocently up at Helen, who returned a weary smile.

'You mean, after all that, he could still perform?'

'Beautifully.'

Helen snorted a small laugh down her nose.

'I think you two could be made for each other.'

'Thank you.' Dahlia took Helen's hand and squeezed it. 'I'd better get back to work. We are in the church today for the funeral of Lord Trimsome. That bloke who won your local talent show has his big close-up today.'

'Oh yes, Tony's big day! I'll see if I can slip in as an extra.'

Helen looked out of the bus window again, scouting for her car or Piran. But there was still no sign.

38

A couple of hours later, there was still no sign of him, so Helen busied herself working on a spreadsheet for Penny. Try as she might to focus, she found herself thinking about Piran every ten minutes or so. She worked through lunch. No one disturbed her.

It wasn't until about two that she pushed her chair back from her desk, stretched her arms above her head and walked to the kitchen to make a cup of tea. As she was putting the bag in the mug, she heard the front door open.

Gray's voice called out, 'Helloo.'

Her shoulders sagged. Just the person she didn't need. She returned to the office.

'Hello, Helen, darling.' At least he had the grace to look sheepish. 'How are you?'

'Fine, Gray, thank you.' She tried to sound breezy. 'Did you enjoy the party?'

'Not much.'

'Liar. Dahlia told me the end of the evening was spectacular.'

Gray immediately perked up. 'Did she? What else did she say?'

'I am not inflating your fat head further. Your black eye and swollen cheek are doing that themselves.'

'Ah yes!' Gray took on an aggressive but wounded

stance, stroking his painful cheek. 'Your caveman boyfriend did this to me. Totally unprovoked. I warn you that if you continue your relationship with him, you will be yet another statistic in the ugly stain of domestic abuse.'

'Nothing to do with you calling him an inbred who should marry his sister then?'

Gray puffed out his chest and pulled himself up to his full six foot three.

'He's a bully-boy who will only make you unhappy. I can look after myself, and I gave him a couple of punches that hurt. But you, Helen, won't be able to defend yourself.'

'I don't need to defend myself from him. He's a sweet, kind man.'

'So was Crippen.'

Helen sighed. 'Have you come here just to warn me off Piran, or is there another reason?'

'As it happens, there is another reason, yes. I wanted to do the honourable thing and let you know something before anybody else told you. Dahlia and I slept together last night.'

'I know, she told me.'

Gray pulled up a chair and leant forward anxiously. 'Did she really say I was all right?'

'Yep.'

'I'm so sorry if it hurts you, darling.'

'I am completely inoculated against you, Gray.'

'Yes, but . . . a tiny part of you must find this very difficult.'

'No.'

'Not even a bit?'

'No, though that is clearly what you want me to feel.'

Gray sat back in his chair and looked defeated. 'I can't

believe how lucky I was to have you and how stupid not to realise what a treasure you are to me.'

'Gray, you are a huge shit, but I wouldn't have missed any of it. Friends?'

'Friends.'

They stood and gave each other a long hug. Finally they broke apart and Gray said, 'I'm always here for you, you know that.'

'You mean, you're always there for me as long as it's not while you're with Dahlia, or watching the football or going to cricket or . . .'

'OK, you've made your point. Just promise me one thing: that you won't let Piran into your life.'

'I no longer have to promise you anything, Gray.'

*

Another couple of hours went past and the door opened again, bringing with it the damp smell of early spring. Helen looked up hopefully. But it wasn't Piran, it was Simon, looking utterly wretched. His shoulders were hunched, his head down.

'Simon, what on earth's the matter?'

To her astonishment, he burst into tears and leant himself against the wall.

'Here, sit down.'

He sat and put his head in his hands. The tears kept flowing and his breathing was ragged.

'Oh, Helen, I am not worthy of my calling. I can no longer be of spiritual guidance to the village, or call myself a vicar.' Fresh tears sprang from his eyes and heaving sobs left him bent double over his knees.

'Is this about Penny?'

He mumbled something.

'What?'

'Yes, it's Penny.'

'OK. Do you want to tell me about it?'

He sat up and she saw such misery in his beautiful chocolate-brown eyes that she got up and knelt by his side, her hand on his knee.

He took out a handkerchief, blew his nose and wiped his eyes.

'Dear Helen. I have sinned. I slept with Penny in her bed last night.'

Helen pretended not to know this already.

'Is that a sin?'

'Not in itself. But I . . . kissed her. Passionately. I have reneged on my vow to God.' He started crying again.

'I don't think you have. I think you are a normal man who wants to love and be loved in return.'

'Oh, I do, I do. I have had so many disappointments. And then I stupidly scared *you* off as well. I just feel such a failure. A failure to myself, to God . . .' Fresh crying.

'Now that's self-pity. Stop it.' Helen put both hands on his shoulders and turned them towards her. His face followed reluctantly. 'What I see is a lovely person. A sincere man of God. A good vicar. And a handsome, funny, kind man.'

'You do?'

'Yes.'

'Then why did you reject me?'

This was a tough question to answer without hurting him.

'Because . . .' She paused. 'Because I am not right for you. I am selfish and like my own space. I love our friendship because we don't own each other. I want my freedom, and you deserve more than I can offer.'

'Is that the only reason? It's not because of anything else?'

'Nothing else.'

He sat quietly, thinking and wiping his eyes. Her thighs were beginning to ache in her crouched position, so she stood up.

'Would you like me to put the kettle on?'

'No, thank you. But would you do me a huge favour?'

'Anything.'

'Would you talk to Penny about me and find out what she feels? Last night was wonderful and shaming, but I can't stop thinking about her. Only, I don't think I can bear to be hurt again.'

'Should I tell her we have talked?'

'Yes, but please don't tell her I have made a spectacle of myself.'

'What spectacle? You are a human being, just like the rest of us.'

He hugged her hard and kissed her cheek. 'Thank you, dearest Helen.'

She watched his familiar form lope back to the vicarage, red eyes hidden beneath his muffler and specs.

'Bloody Penny!'

It took her a long time to get her mind back on the spreadsheet.

*

It was only a matter of minutes before she was disturbed again. Jako stuck his head round the door and said, 'Helen, your mate Tony is asking for you. We're all set up ready to shoot Trimsome's funeral, and it's his big moment.'

Helen looked at her desk, then thought, *Sod it.* She grabbed her coat and ran after Jako.

The church was warm and bright under the large lights. There were lights out in the churchyard too, shining through the stained glass and making the interior shot look fantastic.

Lord Trimsome's coffin was draped in his red and ermine Lords gown and coronet, with a simple hand-tied posy of garden flowers placed on top.

The pews were full of villagers dressed in their 'extras' costumes. Queenie resplendent in a green velvet cape sitting next to Polly in a deep purple and lace-bodiced gown. They both wore glorious bonnets with dark veils. They didn't see Helen, who kept to the shadows round the edge of the church. Penny found her.

'Hi. Glad you could make it. Piran turned up yet?'

Helen tried to look nonchalant. 'Not yet.'

Seeing the anxiety in Helen's face, Penny changed the subject. 'Tony's remarkably relaxed. I've just had a chat with him. Do you know what he's singing?'

'"Ernie – The Fastest Milkman in the West"?' Helen said with a straight face.

Penny laughed. 'No, you loon. "Dido's Lament" from Purcell's *Dido and Aeneas.* The singing coach says Tony is fantastic, a natural counter tenor. He's worked really hard on it.'

There was a flurry of activity at the vestry door. 'There he is.'

Helen saw an angelic-looking Tony walking to his position in the choir with a dozen other men and boys dressed appropriately. Tony's unmissable dark, sleek head just a fraction taller than everybody else's.

Sven went to chat quietly to the choir. Helen saw Tony listen carefully and nod his head once or twice. He looked very composed.

As Sven walked back to behind the camera, Make-up and Costume stepped in and did their stuff. When they had finished, Gilly called, 'Quiet please. Turnover.'

'Running,' said the camera operator.

'Scene two hundred and seventy-four, shot seventeen, take one. Action.'

The old organ began playing the opening bars and suddenly Tony's voice flew like a dove up into the beautifully vaulted ceiling, sweeping around the heads of the awestruck audience, and straight into their hearts. Polly was the first to start weeping, followed by Helen, Penny, Gilly and Sven. Queenie sat ramrod straight with a proud smile on her face.

When the music finished and Gilly said 'Cut', there was a silence and then a storm of applause. Tony shuffled from foot to foot, beaming out at Queenie, who gave him a big wave.

'Was I all right?'

Sven bounded up to him. 'Tony, you were wonderful! We're going to do this several more times and from different angles to make sure we get lots of it. Are you OK for that?'

'Yeah.' Tony laughed. 'I'm with you all the way.'

They did it all again a number of times, and with each take Tony's voice rang out clearly and beautifully. Within the hour, Sven was happy.

He called to everyone, 'We've got it. That was fantastic, everyone. Let's have a very big round of applause for our soloist, Mr Tony Brown.'

The congregation and crew rose to their feet with a noisy appreciation of the star in their midst.

Helen didn't have time to fight through the crowd to congratulate him. She promised herself she'd find him later, but now she really had to finish her work.

The early March sun was starting to set but the nights were definitely getting lighter. As she walked through the churchyard, to the lich-gate and her office beyond, a dark figure stepped out and lightly touched her arm.

It was Piran.

39

'I 've brought your car back. Sorry I'm so late.'

She looked up into his extraordinary face. Tanned, straight nose, desperately kissable lips and his blue eyes full of the sea.

'That's OK.'

'Are you in tonight?'

Her heart skipped a little. 'Yes.'

'Can I come over. About eight?'

'Of course.'

He gave her her keys back.

'See you then.'

She finished her work in record time. When Penny came to check on her, it was all printed off and in a folder.

'There you go.'

'Thank you, Hels.' Penny looked suspiciously at her radiant, smiley friend. 'Piran's been then, I take it?'

'What makes you think that?'

'The radio is on, you are singing and your desk is clear. I get the feeling you want me out of here so that you can lock up. Oh, and your car is parked outside your house again!'

'Penny, I'm so excited. He's coming over to see me tonight!'

'Is he? Oohh! Promise to tell me all tomorrow?'

'Maybe.' Helen was suddenly serious. 'But there is something I nearly forgot in my excitement. Simon came round in a very bad way. He wants me to talk to you about him.'

'A bad way? You mean, regretting what happened last night?'

'No, no. But, I think you have tested his faith. In himself and in his calling. He wants me to test the water with you, I think. To see if you are serious about a relationship with him.'

Penny stared at Helen. 'Oh my God! He wants commitment?'

'Simon is a man of God, Penny, and not given to throwing himself into casual relationships. He has been hurt before, very badly, and if you can't treat him in the right way then you should just walk away now and leave him alone.'

'Oh, crap. I don't know. I like him. A lot, as it happens. The first decent man I've ever met who wasn't already spoken for. But it's complicated. I mean, he lives here and I live in London, sometimes LA, and long-distance stuff is difficult, isn't it? Anyway, I can't quite see myself as a vicar's wife, can you?'

'Don't jump the gun! But don't toy with him, either. What about if you took it slowly?'

'You're right. Shall I call him tonight?'

'Yes.'

'OK, I will. See you tomorrow then. Have a good night yourself.'

'I won't, if you don't go right now! Bye!'

*

'Mummy, would you like me to stay in case things get violent?'

Helen looked up sharply. 'What's Daddy been saying?'

'He's a bit worried about you, that's all. You must admit, Piran is an unknown quantity . . . apart from being given to unprovoked attacks.'

'Daddy started it, not Piran. But if you want to hang about, then be my guest. I have nothing to hide.'

'Well, Mack and the lads are coming over in about half an hour, but I could put them off.'

Helen smiled. 'Go out with the boys. I'll be fine.'

Dear, sweet Chloe. She had decided she wasn't going back to Bristol or her job. She had given her landlord notice on her flat and was spending every minute with Jako, Haz and Mack (short for Mackerel, apparently), planning their three-month trip to the other side of the world. Chloe was changing every day. Her skin was gently tanned by the wind, her freckles blooming on her nose. Her hair, always so sleek and shiny before, was now a glorious tangle of stiffened, seasalt-covered curls. She was belatedly turning into a woman, and a beautiful one at that. Helen could see, without having to ask, how bowled over she was by Mack. And he by her. Dorrie had known him since he was six or seven and first started coming down to Cornwall on family holidays. She'd given Helen the full SP on his parents, and proclaimed them good, hard-working people from the Midlands. Mack, she reckoned, could be trusted, adding darkly, 'at least, as far as any young man can be trusted with a beautiful young girl'.

Helen waved Chloe and the boys off as they jumped into the VW camper van with the legend LOVE SURF hand-painted on the side.

She had half an hour to look as if she hadn't bothered to get ready for Piran. Shower, leg shave, minimal make-up, hair piled casually on top of her head, skinny white leggings and over-sized blue-and-white striped man's shirt on top. She undid an extra button to reveal her pretty pink-and-green floral bra, and just as quickly did it up again.

Out of the corner of her eye she saw Piran's Toyota truck pull up outside. Two minutes to eight. Early. A good sign. One last look in the mirror, checking her teeth for lip-gloss, and she went downstairs, opening the front door just as he lifted his hand to knock.

'Hi, come in. Excuse the mess.'

'If this is mess, my house is a landfill.'

His tall bulk blocked the door and cast a shadow over her face. Why didn't he move? She realised she was standing still and blocking his way.

'Come in, come in. What would you like to drink? Gin and tonic? Wine?'

'I'd like a beer.'

Damn, why hadn't she thought of that? 'Oh, I haven't got any beer. Whisky?'

'Aye, just a large one.'

As she moved past him to go to the cupboard by the sink, which was her drinks cabinet, he took her elbow and spun her round to face him.

Helen felt like she was in a scene from a Barbara Cartland novel. Time slowed so that she took in every millimetre of his face, his eyes, his hair, before his mouth bent to hers and finally he kissed her, properly. With passion and a depth she'd not known since the early days of Gray. She pressed herself against him and cupped his face with both hands. His right hand slid round her waist and his left hand reached into her hair, winding his fingers through it.

They broke apart and looked at each other.

'Golly,' she said.

'Good God, woman, is that all you can say? "Golly."' He imitated her London accent and made her laugh.

'What do you want me to say?'

'"Come upstairs, Piran, and make love to me" would be suitable.'

Helen took his hand and without saying anything, took him up to her bedroom.

He closed the door and kissed her again. They undressed each other, the feel of skin on skin so wonderful that they stood and hugged for a moment until Helen took his hand once more and, sitting on the bed, pulled him down to her. She closed her eyes and drank in the scent of his body and the feel of his body on hers. This was the point of no return. For the first time in over twenty-five years, another man made love to her.

*

'Golly,' she said a little while later as she lay in the crook of his arm, her head on his chest.

'How about "Holy shit" for a change?' He kissed the top of her head.

'Holy shit.'

'That's better. Shall I get you a drink?'

'I'd love a cup of tea.'

'I like your style. I'll put the kettle on. Don't move, I'll be back.'

She watched him as he wandered, naked, through the door and downstairs. She could hear him opening cupboards and running the tap. She lay in her bed just as he had left her. Happier than she could remember. Feeling sexy, wanton and wicked. 'Up yours, Gray!' she said to herself.

He came back up the stairs.

'Where shall I put the tray?'

'Just there on the dressing table.'

'I've made you gunpowder tea.'

'Oooh! What's that?'

'Ordinary tea but with a slug of whisky in it.'

He passed her her mug and she tasted it. 'Mmmm, that will put hairs on your chest.'

'You bet.' He climbed back into bed and she settled on to his shoulder again.

They drank the tea in companionable silence for a few minutes.

'Your husband all right today?'

'Black eye and bruised cheek.'

'Good. He was out of order last night.'

'Dahlia told me.' Another silence. 'Have you seen or heard from Dawn?'

He took a great sigh and shifted slightly, making her neck uncomfortable, so she sat up and moved away from him.

'Yes.'

She didn't think she was going to like this. 'And?'

'She wants me back. I came over to say goodbye to you.'

Helen moved like a scalded cat. She sat up and turned to face him, swinging her open palm at his face, but he caught it.

'I'm joking. I'm joking.'

'It's a stupid fucking joke. Don't you ever do that again.'

She got out of bed and put her dressing gown on, feeling suddenly vulnerable.

He got out of bed and held her. 'Hey, I'm sorry. I didn't mean to upset you. I haven't seen her. I don't want to see her, but I must at some stage.' He tilted her head up to his and kissed her gently. 'Forgiven?'

She kissed him back as an answer, but when Chloe got back later that night all she found was two middle-aged, fully dressed people sitting on the sofa eating spaghetti bolognaise from one large bowl and watching *Newsnight*.

40

The following morning was Saturday and the cast and crew had the weekend off. Helen was brewing tea and making porridge as Chloe came in, yawning, her hair like a bird's nest.

'Morning, Mum.'

'Hello, darling, did you have a good night?'

'Yes. Sorry, I was so tired when I got in – I hope Piran didn't think it rude of me to go straight to bed.'

'No. He quite understood.'

Helen turned her back to Chloe to stir the porridge, hiding a ridiculously soppy smile.

'So, what's going on with you two? I thought you didn't like him.'

'Erm . . .' Helen thought quickly. 'He's not too bad once you get to know him and . . .' inspiration came to her: 'He's interested in finding out more about that treasure box, the one that Tony and I found in the garden.'

'Oh, good. When will he start?'

'I'm not sure. Soon, I hope.'

The phone rang. Chloe got there first.

'Hello? . . . Hi, Piran. Yeah, Mum's fine. I hear you're going to be examining her old box . . . What are you laughing for? Oh, you've had a good look at it already. Great. Mum's here, if you want to talk. Bye.'

Helen wrenched the receiver from her daughter's hand.

She could hear Piran's deep laughter coming down the line.

'Mornin', maid. How's that old box of yours? It seemed in pretty good nick to me.' He laughed again, then stopped and said, 'You're a good woman, Helen Merrifield.'

For some reason tears sprang to her eyes. The tenderness of his voice and the fact he was actually bothering to phone caught her unawares. She sat down in her rocking chair by the Aga.

'I was wondering what you might be doing for lunch today,' she asked. 'Would you like to come over?'

He paused then said, 'I must see Dawn and talk to her about everything.'

'Ah. Would you like to come over after?'

'Do you want me to look at your old box again?'

She laughed. 'You're a bad man, Mr Ambrose.'

'I'll be there ASAP. See you later, Helen.'

When she had put the phone down, she sat in a dream, her body warm with sensual thoughts.

'Mum!' Chloe was pointing at the Aga. 'The blinking porridge is burning.'

*

After breakfast, Chloe went back to bed and Helen sat by her Aga with the back door open, letting in the spring sunshine. Tony popped his head round the door.

'Mornin', Mrs M.'

'Hello, Tony.' She jumped up and gave him a huge hug. 'Well done for yesterday. You were amazing!'

He shifted uncomfortably on his feet and scratched an ear.

'They said I'd done all right.'

'You did indeed. I am very proud of you. Fancy a Ribena?'

'Yes, please.' He stood by the back door, refusing her offer of a chair. 'We ought to start talking about potting up the seeds for the vegetable plot, Mrs M.'

'I'm ready when you are, Tony. Only another week before the filming finishes. Then I'm all yours.'

There was a knock at the door.

'Come in,' Helen called.

It was Simon.

'Mornin', vicar.'

'Tony my boy, you were magnificent yesterday. Well done.' He shook Tony's hand.

Tony grinned. 'Mrs M., I'm going to make a start on them seed beds. I can use the new spade you bought me.'

'Good idea,' said Helen. 'If you need anything, give me a shout.'

'Righto.' And with that he wandered back out into the sunshine.

Helen turned to assess Simon.

'You look so much better than yesterday, Simon. How are you feeling?' She moved to the kettle and reached for a couple of mugs.

Simon settled himself against the sink.

'Penny and I had a long talk yesterday.'

'And . . . ?'

'She has agreed to join me for dinner tonight.'

'Excellent. Where are you taking her?'

'Well, that's just it. The Dolphin looks like I haven't bothered and the Starfish is a bit . . . you know, the other night . . . Well, let's say some neutral ground would be best.'

'How about a picnic up on the moor? Dozmary Pool.

Isn't that where Excalibur was thrown? The lady of the lake and all that?'

'It'll be dark.'

'Just the stars, the moon and each other. Tell her to wrap up warm.'

'But what shall we eat?'

'Simon!' She looked at him sternly, her hands on her hips. 'Food should be last thing on her mind!'

He blushed. 'Helen, it's only a picnic!'

'That's easy then. A flask of soup and ham-and-cheese sandwiches.'

'Are you sure?' His anxious chocolate-brown eyes widened through his specs.

'Trust me, they're her favourite.'

'Thank you.'

'My pleasure.'

Helen handed him his cup of coffee and ushered him into the lounge, bright in the morning sun.

He settled into her patchwork armchair, with the air of a man who needed to talk.

'Helen, I need to thank you so very much for everything you've brought to me over these last six or seven months.'

'I haven't done anything.'

'No, no,' he shushed her. 'You have kindly not referred to my embarrassing behaviour on the night of the bishop's dinner.'

'It wasn't embar—'

'Please, let me finish.' He took a deep breath and removed his glasses, polishing them on his handkerchief, before putting them back on again.

'I must share my feelings with you. Helen, you are the first normal woman who has ever been a friend to me. Denise, who jilted me, was a gentle, sweet person, but too tied to her parents' apron strings. Perhaps too immature to take on a husband and . . . the physical side of love.'

Helen nodded sagely.

'And, Hillary . . . well, Hillary just wasn't ever going to live in a heterosexual relationship.'

Helen tuned in more intently.

'Sorry, Simon. What was that?'

'Hillary is a gay woman.'

'Blimey, you kept her quiet, and no wonder!'

'Well, exactly. Which is why I felt I was falling in love with you. You are kind, and affectionate and . . . very attractive.'

'Oh, Simon. I love our friendship and closeness. I want it to continue – but platonically.'

'And so it shall. But here's the difficult part. I've suddenly realised that I have very strong feelings for Penny. I know she's brash and loud and promiscuous . . .'

'Steady on, that's my mate you're talking about.'

'But I find her so incredibly . . . sexy! I don't think I have ever used that word out loud to anyone before.'

Helen laughed. 'Yes, she is sexy. And has been hurt many times because of it. Can I ask you a very personal question?'

'Go ahead.'

'Are you a virgin?'

'I think so.'

'You either are or you aren't,' Helen said gently.

Simon looked very uncomfortable. 'When I was a boy, about fourteen, at the church youth club, we had a leader called Mrs Bening.'

Helen leaned forward, her blood starting to thrum in her ears. She didn't think she'd like what she was going to hear.

'And?'

'We were on a Sunday walk with all the other children and she asked me to stand by a stile in a field, to count the children over it to make sure we hadn't lost anyone. When the last one, my friend Steven, had gone over, she told them all to carry on across the field to the next stile. When they had their backs turned she got up on the stile and sat on the top, holding her hand out for me. I could see Steven walking away and I wanted to catch up with him, so I climbed up, but she stopped me going over the stile. She took my hand and put it on her breast. Then she put her lips on mine and forced her tongue into my mouth. She had horrible breath.'

Simon carefully put his coffee cup down and put his head in his hands. His fingers pressed tight against his eyes. His shoulders started to heave. Helen went to him and put her arm round him.

'Did she do anything else?'

'She undid my shorts and put her mouth around me.' He turned his head up to her and through tear-streaked eyes he said, 'Then she told me we had had sex.'

'And ever since, you've wondered if it was?'

He nodded his head miserably.

'I can categorically tell you, you are still a virgin,' said Helen.

'I remember her touch, and it shames me, but it was nice too. God forgive me.'

'God does forgive you. It's that bloody woman who's going to have a few awkward questions to answer at the pearly gates. Do you know where she is now? It's not too late to bring her to court.'

'I don't want anything to do with her. I just want to cleanse myself of the shame.'

'Did you tell anyone?'

'No. I can't believe I have finally told you.'

'It's nothing for you to feel ashamed of. It is *her* shame. There are people who can help you. Therapists. The doctor.'

'The church might find out.'

'And what will they do? Turn their backs? I think they're pretty used to this sort of thing. I liked the bishop when we met him. I bet he would be really sympathetic, and help you, if you wanted it.'

'I want to tell Penny.'

'Tell her. The good thing about a woman who's been round the block is that she doesn't judge.'

'She might not like me in that way.'

'That's not what she told me about the other night.'

'Oh God no . . . what?'

'You kissed her.'

'I did?'

'Yup, and she liked it very much.'

'But my vow of chastity?'

'It was only kissing and anyway, how big a deal is this vow?'

'It is my vow to God.' He looked at her, shocked that she should ask such a stupid question. She tried a different tack.

'Your last sermon was about the one message God has for us all. And what is that message?'

'Love.'

'Precisely. I think God wants you to have love in your personal and private life. Proper grown-up love. Not weirdo Mrs Bening, lesbian Hillary and ninny Denise-type love. I think, maybe, God has sent Penny to you, and he has sent you to Penny!'

Helen surprised herself with this sudden clarity of thought. Simon and Penny had a chance to really make each other happy. Conveniently forgetting her pangs of jealousy and doubt about them both, she now felt rather smug at having played Eros.

She took his hand and pulled him up. 'Right, Tiger, let's make you a picnic.'

*

She sent him off with a cool box, wine glasses, crockery, cutlery, a clean baked bean tin with a small bunch of daffs in it and a shopping list to include candles, a torch and a waterproof-backed rug.

'Tell me how it goes, won't you?'

'I will, dear Helen. Thank you.' He gave her a squeeze and kiss on the cheek and was off.

41

Helen closed the front door and was about to sink into her comfy armchair the better to think about her night with Piran and what it did or didn't mean, when Chloe shouted from the top of the stairs:

'Mum, Mack's here. Would you let him in while I dry my hair?'

'Yes, love.' She did an about turn and opened the front door to the tall and gorgeous Mack, who bent his head to avoid hitting it on the door lintel.

'Hello, Mrs Merrifield.' He gave her a kiss.

'Hi, Mack. I'll put the kettle on, shall I? Chloe's on her way.' She put the kettle on the stove and then set out a couple of mugs. 'So how are the preparations coming along for Sri Lanka?'

'Yeah, good. Can't wait.' He fiddled with his car keys, then blurted, 'I will look after her, Mrs M.'

She set down the tea caddy and looked at him carefully. 'You'd better!'

*

Once the lovers had gone, and Helen was washing up the umpteenth mug that morning, she heard Tony laughing in the garden.

'Mrs M., come quick like. Mr Ambrose's car looks all funny.'

Oh my God, had he had an accident? She looked out of the kitchen window and started laughing too.

She was still laughing when she met Piran, with a face like thunder, midway down the front path.

'Bloody woman! She's a frigging nutcase. Look what she's done to my car.'

Piran's Toyota truck was unrecognisable. It had a lot of Barbie pink paint thrown all over it. The windscreen wipers were bent at right angles to the bonnet and the radio aerial had been twisted to look like a two-fingered salute.

'Look at the back!' He grabbed Helen's hand and showed her: TOOT IF YOU THINK I'M A TWAT had been painted on the tailgate.

Helen put her hand to her mouth to keep her laughter in. 'Oh dear. Did anyone toot?'

'Only all the way here.'

'So, Dawn took the news well then?'

Piran gave Helen a chilling look. 'Sorry, Piran. It was just a joke.'

'I know. It just pisses me off that that woman should be so petty.'

'It is funny, though.'

'It might be later.' A wry smile threatened to break through his thundery expression.

She put her arm round his waist and led him back into the cottage.

Tony, who had been standing there taking it all in, called out, 'Would you like me to wash it for you?'

Piran stopped at the front door and smiled gratefully.

'That would be a very kind thing. Yes please, young Tony. I'll pay you for your time.'

*

They were back in Helen's big comfy bed, the afternoon sun slanting through the gap in her curtains and warming the room.

'So what happened?' Helen asked Piran.

'The earth moved.'

She dug him in the ribs. 'Not that! When you saw Dawn.'

'She bashed me with a tea tray, and set about my car. That's about it.'

'What did you see in her in the first place?'

Piran took a deep breath then blew it out through puffed cheeks. 'She was a client. I sometimes do people's family trees. It's a pain in the arse and takes ages, but she was paying me well and I had decided it would be the last one I'd do. When I saw you and Penny at the Starfish that night, it was the first time I'd gone out with her. She invited me over to talk about the research I had, and what she could tell me, and before I knew it she was . . . there. All the time.'

'But you proposed to her?'

He fidgeted uncomfortably and held her a bit tighter.

'We went down to Truro, to have a look at some parish records, and while we were in town she dived into a jeweller's. Before I could open my mouth, she'd chosen a ring – the one she threw at me the other night – a fake diamond. She was all over me in the shop, smiling and joking with the salesgirl and then, when we left, she took me to lunch and made a toast. "To us," she said. And the next thing I know, everyone's congratulating me and I don't know what for.'

'You must have given her some encouragement?'

'Nothing. She came to "Pendruggan's Got Talent" without telling me. She was waiting for me outside in the car park. I couldn't really tell her not to come in. When she was so rude to Tony, I gave her a right talking to.'

The angrier Piran got, the more his Cornish accent came out. 'I'm sorry I left you in the church that night, but I was embarrassed at her behaviour and just wanted to get out of there. It was the same on Christmas night. I wanted to come and have a drink with you, but . . .'

'But . . . well, that was then.'

'Yes, that was the past.' Piran kissed her nose. 'Which reminds me, I think I have found something interesting that may solve some of the mysteries in that old tin box you found.'

'Really! Oh, Piran, how exciting! Let's go down to the kitchen so we can have a look at it.'

In minutes they were sitting beside each other at Helen's kitchen table over steaming mugs of tea, Helen in her dressing gown and Piran in his boxers. In front of them was the open tin box, revealing its contents.

'Right. Tell me what you think you've found?' Helen was all ears.

Piran started: 'There are nine graves in the churchyard that I could not identify. The headstones had disappeared – most likely they'd have been wooden crosses that rotted away over time. Three of the coffins I came across had brass nameplates on them, and they are being cleaned up now to see if we can make out who they belong to. I also found an old urn, which I am assuming contains ashes, though I haven't looked. And it had a brass name-plate on it too, which I got the restorer to have a go at first.'

'And?'

'This is where it gets interesting. When the results came back, it had two names on it. H.A. Wingham and B.G. Wingham with the date fifteenth April 1912. What does that tell you?'

'Nothing.'

'Think, woman! What did they teach you at school?'

'I don't know! You'll have to tell me.'

'It's the date that the *Titanic* sank, with the loss of around fifteen hundred lives.'

Helen looked at him, totally lost. 'And what? The shock of hearing about it caused these two people to die in Pendruggan?'

She could tell Piran was irritated. He banged his fist on the table, causing the teapot to jump.

'For Heaven's sake, Helen! It wasn't as common in those days for bodies to be cremated. So, perhaps these two poor souls perished at sea and their bodies were taken by rescue ships to Halifax in Nova Scotia, where they'd have been put in a makeshift mortuary to be identified. Maybe the relatives back in Pendruggan couldn't afford to have two bodies repatriated, so they had them cremated and the urn sent back instead. Much less space to take up in a ship's hold, and lighter too. Then their relatives had them interred here in the churchyard.'

Helen was agog. 'And what does this tin box have to do with it?'

'Do I have to spell it out for you?'

'Yes.'

'Their surname is Wingham . . . Ring any bells?'

'The old lady who used to live here was called Wingham. Violet Wingham. A relative, you think?'

'Yes. All I've got to do is find the proof and discover exactly how she's related to them. Look at this old photo.'

Together, they examined the old photograph with its slightly orange spots of age.

'Do you think,' asked Helen cautiously, 'that Violet Wingham is the baby girl in this photo and that maybe she survived the sinking of the *Titanic* while her parents died? And perhaps the little boy in the photograph could be Violet's brother – who also perished?'

'At last, she's bloody got it!'

'So, where do we go from here?' Helen asked.

'I'll need to do a little more digging, find out some more. But right now . . .' He drew a trail lightly up her arm with his finger. '. . . I'd like to discover a bit more about you.'

*

Chloe phoned a little later to tell Helen she wasn't coming home that night. Apparently Mack wanted her to meet his parents, who'd come down for a few days.

Suddenly a free agent, Helen boldly asked Piran to stay.

'My truck's outside. Everyone will start talking. Besides, I've got to feed my cats and let Jack out.'

'Well, suppose you go home, feed the cats, and then I come and pick you up and bring you and Jack home for supper?'

He looked at her and smiled. 'You'll wear me out, woman.'

*

Helen had forgotten how wonderful it was to spend a whole illicit night with a man she barely knew. The way he ran his hands over her imperfect body, with such tenderness and wonder, made her feel like a goddess. When she woke, it was to the gentle sound of him creeping downstairs and putting the kettle on.

They lay in bed drinking tea and chatting till they heard the soft plop of the Sunday papers on the mat.

'I'll get them.' He kissed her hand and went downstairs.

When he came back, he was clutching a copy of the day's paper and his face had turned almost white.

'That bloody witch!'

'What. Show me?'

He gave her the paper and on the front page there was the headline: DRUG AND SEX SCANDAL OF MAVIS CREWE ACTORS.

It was accompanied by a photo of David Cunningham and Dahlia Dahling, looking tired and seedy, getting into a location car. And a photo of Dawn, looking as if butter wouldn't melt in her mouth. The caption was: *Jilted lover shocked by sex party. See pages 4, 5, 6, 7 and 8.*

Ice gripped at Helen's heart as she turned the first page and read aloud to a shaking Piran.

I LOST MY LOVER TO SEX-STARVED DAHLIA DAHLING
WHILE DRUGGY DAVID CUNNINGHAM LOOKED ON
by Mandy Pratell

Beautiful Dawn Winterbottom told yesterday of the sleazy goings-on behind the scenes of TV7's long-awaited dramatisation of the Mavis Crewe novel, *Mr Tibbs and the Hidden Treasure*. Last Thursday, David Cunningham, the star of the drama, held a birthday party at the five-star Starfish Hotel in trendy Trevay, Cornwall. Miss Winterbottom, thirty-two, witnessed him and his co-star, Dahlia Dahling, forty-eight, go into the gents' toilet with what appeared to be a paper-wrapped bag of drugs. Shortly after, they returned to the party, giggling and glassy-eyed.

Miss Dahling, famous as Bond girl Candy Floss, then proceeded to sing a highly charged version of 'Big Spender' while Cunningham egged her on. At one stage Dahling dragged local historian Piran Ambrose into a hot tub, where they appeared to be having sex.

'I don't know what would have happened if I hadn't challenged them both. Piran is, or was, my fiancée,' a tearful Dawn told this newspaper.

Love-rat Ambrose was later seen leaving the party with TV producer Helen Merrifield, fifty-six.

'Oh, my God. Piran, she's poison!'

Helen scrabbled for the phone.

'Penny? It's Helen, have you seen the—'

Penny spoke very quickly: 'Yes, I've got the lawyers on it already and TV7's press department are on the case too. Not that they care too much. It's all good publicity for the show.'

'Can I do anything?'

'No, darling. I'll call you if there is. At the moment, I have Dahlia and David confined to the hotel with security all over the place. There are plenty of paparazzi outside and I wouldn't put it past them, or some shit of a journo, to try and get in by pretending to be a guest or new waiter or something. Remember Louise, the owner here?'

'Yeah?'

'She's playing a blinder. We're in lock-down.'

'Shit.'

'Quite. Where's Piran? Only you'd better warn him that the press pack will be looking for him.'

'I'll tell him. Actually, he's right next to me.'

'Oh good . . . Hang on, where are you?'

'At home. In my bed.'

'You lucky cow! No wonder Dawn added ten years to your age! We'll talk about you and Piran later. Got to go now. Love you.'

Immediately, there was a knock at the front door. 'I'll go,' said Piran. Helen stopped him. 'No, look out of the window first.

He crossed the room and shifted the curtain a bit.

'Holy shit, there's a crowd of them out there.'

Helen padded over to Piran and took a peek.

'Oh, for fuck's sake!' She counted them. There were four photographers standing by the gate and a young man and woman knocking at the front door, who, Helen surmised, were probably journalists from one of the red-tops.

'Are the curtains in the sitting room and kitchen still drawn shut?' she asked Piran.

'Yeah.'

'Right, we'll sellotape a newspaper over the porthole in the front door and cook some bacon and eggs to tantalise them with the smell. We have the loo, the telly and each other, so we can stay in all day.'

He kissed her. 'I like your style, maid.'

Helen phoned Chloe to tell her to keep away for another evening, which was no hardship for the loved-up Chloe, and Piran rang Simon to ask him to feed his cats.

'Of course, Piran. This is a terrible business. Where are you now?'

Piran coughed delicately. 'At Helen's.'

'Oh good, I'm glad you're there to look after her. I am worried about poor Penny. May I speak to Helen?'

Piran handed the phone to Helen. 'Hi, Simon! How was last night's date?'

'I told Penny about . . . Mrs Bening.'

'And?'

'She listened and asked me questions. No embarrassment. No shock.'

'Told you.'

'I felt so much better – until all of this stuff with the press happened this morning. After I've fed Bosun and Sprat, I'll go down to the Starfish. They've given me the secret codeword to get in, and I shall defend our dear Penny.'

'She's lucky to have you.'

'And I'm glad Piran happened to be in Pendruggan to look after you! When did he drop in?'

'Umm. Last night.'

There was a short silence. Then, 'Oh! My goodness. Well. Jolly good. Speak later, bye.'

42

By the time the sun had gone down and the temperature had dropped, the last of the snappers and journos had left Pendruggan. Penny phoned to say that the police had cleared the majority of the press pack from outside the Starfish too. The show's lawyers had released statements denying all reports of indecency and lewd behaviour, while being careful not to mention the cocaine element.

Helen and Piran turned on the six o'clock local news to find a lone reporter, looking cold and fed up, outside the Starfish. His filmed report contained two interviews, both with holidaymakers, who had nothing to say other than it had added a bit of a thrill to their stay. Finally the hapless hack threw back to the studio, where the presenter had some breaking news.

'Thank you, Rory. News just in, the author of the Mr Tibbs novels, Mavis Crewe, has called a press conference for tomorrow morning at the Starfish Hotel in Trevay. Miss Crewe, a virtual recluse for the past four decades, is understood to have cut short her world cruise in order to save this new and career-reviving television production from scandal.

'And now, the weather.'

*

The following morning, filming was postponed until after the press conference. Helen, Piran and Jack climbed over Helen's back garden wall and slunk through the church-yard before getting to the lane and Simon's waiting car.

He told them, 'I think the coast is clear here in the village, but the hotel will be surrounded. Penny and Louise have arranged for us to drive into the delivery entrance and through the kitchens.'

The plan worked well and all three of them got up to Penny's room without being spotted. Penny was at her most fearsome. She wore black Louboutin heels with skin-tight leather trousers and a white ruffled blouse. With all her make-up on she looked a bit like Adam Ant in his Prince Charming phase.

She was looking calm, but her rapid speech gave away her nerves.

'Mavis isn't here yet. She's being helicoptered in at ten a.m. The press call is for ten-thirty so she, Dahlia, David and I will have a chance to get our story straight. She phoned me last night. Formidable doesn't touch it. She's a powerhouse.'

'Have you ever met her?' asked Helen.

'No, all of our negotiations were done by the lawyers. This is no sweet little old lady we're dealing with. She drove a hard price for the TV rights while still retaining control over international sales, merchandise, you name it.'

'So that's how she can afford a world cruise? Is she married?'

'Widowed ages ago. She was left with three children to bring up. The writing did a lot for her and the children's security, but since then she has been living a quiet life in Eastbourne.'

'So who's paying for the helicopter?'

'As long as it's not me, I don't care.'

As they spoke, they heard the unmistakable sound of a helicopter overhead.

'Here she comes!'

Penny opened the curtain just a fraction, 'so that's who paid for it!'

On the side of the helicopter, in gilt letters on a royal blue background was written *The Intruder Magazine: we get to the inside.*

'Uh-oh. TV7 and the press office have done a deal with the devil.' Penny looked upset.

'It's good, isn't it? Everybody reads *The Intruder*,' Helen managed to shout above the noise and gust of the downforce.

'It means someone has sold our soul. *The Intruder* will have secured inside stories, exclusive photo shoots, David's drug confession . . . you name it.'

As the helicopter landed on the hotel's small lawn, two uniformed security men ran forward, ducking under the rotors and signing to the pilot. As the rotors stopped, the door was opened and the security men helped out a tiny, immaculately turned out woman in her seventies, with severely coiffed platinum blonde hair. She shook hands with her helpers, gave a jaunty wave to the pilot and stepped forward to greet Louise Lonsdale, who almost curtseyed to her.

'I'd better get down there and start fawning. She's the ace in our hand at the moment.' Penny closed the curtains again.

'Do I look all right?'

Her three friends all made approving noises and with a flourish of her ruffled sleeves, Penny was gone.

*

Mavis Crewe stood in the private dining room, the *Intruder* team, ranged behind her. She looked round the seated faces of David, Dahlia and the TV7 publicity assistant Ben, who looked on in awe.

Mavis started, 'Miss Leighton, I entrusted you with the good reputation of my books and Mr Tibbs. You have disappointed me.'

Penny tried an apologetic smile which was ignored.

'Mr Cunningham, Miss Dahling, you have both behaved reprehensibly.' David started as if to defend himself, but Mavis cut him off: 'I am not interested in feeble excuses. I am here for the purpose of damage limitation. You will, all three, say nothing at this press conference other than the scripted statements I shall give you in a moment. Miss Dahling and Mr Cunningham, you are to spend this afternoon giving your interviews and having your photographs taken for *The Intruder* magazine. I have secured an exclusive deal whereby no other publication or TV news channel will get to you. You will restore the brand of Mavis Crewe and Mr Tibbs, giving us all the chance of a wealthier future. Do you understand?'

They nodded. Dahlia asked, 'How much will we be getting from the magazine for all this?'

Mavis's pencilled eyebrows drew themselves into a stern line. 'That is none of your business. I am saving your arses here.'

'Right. Of course.' Dahlia tried not to look disappointed.

Mavis turned her attention to Penny. 'Miss Leighton, are you able to continue shooting scenes without our two main characters this afternoon?'

'Yes. I shall get Gilly and Sven on to it right away.'

'Good. And while these two are having their photos

taken, you and I shall watch the rushes you have already shot.'

'OK.' Penny felt she was back at school.

'Miss Dahling, Mr Cunningham, here are your prepared statements. Go and learn them. I shall see you in ten minutes in the hotel lounge.'

Looking like school children, the two actors, accompanied by Ben and a couple of *Intruder* security men, left the room.

Mavis straightened the skirt of her electric-blue power suit and sat down.

'God, I could do with a Scotch. Would you join me?'

'Damn right,' replied Penny.

One of the three remaining members of the *Intruder* team disappeared to find the bar.

'I wasn't too hard on them, was I?' Mavis asked Penny, who smiled.

'You were bloody fantastic.'

'Bless you. It's much easier to just tell them what to do. We don't have time for fannying around.'

'Couldn't agree more.'

When the whiskies arrived, Mavis asked the *Intruder* men to leave them in private for a few a moments, then she turned to Penny.

'So what really happened at David's party, Penny?'

Penny filled Mavis in.

'Not too bad then,' said Mavis.

'No, but the *Intruder* hack will try to trip them both up with trick questions, and David, bless him, isn't always a quick thinker.'

'Then it's a good job that I know the *Intruder* journalist in question really well.'

'Do you? Great! Who is it?'

'Me.'

Penny burst out laughing. 'Miss Crewe, I take my hat off to you!'

They clinked their glasses, downed the Scotch in one and went to face the press.

*

Mavis Crewe played a blinder at the press conference. She beguiled the journalists with her wit and charm, while school-marming the actors in front of them. Watching her, Penny couldn't help but be impressed. Mavis was part Mrs Thatcher, part Helen Mirren, but with a dash of Barbara Windsor thrown in.

The press lapped it up and the photographers got all the snaps they needed for tomorrow's papers. David and Dahlia had learned their written responses quickly and delivered them with sincerity and self-deprecation. As far as everyone was concerned, the story had run its course. Just a bit of high jinks at a showbiz party, hyped up by a scorned girlfriend, who, shocked and frightened by the press hassle she was receiving at home, had gone away on a long holiday, presumably with the cash she had been paid for her story.

The afternoon's exclusive interview with Mavis for *The Intruder* was as open and honest as it needed to be, which meant that David alluded to a brief dabble in drugs at a stressed time of his life, and Dahlia thoroughly enjoyed the glamorous photo shoot which was to accompany it.

Later, Mavis watched the rushes already shot and couldn't praise Penny and the team enough. 'It's exactly as I wrote it. Marvellous.'

That night, everyone slept a lot better, and a positive energy returned to the set.

*

The following day, it was business as usual down in Pendruggan, apart from the odd extra gawker and a couple of freelance paps. Queenie was happy with the extra business and the local constabulary enjoyed the extra patrols they could make through the village.

Two days later, *The Intruder* hit the newsstands. The front page and the full story inside did everybody proud. A publicity coup if ever there was one.

Mavis was the hero of the hour. She had stayed on, getting to know all the actors and crew, and she was universally worshipped.

The day after publication, she deemed that her work there was done and flew back to her ship, currently in Sydney, to continue her cruise.

43

The final few days of filming flew by. Sven and Gilly were working their socks off. Sven coaxing and encouraging the actors to keep up their energies and attention, Gilly like a sheepdog constantly trying to herd ill-disciplined cats. Gray, who had taken the vintage cars back up to London the day the story broke, missed all the commotion but was back in time to watch Dahlia's photo shoot. Standing watching her, slithering on satin sheets for one shot, then winding herself round the tall phallic shape of the banister end for another, he couldn't wait to soothe her frayed nerves the best way he knew how.

Helen was kept a virtual prisoner in her office. Not only was she dealing with the day-to-day admin, she was now the main contact for all the companies who were involved in dismantling the village of St Brewey. Its shops, flowers, trees, furniture, costumes and props all needed to go back to whence they'd come, ready for the next job.

On the penultimate day of filming, Helen and Penny were in the production office packing boxes of stationery when Dahlia came over, trailing Jako and Haz, who were crumpling under the weight of several bags and boxes.

She greeted the two women with her usual extravagant air-kissing.

'Hello, darlings! Mwah, mwah, I'm clearing out my Winnebago and thought you two might like some of the contents of the glorious gift bags that have arrived.'

She indicated for the two wilting boys to put them on the floor. 'I can't take it all back with me. Who wants these St Eval candles? The seasalt and the carnation are amazing.'

'Our mum would love those!' Jako and Haz said in unison. Dahlia handed a box to each of them. 'And, Helen, would your daughter like this voucher for Sea Breeze boutique? It's for swimwear. Gray tells me she's off with the surf dudes to the sun.'

'She'd love it. Thank you, Dahlia.'

'Well, it's small recompense for leading me to Gray.'

'I'll take the voucher every time!' said Helen and Dahlia joined in the laughter.

Dahlia kept digging around in the bags and boxes until both Helen and Penny's desks were covered in expensive pots of face cream, perfumes, thermal underwear, Cornish chocolate, lavender pillows, cashmere socks, an evening watch, sheepskin boots and a RNLI jumper from the Trevay Lifeboatmen.

'Wow. This is like Christmas. Are you sure you don't want any of it?' asked Helen.

'Well, let's say I cherry-pick all I want and the rest I like to spread around. I've got this for Queenie.'

She held up a signed photograph of Queenie standing outside her shop in between David, Dahlia and Mavis Crewe.

Penny laughed, 'That's fab. The old boot will love it.'

'And,' Dahlia was deep into the bottom of the last bag, 'I have this to put it in. *Voilà!*'

From a thick wadding of bubblewrap, she produced a

solid-silver picture frame. 'I got it in an antique shop in Lostwithiel. Isn't it lovely?'

Penny picked up the watch and the sheepskin boots. 'Would you mind if I gave these to Simon for the summer fête? He's looking for stuff for the tombola.'

'Of course. Tell you what, I'll see what else I can gather up for you over the next couple of days before we finish.'

'How are things with Gray?' Helen asked Dahlia.

'Good. He's keen and I'm mean, so . . .' She looked at Helen astutely. 'You are OK with it, aren't you?'

Helen looked back into Dahlia's beautiful eyes, fully made up for filming. 'Yes, I really am. I never had him to myself anyway. I think you can handle him beautifully.'

'You bet your sweet bippy, girl! I am much smarter than he is!' She laughed and looked at Penny. 'And you, sweet cheeks – how's it going with the rev?'

Helen wanted to hear this too. Penny looked slightly uncomfortable under two sets of eyes.

'Well, it's early days, but I like him. A lot. He doesn't take advantage of me. He's kind, sincere and trustworthy. I've told him things I haven't even told you, Helen! But . . . I'll be going back to London at the weekend and so maybe that's that. I don't know what is going to happen now.' Penny looked crestfallen.

Helen and Dahlia didn't know what to say. They didn't want to comfort her with false hopes – they knew a long-distance relationship would be really difficult for both of them.

After a small, empty silence, Dahlia changed the subject: 'And what about you, Helen? I can't help but notice that young Piran's delightfully *outré* vehicle is very often parked outside your love nest.'

'You are too nosy for your own good, Miss Dahling.

Oh dear, look, Gilly is marching this way with a look that says she wants you to get on and do some of what you're paid for!'

44

The final day of filming arrived. Helen was asked to join everyone who had been involved to come and watch the final scene. It was only a short one: David and Dahlia as Mr Tibbs and Nancy Trumpet, walking out of the South-West Friendly Bank's front door, strolling down the street to the tea rooms.

The familiar command of orders from Gilly and the crew now sounded poignant to Helen.

'Final checks, quiet please, action . . . And cut.'

Helen watched as David and Dahlia waited for their cue and did their stuff a couple of times. Sven had a quiet chat with the cameraman and then he called, 'Ladies and gentlemen, that is a wrap.'

A huge cheer went up and everybody kissed everybody else, before going back to their Winnebagos and trucks to gather their things and get the hell back to London.

*

Helen and Penny were hosting a small supper that night at Gull's Cry for Dahlia, Gray, Simon and Piran. Chloe had promised to cook and clean and make it as special as possible.

When Helen finally locked her now empty office and walked back home, she hardly recognised the place.

'Chloe!' She put her bags down and stood and stared. 'It looks wonderful!'

'Thanks, Mum. Mack and the boys helped.'

They'd taken the kitchen table into the centre of the sitting room and, in the empty fireplace, they'd put a huge lobster pot covered in fairy lights with extra tea lights around it. The small sofa and Helen's armchair, which usually lived in that room, were now out in the garden, creating an outdoor room on the small paved area by the back door. Mack, Jako, Haz and a happy Tony were busy lighting the chiminea.

They had also laid some rush matting down on the cold stones to add extra luxury. Jam jars of tea lights were dotted on the walls, the flower beds, and in the tree branches.

'What have I done to deserve you?' She kissed them all in turn.

'Mrs Merrifield, Helen, we wanted to give you a small gift for all your kindness and hospitality.' And with that Mack produced from behind the sofa a battered surfboard.

'It's my old one, but it's caught some great waves.'

Helen couldn't speak for fear of tears, so she hugged them all again and called for Chloe.

'Come and see what the lads have got for me.'

Chloe stuck her head round the back door. 'Great, isn't it! We thought that maybe, once you'd got a bit more practice in, you would like to come and join us for a couple of weeks in Sri Lanka?'

Now the tears did come. Helen sat on the sofa and cried and laughed in equal measure.

'I would love to, and I promise not to cramp your style.'

Back inside, the kitchen, so spacious without the table,

had paper chains of Cornish pixies looped around the ceiling. On the Aga a big pan of Cornish new potatoes were gently simmering and on the side was a huge salmon, poached by Chloe earlier.

'I've got salad with the salmon and early asparagus for starters. Then for pud a very alcoholic sherry trifle with extra clotted cream.'

'Darling, it's amazing.'

The boys came in from the garden. 'Right, you two, we're off to the pub. See you later, Cinders.' Mack leant down and kissed Chloe, who visibly glowed with love.

Helen looked at Tony. 'Are you going too, Tony?'

'Going to what, Mrs M.?'

'To the pub?'

He nodded vigorously. Haz and Jako put their arms round his shoulders. 'We'll look after him, Helen. Don't worry.'

*

Later, Gray loomed in through the front door. He was wearing a turquoise linen shirt and well-cut navy linen trousers. A combo guaranteed to enhance his sparkling blue eyes.

'Hi, Dad.' Chloe wiped her hands on her apron and kissed him. 'On your own?'

'Yuh, I came ahead of the others to be in the bosom of my family and to see if there's anything I can do?'

Helen came down from upstairs, looking sensational in a simple black sleeveless shift dress with her auburn curls and freckled cheeks and shoulders shimmering in the candlelight. Gray gave a low whistle.

'Thank you. I dare you to do that when Dahlia's here.'

'I don't have a death wish.'

Chloe was getting clean glasses from the cupboard. 'Dad, there's a bottle of champagne in the fridge. Bring it out to the garden, would you?'

Gray opened the bottle expertly and poured the bubbles into their glasses. Chloe made a toast.

'To my mum and my dad. I love you both and I am very proud of you both. I can't lie and say that I am happy you are no longer together, but as long as we can always be like this, on good terms and friendly, Sean and I are OK. To you.' She raised her glass and drank.

'Group hug?' suggested Gray.

'You bet,' said Helen.

As they stood locked in an embrace, a voice came from the back door:

'Can anyone join in?' Penny arrived with her arm through Simon's.

'Hello, darlings!' Dahlia appeared too. 'Look who I found loitering with intent.'

Piran stood behind her, looking drop-dead handsome in his oldest jeans and threadbare denim shirt. Little Jack ran in to sniff the food bin. Piran smiled at Helen, his eyes making her tummy, toes and . . . good Lord . . . other bits tingle. 'Hello, Helen.'

'Piran!' She went to his side and kissed him quickly. 'Let's get you a glass.'

She thought she could feel Gray's eyes watching her, but when she turned back, he had his arm round Dahlia's waist and was nibbling her ear.

'Supper's ready,' called Chloe. 'Sit where you want, as long as it's next to somebody you like!'

*

Helen sat next to Piran, and Gray nonchalantly placed himself on her other side. Dahlia sat between Gray and Simon, and Penny between Simon and Piran.

The asparagus went down very well, Dahlia eating it lasciviously for Gray's benefit. As soon as the salmon was served and Chloe had returned to the kitchen, Gray started.

'So, Piran. What do you actually do? Do you have a proper job?'

All eyes turned to Piran, who gave Gray a small smile laced with a touch of menace.

'I'm a doctor of archaeology and Celtic history. You?'

Gray set his jaw and shoulders. 'I'm in the classic car trade.'

'Ideal.' Piran placed a forkful of salmon in his mouth. Helen and Penny exchanged glances.

Gray again: 'So you dig up old bits of bone, do you?'

Piran swallowed and picked up his wine glass. 'Yep. And you pick up old bits of metal.'

Gray tensed, but Dahlia intervened, 'Tell us more about your work, Piran.'

'Well, I've just finished a big project in the graveyard here. Some of the graves date back to the seventeenth century and are pretty dilapidated. We're going to repair and restore as many as we can, but some, unidentified, we have to refer to the coroner in order to get them exhumed and re-sited out of the way. It's quite a lot of detective work.'

'He's really an expert in this, aren't you, Piran?' Simon confirmed.

Piran shrugged his shoulders.

'So how did you meet my ex-wife?' Gray topping up his red wine, seemed to be winding up for a confrontation.

'It's a long story,' said Piran, smiling at Helen.

'But you made short work of getting your feet under the table?' Gray wouldn't stop.

'Gray, if you have something to say, come right out and say it.' Piran's voice had a rumble of danger in it.

'That's quite enough, boys, thank you.' Dahlia's voice had just the right amount of schoolteacher in it. 'Now, Gray darling, pass me the wine, would you?'

The table relaxed a little. The moment passed and the evening was back on safer ground, Dahlia regaling them with filthy jokes and slanderous gossip. While the others laughed and chatted, Simon and Penny sat quietly next to each other, holding hands under the table with desperation in their eyes.

*

When it was time for coffee, they all went and sat in the garden, the background noises of Chloe clearing away punctuating the still evening.

Stretching her legs towards the chiminea, Dahlia spoke first, 'Well, old man,' she patted Gray's knee affectionately, 'I'd better get you back to the hotel. What time do you want to leave for London tomorrow?'

'About midday? We can have some lunch on the way.'

'Whereabouts do you live, Dahlia?' Simon asked.

'Virginia Water. I have a bijou cottage on the Thames. Very pretty. You must drop in when you come up to town to see Penny.'

'That might not be for a while,' said Simon.

Penny picked up quickly, 'Well, you see I am going to be working twenty-four-seven editing the tape into a full ninety-minute programme for viewing by the TV7 lot.

Then there'll be extra post-production work and I just won't have the time to see Simon . . . or anyone.'

Everybody looked at Simon, who smiled back as if he didn't have a care in the world, but whose heart was clearly breaking. 'She's a busy woman. She'll forget all about us.'

'No I won't.' Penny took Simon's hand. 'And I will be back for the night of the premiere. By the way, Dahlia, it was very generous of you and David to hire a big screen so everyone can watch it on the village green.'

Dahlia bowed her head graciously. 'The least we could do. And I promise I shall drag David's skinny arse down here for the whole weekend. We'll definitely make the Pendruggan carnival too.'

'Oh, that's splendid,' said Simon. 'I was wondering if I could call on you to judge the entrants in the home produce tent and the horticultural tent?'

'I'd be upset if I wasn't asked! Happy to do that, Simon.' Dahlia got to her feet and pulled Gray up on to his. 'Come on, tiger. I'd better drive you back.'

Penny and Simon got their things together too and at the front door they all said their fond goodbyes. Gray, slightly swaying, told Piran, 'You just bloody well look after her, that's all. She's one of life's treasures and I threw her away.'

Piran slapped Gray on the back. 'I'll make sure she doesn't fall in with any bad 'uns.'

'Thanks, mate. I love you, Helen.' Gray gave her a sloppy kiss.

'That's it.' Dahlia took his arm. 'Home, boy, before you tell the whole village you love them.'

'But I do. I love this place. And I love you too, Dahlia, you sexy top bird.' Again Gray swayed on his feet; the act of standing up in fresh air had definitely gone to his head.

'Bye, everybody. Bye.' Dahlia helped him down the path.

Helen kissed Simon and Penny. 'Look after Simon for me, won't you, Helen?'

'You bet. We'll be here waiting for you when you return.'

Helen stood watching Simon and Penny as they walked down the path and to Penny's car. Until Chloe whispered to her, 'Close the door, Mum. They don't want you watching them say their goodbyes.'

'Oh, yes, right. Of course.'

She closed the door and looked at Piran, longing to take him upstairs and sleep in his arms, but knowing he wouldn't with Chloe there.

'I'd best be off too. Thank you, Chloe, for great grub,' he said.

Chloe replied, 'Where do you think you're going?'

'Home.'

'Don't be silly. Stay here with Mum. I'm going over to Mack's, so see you in the morning.'

45

Within four days the village had once again become Pendruggan. St Brewey had gone, leaving only yellowing patches of grass where the crew village had been, and a few deep wheel ruts on the green.

Life returned to its former rhythm.

The weather was turning warm now and Simon took Helen for surf lessons as often as he could.

After one particularly good lesson they sat on the beach in their wetsuits, using Mack's old board as a seat.

'Are you ready for a pasty?' Helen rootled about in her bag for the two pasties Queenie had given her earlier. Simon nodded, but when she passed it to him he left it by his side.

After a couple of minutes of silent chomping from Helen, she asked, 'What's wrong, Simon?'

He laughed quietly. 'You know me too well.'

'When did you last hear from Penny?'

'The end of last week. She's full on working with her editor and I think she doesn't notice the days slipping past.'

'As you do?'

'Yes.'

'If there's one thing I know about Penny, it's that she is loyal. If she says she's working, she's working.'

Simon's face was suddenly full of pain. 'Supposing she

meets someone else? Supposing she realises that I'm just not right for her?'

'Now you're torturing yourself. Absence makes the heart grow fonder.'

'What about "out of sight, out of mind"?'

'Simon! Stop! Do you want me to have a word with her?'

He turned, panic in his eyes. 'No, don't do that. I've been giving her her space and purposely not hassling her.'

'Ah, so she might think you have changed your mind?'

'I haven't!'

'No, I know that, but . . . Look, you are a little behind in the relationship studies. At your ages, you don't have time for mind games. Ring her up and bloody well tell her how you feel. If you get the answerphone, don't hang up. Leave a short, sincere message. She'll love it. Trust me.'

'OK, Helen, I trust your advice.' He picked up his pasty and began to eat.

46

Now that shooting was over, Helen and Piran had found time to pick up their research into the old tin box and the mystery of Violet Wingham's family. Over coffee and a couple of Queenie's latest apple pies, the two of them were trawling online to see what else they could learn about the events of the night of the fifteenth of April 1912.

Helen's five-year-old laptop was sitting on the kitchen table, Piran tapping away, his half-moon reading glasses on the end of his nose.

'Here we are,' he said, moving a little to allow Helen to look over his shoulder and see a list of websites devoted to the sinking of Royal Mail steamer.

He clicked on a reputable-looking site and went into the page titled 'Victims'. Finally he tapped in Wingham.

'Look – Doctor Henry Arthur Wingham, born 1880 Somerset, travelling second class with Bluebell Grace Wingham, born 1884 Cornwall, and their two children, Violet Teresa born 1911 and Falcon Henry born 1907. Ticket cost thirty-nine pounds.'

'What's that equivalent to today?' asked Helen.

'I don't know – a lot. Maybe three thousand pounds?'

He clicked on Henry's name which had the word BIOG attached to it.

'Doctor Wingham, his wife and son all perished. Doctor

and Mrs Wingham's bodies being recovered by rescue ship *Mackay-Bennett* and taken to Halifax, Nova Scotia. Their ashes were returned to England. Resting place unknown. Their daughter Violet was given into the care of an unknown woman in lifeboat eleven by Mrs Wingham. Eyewitness accounts suggest Mrs Wingham did not get into the lifeboat but went back to find her son, Falcon. The lifeboat was lowered before she returned. Falcon's body was never recovered. Baby Violet, however, was collected by the *Carpathia* and arrived in New York City on the eighteenth of April 1912. She was cared for in Bellevue Hospital, Kips Bay, Manhattan. The same hospital where her father was to have taken up his new position as general surgeon. She was later returned to care in England.'

'My God.' Helen sat down and with her elbows on the table put her head in her hands. 'How many people were there on board?'

He read again: 'It is estimated there were 2,218 people on board, 337 first class, 285 second class, 712 third class and 885 crew. Only 705 survived with 1,514 dying, but numbers are hard to confirm.'

Helen went to the fridge and brought out a bottle of wine. Pouring it into two glasses, she looked at the Peek Frean's tin, on which 'Falcon' was written on a faded and yellowing sticky label. 'How did Falcon get into the tin?'

'Supposing it *is* Falcon.'

'How do we find out?'

'I'll talk to the coroner. He knows the forensic people. I'm sure they'll tell us.'

*

338

The following evening, Helen went round to see Simon.

'Hello, Helen. Come in, come in.' Simon opened the vicarage door wide, gesturing for Helen to go into the drawing room, where the six o'clock news was on the radio. He turned the sound down.

'Take a seat. So, what did Piran find out about the tin box?'

When Helen had told him as much as she could, he sat forward, blinking his big chocolate eyes through his new specs.

'Good Lord! What a story! What happens next?'

'We're going to see if the ashes labelled Falcon can be identified as human first. But I am hoping you may be able to help us in tracing the people who looked after Violet when she came home as a baby.'

'I'll ask the bishop. Remember I told you he's the one Miss Wingham's solicitors have been dealing with?'

'Simon, call the bishop immediately!'

Simon thumped his knees with his palms. 'Quite right! Let's get this sorted.'

A few minutes later, he put the receiver down, looking disappointed. 'I'd forgotten – he's gone to see a mission in Ethiopia. He's not back for a month.'

'Bugger.'

'Quite.' He looked at her. 'How about I have a look in the church register? That may turn something up.'

Unlocking the large and ancient safe, Simon bent down and riffled through half a dozen old ledgers. 'Let's start here. Parish records 1880 to 1920.'

It took a while to get used to the fine copperplate handwriting, but once their eyes had attuned to it they began to decipher the entries more clearly.

'Here. Fifteenth July 1912, baptism of Violet Teresa Wingham. Daughter of the late Henry and Bluebell Wingham. There are two signatures as well: Mr Charles and Mrs Amy Frank, of Pendruggan Farm.'

Helen jumped on the spot with excitement. 'So she was brought to Pendruggan and cared for by the family in the farm across from Gull's Cry!' She hugged Simon round the neck. 'This is so exciting!' She let go of him. 'Can I use your computer?'

'Be my guest. It's in the study.'

It took only a couple of minutes for Helen to get into the census for 1911. 'It's the nearest to 1912. Fingers crossed.'

Typing in Charles and Amy Frank's names and the farm address, she only had to wait a few moments before an ancient copy of their census entry appeared on screen.

'Charles Frank, farm manager, Amy Frank née Wingham, servant. Childless. It fits! So, Charles and Amy were working for the farmer and his wife. Amy must have been Henry's sister. Blimey, Henry did well to become a doctor, didn't he? So when Henry died, Amy and Charles looked after Violet. I must tell Piran.'

*

'Now don't go jumping to conclusions. We have to check and double check,' said Piran, when she spoke to him later back at her house.

'Yes, but they were the ones who had Violet baptised in 1912. As soon as she'd been brought back from America.'

'It does all look as if it fits, but we just need a bit more.'

'But where from?'

Piran tapped the side of his nose. 'Local knowledge.'

He picked up his keys and walked to the front door. 'Back later.'

An hour later he returned, this time with Queenie. Helen was in the kitchen boiling eggs for a salad Niçoise for Chloe's supper. She looked round.

'Hello, Queenie. This is a nice surprise.'

Piran held a chair out for Queenie. 'She is the invaluable local knowledge I was looking for.'

Queenie sat down and lit a roll-up that she'd dug from inside her coat pocket.

Piran said to Helen, 'Now don't go getting a big head, but it looks like you're right.' Helen couldn't hide her smug smile. 'Charles and Amy Frank *did* look after Violet until she was nineteen, when she bought this house.'

'Ha ha! Didn't I tell you!' Helen did a little jig, running on the spot laughing.

'What's going on?' came Chloe's voice from the sitting room where she was watching TV.

'Come in and listen.'

The two women sat in rapt attention as Piran continued:

'Queenie had the key to it all the time, but she just didn't realise it. Go on, Queenie. Tell them.'

Delighted to be in the spotlight, Queenie began:

'When I was evacuated from London in 1940, I was only ten. My Cornish family were all right. Hardworking, decent types. He was a farmhand, working with Charles, and she was a dairy maid. Making all the butter and cream. It's 'ow I learnt to cook me pasties from 'er, you know.'

They all nodded appreciatively.

'Anyways, they was all friends together, my Cornish Ma and Da – that's what I called 'em, see – and Charles and Amy Franks. On occasion they might go out for the night, down Trevay or summink. That's when Violet would babysit me, right 'ere in Gull's Cry.'

Helen and Chloe looked at their surroundings, picturing the house as it must have been.

'Course, it weren't like you've got it now, 'elen. It were a dirt floor and an old range in 'ere, and 'er lovely cat – ever so fond of him, she was, what was 'is name . . .'

'Falcon?' asked Helen, making Chloe jump.

'Yes! That's 'im. 'Owd you know?'

'Tell you in a minute. Carry on.'

'Falcon. That's it. Named after 'er brother what died. I said to 'er, what kind of a name's that? She said, "That is a fine name. It was what Captain Scott of the Antarctic was called."'

Queenie looked at her audience, 'Come to think of it, 'e died an' all, didn't 'e?'

'Yes. Did she tell you how her brother Falcon died?'

'No. She was a closed book when it came to 'er family. I 'eard, from listening at doors as youngsters do, that she survived the *Titanic* sinking, but she would never say a word. About twenty years ago, a newspaper fella came lookin for her 'cos they'd found the wreck of the *Titanic* an' 'e wanted stories from survivors, but she wouldn't open 'er door to him. Oh no.'

Helen pushed a saucer towards Queenie to catch the ash about to spill from the roll-up.

'Violet was very fond of her cat though. 'E loved sitting in 'ere by the range. She loved all 'er cats, but 'e was first so 'e was special. Anyway, I did 'ear Ma and Da talking once, about Violet's dad.'

'Yes?' Helen and Chloe visibly leant in to hear more. Piran was resting against the Aga.

''E done very well for himself and was a doctor.

Qualified in London. 'E was taking the family to New York so 'e could work in one of those smart new hospitals they had over there. But . . .' She shrugged her shoulders and coughed. 'They never made it. Still, the Franks were canny like and, being the only relative, Amy got compensation or insurance or summink from the White Star line. It was a lot. As I remember, about a thousand pounds! I think they gave it to Violet so she could buy this cottage, and have a few bob in the bank. Put the kettle on, Chloe, there's a good girl.'

Queenie had finished her story and was leaning back in satisfaction at the look of stunned amazement on the faces of Helen and Chloe.

'What a story,' said Helen. 'Why didn't you tell me all this before, Queenie?'

'You know me, I'm not one to gossip. And anyway,' she sniffed, 'you never asked.'

She stubbed her skinny cigarette out on the saucer. 'Now tell me 'ow you know about the cat called Falcon?'

'Have a look at this.' Penny pushed the Peek Frean's tin towards Queenie, who read the label, picked the tin up and shook it. 'Oh my good gawd. You don't think this is the cat, do you?'

'We were wondering whether it might be Falcon the brother.'

Queenie put the tin down quickly. 'Bleedin 'ell, I 'ope not!'

*

The four of them shared the salad Niçoise, Queenie not enjoying it much but perking up when Helen poured a glass of sherry for her. By 10 p.m. they were all tired and Piran offered to walk Queenie home.

He stooped to kiss Helen and Chloe. 'I'll see you tomorrow some time.'

Helen kissed him back and was surprised at how relaxed she felt about him not staying the night. She was almost looking forward to having the bed to herself.

But Chloe soon put the kibosh on that. 'Just you and me tonight then, Mum.'

47

Piran had put a call in to his coroner friend, but he was away with his children for the spring school holiday, so they came to a halt with the ashes mystery for a couple of weeks.

But there was still a lot for Helen to think about. The village carnival was only eight weeks away and Tony and she were busy bringing on the early sweet peas and staking the delphiniums. These were the two flowers that Tony thought Helen would have the best chance of winning a prize for. Helen's mint bed was at its best now too, so she dug out an old handwritten recipe for mint jelly and went to work on boiling and bottling it.

'That'll sell well, Mrs M. We should put it on the farm shop stall, to go with the new lamb.'

'Good idea, Mr B. Would you like a pot?'

'No, thank you. I went before I came.'

She smiled at him. 'How about a Ribena then?'

'Yes, ta.'

*

Chloe was rarely in these days. And when she was it was to use the shower or the washing machine.

'Mum,' she said on one of her days at home, 'Mack and I are booking our tickets to Sri Lanka this afternoon.'

'When are you going?'

'After the carnival.'

'So I've got another few weeks of looking at your beach towels and bikinis on the washing line, have I?'

Chloe gave her mum a friendly shove. 'Will you miss me?'

'No.'

'Do you think I'm doing the right thing?'

'Probably.'

'Do you like Mack?'

'Does he make you happy?'

'Yes.'

'Then, yes, I like him. Darling, you are a fully fledged adult now. Go out and try the world for size. I chose to marry and have you and Sean at your age. I don't regret any of it, but I am so glad I am spreading my wings now.'

'Hmm.' Chloe looked at her mum. 'So what's the deal with Piran? He's not over here as much as he was.'

'We speak on the phone and anyway, he's busy, I'm busy. It's a good thing. I really like him, but I don't want to be owned by a man any more.'

'Have you told him that?'

'No.'

'Don't you think you should? So that he can be free to do what he wants?'

'What do you mean?'

'Well, he might think you playing it cool means you've gone off him. His eye might wander.'

Helen hadn't thought of this and was discomforted by the idea. 'Do you think it might?'

'It might.'

*

Piran called a bit later. 'Fancy a drink in the Dolphin, girl?'

'Great. What time?'

'I'll meet you in there about seven.'

'You're not going to pick me up?'

'Not tonight. I'm a bit tired. See you later.'

He hung up. *Oh my God. He's getting tired of you, Helen,* she thought to herself. *When was the last time he stayed over? When was the last time you made love? At least a week ago. Blimey. What's going on?*

She dressed very carefully for him. Pretty, matching bra and pants. Nothing too sexy. But not too ordinary either. She pulled on her new three-quarter-length jeans and added a heel. Then took them off and put on a rope-soled wedge. Better. She shrugged into a well-cut white T-shirt and added a hip-length navy cashmere cardigan. She knew he liked this look.

Chloe whistled as she came down the stairs. 'Looking hot, Mum.'

*

It was a gorgeous late April evening. As she turned her little Mini into the Dolphin car park, she could see Piran sitting at one of the outside tables with a group of male friends.

He had a thick jumper tied round his shoulders, over a blue-and-white striped shirt. His denim-clad legs were planted wide apart and his dark curls were hanging over his collar. As he laughed at someone's story, he saw her, but didn't acknowledge her. She got out of the car and joined him, feeling faintly annoyed. He reached up and squeezed her bum.

'Hello, Helen. This is Mick, John and Merv.'

They all said hello and then carried on talking to each other. She interrupted, 'Anyone want a drink?'

'No thanks. Just got one in,' they replied, and again ignored her.

She pursed her lips and went inside to the bar. Dorrie was serving.

'Hello, Helen. Long time no see. How are you?' She stretched over the bar to kiss Helen. 'Piran's outside, didn't you see him?'

'Yes, I saw him, but he's busy chatting.'

'Like Don. When men get together they gas worse than any woman. What'll you have?'

'A large gin and tonic, please.'

The rest of the evening swam in a blur of juniper berries and quinine. And when Piran finally came into the pub, about an hour and a half later, she was less than gracious.

'Oh, hello, Piran. Fancy seeing you here. I was just enjoying a little drink on my own.'

He looked at her with his ocean eyes. 'Well, I won't disturb you. I've just come in for a pee.' And he walked off to the gents'.

'Another G and T please, Dorrie.' Dorrie obliged and, as she put the drink down in front of Helen, said, "E's a man, that's all. Just flexing his muscles. Drink up and I'll get Don to run you home. Collect the car tomorrow.'

Humiliation swept through Helen. Another man was deserting her. She got in the car with Don, finding the seat-belt buckle impossible to do up.

'Here, let me do it for you, Helen.' He started up his car and began the short journey down to Pendruggan.

After a few minutes, Helen sighed and said, 'What's wrong with me, Don?'

Don shifted uncomfortably. Women were a mystery at the best of times, but when drunk . . .

'Nothin' wrong with you, maid.'

'Then why is Piran ignoring me?'

'I'm sure 'e's not. He didn't want to disturb you while you were chatting with Dorrie. That's all.'

'Huh. You're sticking up for him.'

'No. I think you're a bit tired and in the morning it'll all look all right.' He stopped the car. 'Here you are. Do you want me to take you to the door?'

'No thank you. I don't need a man.' And Helen swaggered off up the path to her front door.

It took a long time for her to fall asleep. Her mind was in a mess. Yes, she wanted Piran, but no, she didn't want him living with her, but yes she wanted him to be hers exclusively, but no that didn't mean he could control her, and yes it certainly meant that he had to be faithful to her . . .

Finally she slept and woke with a whopper of a hangover.

48

She'd had a bath and a large coffee but was feeling a bit sick. Thank God Chloe hadn't stayed over last night. She'd have been unbearably sanctimonious about her mother's drinking.

Taking a moment's respite, Helen sat at the top of her stairs looking out at her garden. What a difference a year makes. What had been an overgrown heap was now tidy and verdant. The beds were bursting with the new growth on her lavender, lilies, roses and peonies. Tony was already weeding the immaculate vegetable bed. He was determined he'd get a prize for his early peas.

Helen roused herself. She had to get up to the pub and collect her car. Standing up, she walked gently down the stairs, her poor head feeling as if a marble was rolling and banging around the inside of her skull.

She steadied herself at the front door, then stepped out into the bright spring day. It burnt into the back of her eyeballs. She shut her eyes in reflex and walked straight into a large, familiar body.

'Ha ha. Poor old Helen. You look terrible!'

'Piss off, Piran.' She opened one eye, her hand shading the other and squinted up at him.

'Lovely welcome.' He put his hands on his hips and looked up at the sky. 'Thing is, Helen, I think we need a chat.'

Helen's stomach squirted adrenalin into her already contaminated system. A wave of nausea passed over her. Was he going to dump her?

'I'm just going to walk over to the Dolphin to get my car, actually.'

'I'll give you a lift after we've had a chat.'

He led her back into the cottage and sat her on her little sofa, while he took the armchair.

'Helen, I think a lot of you. You know that.'

'Do I?'

'Don't be petulant. Yes, I do think a lot of you.'

'Then why have you never invited me round to your place to stay?'

He looked surprised, 'Because it's not as comfortable as here and—'

'You wanted to get your feet under my table. Gray was right.'

His ocean eyes turned stormy. 'The reason I have not invited you to stay at my place is because . . . no woman has. It was meant for me and Jenna.'

'So now I'm competing with a dead woman.'

He stood up very fast and stepped towards her. 'I'll shake the teeth out of your head if you ever speak like that again, do you hear?'

She held her own and met his gaze. 'You wouldn't dare!'

He sat back down and sighed. 'I'm sorry, Helen. But I'm not used to the idea of another woman around and I like my own space.'

'And so do I,' she replied hotly.

'And I don't want to have to share my house and my life with anyone a hundred per cent of the time.'

'Nor do I.'

'But I am a loyal man.'

'And I am a loyal woman.'

'So, what I am trying to say is . . .'

'You don't want a relationship with me.'

He looked at her, exasperated. 'No. Listen. You are a lovely woman and, for all your stupidity, I am really fond of you. But, I like things the way they are. You and me. Separate houses, separate friends, but . . . together. Loyal. Nobody else.'

'So you want your cake and to eat it, too?'

'That's not what I'm saying and you know it. And anyway, you've always given the impression that you like your independence.'

'I do. So if that is all you have to say, then I don't think there is anything left to talk about.'

Piran looked exasperated. 'Helen, you're not listening to me.'

'No, I don't want to hear any more.' Helen's voice caught in her throat. 'Just leave.'

'All right, I will, but you're making a big mistake.'

With that, Piran walked out of Gull's Cry and drove off in his car.

A couple of hours later, when she had finished crying, she called Chloe on her mobile and asked her to come and pick her up with Mack so she could collect her car. She was sombre when they came for her and didn't speak for the entire journey.

*

Over the next two or three weeks the carnival committee swung into the final countdown. Helen buried her heartbreak and tried to concentrate on the event. She knew it could never work with Piran; he was the most irritating and pig-headed man she had ever met, and she told herself she was glad to be rid of him. But deep down inside, Helen didn't feel glad.

Raffle prizes were collected from local businesses, the WI were cadging empty jam jars off everybody for their preserve and pickle stall and the children were thinking up their fancy-dress costumes. Helen spent a lot of her time at the vicarage, sitting at Simon's desk working on coordinating everything from Simon's end. Apart from everything else that had to be sorted out, the church needed a spring clean because it would be open for a local art sale on the day of the carnival.

She turned over a page of her notebook and began a fresh To Do list. The phone rang:

'Hi, Ma, how are things?'

'Hi, Sean, darling. How did you know I was on this number?'

'Chloe is the fountain of all knowledge.'

'Has she told you she's booked her tickets for Sri Lanka?'

'Yeah. Which is why I thought I'd better make a date to come and see you and her before she jets off.'

'Have you seen Daddy?'

'He called. He wants me and Terri to go out to dinner with him and Daisy Doodah.'

'Dahlia Dahling!' she corrected him, laughing. 'You should meet her. She's great fun. More than a match for your father.'

'Yeah. Maybe. Anyway, Dad says you've got some bloke in tow.'

'Well, he's wrong, that is over. It was the man you met at Christmas. In church. Piran.'

'The bloody pirate? Chloe did mention him. What went wrong?'

'We're too different and we like our own space. Neither of us were ready for a relationship, that's all.'

'Well, Ma, you're sounding very chilled about it all, I must say. So, when would be good for Terri and me to come down?'

'What about for the carnival?'

'Yeah. We were talking to Chloe and she told us about the carnival. Is it true you've got a big screen broadcasting the *Mr Tibbs* thing to the village?'

'Yes. It should be fun, if the weather holds. Oh, and ask Terri to bring some of her paintings down, if she would like to, because we've got an art sale in the church.'

'Sounds good. We'll come down on the Friday night then. I'll phone Don and book a room and see if he can fit in some fishing too.'

'Great fun. Looking forward to it. Love to you both. Bye.'

She put the phone down and looked out of Simon's study window. The vicarage lawn needed mowing before it could be used as the cream tea garden at the carnival. She looked beyond to the church, which was looking gorgeous, dappled in sunshine and shade with the rooks snoozing on the roof pitch. Next she turned her eye to the ramshackle churchyard and thought of Piran and the work that still needed to be done there.

To her surprise, she saw Piran's Toyota turn in through the gate. As he stepped out of his truck, which had never fully recovered from Dawn's assault, Jack jumped down, cocked his leg on the gate post and followed his master towards the vicarage back door.

As he stepped into the cool of the kitchen, she stood up to meet him, her heart thumping in her chest.

'Piran! Simon didn't mention you were coming.'

Piran looked at Helen intensely for a moment. She felt herself grow pink under his scrutiny.

'Want a cuppa?' She tried to sound breezy. 'I'm making one for myself and Simon.'

'No, thank you. I can't stop. I popped in to speak to Simon about some of the church records, but now that you are here – I've got news for you that may be of interest. That is, if you want to hear it?'

'Go on,' she said.

'I've had some news from my friend in the coroner's office.'

'About Falcon's ashes?' Helen turned from filling the kettle and lighting the gas hob. Despite herself, she was interested.

'Yes. DNA is destroyed by fire. Human or animal, it's not possible to tell them apart.'

'Oh dear. I should have thought of that.'

'But . . .' he paused.

'Go on.'

'Teeth can sometimes survive the flames. If we riddle the ashes through a sieve, we might find something.'

'Can we do it?'

'I've already done it.' He opened his big calloused palm and sitting in the middle was a small, sharp tooth. 'Coroner says it's definitely not human.'

49

Helen was quiet. 'I almost hoped it was Violet's brother. This means his little body is still at the bottom of the sea.'

They both looked sadly at the tooth.

The phone in Simon's study rang, breaking the melancholy mood. Helen took a few seconds before moving to answer it.

'Hello, Holy Trinity vicarage. How may I help you?'

A woman's voice boomed down the phone: 'Who is this?'

'Helen Merrifield.'

'Ah, Mrs Merrifield. The location of the horticultural tent won't do at all. I always like to be on the left side of the green. It stays so much cooler for the plants.'

'Hello, Mrs Tipton. What would you like me to do?'

During this interruption, Piran wrote a note on Helen's pad and quietly let himself out. Helen scanned the note: *TALK TO ME.*

'Yes, Mrs Tipton, I am still here.' She lifted the note to her lips and gently pressed them against it. Then, resting the phone between her shoulder and ear, she folded the note carefully into her purse. 'Mrs Tipton, you may have what you want, where you want it. Life is just too short, isn't it?'

*

The night before the carnival, the hard-working committee members were busy out on the village green. The huge marquees had gone up the day before, taking up three sides of the rectangle but with one wall open to the middle. Now the insides were being dressed with trestles, calligraphied signs and bunting.

Queenie was faffing around with the display units for her pasties. 'I'm too close to the barbecue, 'elen dear. All that smoke ain't good for me lungs.'

'It's just the same smoke as your roll-ups, Queenie,' Helen responded.

'Oh no, dear. Me fags is pure. This cooking smoke is pure fat settling in me lungs.'

'Would you like me to move you?'

'No. I'd like you to move the barbecue, dear.'

Helen didn't need asking twice. She found the leader of the Rotary Club, who was in charge of the cooking: 'I don't think you're in the best spot here, Mike. I think you'd be better over by church. It'll lure people in and out of the art show.'

'OK, boss.'

And to Helen's surprise, he and the other men moved it willingly.

Outside the tents, and circling the centre show ring, were several stalls. One was signed GUESS THE WEIGHT OF THE VICAR, others FERRET RACING and BOWL FOR A PIG.

The centre show ring was reserved for the dog show, tug of war, the pipe band and the drum majorettes. In the evening, it would become the auditorium for the big-screen showing of *Mr Tibbs and the Hidden Treasure*.

As Helen walked around helping, cajoling and congratulating everyone, her back pocket began to vibrate. Her mobile phone very rarely worked in the village, but some stray signal must have blown in on the breeze. She answered, 'Hello?'

The line was very bad.

'Hel . . . it's Penny. Mavis is coming down for the . . . nival . . . bringing special frien . . . don't tell Queenie, but it's Al . . . . . . chmar . . .' The line went dead.

Helen made a mental note to call Penny back on the landline at home later, but naturally forgot as soon as she saw Sean and Terri turn into the village in his little Porsche with the roof off and several canvases strapped on to the roof.

She ran towards them and hugged them both tight as they leapt out of the car to hug her in return.

'Go indoors and put the kettle on while I just do my last rounds of the tents and stalls,' she instructed them.

When she was satisfied that everything for the carnival was on schedule, she went home to Gull's Cry. Mack and Chloe were home and, together with Sean and Terri, were sitting out in the garden on the old bench and the low walls. A tea-cosied teapot was sitting on a tray surrounded by mugs, milk jug and plate of ginger nuts.

Chloe and Terri started to pour and hand round the mugs. Mack was telling Sean about the big screen that was to be fitted at first light the following morning.

'It's gonna be so cool, Seano. The carnival has a licence for the beer tent to serve through the evening until ten-thirty.'

'Will they need any help putting the big screen up?' asked Sean.

'No,' said Helen, laughing. 'They are professional

engineers. But I'm sure you'll be allowed to watch if you're good boys! Let's just pray for dry weather.'

*

She woke at half past five to find her prayers were answered. Little white clouds drifted lazily in the azure May sky. A cuckoo, a pair of blackbirds and a skylark were singing, and on the gentle breeze, Helen could just hear the waves breaking on Shellsand beach.

The house was still and quiet. Chloe had gone back to Mack's, as usual, and Sean and Terri were in Dorrie's best room at the Dolphin.

Helen padded downstairs, pulling on an old cardigan over her nightie. She put the kettle on and collected the papers from the mat.

Hearing a vehicle on the road outside, she looked out and saw that it was the big screen men. She'd take them some coffee later, but decided to let them get on with it for an hour or so.

By 7 a.m., most of the village males were out in force discussing technology, high definition, 3-D and other blokey stuff. All of them had a coffee in their hands, as did the engineers. By 9 a.m. BBC1 was broadcasting loud and clear throughout Pendruggan.

Helen stepped out into the hum of anticipation. First stop the marquees.

They were each brimming with flowers, vegetables, home-made jams and chutneys, the Stitch and Bitch society's fabulous quilts, the Wood Workers' society with their turned light-pulls and salad bowls, and the long trestles with pale-pink cloths ready for the home-made cake entries.

Mr Audrey Tipton was on the public address system:

'One two. One two. Can anyone hear me?' Several people turned and shouted back, 'Nooo.'

Outside, Helen spotted some extra stalls. One was a jolly striped tent with the sign PSYCHIC POLLY – ASK ME YOUR FUTURE AND I SHALL SHOW YOU THE WAY pegged outside. The other was an attractive antique side table with two regency chairs on a raised dais.

Simon approached her, wreathed in smiles. 'I've got a surprise for you!' He pointed, and she turned to see Penny standing behind her.

'Pen! We've missed you! When did you get here? How are you? How has the edit gone? Are you nervous about tonight?'

'Give me a chance! I came down late last night to surprise Simon and check Mavis and her guest into the Starfish. Yes, the edit has gone well and I'm really excited. Doesn't all of this look amazing!' Penny swung her arms wide as if to embrace the whole village.

'It's great, isn't it,' Helen said. 'But I'm just wondering who this table is for.'

'Ah,' said Simon. 'That's for Mavis and her guest to sign books. Mavis's publisher has decided to reprint her back catalogue, hoping to make a healthy return. And as for her guest, well, he's no stranger to bestsellers, is he?'

'But who is he?' said Helen.

She never heard the answer as piercing feedback from the speakers drowned out Penny's words, and then she and Simon headed off towards the GUESS THE WEIGHT OF THE VICAR stall, before she could ask her to repeat it. Exasperated, Helen turned away and then saw Terri and Sean walking towards her carrying half a dozen canvases.

'Where do you want these, Ma?'

50

The carnival was due to be opened by Mavis Crewe at midday. By half-past eleven, Terri's pictures were hanging in the church and an enormous crowd was waiting on the village green for the attractions to open. Several of the Rotary Club men were stewarding the tents and not allowing anyone in to peek at who the prize-winners were.

The boy scouts were doing a grand job directing a large queue of traffic into the farmer's top field, which had been set aside as a car park.

Walking back from the church, Helen was joined by Queenie. She was wearing the costume she'd worn for the filming, a fabulous green cloak and veiled hat.

'What have you come as?' asked Helen.

'It's to add a bit of authenticity to me pasty stall, innit. Don't tell your mate Penny, but I accidentally forgot to 'and it back after me day's acting.'

*

At five to twelve, a blacked-out people carrier turned on to the village green with two police motorcycle outriders. Mavis Crewe stepped out first, clad in pillar-box red. To everyone's astonishment, she was accompanied by her star guest, Alan Titchmarsh.

Queenie took one look and said, 'Oh my good Gawd, it's 'im. It's Alan.' Thankfully, Polly, dressed in a multi-coloured kaftan with numerous strands of beads and a turban, was on hand to step in and administer medical attention.

Mavis and Alan approached the microphone. Mavis went first.

'Ladies and gentlemen of Pendruggan . . . Or should I say, St Brewey!' A loud cheer went up from the crowd. 'I thank you from the bottom of my heart for your outstanding generosity and willingness to allow the producers, cast and crew of *Hidden Treasure* to take over your beautiful village and make such a success of the filming. I shall be signing Mr Tibbs books later at a special discount: buy one and get the second at half price!'

'Tight old bitch,' said Queenie, pushing Polly's bottle of smelling salts aside.

Mavis continued: 'I have just returned from cruising the world, which was an unforgettable experience. I made many new friends, including this gentleman standing next to me.' Loud cheers. 'May I introduce a man who needs no introduction. The man who will officially open today's proceedings . . . Ladies and gentlemen, Alan Titchmarsh.'

'Get me to the front, Helen. I want to see if 'is hair is real,' said Queenie.

'You stay put, Queenie,' said Polly. 'We'll see him soon enough.' Polly whispered to Helen, 'Just keep an eye on her, would you? I've got to get to my tent. She'll be all right in a minute.'

Alan started to speak: 'Ladies and gentlemen, I am delighted to be here in Pendruggan and very much looking forward to visiting the horticultural tents. Mind you, I like a bit of fruit cake too, so if the ladies on the cake stall will keep one back for me, I will pay you as I come round. Enjoy the day, the weather and being among good friends. I now proclaim this carnival well and truly open.'

His timing was immaculate. The church clock struck midday just as he said his final words.

An immediate scrum ensued. Queenie broke loose and headed towards the mêlée. Helen tried to stop her, but gave up.

While one crowd, led by Queenie, swamped Alan, another surged towards the tents.

Helen made for the flower tent. It took a while to push through, but when she got to the delphinium display, her own entry had won nothing. She edged through to the sweet pea table and found she'd come third out of ten entries.

'Well done, Mrs M.' Tony appeared beside her.

'We must find the vegetables to see if your peas have won anything.' Helen took Tony's arm and led him over to the vegetable display. 'Oh wow, look! You've got second and a highly commended.'

Before long, Tony was deep in conversation with Alan Titchmarsh, who was cradling a fruit cake, so Helen moved off, not wanting to interrupt.

She wandered out of the tent and bumped into Dahlia, David Cunningham and Gray.

'What's happened to Captain Pugwash these days?' said Gray, obviously referring to Piran.

'Mind your own business,' replied Helen. 'Hello, Dahlia. Hasn't this old git bored you stupid yet?'

Returning her kiss, Dahlia answered, 'He's a silly old fart, but I like having him around. He makes me look young.' She grabbed Gray's arm and kissed him affectionately. Gray looked wounded, then rather smug as a couple of old fellows walked past looking envious.

'Hello, David. How are you?' Helen greeted David Cunningham.

'Fine. Fine. I've brought my wife and kids with me. They're here somewhere. I'll introduce you later. But first, I'm going for a pint. Coming, Gray?'

Dahlia gave Gray a look which he interpreted correctly. 'No thanks, old man. Maybe later.'

As David took off towards the booze, Helen asked Dahlia, 'Are you both still on to judge the fancy dress in the main ring? About three p.m.?'

'Of course. Love to.' Dahlia spotted something that caught her eye. 'Look, Gray – a fortune teller. Let's go and see what the future holds for us.' And she dragged a less-than-excited Gray off.

*

'Oh my God! Polly is brilliant!' An excited Chloe plonked next to Helen, who was sitting on the bench by the phone box. 'She told me that going to Sri Lanka was just the first of many travels, and that Mack and I had a real future together. She told me I'd have two children and come back here to live once I was settled. Isn't that great!'

'Genius,' replied Helen.

'Sean and Terri are in there now. Can't wait to see what she's told them.'

They waited ten minutes, then Chloe went to get Sean and his girlfriend to drag them back to Helen.

'So what did Polly say?' Chloe was clapping her hands like she used to when she was little.

'Ma, Chloe . . .' Sean suddenly looked serious and Helen noticed that Terri was a little pale.

'What?'

'We are going to have a baby.'

'How lovely. And when does Polly say this will happen?'

Terri turned to Helen. 'It's already happened. We were going to tell you tonight, but Polly has just seen the baby in my palm. She says it's a little girl.'

Helen clutched both Sean and Terri's hands. 'You mean, you already know you are pregnant. Definitely?'

'Yes. Four months. Congratulations, Granny!' beamed Sean.

Helen leapt to her feet with her hand at her mouth. 'Oh my goodness. Oh. Oh.' Tears of shock and happiness overwhelmed her inexplicably. She sat down again and Terri and Sean both put their arms round her. She managed to say, 'Does Dad know yet?'

'Not yet, we wanted you to know first.'

'Hello, kids!' Gray strode up behind them, grinning like a Cheshire cat with Dahlia, looking less than happy, on his arm. 'I've just had my fortune told and apparently old Dahlia and I are a match made in heaven. We even have the sound of tiny feet to come in the not-too-distant future.'

'I feel rather faint. Can I sit down next to you, Helen?' said Dahlia.

'Dad,' said Sean, 'you definitely will be hearing the patter of tiny feet – around November. You're going to be a granddad.'

'Thank God!' Dahlia and Gray said together, making the whole party laugh.

*

By 2 p.m. most of the stalls had sold out. All Queenie's pasties were gone and the Rotary men's barbecue had been a huge success. Polly had a steady stream of people queuing up outside her tent and poor Simon had been picked up so many times by people trying to assess his weight that his hips were feeling bruised.

The pipe band, dog show and majorettes' display in the main arena had slightly overrun, so it was a little later than advertised that David and Dahlia entered the ring to judge the fancy-dress competition.

'The ring of doom,' said David, off mic. 'No matter who wins, the others will all hate me.'

'Don't worry, there's a prize for everyone. It's first, second and third, and then everyone gets a lollipop.' Helen handed him the three envelopes containing book tokens and gave Dahlia a large plastic sweet jar full of brightly coloured lollies.

The winners were a five-year-old girl dressed as Roadrunner, a ten-year-old boy as Mr Tibbs, and fifteen-year-old twins who came as Fish and Chips. After lots of photos and time spent charming the losers and their parents, Dahlia and David left the show ring unscathed, and to massive applause.

Next was the tug of war. Two teams of huge young men entered the ring and were cheered by every female available. Mr Audrey Tipton gave the order for battle to commence and Helen left them to it.

She found herself outside Polly's tent. There was no queue, so she ducked her head through the flap to ask how Polly was doing. She was snoozing quietly in her deckchair, her turban on the table by her crystal ball and tarot cards, her hair damp with sweat. She stirred as she sensed someone watching.

'Hello, Helen. Do you want your fortune told?'

'No, I just wanted to see how you are. You've done a roaring trade.'

'Always do. Sit down and I'll have a look at your hand.'

Helen sat. Polly put her specs on and took Helen's hands. 'Don't mind if I don't put me turban back on, do you? Right, let's have a look. Mmm . . .' The feeling of Polly's gentle fingers tracing the lines on her palms was very soothing. Helen relaxed for the first time that day. 'You know already that you're going to be a grandma, a little girl who will bring great happiness to you all.

'Now, your first husband, Gray, he's going to be fine with Dahlia. There may be times he'll want refuge at your place because she'll give him a hard time, but don't feel sorry for him. Mmm . . . Chloe. She's a great girl. She'll travel, but will settle back here and always be close to you. She'll need you when she's had her little ones. Let me have a look at my crystal ball . . .'

She dropped Helen's hands and picked up the smooth, clear orb, polishing it with one hand and looking deeply into its magnified depths. 'Ah, now. This is interesting. I don't see a marriage as such, but you aren't on your own. And there is wedding news. News that will make you very happy.'

'Chloe and Mack? Sean and Terri?' Helen ventured.

'No. Not them. An older couple.'

'Gray and Dahlia?'

'No, it's . . . well, I can see Holy Trinity. It's here in the village. But I can't see who. Oh, and . . . what's that?' Polly looked up and to the right of Helen. 'OK. Yes. I'll tell her.' She returned her gaze to Helen. 'My guide has given me a message from the spirit world: "Violet says thank you."'

A chill spread up Helen's spine.

'Polly, please don't tell anyone you said that, will you.'

'No, of course not.' Polly smiled and tapped her nose. 'The spirits and me operate in strict confidence. Like doctors and priests! I think we both know who Violet is, don't we? I believe that she's happy you have looked after her house and garden so well. That's all. I see only happiness ahead for you – rejoice!'

Helen stood up, still feeling rather shaken. She wasn't entirely sure that Polly's explanation was the right one. She felt instinctively it was something to do with Falcon's ashes and the other contents of the tin box. She swept her hair from her face and said, 'Thanks, Polly.' Then, after a pause. 'Are you coming to the big-screen broadcast tonight?'

'Try keeping me away!'

The two women kissed and Helen left the humid little tent, glad of the cooler afternoon air outside. She immediately heard a familiar voice, one that she had been secretly longing to hear.

'So, maid, did Polly see me in your future?'

It was Piran. He put his hands on her shoulders and spoke: 'Why haven't you been in touch, Helen? I wanted to talk to you.'

'I wasn't sure what we had to say to each other. You seem to be intent on clinging to the ghost of Jenna. There's no room for me.'

Piran sighed and looked at Helen, his face serious.

'When Jenna died, my heart was ripped out. It has taken me a long time to get back on an even keel, and even now I have my dark days. But I want you, Helen. I've not felt like this about any woman since Jenna, but I need to take it slowly. You have to understand that.'

He took her hand and held it to his chest. 'So, Mrs Merrifield, on those terms, will you be my girlfriend?'

She looked deeply into his beautiful, sincere eyes and nodded her head. He kissed her softly, then more deeply.

He put his arm around her and they walked quietly away from Polly's tent.

As they wandered together through the sounds and smells of the country fair, a feeling of a deep connection with Piran, this village and its people overwhelmed Helen. This was the right place for her. She had come home.

51

By 6 p.m., the village green was virtually deserted, the carnival committee had almost cleared up all the debris, and the tents were empty of their displays. In the church, several of the paintings had red stickers on them, including three of Terri's.

Helen's little house was filled with the usual crowd: Simon and Penny, Gray and Dahlia, Chloe and Mack, Sean and Terri, and of course Piran, who was pouring drinks for everybody. When he'd finished, he made a little speech:

'I'd like everybody here to raise their glasses to Simon and Helen for all their efforts in making today such a success. Cheers!'

Simon blushed and looked at his feet while Helen gratefully took a swallow of her Scotch on the rocks.

'I should like to make a toast too.' Simon spoke softly: 'To Penny Leighton. She has brought great excitement to Pendruggan and much happiness to me. Here's to her and the stars of tonight's big entertainment.'

Penny quietly stood next to him and put her arm through his, giving it a squeeze. 'May I say something too?' she asked.

Gray interjected, 'Oh, bloody hell, no, Pen. We all get the message. What time shall we gather tonight? Dahlia's got to get her face on.' He playfully pinched

Dahlia's bottom, then as quickly ducked as she swung a slap towards his cheek.

'The show starts at nine, so let's meet on the green at eight forty-five,' said Penny. 'I've got a row of chairs reserved for us lot and the diva known as Mavis Crewe.'

*

Helen and her friends left Gull's Cry at 8.30, carefully wrapped in warm jumpers and insect repellent. The big screen was showing the final reel of a James Bond film and the green had become a makeshift auditorium. Hundreds of people had arrived with deckchairs and kitchen chairs and claimed their spot. In the middle, and roped off from the others, was a row of a dozen comfortably cushioned garden chairs. On the end was a ruby-red velveteen reclining armchair in which Queenie was firmly ensconced.

''Ello, me ducks. Some of the boys brought me chair out for me. I can't sit on nuffin' else. Not with me asparagus veins.'

'Do you need a drink?' offered Piran, tongue in cheek.

'Bless you, no, I've got me bottle of brandy in me bag.' She tapped her ancient cream leather handbag with a gnarled hand. 'I'll have a packet of crisps, though.'

David Cunningham, Dahlia, Gray, Penny and Mavis all arrived at that moment. Piran took the drinks order for everyone, with soft drinks for Terri and Chloe, and David sauntered off with him to help carry the load back.

Waiting those final few minutes for the programme to start seemed endless. At last the James Bond credits rolled and as a commercial break began, the beer tent had one last anxious push to get everyone served before the continuity announcer spoke: 'And now on TV7 the epitome of the amateur English detective – it's *Mr Tibbs and the Hidden Treasure!*'

The theme music started and as shots of Pendruggan and Trevay appeared on the screen, the crowd started to whistle and cheer. Just as quickly there fell a hush, as the story unfolded and shots of their friends or themselves came up on the enormous screen. Tony's scene stole the show, naturally, and was met with a lot of 'aaah's and one shout of 'Well done, Tony' from the back. But it was the central roles of Mr Tibbs and Nancy Trumpet that kept the audience spellbound. Their relationship on screen was tangible and sincere. The banter, the flirting and the razor-sharpness of their brains guaranteed the show would be a success. As the final scene faded away, the audience applause must have been heard in Truro.

Dahlia, David and Mavis were swamped by local journalists, all wanting instant quotes and photos, while a TV crew was filming the carnival atmosphere.

Penny stood back, unrecognised, Helen by her side. 'Well done, Pen. You did it.'

'It's gone well,' said Penny, 'but remember, this is a friendly crowd. What did those who were watching in the middle of cities or way up north think of it? We might not be relevant to them.'

'How will you know?'

'We'll get an early indication tomorrow from the overnight figures. They'll tell us how many people watched and, more importantly, what share of the audience we got. The BBC are very strong tonight with their new drama. But they didn't have a big name for it, whereas we had the double Ds! David and Dahlia.'

'Will you let me know as soon as you find out?'

'Yes, I'll walk over in the morning.'

'From the Starfish?'

Penny looked a bit sheepish. 'From Simon's.'

'Oh my God! You mean, you and—'

'Keep your voice down!'

Helen whispered, 'You mean, you and Simon are spending the night together . . . properly?'

'Yep.'

'Wowzer!'

*

The next morning, Helen left Piran sleeping. They had spent a glorious night talking, kissing, making love and talking again. She nipped over to Queenie's to get the papers and search for reviews.

'The bloke on the breakfast news said it was a classic of its kind,' said Queenie. 'And that Mavis Crewe books were gonna fly off the shelves. Good, innit?'

'Brilliant! I'll have all these papers and a pint of milk, please.'

Helen paid Queenie and sped back to Gull's Cry. Piran was in the kitchen wearing her pink cotton dressing gown and making a pot of coffee.

'Anything in the papers?'

They both sat down and searched. They found three reviews and read extracts to each other.

'"Move over Miss Marple, Mr Tibbs is in town." That's the *Express*.'

'The *Observer* says: "David Cunningham brings his big-screen charm and sexiness to a small-screen role that will surely bankroll the rest of his career."'

'And the bloke in the *People* says, "Dahlia Dahling is

astonishingly good as the sexy, feisty, warm and funny Nancy Trumpet. The only question is, will old Tibbs let his Trumpet get the better of him?"'

Helen was thrilled. 'Golly! Penny's got a hit on her hands. I can't wait to hear what the viewing figures are.'

An hour later and a jubilant Penny ran in to Helen's kitchen. 'Get the champagne out! We beat the BBC! We beat everything! We won the slot with the largest share of the audience and almost nine million viewers. I can hardly breathe. Quick, alcohol, alcohol!'

Helen was at the fridge, which was not yielding champagne. 'Rosé any good?' She brandished a half-empty bottle.

'Anything! I can't wait to tell Simon. He's in church for another twenty minutes. There really is a God!' She grabbed the glass of rosé and took a slug. 'Thanks, darling. Got to go. Waiting for Simon and a call from Jack Bradbury, TV7's Director of Programmes. Said he'd call before lunch. See you later.' Draining her glass and plonking it on the table, she ran back over to the vicarage.

Helen and Piran, still wearing Helen's dressing gown, stood looking after her and then burst out laughing.

'She's a live wire, that one,' laughed Piran. 'Is she always like that?'

'Yep. You should see her when she's really excited.'

It wasn't too long before Piran did see Penny really excited. Again she threw herself into the kitchen, this time accompanied by a beaming Simon.

'They want a series! They want *all* the Mr Tibbs books – and there are eighteen! Over the next six years! And all to be made here in Pendruggan!' She stopped, looking worried. 'If they'll have us. Have we pissed many people off? Could the locals put up with the intrusion? What about the local council? Will they give me permission again? Oh my God.' She dropped into Helen's rocking chair and put her head in her hands. 'Will Dahlia and David want to renew their contracts? Will I manage the travelling . . .'

'Will you marry me?' Simon spoke so clearly that they all turned to look at him.

'What?' asked a stunned Penny.

'Will you marry me? You could live here and not have to travel. You could have your office here. Bring the whole business down?'

Penny continued to look at him. She frowned, she blinked, she put her hand to her mouth and then she replied:

'Yes, Simon. Yes, please.'

*

When Helen and Piran finally got to bed after a long celebratory lunch at the Dolphin with too much champagne, Helen fell into a restless sleep.

A woman with old-fashioned clothes and a silver-haired bun came to her in a dream. She told Helen that she was Violet Wingham. She thanked her for finding Falcon, 'My favourite cat.' And asked her to bring her family together again. 'It's time we were all together after such a long time.' Then Helen found herself on board a large ship, but she felt cold and when she looked down her feet were in the sea. A little boy was trying to swim to the surface. She put her hands in to pull him out, but she couldn't reach him as he sank out of reach and finally out of sight.

*

Piran switched the light on, 'What is it? Wake up, it's a dream.'

Helen opened her eyes and adjusted to the present, then cuddled close to Piran, trembling.

'What's happened, my love? A nightmare?' he asked.

'It was something that Polly said to me at the carnival.' Helen told Piran the story, watching to see if he'd laugh at her. He didn't.

'When Jenna died, little odd things round the house happened. I remember I couldn't find my passport. I was angry at Jenna because she was always damn well tidying up. I shouted out her name in the house. Angry she'd left me and missing her so much it hurt. Anyway, the next day, there was my passport, on the toaster. I'm sure it hadn't been there before, but . . .'

'I don't want to lose you.'

'You're not going to.'

'How do you really feel about me?'

'You must know by now, Helen.'

'Please say the words.'

'You first.'

'I love you, Piran Ambrose.'

'Good. I love you, Helen Merrifield. Now let's get back to sleep.'

52

It was about a week later that Simon phoned Piran and asked him and Helen over for an important meeting that evening, at the vicarage, six o'clock.

Early summer was now in full swing in Pendruggan. The wisteria hung heavily from the dark eaves of the vicarage, its deep scent nudged through the open windows by a delicate, warm breeze. The house martins and the swallows were chattering above, then swooping low over the lawn and catching insects on the wing.

As Helen and Piran stepped over the threshold and into the hall, signs that a woman was once again in charge of the house were subtle but clear to Helen's eyes. Gone was the smell of musty books, replaced with the freshness of new paint. The walls were light and creamy, the flagstone floors polished, the large drawing room had two new squishy café au lait sofas and a large rug in a contemporary pattern woven in turquoise, lapis and coral. The ancient kitchen had been replaced with washed driftwood cupboards, a deep butler's sink and neon-pink Aga, a large scrubbed pine kitchen table with mismatched, cushioned chairs round it. It was Penny. It even smelt like Penny. The only things she hadn't touched were Simon's office and Simon himself.

'I love them just as they are,' she had told Helen.

Now she was coming towards Helen in bare feet, denim shorts and her hair clipped on top of her head, and not a scrap of make-up.

'Darlings!' she said, her eyes wide with excitement. 'Something *amazing* has happened. Come through.'

They walked into the revamped drawing room. The bishop was settled on the sofa with a glass of sherry, but stood up and gave Helen a welcome hug and Piran a warm handshake.

Simon poured a sherry for everybody and then said, 'This morning the bishop phoned with some interesting information . . .' He stopped and looked at his audience.

'Come on, man. Spit it out,' said Piran.

'Sorry, yes. Miss Violet Wingham's solicitors have been searching for any living claimants to her estate and have found none. Therefore, and this is the exciting bit . . .'

'Oh, it is, it is!' said Penny, jiggling her toes on the rug.

'Miss Wingham instructed the lawyers that, on finding no living claimants, they should give her entire estate to . . . Holy Trinity church!'

Helen's mouth fell open. 'You mean, the church inherits her money?'

'Yes. And, it turns out that Miss Wingham never spent any of the money that her aunt got for her as compensation from the White Star line when the *Titanic* was lost. She invested it – wisely, as it happens – and that, plus the sale price of Gull's Cry, brings the total to almost a quarter of a million pounds.'

Piran stood up. 'To use for the churchyard restoration?'

'Yes,' said Simon, shaking Piran's hand. 'And we might have a little left over, after the success of the carnival.'

'Isn't it wonderful?' beamed Penny.

'God moves in mysterious ways,' added the bishop.

Helen spoke: 'I have had an idea and I'd like to run it past you all . . .'

Epilogue

On a sunny day in July the entire village gathered in the churchyard, the better to see the ceremony. The bishop, Piran and Simon stood next to the simple rough-hewn granite cross. The bishop raised his voice to quieten the crowd and when he had their attention said, 'Welcome to the newly restored churchyard of Holy Trinity. May it be a place of joy and healing to all who visit here.' Then he took the first of two beautiful wooden boxes from Simon and placed it into the freshly dug earth. When he had done the same with the second box, Piran scattered violet flowers over it and then gave the bishop a smaller urn, which he blessed quietly and placed next to the larger box.

Queenie nudged Tony. 'Where's Helen and Penny?'

Tony shrugged.

'Let this be the last resting place of Miss Violet Wingham, a survivor of the *Titanic* sinking, and her parents Henry and Bluebell Wingham, who lost their lives. Next to them lies Violet's faithful feline companion, Falcon. Named after her older brother, who perished before she could know him. His resting place is known only to God. Let us pray . . .'

When the service was complete, the bishop called to the crowd again. 'Before you leave here, Simon Canter has asked me to invite you all inside the church for a joyful surprise.'

Intrigued, everyone filed in to find the church full of gardenias and Miss Audrey Tipton beaming with pride at her work. Every seat was taken by the time the old organ wheezed into life playing the Wedding March. There were some mystified glances until, turning round, they saw Penny dressed in a simple cream wedding dress, followed by her maid of honour, Helen.

As one, the congregation turned to the altar to see the groom – Simon, standing looking in wonder at his bride walking towards him – with Piran at his side as best man.

Never had Holy Trinity seen a more joyful wedding. No one would sit down, everyone was singing, clapping, laughing and finally spilling back out into the sunshine of the churchyard.

Simon and Penny kissed deeply at the doorway. Queenie's voice rang out, 'Ain't you going to chuck your bouquet, Penny?' Letting go of Simon, Penny turned her back and threw it. Helen tried not to catch it, but it landed on her anyway.

She looked quickly at Piran and mouthed, 'What shall I do?'

Piran took the posy from her and, reaching for her hand led her over to the new memorial stone to Violet and her family. The inscription read:

In memory of all those lost who sailed on the Titanic
15 April 1912 including friends of this parish
Violet Wingham 1911–2008
Her father Henry Wingham 1880–1912
Her mother Bluebell Wingham 1884–1912

and her brother Falcon Wingham 1907–1912
Lost at sea but not forgotten.

And below, in smaller, letters:

Also 'Falcon' the cat, a faithful companion.

*

Piran and Helen gently laid the flowers on the fresh mound of soil.

Helen sent a silent thank-you to Violet and was then engulfed by handfuls of confetti clinging on the wind from Simon and Penny's photographs.

She took Piran's hand. 'Come on. You and I have a lot of life ahead of us. Let's live it!' And they ran to join the crowd.